1/2r

GO BACK
AT ONCE

Go Back at Once

ROBERT AICKMAN

With an introduction by
Brian Evenson

SHEFFIELD – LONDON – NEW YORK

And Other Stories
Sheffield – London – New York
www.andotherstories.org

Originally published in 2020 by Tartarus Press, UK
First paperback edition 2022, And Other Stories

1 3 5 7 9 8 6 4 2

ISBN: 9781913505202
eBook ISBN: 9781913505219

Typesetter: Tetragon, London; Typefaces: Albertan Pro and Linotype Syntax; Cover Design:
Travis Brun. Printed and bound by the CPI Group (UK) Ltd, Croydon, CR0 4YY.

A catalogue record for this book is available from the British Library.

And Other Stories gratefully acknowledge that our work is supported
using public funding by Arts Council England.

And Other Stories would like to thank Rosalie Parker, R. B. Russell, S.T. Joshi
and Jim Rockhill for their help in the preparation of this volume.

INTRODUCTION

Readers know Robert Aickman, if they know him at all, as a writer of 'strange stories': tales that don't quite descend fully into a territory that might rightly be called horror but which are, nonetheless, unsettling and, well, strange. They're stories that leave you off balance and unsure, stories with the potential to haunt you for a long time after you finish reading them.

Yet there's an entirely other Robert Aickman out there, more ambitious, no less strange, harder still to classify: Aickman the novelist. In his longer fiction, we meet a writer born into the wrong era – someone who wouldn't be out of his element trading bon mots with Noël Coward, someone whose work wouldn't be out of place beside Waugh's and Wilde's. His writing here is funny and charming, satirical and playful in a way we get only the briefest glimpses of in his stories. Where many (though not all) of his stories have somewhat hapless male protagonists, he offers, in the two novels and one novella of his that have been published, female focal characters: young women and girls coming into their own. He proves surprisingly good at ventriloquising the voices of these female characters, though also perhaps a little bit unhealthily fascinated by the different outfits he imagines them wearing.

Only one novel of Aickman's was published in his lifetime, *The Late Breakfasters* (1964). Hardly a success when it first appeared, it garnered little attention in the years that followed. Now, it may be cursed by lying too much in the shadow of the strangeness Aickman is known for – when it was reissued by Valancourt a few years ago, it was packaged as *The Late Breakfasters and Other Strange Stories*, and was followed by six tales in Aickman's typical mode. But *The Late Breakfasters* is hardly strange in the classical, supernatural sense, and to present it as such is an encouragement to misread. It's a bit like packaging a banana together with a half-dozen nails and calling the results lunch. Rather than being chilling or unnerving, *The Late Breakfasters* is delightful, melancholy, and full of wit. It more resembles what might have resulted in the unlikely event of Evelyn Waugh and Ronald Firbank collaborating on a novel about semi-unrequited lesbian passion.

Another novel, or more like a novella, *The Model*, was only published six years after Aickman's death, in 1987. Reading something like a fable, it tells the story of a young girl named Elena who wants to train as a ballerina. When she discovers she is to be given in marriage by her father to settle his debts, she flees to pursue her dream. Yet the tone is anything but grim, and as she travels things become very odd indeed, the reality of the world feeling increasingly contingent.

Both of these books arguably do have their fantastical moments – briefly (and tenuously) in *The Late Breakfasters* and more pervasively in *The Model* – but such supernatural developments are deployed differently than the unnerving and certainty-eroding oddness that undergirds Aickman's best stories. And yet the novels have a deftness to them, a lightness, not so dissimilar from the stories as to be unrecognisable, but given a prominence that makes them into supreme pleasures for those readers who can tune into their anti-modern wavelength . . . especially if they can, for the duration, set aside the expectation of 'spookiness' bred by Aickman's reputation.

For many years, *The Late Breakfasters* and *The Model* were Aickman's only longer pieces available. Now there's one more: *Go Back at Once*. Originally written in 1975 but left unpublished, the novel languished in Aickman's archives for decades as a typescript until Tartarus Press, the most committed publisher of Aickman's work, issued it in a limited collector's edition. The edition you hold is the first trade edition.

In *Go Back at Once*, Aickman managed to write something that initially seems like a satirical sort of Bildungsroman, but quickly exceeds those bounds. The novel is ostensibly about Cressida Hazeborough and her friendship with Vivien, a wealthy upper-class schoolfriend with whom she is quite close. It takes place in the aftermath of war, with Cressida having lost her brother, Hugh, to combat. Unsure of what to do with herself but knowing the last thing she wants is to stay home and slip into marriage with a boy she's known for years (who both she and Vivien refer to by the moniker Tiddleywinks) she comes to London with Vivien to live with Vivien's Aunt Agnes. Aunt Agnes is the first divorced person that Cressida has met, which gives her a curious allure. Cressida knows her father would not approve of her living with a divorcee – after all, he also disapproves of short hair on women, short dresses, and drinking cocktails – so she keeps this information to herself when asking her parents for permission to go. She takes a job in a shop called Perdita, where she works with someone who is also named Perdita. Meanwhile, Vivien works as the receptionist for a psychoanalyst (who she convinces to see Cressida without charging her) and attempts to write a novel.

Everything seems set up for Cressida to become increasingly aware of herself, fall in love, and blossom fully into adulthood, and for Vivien to serve as her foil in this. In a more traditional novel, this is precisely what would happen. But Aickman has little interest in pursuing this arc. Instead, he's interested in the way Cressida converses with those around her, interested in the dynamics of the characters, but less and less focused on writing a Bildungsroman in a predictable sense. And so, a quarter of the way into the novel, Aickman abandons London altogether and dizzyingly propels his characters to Trino, a makeshift country that's been carved out of a patch of Italy by someone named Virgilio Vittore.

Vittore is a little like Harry Lime in the movie *The Third Man*: we are told a great many things about him, some accurate, some mere rumour, before he appears 'in person'. He's first mentioned at the dinner table, and everyone seems to know who he is except for Cressida. We know that his name circulates in the newspapers, that everyone is conscious of him, that many of the stodgier of Aunt Agnes's guests disapprove of him. Eventually Cressida and Vivien encounter his face on a stamp. In time they come to understand that he's a dreamer, a romantic, that he's rumoured to own houses in every capital in Europe, that he's physically unattractive yet irresistible to women, that he 'governs according to the laws of music', and that he has had some sort of past connection to Aunt Agnes, the specifics of which she takes a certain pleasure in feeding to Cressida and Vivien in dribs and drabs.

Unlike Cressida, Vivien seems to know a little bit about Vittore. When Cressida asks in frustration who exactly this Vittore is, she responds, 'with emphasis', 'He is a *man*,' but goes on to qualify this: 'At least I think so.' The source of her information is an article she read in *Woman's Own*. Drawing on the words of that esteemed publication, Vivien proclaims that 'Vittore is a great poet, and a great playwright, and a great athlete, and a great soldier, and a great leader, and a great aviator, and a great lover. That most of all.' He has all the dangerous fascination of a carefully constructed charismatic authoritarian leader – which in fact he is, though Cressida and Vivien cling to his idea of ruling by music and believe this might redeem him. Fascinated by rumours of him in London, once in Trino Cressida and Vivien continue to circle Vittore, drawing closer and closer to him – though Cressida fears she might never actually set eyes upon him.

The majority of the book takes place in Trino. It involves the exploration of an artificial country run by way of romantic notions and enthusiasms, but without an excess of organisa-tional principles. Vittore's endeavour is supported by a motley assortment of folk from everywhere, who each seem to have arrived in Trino for their own peculiar reasons. Cressida's coming of age in London is replaced by a madcap, parodic, and often very funny version of the same in Trino. This portion of the novel, particularly in the way it describes the place and the people in it, strikes me as reminiscent of Anthony Powell's *Venusberg* (1932), about a journalist who secures a position in a Baltic country and his misadventures there, though that novel doesn't have nearly the humour that Aickman's does.

In a way Cressida is no more at sea in Trino – where at one point she is quite literally at sea – than she was in London. Resourceful, she manages to pick her way through a number of prickly situations. But we as readers are more lost: we might have been able to feel superior to her struggles with certain social circles in London because we have already surmounted such struggles in our own lives or experienced them in books. But in Trino we'd be as off balance as she is and would probably operate with a great deal less aplomb.

One of the strengths of *Go Back at Once* is the closeness of the third-person narrative to Cressida herself, the care with which Aickman touches on her sometimes ingenuous manner of thinking and speaking, allowing it to permeate the entirety of the narrative, sometimes through free indirect discourse, sometimes through more complex means. For instance, it may be the narrator who tells us that 'The walls were hung with boudoir-coloured silk, and there were boudoir-designed furnishings, the colour of dried skeletons on the steppes,' but the whole phrasing of that description, its repetitions, what it chooses to notice, is imbued with Cressida's often amusing way of looking at the world. Or is it? Perhaps this is as much the narrator giving his own words to things that Cressida may be inchoately feeling or thinking, and perhaps he's getting it wrong. The line between the narrator's satire and the young woman's own feelings becomes very blurry indeed, and Aickman knows how to exploit that ambiguity to maximum effect.

Go Back at Once, like Aickman's other novel-length works, has a certain lightness, in the positive sense that Italo Calvino uses the term. There's a buoyancy to the prose that allows Aickman to move from absurdity to absurdity with a deft touch that keeps the balloon that is the novel aloft. There's something gleeful and slightly dangerous about the satire of the book, partly because it's not always clear where the satire is meant to start or stop. It's a novel full of contradictions – Aickman, quite conservative, does seem genuinely to admire this impossible romantico-fascist state that follows the laws of music, but he also can't help but be sceptical of it. It's a glorious dream for him (with more than hints of nightmare to us), but even when he's only dreaming his pessimistic streak wins out. He can't resist breaking his dream apart, which ends up making his Trino feel like more of a critique than he perhaps intended.

Such tensions give the novel a kind of innate dynamism. The effect is similar to what the best satire gains when (as is the case with Swift's work, for instance) the connection of the writer to what he or she is satirising becomes less important than his or her delight in the world being created. *Go Back at Once* is a wonderfully readable book, full of deft and often very funny turns of phrase. It may not be strange in the sense of Aickman's stories, but it's well and truly strange in its own unique way – thoroughly mischievous, sly, and inviting.

BRIAN EVENSON

CHAPTER ONE

The Hero

Once upon a time everyone knew that Sawbridgeworth was pronounced Sapsworth, that Daventry was pronounced Danetree, that Cirencester was pronounced Cissiter, that Derby was pronounced Darby, and, on the same principle, that beautiful, remote Happisburgh, at the very furthest corner of Norfolk, was pronounced Hazeborough, and had been since the days of its greatness. When times were swiftly changing, Mr Vernon Happisburgh had been faced with a difficult decision. Should he begin to pronounce himself Happ-is-burg or spell himself Hazeborough?

He decided upon the latter, largely so that there should be no confusion with the Imperial Family that had now fallen on difficult times.

When Isaac Disraeli decided to become a Christian, he took all his family with him, hand in hand. So, necessarily, it was with the name-change in Mr Hazeborough's family, who, however numbered only two: his wife, whose name was Phyllis, and his daughter, whose names were Cressida Hermione Helena. Until a year or two before, there had also been a son, Cressida's older brother Hugh, but he had been killed within mere months of being conscripted, and within mere weeks of the war's end. The three survivors became Mr, Mrs, and Miss Hazeborough.

Cressida had loved her brother, who, indeed, had been a god among youths, captain of cricket, stand-off half in the second fifteen, and the first to win the open hundred yards three years running. He had been a strong and impressively competitive swimmer, a rider to hounds of more than promise (as the elderly Master had expressed it), and a dab hand with the foils, though not actually Captain of Fencing. He had danced like Vernon Castle (when given the chance).

It was in memory of him, though he had been six years older, that Cressida later took up fencing herself. There were a number of girls who went in for it at Riverdale House. First the class had been taken by Mrs Hobbs, but soon a male instructor had had to be sent for. Cressida had excelled from the first, all the time half-imagining herself to be Hugh; and in the end she had fenced for the school. The team might well have carried all before it if the others had been as good as Cressida. Alas, those very things in which we excel at school are precisely those of least application when we are compelled to drag ourselves away.

At Riverdale House, Cressida's great preoccupations, other than the memory of Hugh, had been poetry, and a dark-haired girl named Vivien, who loved poetry too. Both girls wrote it, read it, and especially read it aloud to one another. In the end Cressida came upon some lines that summed up the situation:—

'The Wily Vivien stole from Arthur's court:
She hated all the knights, and heard in thought
Their lavish comment when her name was named.'

Vivien was the younger by slightly more than a year when the two found one another in the fourth form under Miss Elm, who was not merely silly, as are so many schoolteachers, of all sexes, but simply mental. Vivien was even cleverer than Cressida and seemed likely one day to be even more beautiful. Neither of these considerations stood at all in the way. Indeed, Cressida positively preferred things to be as they were. It seems likely that Cressida would never have encountered the greatest man of his age (some, including the man himself, said, of any age) but for Vivien's enthusiasm and drive in the early stages of the project.

With the consent of the authorities and of Mr and Mrs Hazeborough, Vivien accompanied Cressida to the unveiling of the tablet to Hugh in his school chapel. After Tea, which was dull (the cakes and biscuits, like the partakers, were past their prime), the two slipped back into the high, red-brick chapel and read all the memorials to the great men: poets, generals, secretaries of state, colonial governors, prison governors, governors of the Bank of England.

'Lives of great men oft remind us,' remarked Vivien. Cressida was not used to seeing her in a plain black dress.

'*He* was only a headmaster,' said Cressida, examining a tablet, large, Latinate, and cracked.

'They also serve who only stand and wait,' Vivien pointed out.

'That's just about all that women *can* do,' said Cressida.

'Nonsense,' said Vivien. 'You're going to do much more.'

'I hope so,' said Cressida, doubtfully but dutifully. 'At least I think I hope so.'

'Of course you hope so,' said Vivien. 'It's much better to be a woman than a man.'

A little later, the elderly verger entered, having heard voices.

'Oh!' he exclaimed when he saw who it was. 'Enjoying your-selves, are you?' He did not know how to make the best of girls.

'Yes, thank you,' said Vivien. 'Very much.'

It would not have been proper for Cressida to reply, seeing what they were there for that day.

They continued their purposeful examination of all the memorials.

The verger stood about.

'Don't you feel cold?' he asked after a bit.

'No,' said Cressida. 'We never feel cold.'

It was a point upon which she and Vivien particularly prided themselves, at least in comparison with some of the silly geese at Riverdale House.

CHAPTER TWO

The Problem

It was unthinkable that Vivien should stay on after Cressida had left.

At their last prize-giving, Vivien had won the prize for Latin (that was how she had had no difficulty with the inscriptions) and Cressida the prize for elocution. At a later phase of the ceremony, Cressida had been called upon to manifest her art, and she had recited 'The Listeners' by Walter de la Mare; 'The Great Lover' by Rupert Brooke; and, more daringly, William Morris's 'I know a little garden close'. She was loudly applauded by the entire audience, tightly packed in the hot room and with many of the males in morning dress with spats. She seemed to appeal more than either the scene from a well-known play by Molière which had preceded her or the girl who played Bach on the violin after her. Then came a surprise. At the very end, the headmistress, Miss Grindleford, rose yet again and said that while Riverdale House did not regularly present a Good Conduct Prize but only when quite exceptional merit seemed to compel, yet that year the staff felt there was such merit, and that it had been displayed by Cressida Hazeborough. So as well as a *Popular Reciter*, bound in red, Cressida received a *Meditations of Marcus Aurelius Antonius* bound in green, and translated idiomatically by a Clerk in Holy Orders. The head girl, Mary Daimler, looked sour, without being particularly successful in concealing the fact; and Cressida was considerably at a loss, then and thereafter, as to why she had been picked on. Of course her behaviour had been perfectly reasonable, because only silly geese flaunt themselves or make any kind of overt challenge. Vivien, who had sat near the back in her sixth-form dress, pointed out later that there is little known correlation between conduct and reward anywhere in this world, though it may be different in the next: 'Like flies to wanton boys are we to the gods,' she said. Vivien's parents could not attend because they were in the Caribbean. This was not for pleasure, but because Vivien's father, Sir Neville, held an appointment there.

Both Cressida and Vivien were perfectly clever enough to go on to a university and, having arrived there, to excel; but there was no question of that for either of them. Cressida, indeed, was intended (in so far as intention entered into it) simply to return to Rutland and there await picking on for matrimony. Vivien, on the other hand, was positively not wanted in the West Indies. Her mother pointed out that her father and herself would soon be back in any case, because they always were, and suggested that in the meantime Vivien move into her aunt's house near Gloucester Road and perhaps look for a job of some kind. Her mother added that she had already written on the subject to Aunt Agnes (who was her husband's sister, not her own). She did not say whether or not Aunt Agnes had replied in any way.

Cressida and Vivien had discussed the whole matter before the end of the term; though not long enough before for complete convenience. The casual attitude of their respective parents strongly suggested that they would have preferred their daughters to remain safely at school for all time, even though they, the parents, had to pay for it. Vivien too had an elder brother, Paul, but he had already vanished into the Palestine Police, where he led a life of excitement.

The best they could think of was that Cressida should move in on Aunt Agnes also.

'Would your parents mind if you didn't go straight back home?'

'I don't think so,' said Cressida. 'But wouldn't Aunt Agnes mind?'

'Aunt Agnes is a good sport in her own way,' replied Vivien.

'What way is that?'

'Well, to start with, she's divorced.'

'Daddy wouldn't like that!'

'My daddy didn't like it either. It nearly finished his career. That's supposed to be why he's stuck away where he is.'

'I've never known anyone who's been divorced,' said Cressida.

'You'll meet plenty more when you know Aunt Agnes.'

'Really?'

'The house is always full of them. They're the sort of people Aunt Agnes likes best. She told me so.'

'She can't have *told* you a thing like that!'

'Of course, she did. Don't be a goose, Cressida. If Aunt Agnes weren't the type she is, she might make difficulties about taking you in. So thank your stars.'

'I'll have to *ask* Mummy and Daddy,' said Cressida.

'Well, don't say too much. Just tell them that your hostess's brother is a K.C.M.G.'

Vivien bought each of them a banana sundae to settle the matter.

CHAPTER THREE

The New Home

'Should your aunt still call herself a countess when she's no longer married to the man who's the earl? Not that I don't think she's wonderful all the same.'

The room provided for Vivien contained a large sofa as well as a bed, and on it Cressida sprawled. In her own room, though there was a bigger bed than Vivien's, there was no sofa. Cressida had rather expected to be sharing a room. She did not know whether to be glad or sorry about things as they were. At Riverdale House, they had contrived adjoining cubicles, separated only by a cretonne curtain. It was always said that there were many changes in one's life when one left.

'Why ever not?' replied Vivien. 'Once a countess, always a countess. Not all the water in the wide rough sea can wash the grace from an anointed king.'

'That's a bit different. Aunt Agnes hasn't been anointed.'

'Who has, nowadays?' said Vivien. 'Have a cigarette.'

'I don't really like them,' said Cressida, taking and lighting one all the same.

'These are special. One of Aunt Agnes's friends supplies them. They're Balkan or something. Gaston says they wouldn't kill a kitten.'

'Is Gaston French?'

'Yes, he's at the embassy or somewhere. I don't like him.'

'Have you seen much of him?'

'I've seen him twice.'

'Is that often enough?'

'Too often,' replied Vivien.

Later, Cressida changed into her first really short dress. She had bought it that afternoon in Kensington High Street. Neither Mrs Hazeborough nor her husband liked short dresses. This one had been very cheap, but Cressida felt that it was hard to see why one should pay more when in any case so very little stuff was involved. The dress was mainly a pale pink.

Vivien's dress was scarlet. It had not been bought at the same time. Vivien always wore either red or black when she possibly could, which was most of the time, because her parents were mostly out of the country.

Cressida's figure, however, was more in the fashion than Vivien's.

'We must do something about our hair tomorrow,' said Vivien, eyeing Cressida's figure in her new dress.

'My father hates short hair on women,' said Cressida.

'None the less, this is London, darling,' said Vivien patiently, 'and we are about to meet the cream of society.'

'Really? I hadn't realised.'

'You look fine, Cressida,' said Vivien. 'Really beautiful.'

Cressida let Vivien descend the staircase first.

Gaston apparently was not there. At least, Cressida thought not, but the introductions were exceedingly confusing, as the two girls had entered after the company had become quite animate, following several drinks. These appeared to be largely cocktails, and there was an actual Negro in a white jacket to shake them up. Cressida's father did not approve of cocktails, and, in fact, she had never consumed one.

'Cocktail, darling?' asked Lady Luce. Cressida accepted at once.

She and Vivien sometimes called one another darling, but the promiscuous use of the endearment by adults was still another thing that Mr Hazeborough quite specifically objected to.

At that moment, Cressida deliberately resolved henceforth to waive every single one of her parents' objections, or very nearly so. It really had become a matter which needed a decision, one way or the other.

There were more men than women. All the men were in dinner jackets, but some of the women struck Cressida as being less well dressed than she and Vivien. This was disillusioning.

Nor could it be said that any of the men was yet making eyes at her, or at Vivien either. Perhaps Lady Luce, Vivien's Aunt Agnes, would not have liked it in either of their cases, Cressida reflected. Perhaps, too, all the men had known Vivien since she was a child.

It continued to be quite easy to go on merely talking to Vivien.

'Is that man really black or is he a white man with black on his face?'

'He's black,' replied Vivien. 'But he's not here all the time.'

'There wouldn't be enough for him to do,' said Cressida.

'Possibly not,' said Vivien. 'I must say that Aunt Agnes might do more to mix us up. That little more and how much it is; that little less and what worlds away.'

23

But the more Cressida gazed around, the less sure she felt that she wanted to be mixed, least of all artificially.

The disconcerting thing was that these people seemed to have more in common with the people she was accustomed to in Rutland than they had anything distinctive of their own. Even the legendary cocktail had failed, as far as she could tell, to exhilarate. Probably Vivien's Aunt deemed herself too judicious to offer her another one.

A man did speak to her, but in a tone adapted not so much to a friend of his daughter's (supposing he had a daughter) as to a child at the village school. Cressida, fresh from Riverdale House, with all its sophistication, could have snapped at him, though she just managed not to, through the expedient of not speaking at all. So far in life she had found middle-aged men more interesting than young men, in so far as she had met either; but this middle-aged man was an exception. Perhaps he was divorced, and this had saddened him.

Vivien had drifted away and was now talking to a man with white hair and a red face who had even risen to his feet for her benefit.

Dinner, however, really was succulent; unimaginably better than Rutland. Some of the girls had deemed it immodest to think of nothing but food and drink. Vivien, on the other hand, had tended to cite Tolstoy (despite his apelike and toothless appearance): 'People with exceptional talents have exceptional appetites.' It was the only thing by Tolstoy she could remember reading.

Cressida had never encountered such food as this before, and the men on either side of her were so impossible that she was able to do it full justice. The men kept addressing one another

24

over Cressida's head, though only literally. The wives who were present tended to shout at one another also, Cressida noticed, rather than address the men next to them. Altogether, the noise in the room was tremendous. The conversation, Cressida adumbrated, was full of sound and fury; signifying nothing. Would her own life offer no more than this? So frequently she doubted both life and herself, whatever Vivien might proclaim.

Vivien had been placed by her aunt between two of the younger men. Perhaps both had been brought forward for Vivien's sake. One had dark, wavy hair and a large, pale flower in his buttonhole. Cressida supposed that he looked quite interesting, though Vivien's expression as she listened to him was, as so often, enigmatic.

'If one is at the bar,' Cressida could hear him saying, 'the grind is just murder. One hardly sees one's wife and kids from year's end to year's end.'

Cressida was surprised that he should already be thinking of things like that. But then she might not be the only person of more or less her age to be doubtful about the most that life could possibly offer. She had never before met another such person (Vivien was always a blaze of confidence), but here might be one. Intermittently, she eyed the young man opposite. Of course it was hardly to be expected that Lady Luce should provide two equivalent young men for her, Cressida, who had never been properly invited to the house at all. Even though Lady Luce had been kindness itself to her, she really knew nothing about her, except what Vivien had proffered, which was often distorted, to say the least.

Cressida picked away the last little scraps of fish from the bone. At procedures like this she must learn to be effortlessly proficient, in case she should one day find herself seated between cabinet ministers or ambassadors. Her two actual neighbours seemed interested mainly in catching fish rather than in eating them.

'If one goes in for medicine,' said Vivien's young man, 'it's simply slavery. One can give almost nothing to one's home-life at all.'

Cressida thought that, of the two careers, the bar would be better for him, owing to the clarity of his diction. At the bar one has to speak in a loud voice for hours at a time, for days on end, sometimes for months and years, as in the Tichborne case. Her father frequently referred to that great legal battle.

'Not until it's too late,' put in the other young man, who had sandy hair, already waning, and very small spectacles, before very small eyes.

'Too late, Jeremy? What do you mean?' asked the first young man, put completely off his theme, and speaking across Vivien.

'A doctor has no time of his own until it's too late to be of any use to him.'

'That's precisely what I was saying, Jeremy. One even thinks of the church, like Alastair. But really one can't quite.'

Cressida failed to hear why that was; because at that moment both her neighbours, having finished their fish course, spoke to her simultaneously.

At a subsequent stage, the late night edition of the evening paper appeared. It was brought to Lady Luce on a salver by a man who had helped with the serving; white, not black.

Lady Luce held the paper before her and glanced at the front page. There was an almost universal hush, lest the oracle might impart.

26

'Vittore has dashed off and captured somewhere else,' imparted Lady Luce conclusively, and as if some announcement simply had to be made.

'Bloody mountebank!' exclaimed the man with the white hair and red face. 'If you'll excuse the language, Agnes.'

'He did fight on our side in the war,' said one of the married women.

'If you call what he did fighting,' said another guest, masculine, formless, average.

'Really, Tomlins,' said the same married woman. 'I don't see how we are in a position to know.' Presumably she was the man's wife; presumably this was one couple where there had been no question of a divorce for either party; presumably Tomlins was the husband's Christian name.

'Some of us know,' said another man, quietly, but, as he intended, lethally.

Cressida might have guessed who would settle the matter.

Vivien spoke up. Though she had a clear enough voice, Cressida had not previously heard her during dinner. Perhaps she had not uttered.

'Virgilio Vittore is the greatest man in the world,' said Vivien.

All laughed tolerantly.

'How do you *know*, dear?' asked Lady Luce.

'Everyone knows,' said Vivien. 'That's just the trouble.'

'I'm not sure *I* know,' said Lady Luce, to ease the tiny tension. She was smiling suitably. Among other things, she conveyed that no one knew what she really knew.

Cressida much regretted that she had no views on the matter, in that she did not at all clearly know who Virgilio Vittore was, though she too had seen the name every now and then in the newspapers.

The trouble was that, at Cressida's age, one could not take in and concentrate equally upon every topic reported. Cressida had thought it best to seek a convincing grasp upon selected subjects. In due course, she would take up further subjects, perhaps when she had grasped all there was to grasp about the present subjects, so that they had become a little boring. New subjects sometimes even imposed themselves and spread out on their own, as she had already noticed. It seemed likely that one day she would have grasped all that she would wish to grasp, and perhaps be a little bored with everything there was.

In the drawing room, Lady Luce explained to Cressida that, when the men appeared, they were all going to play bridge, so that Cressida might prefer to go up to her room. Cressida did not particularly want to go to her room, but it seemed difficult to demur.

'I forget, Vivien,' said Lady Luce. 'Do you play bridge?'

'No, Aunt Agnes,' said Vivien. I haven't the brains.'

'Of course you have, dear,' said an elderly lady, whom the new fashion did not entirely suit. 'Bridge is nothing like as difficult as people say. I managed to teach the man who came to mend the chairs.'

'Beatrice Basingstoke,' remarked another woman, 'managed to teach her Pekingese.'

'I think you *should* learn bridge, Vivien,' said Lady Luce. 'I'll see what can be done about it before your parents come back. In the meantime, perhaps you and Cressida would like to sit in one of the corners and play something else?'

'Don't *worry* about us, Aunt Agnes,' said Vivien. 'We both know that we still have much to learn.'

The men held back for what Cressida thought a surprisingly long time. The first pot of coffee had had to be consumed lest it grow cold; and now there was anxiety about the second pot. Cressida had always supposed that the conversation of women among women was what it was, owing to her being there, a mere schoolgirl; but in Lady Luce's house she began to wonder whether it was not much the same whether she was there or not. Certainly the women seemed to take very little notice of her. What was more, she began to doubt also whether the conversation of men among men could be anything much preferable. Most of the adult men she had met so far had merely depressed her. She was relieved to reflect that Vivien seemed to feel the same. Now all the youth of England is on fire, Vivien sometimes remarked sarcastically at suitable moments.

Already, Cressida had very nearly come to the conclusion that divorced people were hardly distinguishable from other people. But that, she suddenly realised, might be precisely the danger; the element in the divorce situation that most disturbed her father. It seemed very probable. Like confirmation, the whole thing was perhaps difficult to grasp until one had been divorced oneself, which Heaven forfend. But to think of having even once to marry one of those men in the dining room! Even though many of them had been married twice, or much more! Not even the youth who 'really couldn't quite' take holy orders appealed to Cressida. In fact, she was pretty sure that he was not even the one she would pick, if pick she had to. And one day the compulsion was going to be difficult to avoid—or to evade. The evening had brought the matter home to Cressida as nothing before had done. It was marvellous that people managed to grow up, thunderstroke after thunderstroke, without more nervous breakdowns.

There was a woman talking endlessly about the taxes and raising her tone menacingly whenever another attempted to intrude. What the woman said was perfectly true, of course; or at least substantially so. Cressida knew enough to know that, as taxation was one of the most frequent themes at home. The troubles were that the woman was using all the wrong arguments, both silly and offensive ones; and that she would have been such a poor advocate even for the right arguments. The arguer is the greater part of the argument, Cressida reflected.

When even the second pot of coffee was nearly cold, most of the men dribbled back, in many cases tottery and truculent. Cressida assumed that the absentees were queued up around the bathroom.

Lady Luce was too good-natured to refer to the state of the coffee. She simply poured it out, and one of the men passed it round among the other men, as if nothing were wrong. It was too late for a third pot in any case; the servants having gone to bed or gone somewhere else.

'Sorry we hung about, Agnes,' said one of the men. 'We were talking about the All Blacks.'

'If we're going to play bridge,' said Lady Luce, 'we'd better hurry up and organise ourselves.'

'*You* organise us, Agnes!'

There was much conflictual moving of furniture and opening up of objects hitherto closed in on themselves; much sitting down in wrong places and standing up again; much abnegation and some assertion: while all the time missing men were sauntering back, and ladies flitting out to make themselves even lovelier.

It was easy for Cressida and Vivien to go unnoticed, especially as one of the men, upon his return, had left the door open.

They went up to Vivien's room.

'What are the All Blacks? Are they a jazz band?'

'They are a football team,' said Vivien. 'I was taken to see them once. Rugger. Twickenham.'

'Is all conversation like that when one has left school?'

'All the conversation I've heard,' said Vivien. 'It's a mask, you know.' Vivien was smoking again.

'Then there's something more exciting behind the mask? Is there *really*, Vivien?'

'Of course men talk shop a lot, when we're not there—and most of the time when we are. You mustn't expect the Art of Conversation at Aunt Agnes's bridge evenings.'

'No, of course not,' said Cressida, blushing slightly. 'Were *all* those people divorced?'

'I think so. I don't know any of them very well.'

There was a pause.

Then Cressida asked, 'What exactly are we going to do about it, Vivien? We'll be sucked in, else. Sucked down, more likely.'

'Not me,' said Vivien, stubbing her cigarette, less than half smoked. 'And not you either. We're going to fight. We need a strategy.'

'Send me word,' said Cressida, 'when we've got one.'

'I don't know enough yet. Paul always said you can't work out a proper strategy unless you have the knowledge. But I'm going to learn, Cress. And so are you. We're in this together, and well you know it.'

Cressida considered. The matter had never before been put so plainly to her.

'I suppose so,' she said cautiously. 'I'm not sure where I am.'

'You had your chance when Tiddleywinks proposed to you. Did you want to marry Tiddleywinks? Well, then.'

'Vivien,' Cressida protested. 'It wasn't a proper proposal. I keep telling you. Tiddleywinks simply asked if he might propose when we were both older and when he was fully trained. You must remember that I've known him ever since we were babes.'

'I know one thing, Cressida,' said Vivien. 'When it comes to the opposite sex, I am interested only in a Man, and neither you nor I have ever met one.'

'Give me that man that is not passion's slave,' cited Cressida.

'Or that is,' said Vivien.

They then read their books, while Vivien smoked cigarettes, one after another, none of them completely finished.

'Vivien,' said Cressida, when it was long past midnight. 'I'm going.'

Vivien seemed still absorbed, though much time had passed.

'What book is it?' asked Cressida. They made a particular point of not trying to influence one another about books.

Vivien smiled and held the cover towards Cressida. Cressida read: Castiglione, *The Courtier*.

'Can you understand it?'

'It's not in Italian, idiot, it's translated.'

'Even then. Do you understand it?'

'Some of it,' said Vivien. 'Say not the struggle naught availeth.'

Cressida said goodnight and they kissed.

'No good asking if you want anything,' said Vivien, 'because you won't get it even if you do.'

'D'you mean they're still playing bridge?'

'I should think so. Once they've started they don't stop. When I was a kid, I used to creep down and find them with the curtains drawn and the lights on hours after it was daylight outside. I think that bridge is all Aunt Agnes really cares about.'

'I suppose she's very good at it.'

'I don't think so,' said Vivien. 'Daddy says she loses every time.'

CHAPTER FOUR

The Conversation

None the less, what amounted to an alternative view of Aunt Agnes was offered to Cressida that very same night.

Though Vivien had trouble in sleeping, Cressida slept like a little bird, as her mother often put it. Notwithstanding, she woke up at once when Aunt Agnes entered her room, quietly though Aunt Agnes did it. Aunt Agnes was carrying a lighted candle in a large silver candlestick. Cressida was accustomed to the nocturnal use of candles in Rutland, but in Central London it surprised her.

'I didn't want to wake you up,' said Aunt Agnes softly. 'Perhaps you were awake already. Like me.'

'You didn't wake me up,' said Cressida politely.

'I'm glad,' said Aunt Agnes. 'After all, you are my guest.'

'It's very nice of you,' said Cressida.

'It's very nice *for* me,' said Aunt Agnes. She seemed a different person; a gentler and (to be honest) nicer person. Not that Cressida had felt any serious lack of gratitude, or of respectful fascination.

Aunt Agnes wore eau-de-nil silk pyjamas and a matching silk peignoir. Embarrassingly, Cressida wore only a pale-blue nightdress with dog roses on it. Vivien had long objected to this garment, and to others like it, but Cressida's parents were not made of money, let alone Cressida herself, who had virtually none at her free disposal; nor was she going to accept presents of clothes from Vivien, even had they been offered, which, judiciously, they had not been.

Aunt Agnes's bobbed hair was tied up in an eau-de-nil bandeau-de-nuit, which suited her.

'I can't sleep, Cressida,' said Aunt Agnes. 'Those frightful cards. I hate them. Do you mind if I sit down?'

'Please sit down,' said Cressida.

Aunt Agnes seated herself in the chintz-covered armchair.

'Those frightful people, too,' said Aunt Agnes. 'Just between the two of us, Cressida, don't you agree with me? *Aren't* they frightful?'

'I don't know them well enough.'

'You don't have to know people well in order to know them.'

'That's what Vivien says.'

'It's true,' said Aunt Agnes. 'It's true with most people, anyway.'

'*You* seem different.'

'I am Vivien's aunt, and can't help behaving like an aunt when she's there. Her parents expect it of me. I'm not *your* aunt.'

'I should like it very much if you were,' said Cressida.

'That's nice of you but I'm not sure that I want another niece. Perhaps we could just be friends?'

'I should like that,' said Cressida.

'But it's not only being Vivien's aunt that's wrong. The trouble with me is that I just don't like crowds. With a crowd of people I'm at my worst. They make me hate myself as well as them.'

'Vivien says she doesn't like people.'

'You're very fond of Vivien, aren't you?'

'Yes. She's my best friend and always will be.'

Aunt Agnes smiled. 'You're quite right. Vivien is a very clever girl.'

'Not clever *only*,' said Cressida.

'I'm sure not. But the cleverness is important. Because it will prevent Vivien ever being happy—or quite happy.'

'Yes,' said Cressida. 'I know that.'

'So from time to time she may very much depend upon you.'

'Oh, Lady Luce, do you think so? I feel that I'm the one who depends on her.'

'Cressida,' said Aunt Agnes, 'I wish I could suggest that you called me something other than Lady Luce, but I won't have Aunt Agnes, and I can't permit you to call me by my Christian name while my niece is around and is your best friend too, so I fear that there is absolutely nothing to be done about it.'

Cressida could think of no instant reply to that, so it was fortunate that Aunt Agnes continued speaking.

'Vivien has not had a very happy childhood, because her parents are not well-suited. It is largely my brother's fault, but there it is. So I am particularly glad that she has a good friend in you.'

'I still miss *my* brother very much,' said Cressida. 'He was killed in the war.'

'Oh,' said Aunt Agnes. 'So many people were killed in the war.'

'My uncle too. My father's younger brother. He was a colonel, but apparently it made no difference.'

'Nothing made any difference. I lost the man I loved, Cressida.'

'Oh, but you found someone else, Lady Luce!' cried Cressida, much wanting it to be so, very glad it was so, thinking no further.

'Yes, of course. Most of us do that in the end.'

Remembering that Aunt Agnes was, after all, divorced, Cressida, once more, did not quite know what to say.

'There should never have been a war, all the same,' said Aunt Agnes.

'There must never be another one, Lady Luce,' said Cressida with great firmness. 'Never.'

'Of course not,' said Aunt Agnes. 'And now would you like me to go?'

'I *am* a bit sleepy,' said Cressida, all manners forgotten.

'I expect I am too,' said Aunt Agnes.

She rose to her feet, retied the wide cincture of her peignoir, crossed to the bed, and lightly kissed Cressida on the brow. 'I want you to stay as long as you like, or as long as you need to,' she said. 'However long it may be. I can't say that in the clear light of day. But remember. It's something understood and settled.'

Quietly opening and shutting the door, Aunt Agnes departed, leaving in the room impressions of languor and sentiment which Cressida found so overpowering that she fell asleep almost immediately.

She dreamed that she was in a desert, tied naked to a tree, the only tree there was, or the only one she could discern from her disadvantageous position. Her hands were tied together behind the tree, and it was very hot, though not so much with the dry heat one would expect to rise from sand as with the damp heat one would expect to fall from rainforest. In front of her, seated on the sand, were a group of men, ten or twelve of them, all in mud-of-Flanders uniforms, however incongruous. In fact, there were actual grey streaks on them now; blanched, very nearly, by the sun. Cressida was perspiring all over, and her damp hair fell into her eyes, about which she could do nothing. Someone had said that she should have had her hair cut shorter, that it was expected of her; but plainly she had done nothing about it. The men were listlessly chucking cards and dice about on the sand, and speaking nothing but obscenities. Some were words that Cressida vaguely knew to exist; some were words she had never before heard or heard of. On the face of it, the only communication between the men consisted in competitive snarling; but it was the matey form of snarling which Cressida had observed men to go in for when on their own. Probably the men had been isolated for a long time, so that the maleness of their behaviour had been intensified. The whole desert was littered with empty brown bottles and cartridge cases. The men were very huddled, so that it took some time for Cressida to realise that the faces of many were disfigured by ghastly wounds, crimson and twisting. As for her own situation, it was not so much that Cressida had no explanation for it, as that it did not occur to her to need one. But in due course, in ten seconds, ten hours, ten years, no time at all, the growling and bickering men seemed to be taking one another more seriously: the backchat was becoming abuse, conventionalised no longer. A possible explanation was that the beer, and the rations, and such slaughterable game as there might ever have been, had run out; because soon the men were actually fighting, each against all. They were packed closely together and milling unpredictably: like a rugger scrum on Pathé Pictorial. Cressida began to feel fright. The sweat of fear augmented the sweat of the sun. Then she realised that the men had drawn their bayonets, and had fully committed themselves. They were slashing and hacking at one another. Their salacious words were no longer tired and almost meaningless: they had become choice stimuli to frenzied action, like the liturgical shrieks of Islamic fanatics. One after another the men were dropping to the dirty sand, overcome, lacerated, inert. So much defeat within only a few feet of her almost made Cressida dissolve with terror. 'Hugh,' she cried. 'Oh, Hugh.'

She was awake. She realised that she had fallen asleep while lying on her back and with her hands locked together beneath her body; the position from which she had been addressing Aunt Agnes, and in which Aunt Agnes had kissed her. She was terribly hot.

While she was slowly releasing herself, there was a light tap on the door and Vivien entered.

'What is it, Cressy?'

'A dream.'

'I thought you were being strangled.'

'Did I wake you up? Sorry.'

'No. I wasn't asleep.'

'Well, I'm sorry about that then.'

'Yes. I think my mind's too active.'

'Vivien, you realise we don't really know how Hugh died. We don't actually know at all. I suppose some people know, but *we* never shall. I never properly thought of it before. I believed what they all said.'

'Probably better *not* to know, Cressida.'

'I don't agree with that. It's going to haunt me. I absolutely need to know.'

'You're much too hot, Cressy. People always are in this house. It's one of the worst things about it.'

Vivien was still wearing one of her school nightdresses, but at least it was in a single colour, and a strong one: red, of course. At Riverdale House, it had considerably divided opinion among the girls; and had even elicited a puzzled comment from one of the mistresses.

'It *is* rather hot, but I'm very lucky to be here,' said Cressida. She did not mention Aunt Agnes, and without even having to decide not to.

'None the less, life does not end with bridge parties. We must keep our eyes and ears open, Cressy. Four eyes. Four ears.'

Cressida resolved immediately that she would do her best.

Chapter Five

The Shop

It was all very well for Vivien to keep saying things, but acting upon them was so difficult. This did at all not surprise Cressida.

One obvious problem was that it was so easy to shed present advantages, considerable even though unsatisfying; so hard to acquire and be reasonably sure of keeping a single new advantage of any kind, however trivial, in exchange. Cressida already had a fairly splendid new home, especially after what Aunt Agnes had said; a tiny independence, now that she had a job; even a tiny freedom, possibly quite enough (as many would certainly point out) for one of her years, inexperience, and deep provinciality. She had had her hair cut off and had bought several new dresses. In so far as she mixed with anyone, she mixed mainly with people who were supposedly prosperous and successful. Aunt Agnes, at moments, was a new mother; and, at those moments, far more exciting than the lady Cressida had taken to describing as her 'real mother'. Cressida felt almost certain that Aunt Agnes was therefore more dependable also. To be less exciting is so often to be more calculating, and when one's parents start to calculate, one never knows with what conclusion they will bring the process to an end.

As Cressida could not yet do anything of major commercial consequence, she had accepted the offer of a job in a flower shop, which had been proffered by one of Lady Luce's apparently closest friends, a man named Mr Bobby Ravenscourt.

The proposition had been entirely above board: Lady Luce had been present when it had been put forward. On the other hand, there had been no question of Mr Ravenscourt having been even partly influenced by considerations of charity: he had taken the entire initiative in the matter without its having been even hinted that Cressida might need paid employment of any kind.

It was true that Lady Luce had said, 'That's very sweet of you, Bobby,' but she often said that sort of thing when speaking to men.

It was true, too, that the shop was not in S.W.7, where Lady Luce resided, but in S.W.10. However, some of Lady Luce's visitors refused on principle to give any heed to the new system of sub-dividing postal districts by numbers. They predicted that in any case it would not last.

The shop was named Perdita. 'Ah, *A Winter's Tale*,' Cressida had said at once. 'Violets dim, but sweeter than the lids of Juno's eyes.' But Lady Luce had said, 'I expect Mr Ravenscourt's forgotten *The Winter's Tale*. Haven't you forgotten *The Winter's Tale*, Bobby?' And while Mr Ravenscourt was trying to utter something brazen, Vivien, who had been in the room too, had said 'Not *The* Winter's Tale, Aunt Agnes. *A* Winter's Tale.' Whereupon Lady Luce had said, 'I think you are mistaken, Vivien,' and offered her another sponge cake, which Vivien had accepted. They were all consuming matutinal Madeira, one of the many matters in which Lady Luce insisted upon treating the girls as fully adult, whatever their real parents might think or do.

Perdita herself was a rather gaunt woman of at least thirty-two. Vivien had alleged that night to Cressida, when they were reading their books, that Perdita was 'really' Mr Ravenscourt's daughter; though Cressida had replied that in that case Mr Ravenscourt must have been remarkably young at the time: at which point they decided to leave it for the present in absence of anything very positive.

Perdita the shop seemed quite busy, and Cressida was not surprised that an assistant saleswoman had been needed for some time. Cressida was not asked either to keep the books or to do the cleaning.

Many of the customers were elderly. There was a steady demand for monochrome flowers in bulk, leaves and all. They were applied to brightening up the apartments, and (in some cases) houses of people whose children had left the nest; and, often, whose spouses had gone off too. Of course there were also young women who lived in flatlets (a new trend) and bought daffodils; and young men buying single carnations for their jackets and overcoats.

Perdita the proprietor usually wore a grey dress, a long, narrow rectangle. Cressida supposed it was to mark her off from the customers, so that people should not bring their bundles of peonies to the wrong person; and wondered whether she, Cressida, should dress similarly. She would rather have liked it, and it would certainly have saved both money and trouble, but as Perdita did not suggest it, Cressida could see that Perdita might not solicit more direct competition, especially from someone younger. She had not had to bother much with such problems.

Perdita always very kindly produced a light luncheon for them both, shutting the shop for half-an-hour for the purpose. It was one of Cressida's tasks to turn the key in the lock of the outer door and hang up a notice reading CLOSED UNTIL THREE O'CLOCK. Perdita herself removed the notice and unlocked the door when all the litter and scraps had been rendered invisible. To shut for a full hour would have been both uneconomic and unnecessary. Luncheon consisted in fish paste or meat paste sandwiches, an éclair, and milky coffee from a thermos. Perdita made the sandwiches in her flat, and each morning bought the two éclairs at the same shop, where she had become known in no time, so that the little packet was waiting for her each day, only needing to be paid for. Perdita made no secret of preferring coffee éclairs to chocolate éclairs.

'I am sure that I could be the one who brings lunch every other day,' said Cressida soon; confident in, among other things, Lady Luce.

'That's nice of you, Cressida, but it's simpler if I do it.'

'But why?'

'I'm in the habit of it,' said Perdita, with a faint but firm smile.

Cressida realised that she wanted it like that. People become set in their ways.

One day, Perdita had not had time to make sandwiches, so had bought sausage rolls at the éclair shop, causing surprise, and hope for the future.

While they were eating them, Cressida said: 'What a beautiful name you have! Perdita! Much nicer than mine.'

'Do you think so?' responded Perdita. 'I always think it's rather a silly name. It means "lost", doesn't it? And no one likes to be called lost.' She smiled her smile, not really wishing to seem unfriendly.

'Well,' said Cressida, keeping things up, 'Cressida was really a little tart, and that's not very nice either, is it? Though fortunately almost no one knows.'

But Perdita clearly did not care for words like that, even between two women in a locked-up shop.

However, she pulled herself together, and, trying to play her part too, asked, 'Why did your parents call you that?'

'My mother just liked the name,' said Cressida, picking up her éclair; chocolate, that day of confrontation and soul-bearing.

'Parents should think more of what a child will have to go through later,' said Perdita.

'Sometimes it's worse to be found than lost,' observed Cressida. 'Just as there are worse things to be than—what Cressida was.'

'You shouldn't try to be witty, Cressida,' said Perdita. 'People don't like it.'

'You mean they don't like it in women?' asked Cressida cheekily.

'They don't like it in anyone. It upsets people.'

'Do you like people, Perdita?'

'Not much. But we all have to make the best of them.'

Cressida had finished her éclair. 'Perdita,' she said. 'What do you want most in the world?'

Perdita was pouring the coffee. She always poured it at exactly the same, well-judged speed.

'Why do you ask me?'

'Vivien says it's the greatest test of anyone's character.'

Perdita never agreed with anything Vivien had said. For one thing (though only one), she had known Vivien, albeit slightly, for longer than had Cressida.

'Vivien says that when you ask most people, they have no answer. That speaks for itself.'

'I'm perfectly able to answer,' said Perdita. 'What I want most is a small cottage in some nice place, Sussex or Hampshire, but not too near other people. I don't mind what it looks like provided it can be kept very warm, and has a fair-sized garden. That's what I want, and I'm working hard and saving up so that I can get it.'

'But what would you *do* all day?'

'I never lack for occupation, Cressida.' Perdita smiled. Then she added, 'I should have time for my research.'

'What are you looking for? The Philosopher's Stone? The Fountain of Youth?' Those seemed to be the only things one could possibly research into day and night in a small isolated overheated cottage that looked like nothing on earth. There had been a mistress at Riverdale House who was just like that: Miss Rossetti. She it had been, in fact, who had told the class about those very quests. Vivien had been fascinated, Cressida rather more sceptical.

'Well, yes, in a way, I suppose I am,' replied Perdita, now smiling a quite different smile. 'I research into the history of my family, and there's no possible end to that.'

CHAPTER SIX

The Healer

Vivien was working as a receptionist to a psychoanalyst. As there was seldom a new patient, but only the same old people (though not always old in years), the job was a comparatively light one. All the same, it was essential: Dr Blattner could hardly himself admit the patients into the house and dismiss them from it at the end of each one's 'session'. It would have undermined all confidence.

Vivien was not even called upon to type out the notes that Dr Blattner occasionally set down as the patient ran on. In the first place, complete confidentiality was essential to the success of the treatment ('Complete! Total! Absolute!' as the Doctor described it to each patient at the outset of the long ordeal). In the second place, Dr Blattner's shorthand had been specially designed for him by a tachygraphist in Vienna, and was thus decipherable, if at all, only by him; even the expert having long ago forgotten most of the system. In the third place, Vivien could not type, though she was learning fast.

Vivien first employed her spare time in making notes of her own from books in Dr Blattner's professional library. When she came to the end of the books that were in English, and had looked through the illustrations in the others, she thought that the time had come to start writing and illustrating something herself. After thinking for nearly an hour (each 'session' lasted for a precise fifty minutes, and when she heard through the wall the sharp ping of Dr Blattner's machine, she rose to her feet, prepared for being quietly sympathetic), and after realising that complete originality could not by this stage in human history be expected of anyone, she decided to begin with a short novel about two girls at Court, one poor because only the daughter of the Court Physician, the other rich because the daughter of the Chancellor of the Realm, who, had necessarily, all the contracts to allot. Vivien dashed off simple drawings of the two girls and wrote half the first chapter in longhand all in one day. It had been explained by the new English literature mistress that the long exposés of history and geography which come first in so many of Sir Walter Scott's novels were a device for enabling the author to 'warm up', so that in due course, and without being self-conscious about it, he could start the process of true creation. Vivien, however, found that she was being creative from the very first sentence. Already her two girls were withdrawn behind an old arras at the top of the vast marble staircase with jewelled daggers in their belts, while, outside the immense windows, night fell silently and a thousand stars appeared. The one girl was confident, almost cynical. The other was gentle and more dependent. Vivien derived great inspiration from the rough drawings she had made of them: the one dressed as a page, the other in the simplest of black dresses. The next day she drew them dressed the other way round.

Vivien had obtained her job not through influence of any kind, but simply from answering an advertisement in the *Morning Post*, which arrived each morning at Aunt Agnes's abode, and gave people something to talk about through the day. What was more, Vivien did not waste ink and stamp on answering many advertisements; she answered only this one. When she arrived to be looked at and interrogated, Dr Blattner had explained that he always advertised in the *Morning Post*, because, for the sake of his patients, he employed only girls from good families. He spoke as if numberless such girls had passed through, and, as he spoke, he scratched his head, which was almost completely bald, with both hands, which were neither of them bald at all. Vivien realised that many would think her lucky to get the job against such well-connected competition.

'Have you ever been analysed yourself?' enquired Dr Blattner.

'Sorry. No.'

'Or considered the possibility?'

'Never.'

Dr Blattner had then engaged her almost immediately.

He had the hairiest hand that Vivien had ever shaken, let alone held, however involuntarily.

'I am sure we shall reach an understanding,' Dr Blattner had said.

CHAPTER SEVEN

The Invitation

Over the sandwiches one day, Perdita asked Cressida if she would care to come to supper some evening in her flat. Cressida had never been there.

'I should love to.'

'Which evening would you like best?'

'Which evening would you prefer?'

Someone had to decide, and it seemed to Cressida best to settle on a Saturday, because on that day the shop closed at one. (Cressida normally went home for a substantial lunch.)

'Besides,' said Perdita, 'it will be easier for Brian.'

'Is he coming too?'

'I thought you'd be interested in meeting him.'

'Who *is* he?'

'He's a boy I know. Much younger than me, of course. He's very serious, but I thought you mightn't mind that.'

'Anyone else coming? Forgive my asking.'

'My usual crowd,' said Perdita. 'Get there about six, would

you? I need time for the cooking and want to be able to look after everyone properly.'

Cressida already knew the address, because Perdita had told it her on the day of her arrival, lest she might need to report that the shop had caught fire, or something like that, when Perdita hadn't been there. So far, however, there had been no period when Perdita had been absent and Cressida present. Cressida occasionally regretted this.

Perdita resided neither in S.W.7 nor even in S.W.10 but in S.W.6, where Cressida had never before heard of anyone living. Why S.W.6 should be the furthest out, she was unable to imagine, however hard she tried. She had to go to a little known station named Parsons Green, and thereafter cope with Vivien's street-plan, while men stood about outside public houses and eyed her.

She had been in the job for three months and now it was October. Still there was a suggestion remaining of the interminable London twilight. There always was.

The house was purplish red and adorned with moulded strips. Perdita had said she lived on the third floor. The front door of the house was open. The communal staircase was fragrant with cleanliness. The lights were perfectly adequate.

Cressida read 'Miss Perdita Stanley-Smith'. She rang.

Perdita opened the door. She was wearing an orange dress with green sprigs. Her arms were bare, though, as Cressida had noticed before, they were rather thin arms.

'Come in, Cressida.'

There was a tiny hall.

'Would you like to leave your coat in my bedroom?'

The bedroom opened up on the right. There was a slender bed, and a picture of seraphs among pale yellow flowers.

'Do you want anything else?'

'No thank you. What a pretty room!'

'Thank you. Come into the sitting-room.'

Perdita entered first. 'Bobby,' she said, 'you remember Cressida?'

Him Cressida had not expected, had not so much as thought of.

'Of course I do,' said Mr Ravenscourt, rising to his feet. 'How are you, Cressida?'

'Very well, thank you.'

'Come and sit next to me on the sofa.' He wore a business suit and looked dependable in the extreme. A fire flickered in the grate. Cressida sat down.

'Brian's late,' said Perdita.

'Brian's always late,' said Mr Ravenscourt gravely.

'He works so hard,' said Perdita.

'He loves his job,' said Mr Ravenscourt very earnestly.

'What does Brian do?' enquired Cressida.

Mr Ravenscourt laughed. 'What *doesn't* Brian do? That's more the question to ask, isn't it, Perdita?'

'Brian's actual job's with the Council,' said Perdita, 'but what he does goes far beyond that.'

'It's a little difficult to describe if you don't know Brian,' explained Mr Ravenscourt.

'Brian is one man who leads a really serious life,' added Perdita.

'He gives a mere businessman like me something to look up to, Cressida. I can tell you that. If I had a son, I should wish him to be just like Brian.'

'You have no children, Mr Ravenscourt?' enquired Cressida.

'I'm a poor lonely divorcé, Cressida,' replied Mr Ravenscourt. 'I have nothing and no one to care for except the money I make and this little circle that Perdita has created.'

Cressida suspected that she was more at the age for a straight line.

'Perdita and I and the rest of us here, we ask nothing of one another, we expect nothing, we are simply ourselves.' Mr Ravenscourt paused. 'Do you understand that, Cressida?'

'I *think* I do,' said Cressida. 'I'll try to.'

'Possibly Cressida may understand better before the evening's over?' Mr Ravenscourt suggested to Perdita.

'Possibly,' said Perdita, with no special eagerness, let alone conviction.

'We shall see!' said Mr Ravenscourt archly. 'We can only observe!'

So far Cressida could not understand why Perdita had involved her, why she had been invited. Could it be that Perdita also had aspired to enrol her, but that somewhere en route, she, Cressida, had done or said something unsuitable? So often in life one did that, and so seldom did one know.

A Mr and Mrs Stanley Barrington arrived; then a Miss Elvin; then a Mr and Mrs Matthew Makepeace; then a Mr Parker. In the shop, Cressida had become quite good with names.

All these people were appreciably older than she. She realised that they belonged to much the same intermediate, indefinable generation as Perdita. The way they were dressed confirmed this. They all seemed exhilarated to see one another, and it was not to be expected that they could bestow an equal amount of time and attention upon a very young female newcomer. For just about the first time in her life, Cressida felt fashionably dressed to the point of embarrassment. Her legs alone were in a different class from any of the others, and her stockings even more so.

'When Brian arrives, I'll get out the sherry,' said Perdita.

'Give the fire a poke, will you, Clementine,' said Miss Elvin. 'I'm shivering.' Cressida did not feel in the least cold and, as far as the eye could see, Miss Elvin was enveloped in thick wool. Cressida's response, therefore, was of little more than a token character.

'Let me,' said Perdita, snatching the small poker and proceeding to bash away at the top of the fire as if it were the bottom of an infuriating child. 'We don't want anyone here to be cold.'

'Indeed, no,' said Mr Ravenscourt. 'Shall I go round the corner and bring up some more logs?'

'It must be miles away,' said Mrs Stanley Barrington, who was wearing a rabbit coat, which she had not yet removed.

'Only about three hundred yards, when once you're in the street,' said Mr Ravenscourt. 'Exercise does us sedentary folk good. I'll bring up a big armful.'

'Better put on something over your jacket,' said Mrs Barrington. 'The logs will be messy after all the rain we've been having.'

'It's been raining for weeks,' said Mr Matthew Makepeace.

Cressida was surprised. She had not noticed that.

'Will they burn if they're damp?' enquired Miss Elvin.

'We could let them dry out for a bit in the heat of the room,' suggested Mr Stanley Barrington.

'Better still, fish out the dry ones from the bottom of the stack,' said Mr Makepeace. 'From the back at the bottom.'

'From the bottom at the back,' said Mr Parker, who had not noticeably spoken before. Spills of greying hair protruded from his ears. It was all one noticed, apart, perhaps, from a continuous smile.

'Please let no one go to all this trouble simply for my sake,' cried Miss Elvin. 'I'm perfectly all right. Really.' But her tone was tense.

'No trouble at all, Millicent,' said Mr Ravenscourt, 'but I wonder if you could lend me a mackintosh, Perdita?'

Perdita produced one from a cupboard in the hall. Cressida assumed that Mr Ravenscourt would look a little ludicrous in it, but, to her surprise, it seemed to be a male mackintosh.

As Perdita helped him on with it, Cressida could compare the two left profiles fairly close together. Unfortunately, she was unable to decide whether or not she found support for Vivien's assertions. She supposed that more time was needed; a patient and reflective comparison of structure and mien, to say nothing of clinical measurements with specially designed instruments. So often was this true in life. Each moment had fled before one had even grasped its import.

But then Brian appeared. Everybody cried out, and some even stood up.

In a flash, Brian had grasped the entire situation. 'Don't think of it, Mr Ravenscourt,' he cried. 'I'm here now. Let me do it.'

Before he could be stopped (if anyone had wished to stop him), he was gone. He had been a small, pale man with a funny voice and very big spectacles, in the new American style. His clothes were similar in general concept to Mr Ravenscourt's. All the other men present were less tidily arrayed; less formally, as they themselves might have put it.

Mr Ravenscourt was taking off the mysterious mackintosh. Cressida wondered how Brian was providing against the elements. Probably he had brought his own protective garment. Almost certainly that could be depended upon.

'I was quite ready to do it, Perdita,' said Mr Ravenscourt, looking, or half-looking, into her eyes.

This time his left profile married with her right profile.

Perdita said nothing.

Cressida looked out of the window. Now, indeed, it was raining.

'Brian's always so good,' said Mrs Matthew Makepeace.

Her remark might be superfluous, but her voice was a contralto of the kind that is sometimes difficult to control without training. Caverns measureless to man, thought Cressida. If only there were treasure within! Glinting gems! Fiercely phosphorescent fish! In the meantime, a sombre and deep voice was no doubt preferable to dead silence.

Silence, however, was unlikely.

It always had been; but now Perdita had produced the sherry, and Mr Ravenscourt had gone for the glasses. The arrival of Brian had come as a release.

They were talking excitedly about past holidays, past visits to Sir Oswald Stoll's London Coliseum, past rambles along the foothills of the North Downs. With a gasp (which she succeeded in concealing), Cressida realised that all these things had been undertaken conjointly by all of them. She was in the presence of a collective: a term that she and Vivien had picked up when reading to one another about the changes in Russia. Some of these excursions, to Bordighera, to Sarah Bernhardt in *Daniel*, to Deepdene, near Dorking, must have been carried through before the war; and still they were spoken of.

This chronology was confirmed by references to persons named Stephen and Wilfred, who had plainly perished. Cressida knew the way people spoke in these cases.

Mr Ravenscourt had reached her with the glasses of sherry on a tray from the flower shop. He spoke in her ear. 'It's Empire. South African.'

'A new experience for me,' said Cressida. Then she added: 'More patriotic than we are at home.' But even that did not sound right.

Mr Ravenscourt should properly have moved on. Mr Parker's mouth was perceptibly open, though not for speech. Moreover, the bottle had been less than quite full to start with.

However, Mr Ravenscourt lingered a little moment.

'Cressida,' he said in her ear, 'where *is* your home?'

'In Rutland,' said Cressida.

'A most beautiful county,' said Mr Ravenscourt in the same intimate manner. 'And a most beautiful girl.'

The conversation was so loud that he hardly needed to mutter in that way. All the same, it was pretty well the first proper compliment Cressida had received.

'Thank you,' she said, and half-lifted her glass. This time she was in no doubt. That was the proper gesture. Mr Ravenscourt's kind eyes seemed faintly to gleam.

'Later on,' he muttered vaguely. 'Later on, I hope.'

His eyes fell the length of her dress, then the length of her pretty legs. Naturally, the whole thing took only a second or two.

For that matter, Brian was up again, with what seemed scores of logs. Two of them were placed on the fire, where they sizzled and exploded and made pictures.

CHAPTER EIGHT

The Water Jump

'Cressida,' said Perdita. 'You must meet Brian. Cressida Haze-borough. Brian Hawk. Brian has an awful lot to talk about that you'll be interested in.'

Perdita had spilt sherry down her front, and was mopping at it petulantly.

'Shall I rub it?' enquired Brian.

'No, thank you, Brian,' said Perdita, almost roguishly. It was the first time that Cressida had seen her blush, except sometimes with justified indignation. Brian was so absorbed with Perdita's front that he had not yet shaken hands with Cressida, as had presumably been expected of him. Cressida let her own hand drop to her side.

Perdita expressed the view that she had better disappear for a moment.

'Very pleased to meet you,' said Brian to Cressida. 'I've heard so much about you. You're the help in Perdita's shop, aren't you?'

'At present,' said Cressida.

'Perdita's a fine woman,' said Brian. 'She must be wonderful to work for.'

As it had hardly been expressed as a question, it hardly seemed to call for an answer.

'*You* work for the Council, I believe?'

'You could call it that.' Brian seemed to have difficulty in focussing his eyes as well as his voice.

'And you're terribly busy?'

'I soon become involved,' said Brian. 'I like it that way.'

'No man is an island,' said Cressida.

'That's right,' said Brian. 'That's in the Testament, isn't it? Are you a Christian?' But Brian's tone was perfunctory for such an important question.

'Of course,' said Cressida.

'Good,' said Brian. 'What do you do about it?'

Cressida supposed that it was the trouble Brian had in looking at people which had led to his wearing such peculiar spectacles.

'I try to lead a Christian life,' said Cressida. 'What about you?'

'I have my club, you know,' said Brian, smiling in such a way as to suggest it was something that most people knew.

Cressida was surprised.

'Which club is it? Daddy belongs to the Rag.'

'It's a club for boys. I got the Council to set it up and I have a free hand all round.'

'With money from the rates?' asked Cressida. '*Our* money?'

'You could hardly think of anything better to do with the rates than to turn boys into proper Christians,' said Brian.

'Well, what about girls? Don't they get a club too?'

'Girls don't need clubs,' said Brian, in a suppressed voice, as if he were holding down his luncheon by sheer will power.

'I'm not sure about that,' said Cressida. Her sherry glass had been empty for some time; but Brian plainly was one who did not drink sherry at all, presumably upon principle of some kind. Cressida wondered why then the manifestation of the sherry bottle had been so precisely timed to coincide with Brian's arrival? Life was endlessly full of these mysteries.

'I'm not sure about that,' said Cressida again. 'Girls can get lonely too, you know.'

She knew at once that it was a silly thing to say, however veracious. Girls must never mention loneliness except to other girls.

Fortunately Brian seemed calm. 'Boys have *spiritual* loneliness,' he defined. 'A void. A yearning.'

'You do lots of other things too?' enquired Cressida.

'I try to organise rambles for the group.'

'This group?' solicited Cressida, slightly slanting her eyes.

'Of course.'

'How far do you go? Normally I mean.'

'Not too far. They have to work during the week, you must remember.'

'I like *long* walks,' exclaimed Cressida, with fatal sincerity.

'We should not only think of ourselves.'

Obviously, she had invited something like that.

Still, she saw no reason why she should be done down completely. 'Do you never do anything you like for its own sake?'

Unexpectedly, Brian turned a little greener for an instant. Cressida would have sworn to it.

'I like everything I do,' he said, recovering quickly. 'That's what service consists in.'

Cressida felt out of her depth. Possibly, even, Brian was right in what he said. Almost anything was possible with a man like that.

'Brian!' cried Mrs Stanley Barrington and Mrs Matthew Makepeace. 'Come and sit on the sofa with us.'

Without even attempting to disguise his relief, Brian plumped down between them.

'Wouldn't you like to wash your hands, Brian?' asked Mrs Makepeace.

'Why should I?'

'After carrying all those dirty logs. I thought you might feel more comfortable.'

'Don't nag Brian, Hilda,' said Mrs Barrington. 'I'm sure he just wants to rest quietly after all he's done.'

'I was thinking only of Brian, April,' said Mrs Makepeace. 'I just wanted him to be comfortable before touching anything.'

Cressida, all alone (and she had heard that there was no loneliness compared with loneliness in the midst of a crowd), turned back to the rain for company. She moved over to the window. It was one which the window cleaner found almost impossible to reach, and the drops were making runnels.

With her finger, she tried to write her name on the glass, but of course on that side it would have been visible only if the sun had been shining.

Cressida loved all rain, from single diaphanous drops falling on the bare neck while the air was warm and luminous, to heavy downpour, demanding the stoutest of protection. The demands of external nature, Cressida adored to meet halfway; however differently she might feel about the demands of daily living.

'What's your family motto, Clementine?'

It was Miss Elvin, who had stolen up behind Cressida while she had been lost in the rain.

'"Ne Cedis." But we haven't used it much since the end of the war.'

'What a pity!' said Miss Elvin. Close to, her woollen dress, opaque and clotted, looked inches thick. There were all kinds of sober colours in it, as if it had been knitted from nearly used up lengths of wool. Cressida was frightened to speculate upon how little there must be of Miss Elvin within it, without it.

'I think so too,' said Cressida.

'Mine is "Sempre". Just "Sempre". That's all.' Miss Elvin spoke as if it were an achievement.

'What's that mean?' asked Cressida. 'I'm afraid I don't know.'

'It means "Always". Simply "Always", said Miss Elvin. 'It's Italian, you know.'

'I thought all family mottoes were in Latin.'

'Oh no, Clementine. Some of the very best families have mottoes in Italian. The Russells, for example. Dukes of Bedford, you know.'

'Are you one of those?'

'Oh, dear no. Nothing of the kind. Not that I'm properly an Elvin either. The name Elvin means and stands for absolutely nothing. My mother made a mésalliance, you know, and I am the unhappy product of it.'

'*Are* you unhappy?'

'Of course I'm unhappy, Clementine. I am deprived.'

'Yes, of course. I understand that.'

'I am no one.'

Cressida tried to smile sympathetically.

'I wish Brian would put another log on the fire.' A strange convulsion swept through Miss Elvin. She did not merely shiver. A twisting, writhing convulsion passed from her head to her toes, twisting her, moreover, inside her thick dress, which did not seem to Cressida to twist with her. It was like the Fairy Carabosse in the Leicester pantomime.

'I'm sure he will,' said Cressida soothingly. She noticed that Miss Elvin spoke as if it were Brian's flat, and not Perdita's. She supposed that Brian had that effect in almost every house he visited. Her father had said that something of the same kind appertained when one was honoured by a visit of the monarch.

'I don't know at all,' said Miss Elvin. 'I don't trust Brian as much as some of them do.'

'Oh, but surely?'

'I know what I know. And they don't know. They're not trained observers, as I am.'

'Are you really trained to observe?'

'By the best trainer of all, Clementine. By life. By life itself.'

Miss Elvin paused. It was a ceremonial pause, and Cressida thought it best not to break in. This must have been right because Miss Elvin switched adroitly.

'I should be delighted if you would come and have supper with me one night, Clementine, in my little home.'

'How nice of you!' Time, time was needed.

'It's time I saw a completely new face.'

Cressida tried to smile sympathetically again.

'You won't mind its being right out in S.W.34. There are buses. I'll send you a little time-table.'

'Of course I don't mind. But I'm afraid I don't have many free evenings.'

'You must have *some*. You're only a young girl. What do you do with your evenings?' Already there was a curious change in Miss Elvin.

'Oh, I study with my friend, Vivien, and I sometimes go to dances.' To hell with plausibility!

'What exactly do you study?' Miss Elvin was being quite nastily sarcastic.

'Well, life mainly, I suppose.'

'Are you being insolent, Clementine?'

'Certainly not. It's what *you* said.'

'Be that as it may,' said Miss Elvin, 'name one night you *can* manage?'

'None, I'm afraid, for the rest of this month.'

'*That* doesn't matter,' said Miss Elvin. 'Next month I have every single night free without exception. Would you care to make it the fifth and we could go to the park and watch the fireworks? We all spend months making the Guy.'

'I think I'd prefer the sixth,' said Cressida, in whom desperation was leading to recklessness.

Miss Elvin stared at her.

'I don't believe you want to come at all. I know you don't.'

Miss Elvin's face, never rubicund, had turned horribly pallid. Cressida imagined that this was the colouring known in books as 'a dirty white'.

'Oh, but I do, Miss Elvin. Of course I do. I should simply love to come on the sixth.'

'You're telling lies, Clementine. You're lying to me. Of course you don't want to see me. You hate the sight of me, like everyone else.'

Her expression was beyond any description that Cressida could compass. What made things even stranger was that Miss Elvin was still keeping her voice down, so that her words did not penetrate the general throng, now rendered even breezier by a glass of patriotic sherry, sometimes a glass and a half. Over Miss Elvin's shoulder, Cressida could see the empty bottle on the mantel, no doubt thrown in some kraal by Zulus and Hottentots. She felt that she herself was inside the bottle.

'Miss Elvin, what nonsense!' said Cressida. 'All these people are your friends.'

'You may believe that, Clementine. You are probably too young to know better. One day you will know. No one can escape knowing. No one.' Miss Elvin had become even more upsetting; because now her tone was that of a conspirator forcing out a dreadful secret in dangerous company.

'I'm sorry, but I simply don't understand,' cried Cressida. Nor did she want to. Miss Elvin might be mad, but there was a horrible conviction in her words. Miss Elvin was Carabosse, shapeless, protean, inimical.

'Games now!' cried out Mrs Matthew Makepeace.

Almost everyone began moving the furniture about, with Brian in charge. It might almost have been one of Lady Luce's bridge parties: mutatis mutandis, of course.

'Come on, Millicent,' cried Mr Makepeace. 'Give us a hand.' He sounded perfectly genial and jovial.

Cressida noticed that no one had called upon *her* to help. Of course she did not know the conventions; what was aimed at. The evolution had been a matter of long years.

The hubbub was considerable, the room being smaller than Lady Luce's.

Miss Elvin had failed the call. She was huddling over the fire like a heavily padded witch, her crouched back to the room.

But these mere preliminaries could not be expected to continue for long. What game was it to be? Could what Cressida's mother called 'the bridge craze' reach further in this company than to Mr Ravenscourt? Cressida simply could not imagine Perdita giving a bridge party, and, after all, it was supposed to be her room.

It was not necessary to imagine anything. A wide tract of carpet had been cleared of encumbrance, and upon it Mr Ravenscourt himself was unrolling a long, wide scroll inscribed in full colour with the Race Game. From where she stood, Cressida could see the Water Jump, the Starting Gate, the packed and enthusiastic Stand at the Winning Post, with all the men in grey top hats. But always it was the Water Jump which caused her the worst anxiety.

Perdita was looking after her. 'Would you like to join in? We usually have games when it's a Saturday and people don't have to work the next day.'

Mr Ravenscourt's eyes were quietly on her. Indeed, the whole circle was hushed for a moment before the wildness began.

'Of course I would,' said Cressida. She was aware that presumably it was her well-meant suggestion of a Saturday which on this occasion had involved all of them in a Saturday.

She found herself on the carpet between Perdita, conscious of her responsibility, and Mr Parker. They were all down there except Miss Elvin, who towered over them in a hard chair, like a goddess of justice. Brian was at Perdita's other side. It seemed clearer and clearer that there was some kind of understanding between those two, though Cressida might have hesitated to be at all specific as to what it could be.

'We must all make the best of what fate offers us,' remarked Mr Ravenscourt, apropos of the draw for horses, which had brought him the roan lacking half a back leg.

Somehow, Brian had drawn the showiest horse, the skewbald, though it also looked a trifle like Sanger's Circus. Cressida had drawn the black. She approved of that. Perhaps the best thing was to leave decision on the lap of the gods, after all? In any case, she did not understand how the draw for horses was conducted, and no one had remembered to tell her, even if by now anyone was able clearly to do so, many years having passed.

There were two dice, but Cressida deduced that at some stage a dice had been lost or purloined, because now the two did not quite match. The dice were thrown on the carpet for all to see. At the same time, the person throwing called out, as best he or she could, the total thrown. Miss Elvin, when casting for herself, had each time to compress her middle region in a way some would have found uncomfortable, but in compensation, she had an extra view of the fate attending all others. Authority so often means intermittent anguish.

At first, the horses leapt forward, with Brian's eye-catching skewbald well in the lead from the outset; but then came the disasters, the returns to the starting line, so much less injurious, however, as Cressida was well aware, than what would have occurred had the race been *en plein air*. Needless to say, Cressida's handsome black failed at the Water Jump. Always, Cressida's horse, no matter what its colour, failed at the Water Jump. Cressida hated the Water Jump. It played a large part in her ever-intensifying distrust of all activities that involved animals.

'Hard luck, Cressida,' said Mr Ravenscourt, opposite her on the other side of the course.

'Poor Cressida!' said Perdita, but from a certain spiritual altitude.

'It'll happen again,' said Cressida. 'You'll see.'

'Nonsense, Cressida,' said Mr Ravenscourt. 'After all, this is purely a game of chance.'

'We used to put money on the horses when we played it at home,' said Cressida, unexpectedly.

No one responded.

'That was in Rutland,' said Mr Ravenscourt, covering up with a kind smile.

But suddenly Cressida was aware that Miss Elvin was staring at her in another new way. Probably she had been doing so ever since the game started. Cressida had simply not cared to look up at her.

The dice box had drawn near to Cressida, and when Perdita passed it to her, Cressida misstated the total she threw.

'Eleven,' said Cressida, almost stammering on the vowel.

'Ten,' corrected Miss Elvin, in a birdlike screech.

'Ten,' said Cressida. 'So sorry. I added it wrong.' She could not imagine how she had done it. She had been playing these board games almost since the cradle. She must be in a state of utter confusion. She was upset.

'Never mind,' said Perdita, though her tone was still not entirely that of reassurance.

The episode had held up the race for a certain number of seconds, partly because Cressida had also omitted to pass on the shaker to Mr Parker. Doing so with extra emphasis, intended for politeness, she was surprised when Mr Parker failed to shake, but simply transferred the apparatus to Mrs Stanley Barrington, on Mr Parker's other side.

'What about you?' enquired Cressida, courteously, though looking at Mr Parker's ear. She did not think she had spoken to him before in the whole course of the party.

Mr Parker shook his head, smiling contentedly.

'I have no horse, my dear.'

And she had not noticed even that!

'Oh, but why?'

'There are not enough horses in the box, and there's one extra person tonight, you know.'

'How dreadful, I feel terribly ashamed.'

'No need to, my dear,' said Mr Parker. 'It's happened before in the world.'

'We should have drawn lots as to who should be left out!'

Miss Elvin was still gazing at her. It struck Cressida that almost everything Miss Elvin did might have an element of the unpleasant for the rest of the world, poor thing.

'Not a bit,' said Mr Parker. 'When it's necessary for someone to stand down, I always do it.'

'That's most unfair,' cried Cressida.

'It's the spirit we all like to keep to,' said Brian from the other side of Perdita. His voice seemed somewhat expressionless, perhaps because he was concentrating upon his skewbald horse, now even farther ahead of the rest. 'If it's not one, it's another.'

Just exactly not that, thought Cressida, now merely squinting at Mr Parker's ear from the furthest corner of her eye.

Under slightly other circumstances, her blood could easily have boiled. But the dice box had made another round, and had reached Perdita once more. If Cressida did not get it right this time, Miss Elvin might well have her burned at the stake as an imposter, a young witch, Cressida la Pucelle.

Chapter Nine

The Uncertainty

And Cressida did not get it right. Or so Miss Elvin claimed. And so they all seemed to accept.

As in many of life's more important situations, the person most concerned never fully grasped or understood either what really happened or what lay behind it.

Cressida threw seven: a five and a two. She moved her black horse, as they were all moving their own horses.

Miss Elvin hissed out, 'She's cheating. That girl cheated. I saw her do it.'

One awful thing was that Cressida, thus challenged, was herself unsure. It was possible that the black horse had somehow gone forward more than seven places. Cressida's mind was on everything else but the game.

If this whole evening was real life, her inner voice never stopped whispering to her, life more real than a child's life, than the life of a very young and protected girl; if this in a general way was what things were to be like in the future . . .

Above all, Cressida was simply terrified of Miss Elvin, who

had long ago seen through to her soul at one glance, though herself hampered and padded into a frightening unreality, a skeleton in the thick fur of a caterpillar, every spine toxic.

For better or for worse, Cressida made not even an attempt at defence.

'You see!' hissed Miss Elvin. Or a hiss it seemed to Cressida in retrospect. 'You all see! She has nothing to say for herself. Just as well. She has told enough lies for one evening.'

Cressida turned sharply to Perdita, but she saw that Perdita's eyes could offer nothing better than reproach. Cressida turned the other way, to Mr Parker; but he was merely grinning. It was neither more nor less than his usual expression. Mr Ravenscourt, opposite, was gazing at the floor.

'She looks down on us,' cried Miss Elvin. 'She thinks she can do what she likes with us.'

Cressida knew quite well that here at least Miss Elvin had found words for the general view. Not that there was reason to suppose much disagreement with anything Miss Elvin proclaimed. Miss Elvin had emerged as a natural leader: one with a gift for enunciating what others merely groped for.

'You do, you know,' Perdita said quietly. 'It's quite true.'

'You have to *work* at friendship,' said Brian, almost sotto voce. Plainly it was one of his more frequent dicta.

Mr Ravenscourt lifted his gaze from the floor, and, carefully not looking at Cressida, said: 'I suggest we call this particular race Honours Even and have some tea. In fact, I'll help to make it.'

'Why?' exclaimed Brian. 'The race is nearly finished.'

'It wouldn't be fair to Brian if we just give up,' said the heavy contralto voice of Mrs Matthew Makepeace. 'We must see things through.' Brian flashed her as much of a grateful look as was possible for him. 'I suggest that someone else take over Cicely's horse until the end of the race. It's quite possible to throw for two horses. We know that.'

'It won't win anyway,' said Mr Stanley Barrington.

Cressida rose to her feet. 'My name is not Cicely. My name is not Clementine. I hate you all.'

She walked to the door with considerable dignity.

'There you are,' said Miss Elvin. 'What did I say? She even admits it. There's a word for girls like her.'

Cressida opened the door slowly and carefully; but, when on the other side, slammed it forcibly. At such moments, such things happen, are even expected.

On her own, Cressida abandoned dignity and raced down the flights of stairs. Only when she had opened the front door of the house did she remember about her coat. She shut the door quietly and stood in the hall, reflecting. She decided that it was impossible to abandon the garment: questions would be asked, and comments made for years and years. Moreover, she might catch something from the autumnal air and be a further burden. People said that happened.

She stole quietly upwards once more. The door to Perdita's bedroom had been shut, and was impossible to open in silence. It must have swollen or something.

The door of the sitting room opened and shut, and Perdita appeared. At some point, she had assumed a fawn cardigan.

'I'm sorry, but you know you did rub them up the wrong way.'

'I hardly spoke the whole evening.'

Perdita smiled her smile. 'That's just it. We're a matey sort of group, you know. Never mind. Least said, soonest mended. Let me help you on with your coat. The rest of them will be going home soon.'

Cressida was unable to evade Perdita's help with the coat.

'Do you believe what that old hag said? I should like to know.'

'You mustn't call poor Millicent an old hag. The trouble with her is that she's in need of love, *real* love, like the rest of us. You will come to understand that, Cressida.'

'She accused me of cheating.'

'It was only a game. And it wasn't as if money was involved, as you foolishly suggested. Now you'll see why we don't play for money. Brian says it's the root of all evil.'

Cressida felt frustrated.

'Who won in the end?' she asked.

'Oh, Brian won. With only a couple more throws. Brian always wins.'

'But it's supposed to be a game of chance.'

'Yes, of course. Brian is just good at games of chance. Some people are, you know.'

'No, I'm not sure I do know.'

'Oh, Cressida!' exclaimed Perdita. 'You must try not to take everything so seriously.'

'I was accused of cheating. Don't you think that *is* serious?'

'Sometimes, of course,' said Perdita. 'But not when it's just Millicent at a party. You must learn to live and let live. Now I must go back to them. See you in the shop on Monday. I expect you'll get better at this sort of thing when you've seen more of it. You must come again when poor Millicent's not here.'

'Is she never not here?'

Cressida had spoken before reflecting.

But the sitting room door had opened again and Mr Ravenscourt appeared. Presumably Perdita's guests were wondering what had become of her.

'Ah,' said Mr Ravenscourt. 'How's our little girl now? If you wouldn't mind waiting ten or fifteen minutes, I could take you in my car.'

At the shop, Perdita had mentioned that she needed time for cooking. Surely they could not eat it all in fifteen minutes, even if she, the disturber, were waiting in outer darkness?

'No, thank you very much,' said Cressida with dignity.

She quite missed the chance of comparing profiles once more.

CHAPTER TEN

The Suggestion

'But it was never made clear whether or not they really accused me of cheating.'

'You'll get used to that sort of thing,' rejoined Vivien. 'Nothing that matters is ever made clear.'

'Do I just go back to the shop on Monday as if nothing had happened?'

'That's it. Not a word will be said.'

'But I shall be marked down. And all for something I never did.'

'You're not sure you didn't.'

'I'm sure I didn't *mean* to do it. And that's what counts.'

'Not really, you know.'

'It's what counts with God.'

'But only when you get to Heaven.'

'The way things are going, I shall *never* get to Heaven.'

Vivien considered that, scraping out the last spoonfuls of vanilla ice cream, now the consistency of baby food. She had been with a quite different aunt for the weekend.

Two days later Cressida was still dishevelled. It was all like the aftermath of an exam in which not one single question has been answerable, even though everything turns on it.

'Would you like a session with Dr Blattner? There's one free the day after tomorrow. Aaron Moss won't be coming: he's gone into the bin.'

'I couldn't afford it, Vivien.'

'I expect that can be fixed.'

'But what ought I to say to Perdita?'

'Tell her you're seeing a doctor. She'll understand that. It's the one thing she will understand.'

Cressida half rose, with her hands on the stone table-top. Now she could see herself in one of the big looking glasses.

'I do look pale. Positively ashen.'

'You've got a sore throat too.'

'*Have* I?' Cressida's arms gave way, and she sat down again with a thud.

'Of course you have. And a temperature.'

'Really?'

'And your ankles are swollen.'

'That's quite true. I noticed it when I got up.'

'And your hair lacks lustre.'

'But it often does, Vivien.'

'11.25 on Wednesday morning. You'll be there until 12.15. Then we might go out and eat. I'll give over writing my novel.'

'I don't want to stand in your way, Vivien. I've caused enough trouble of that kind.'

'As a matter of fact, I'm rather stuck in any case.'

CHAPTER ELEVEN

The Interview

'The trouble, Dr Blattner, is not only that I don't know whether I'm being seriously accused. I don't even know what actually happened. It was mainly there that Vivien thought you might be able to help.' Cressida gave a little gasp.

'Have you ever been analysed, Cressida?'

Cressida was not sure what authority he had to use her Christian name. But having put herself in professional hands, she recognised that she had no further control over anything.

'You mean psychoanalysed?'

'That's what people call it.'

'Of course not.'

'Or considered the possibility?'

'Do you think I should?'

Cressida was blushing. Dr Blattner scratched his bald head even more fiercely for a moment.

'You are about the right age. Most of my patients start too late.'

'Whatever do you do then?'

'I continue. However hopeless, I continue. It is required of us professionally.'

'It must wear you out.'

'It does, Cressida. Not all my patients are pretty young women who have misconducted themselves. In fact, very few of them are.'

'I have *not* misconducted myself, Dr Blattner. At least I don't think so. That's the point. I don't know whether I have or not.'

'I *could* find out. But it might take six, ten, twelve years. You would have to weigh up how important it is to you.' Dr Blattner was now scratching his thigh, or rather, his trousers, instead of his head.

'Can't you do something for me *now*? Before 12.15?'

'You do not understand, Cressida. I am not a quack purveying instant cures. I do not offer cures at all. There are no cures. I explore. I penetrate. Often it is necessary to wander with a patient, to mountaineer with a patient, to starve with a patient, nearly to drown or suffocate with a patient, to wrestle in depth with a patient. My patients are antagonists, Cressida, and I offer nothing whatever that does not have to be worked for, waited for, and watched for with tender anxiety, like a mother watching over a very sick child, who will almost certainly die.'

'I suppose it does some good?'

'It is not my aim to do good. If good results, that is entirely incidental. I have no definable aim of any kind. In analysis, aim is non-existent, irrelevant, distracting. Just as I do not cure, so I do not aim. I am. I simply am.' Dr Blattner made a gesture of amness with both arms, as if opening the doors of the morning. Fully extended like that, they seemed to Cressida very long arms, doubtless a consequence of Dr Blattner having made the same gesture so often.

'Dr Blattner,' cried Cressida, 'why am I here?'

'Now you are disappointed in me. That is good. It is the necessary first step. You have taken that step more quickly than most.'

'Thank you very much,' said Cressida with spirit. 'But it doesn't help much, does it?'

'Quite possibly it is all the help you need. It is a common saying among analysts—possibly the only saying we all share—that in analysis all is revealed at the first interview if only the analyst can divine it, which, of course, the analyst cannot and must not. On the other hand, the patient will often get as much, or more, from the first single interview as from the entire ten-year course.'

'Just now, you said twelve years, Dr Blattner.'

'You are beginning to be irritated with me. That is good also. It is the necessary second step. It would be better still if you were actively infuriated, if you were to strike me, for example, or kick me.'

'I seem never to be properly infuriated, Dr Blattner. I don't know why not.'

'It takes time, Cressida. Everything in analysis takes time.'

Dr Blattner looked at his watch.

There was dead silence for a minute or two.

Cressida, whose sharp hearing had often startled family and friends, wondered if the Doctor's watch was tickless, in order, no doubt, not to upset the patients, perhaps in order not to awaken them.

'You see, Cressida,' said Dr Blattner suddenly, 'in this matter of your little card game—'

'It wasn't cards,' said Cressida. 'I'm not very good at cards. It was the Race Game, with dice and horses.'

'Yes,' said Dr Blattner, rubbing his ankle to erase his mistake. 'Horses. But the point is the same. You expect me to explain the exact relationship between chance and fate, between the conscious and the unconscious, between intention and achievement, and who knows how much more; and all at a single interview. I cannot do it.'

'I understand what you mean, I suppose,' said Cressida cautiously. 'I hadn't seen it like that. You would have to be completely inside me in order to find an answer.'

'If then,' said Dr Blattner, 'if then. But I perceive that you have begun to be attracted by me, to come over to my side, to cleave to me. It is the third step, and the most important of all.'

Cressida found that she was giggling.

'It is good of you to see me without a fee, Dr Blattner,' she said in the hope of covering up.

'Vivien spoke for you, and I rely very much upon Vivien. She is greatly wiser than I am.'

'Really? Isn't Vivien too young?'

'Most people lose all wisdom at about twenty-five, Cressida. Analysis is about reconstitution, like the eggs we bought in wartime. Remember that when you are twenty-five yourself. It will enable you to accept the nature of the universe, and not come to people like me expecting the nature of the universe to be remedied.'

Dr Blattner was filling a graduated glass with almost black fluid from a stoppered bottle. It was difficult to tell whether it was alcoholic or what it was. In any case, the doctor downed the potion, without offering any to Cressida.

'Of course I should not say such a thing to the ordinary paying public. I am speaking to you as an intimate.'

'Thank you very much.'

'We must all let the mask fall on occasion.'

For one moment, Cressida was afraid that this was going to happen literally.

'Mask and face, analyst and patient, you and me: what's the difference?' enquired Dr Blattner.

He had ceased all his former physical activity, varied though it had been. Cressida, who could see almost as well as she could hear, considered that his eyes looked quite different from when she had entered the room. She thought, however, that this might be because heavy clouds had gathered outside the consulting room window. More rain, as Mr Matthew Makepeace would say!

Dr Blattner murmured something further, but it was too arcane even for Cressida's ears.

The door opened and Vivien entered, looking at her watch, as everyone does around psychoanalysis.

'Come on, Cress. Time's up.'

'It can't be.'

'Look for yourself.' Vivien pointed not to her watch but to the doctor.

'Goodbye, Dr Blattner,' said Cressida politely. 'And thank you very much.'

'You can leave that,' said Vivien. 'Dr Blattner won't be attending. It often happens.'

CHAPTER TWELVE

The Dependent

They were in the tea shop.

'What *was* that dark stuff in the bottle?'

'It's a concentrate.'

'It didn't look very concentrated. There was too much of it.'

'Well, it is.'

'How do you know?'

'Sir Johnson Jackson-Johnson told me. He's a specialist. He looks after all kinds of famous people when they're ill: fits, strokes, all that. He said that poor Dr Blattner was dependent on the stuff, but that it was all right, and that I shouldn't worry.'

'Isn't it bad for him?'

'I suppose so.'

'Hasn't Dr Blattner got a wife?'

'He's divorced.'

'Another one!' said Cressida ironically.

'That's why he scratches himself so much.'

'I was watching it the whole time. You can't take your eyes off.'

'The patients get on his nerves too though they all think he's wonderful.'

'He doesn't seem to do much for them.'

'They absolutely depend on him. That's surely something? Not many feel that way about a doctor.'

'Are you sure, Vivien? I think it's quite common.'

Vivien looked at Cressida for a moment. Then she said 'People may want to feel it, but generally they can't manage it.'

Cressida was quite willing to leave it at that. 'Does the waitress come in the end?' she said.

'Sorry,' said Vivien. 'It's always like this. I forgot you had to get back to the shop.'

'I'll tell you something extraordinary,' said Cressida. 'I feel quite differently about the whole business. I have been feeling different ever since we left Dr Blattner. I think he *has* cured me, after all.'

'Shouldn't be surprised,' said Vivien. 'Everyone says he's wonderful.'

'What do you really think, Vivien? Really and truly.'

'He's become very dependent. He's taken to saying he can no longer live without me.'

'But—'

'Yes, I know, Cressida. I know very well. We've both got to get away soon. I keep reminding you.'

'But how, Vivien? Where?'

'Something will happen,' said Vivien.

At long last the waitress arrived. The different delicacies selected by Vivien and Cressida unfortunately proved to be already off.

'Can't think why they don't make more,' said the waitress.

Chapter Thirteen

Fire Engines

Some weeks after Christmas, Cressida dreamed that she was in a very gaudy but very hot room, where businesslike men were sprawling on gilt chairs round a long and polished table. She herself was shut in a narrow cage or cell, and everything had to be seen through the gilt bars, thick and excessively ornamental, which extended before her from above her head to the floor. The compartment was lined with ebony, and the top of it was only an inch above her head. There was no room for movement of any kind, and Cressida was wearing a very heavy golden dress or robe, in which she felt too hot. Despite its weight, the dress did not fit at all closely: possibly one could say that it did not fit at all. It was plainly not a garment personal to Cressida. All the time she felt that it might fall right off; which in some ways would even have been welcome. She could not decide whether she was wearing anything underneath the dress but, beyond doubt, she wore shoes with very high heels. One end of the long table was just in front of her, beyond the bars; and there a gap had been left so that she could see the men on both sides all the way down, at least up to a point, because there was no light but candles, in chandeliers and in random places, which must have contributed greatly to the heat. Even the men kept mopping themselves, but no one seemed to think of opening a window, of throwing off formality. Some of the candles were very thick, and burning unevenly, in niches and on ledges, as if faces were about to emerge. The room was decorated weightily in black and gold and ormolu. At the far end, immediately opposite Cressida, was a picture of a woman in a silk dress hanging from a gibbet: a portrait of the woman, one might say, despite the smoky, flickering light. The men were engaged upon some business but seemed to find great difficulty in making even a start. Some were obviously deaf, others obviously blind; some were injured or crippled, others merely deformed. A few might well have been more or less whole: there was no evidence of allowance being made, on the one hand, or of assertion on the other. The job in hand would have been simpler, however, if the men had been able to communicate more adequately. The deaf screeched, the injured and the deformed whined, the sightless implored. There seemed no one qualified to preside, or even to enforce. Cressida could neither gather nor imagine what they were arguing about; and wondered whether any one of them would have agreed with any other even on that subject. The only thing was that the matter was of urgent importance. The ardour and earnestness of each individual were progressively turning him into the apparition of an animal: here a bull, there a goat, and in one corner a monkey; a whinnying horse, a laughing hyena, a screaming macaw, but all the time a man none the less in each case, veritably a man. In the end, they decided to draw lots: it had been inevitable. A dark, slightly hunchbacked raven among them was cutting an irregular sheet of patchy paper into tiny slivers with very small scissors, so small that Cressida could hardly see them. The slivers were gathered up into the raven-man's fist or claws, and deposited by him (or so it was to be presumed—one could not see exactly) into a tubular hat, an oversize fez, bright red and disgustingly decorated with faded, indeed putrid, flowers of the field and marshland. This object straggled round, while the men snatched and opened. Then, inevitably, the men began to insult one another and jeer. But something unpredictable had happened: while Cressida had not been looking at it, the tubular red object had turned into a screaming baby. It foamed and threshed on the polished table, its face so upside down and convulsed that Cressida never really saw it; until one of the men stood up and drew an immensely long sword, more and more of it as it came up over the edge of the table, indeed so long that Cressida woke in sobs before she had seen the end of it.

Vivien was in the room.

'Cressy,' she said. 'Hold on, for God's sake. It's only the fire engines.'

'Is the house on fire?' spluttered out Cressida through her sobs.

'Not this house. There seems to be something going on up the road.'

'Vivien! I've just had the most frightful dream.'

'I've told you before, it's the heat. *This* house should have been burned down by it long ago.'

'I dreamed I was in a cage having lots drawn for me.'

'Well, you were bellowing out "Hugo, Hugo".'

Cressida's tone changed.

'You mean Hugh, don't you?' Cressida stopped crying.

'Not Hugh. Hugo.'

'It couldn't be. Who's Hugo?'

'How do I know? Except that my Doctor Blattner's name is Hugo.'

'Well, I didn't know that.'

'We all know far more than we know we know. Or so Dr Blattner keeps saying. Now you can see for yourself.'

But Cressida had begun to weep again. 'Oh, Vivien,' she said. 'I do miss Hugh, I do, I do.'

CHAPTER FOURTEEN

The Pets

The fire up the road had been more serious than Vivien had thought. Indeed, several of the domestic pets had perished in it. At least, they had not been seen since. Lady Mallow was said to be heartbroken, and the former governess, who now acted as Lady Mallow's companion, had had to be taken to hospital. Sad notices appeared outside all the police stations, appealing for news of the creatures and proffering uneconomic rewards.

'You don't think we could pass off some other tabby?' postulated Cressida. 'After all, one tabby is much like another.'

'Aunt Agnes says that Ming was hardly able to move. It probably explains what happened to Ming. We should have to find a tabby that was hardly able to move.'

'Well, what about the parrot? Apparently it was only an ordinary grey. There are lots of those about.'

'Aunt Agnes says this grey recited passages from the Koran. Sir Stephen Mallow was in Mesopotamia, you know, before his accident.'

'I didn't know he'd *had* an accident.'

'It was after some party he shouldn't have been at. My father knew him well. Daddy says it was simply bravado.'

'Vivien. Have you read the Koran?'

'Only some of it. I had to because of Daddy. I don't think you'd like it.'

'Why not?'

'I just don't think you would. Daddy always said it was meant mainly for men.'

'Do you mean it's poo?'

'No, of course not. Just long and boring, like *Arrival and Departure in the Dardanelles*.'

They were in Vivien's room, and it was quite late, time, almost, for bed. At heart, Cressida was a little relieved that the Koran was one thing she would not have to bother very much with.

CHAPTER FIFTEEN

The Revelation

'Vivien, who *is* Virgilio Vittore?'

'He is a *man*,' replied Vivien with emphasis. 'At least I think so.'

It was at exactly the same hour the following evening, though now there was a fog outside. They both found it useful to compare notes, to become more themselves; before the one attempted slumber, the other accomplished it. Moreover, unlike their elders, they both rather liked fogs.

'Yes, I remember your saying so at that first bridge evening, Vivien. I'm *never* going to learn bridge. I think it's awful. Look at tonight.'

'That was because Dotty Empson was in such pain the whole time.'

'I suppose so. Lady Luce said she was going to teach you before your parents got back. Has anything more happened?'

'Nothing. People don't always want to let others into the things they're most fond of. Especially kids like us.'

'I suppose Lady Luce really *is* fond of bridge?'

'What do *you* think?'

'I'm not sure. I think there's something sad about her.'

'She's been divorced, and she's got no children, and she's got no proper man, and she doesn't read books, and she doesn't take any exercise. Of course there *are* worse things than all these.'

'You mean like not being able to feed the hungry mouths, or having to work down a mine?'

'Daddy says that most of the miners like the mines. I can understand that.'

'I suppose so,' said Cressida. 'If only one didn't have to do it all the time.'

'No, that's attractive too in a way.'

'Poor Lady Luce!' said Cressida.

'Yes,' said Vivien. 'I've always been sorry for Aunt Agnes. Ever since I can remember. She's the kind of person who can never be happy, however many chances she had.'

'Happiness is not a matter of what happens to us,' said Cressida firmly. 'Don't you remember? We make happiness inside us from the little particles of grace, just as we make bread from yeast.'

'Haven't made much bread lately,' said Vivien. 'I'm glad you like Aunt Agnes. I think you'll be someone she can depend on.'

'But I depend very much on *her*, Vivien!'

'Not in the same way.'

It flitted for a second through Cressida's mind to wonder upon whom *she* could depend. Alas, not upon her parents, whose incommunicativity she more and more suspected to derive from their having nothing to communicate.

'Why are you so sure that Virgilio Vittore is a man, Vivien?'

'It was mainly an article I read about him in *Woman's Own*.'

'In *Woman's Own?*'

'It belonged to Elsie Churchill.'

'That little goose!'

'We all have to start somewhere, Cressy. In any case, Vittore's name's in the paper the whole time. Haven't you noticed?'

'Yes, but I don't know where it all began. It's no good trying to pick up a thing like that halfway through. You get completely the wrong end of the stick. So it's one of the things I've just left, like reparations, and Ireland.'

'Vittore is a great poet, and a great playwright, and a great athlete, and a great soldier, and a great leader, and a great aviator, and a great lover. That most of all. He is always saying that the bays of the poet and the laurels of the victor rust before the single pure white rose of love.'

'Goodness, Vivien! Was that the sort of thing Elsie Churchill went in for?'

'Not particularly. She just bought the paper every week whatever was in it.'

'How can you remember the words, Vivien, after all this time?'

'Don't be a goose yourself, Cressy.'

'I suppose it was Destiny that led you. From what you say, I think Elsie was far too young.'

'Why do you ask about Vittore?'

'Of course it's perfectly true that laurel and bay are evergreens, while white roses often don't last a week. I suppose that's the *point.*'

Vivien smiled.

'I suppose that "rust" is all that evergreens can do?'

Vivien offered no argument.

'And Vittore's all those other things as well?'

'According to *Woman's Own*. What I said at the dinner party was only to annoy, and to point out that there *are* other occupations for men.'

'Don't you remember Miss Grindleford telling us that the height and acme of vulgarity was to be rude about the church?'

'Or any minister of it, however unworthy.' Vivien, as ever, had completed the quotation, and with her usual overall accuracy. 'Even if as unworthy as Alastair Athercliffe,' she added superfluously.

'You must remember,' said Cressida, 'that I don't know him.'

'But you don't know Virgilio Vittore either, Cressy.'

There was the tiniest of silences. Cressida just had time to reflect that mainly in silences is history made and life lived.

'Doesn't he keep dashing off to places?'

'And instantly capturing them. And running up his own flag at the highest possible point.'

'What does he do then?'

'He governs according to the laws of music.'

'You got that out of *Woman's Own* too?'

Vivien nodded.

'Why does he do it?'

'The article didn't really explain. Something to do with politics, I suppose.'

'What else do you remember?'

'That Vittore owes everything—everything in this present cosmos and in the shining cosmos of the future—to beautiful women. Above the earth, on the earth, below the earth.'

'That's all very well, of course, and you can't imagine Brian Hawk saying it—'

'Who's Brian Hawk?'

'Vivien, you remember! Brian Hawk is the one with the funny eyes. But it's all very well for Vittore. What guarantee have the women got in return? Was there a picture of Vittore?'

'No. That's part of it. Apparently he looks terrible.'

'Vivien!'

'But he's irresistible, all the same.'

'How can he be?'

'I don't know, Cressy. He just is. It's not the kind of thing we learnt much about.'

'What a let-down! He's just a common or garden wog on the tiles.'

'Most wogs are *handsome*, Cressy. You must remember that.'

'And what an absurd name! Vittore! Is it his real one?'

'Can't remember. I don't think so.'

'But it was you who said he was the greatest man now living?'

'That was still *Woman's Own*. Or something like that, it said.'

'I could scream with disappointment,' said Cressida.

There was a discreet but steady tapping at the door. Cressida opened it.

Outside was Aunt Agnes, in black silk pyjamas, a matching black peignoir, and a scarlet bandeau-de-nuit, Vivien's colour.

'I don't wish, Vivien, to play the aunt,' said Aunt Agnes, 'but you two can be heard all over the house.'

'Sorry, Aunt Agnes,' said Vivien, 'but we're both getting worked up about Virgilio Vittore.'

'I'm not sure that I want to hear about him,' said Aunt Agnes.

'He's proved to be a washout,' said Cressida. 'He looks like the dog's dinner.'

'Looks aren't *absolutely* the last word in a man,' said Aunt Agnes.

'I think they are very important, Lady Luce,' said Cressida.

'What Vittore has is power,' said Aunt Agnes.

'So you agree that he's attractive,' said Vivien, quite quietly.

'From what I know, I agree,' said Aunt Agnes. 'And I say again I'm not sure that I want to know more.'

'Have you ever been to Trino, Aunt Agnes, before Vittore captured it?'

'No, Vivien, I have never been to Trino. Not before and not since.'

'Wouldn't you like to go to Trino, Aunt Agnes?'

Aunt Agnes smiled. 'I can think of places I should prefer, Vivien.'

'It must be thrilling to live according to the laws of music,' said Cressida.

'If you can manage to do it,' said Aunt Agnes with a smile.

'Is it difficult?'

'How did *you* find it when you were learning music yourself?'

'Slavery,' said Cressida. 'But it's not the same.'

'That was because of Mrs Flitt,' said Vivien. 'It would have been all right if we'd had a kinder teacher.'

'But surely Virgilio Vittore doesn't actually teach music? That's not what he means?' enquired Cressida.

'I shouldn't think so,' said Aunt Agnes. 'Because he's quite unmusical.'

'Aunt Agnes!' cried Vivien. 'Do you actually know Vittore all the time? Is that why you don't want to hear about him?'

'I knew him slightly once, Vivien. That is to say, I met him.'

'Oh, Lady Luce, where? In England or in Italy?'

'It was in Paris, Cressida.'

'Tell us, Lady Luce.'

'Please tell us, Aunt Agnes.'

'Some time, if you like. There's very little to tell. Perhaps I'll tell you on the day Vittore leaves Trino.'

'But must Vittore leave Trino? *Why* must he?'

'Because he has no business whatever to be there, Vivien. If we weren't all worn out with war, he'd have been driven away long ago. He would probably never have been there in the first place.'

'Who would have been there instead?' anxiously enquired Cressida. It was the water jump again.

'The properly constituted authorities, I suppose, Cressida. I'm not quite sure after all the changes there've been. But certainly not Vittore.'

'No more music, Aunt Agnes?' enquired Vivien.

'It's the food of love, Lady Luce.'

'Love plays no part whatever in running the world,' said Aunt Agnes.

'Perhaps that's what Vittore's trying to change?' suggested Cressida.

'I am shivering,' said Aunt Agnes. 'I propose to get out of the draught.'

'Why can't we all go to sunny Italy?' enquired Vivien.

'Bed is where you two had better go. Goodnight, and quietly now.'

'Goodnight, Aunt Agnes.'

'Goodnight, Lady Luce.'

CHAPTER SIXTEEN

The Spell

Immediately the door had shut, Cressida whispered:

'We're going to cast a spell. The way Miss Rossetti showed us.'

'Failed to show us, you mean,' Vivien whispered back. 'In any case, we could never assemble the things without disturbing Aunt Agnes again. None of my family sleeps properly. You know that.'

'It'll be better if I do it. Less trouble if I'm stopped. I'll creep down and see what I can find. You stay here.'

'But some of the things won't be in the kitchen.'

'We must improvise, improvise. Just like the Prince of Wales.'

It was impracticable to turn on the staircase light. Vivien watched with anxiety as Cressida descended through the blackness.

'Watch there are no stair-rods loose.'

'Shshsh.'

Vivien drew back into her bedroom.

In about ten minutes, Cressida returned.

'All clear. Not a mouse stirs.'

Vivien cautiously shut the door behind her.

'I've borrowed the shopping basket.'

'How much did you find?'

'Oh, most.'

'Are we going to do it in here, or in your room?'

'I'm further from Lady Luce.'

So they stole into Cressida's room bearing their burden.

'Do you think we ought to undress first?'

'I don't see why we should.'

'Try not to giggle, Cressy. We don't want Aunt Agnes asking what we're up to.'

'It's more like a cooking class than magic.'

'I wish Miss Rossetti hadn't been interrupted before she showed us the whole thing.'

'It was old Sag did that.'

'I know it was.'

'She always barged in at the psychological moment.'

'She was put up to it.'

'We never really knew that,' said Cressida.

'You mean we weren't actually told it,' said Vivien.

Cressida laid out the contents of her basket on the floor. The two girls stared at them.

'You know, I just don't believe in this,' said Vivien. 'I don't think we're doing any good at all.'

'Oh, Vivien! Let's *try*.'

'I'm sorry about your having to go downstairs in the dark and all that, but it's ludicrous. Just *look*!'

'It's *nature* magic, Vivien, Not black magic. That looks quite different. We don't know what black magic looks like.'

'Not so damned silly as this looks, I hope.'

'It's all very well for you, Vivien. You can *pay* to go to places. At least it's *better* for you.'

'I can't, you know, Cressy.'

'Well, you will be able to one day.'

'So will you.'

'I shall never have a penny. Everything's mortgaged already. It's really all because Daddy's so *stupid*.'

'While I have a penny, Cressy, you'll have a penny. And Aunt Agnes is very fond of you too.'

'I want to see the world. I'm fed up with Perdita's bloody shop.' But Cressida too could not regard the objects on the floor without dismay.

The objects on the floor were so absurdly sad within their context, perhaps within any context, that Cressida began to shed tears. She had to open a drawer to look for a handkerchief.

'Oh, Cressy, I know what you feel!' said Vivien. 'But Miss Rossetti was just a funny spinster.'

'That's what I'll be.'

'*And* she never finished what she had to tell us. Look, Cressy, I'm putting it all back in the basket, and *I'll* be the one who goes down to the kitchen.'

'It had better be me.' Cressida's tears were still flowing.

'It's really the spirit inside us that casts the spell,' said Vivien. 'All this is just means to an end.'

'Let me,' said Cressida, taking the basket. 'Your aunt will ask questions if she meets *you* on the stairs. And I know where the things came from.'

Cressida risked turning on the light. It was too much to be expected to see in the dark with tears in her eyes. In the event of interception, she could always say that she preferred the downstairs lavatory if Lady Luce didn't mind.

CHAPTER SEVENTEEN

The Letter

Of course, Vivien had been right in what she had said about means and end. The crystal, the palm of the hand, the animal entrails, the flight of the rooks, the disposition of the litter in street or park: all are but clarifiers through which the glass becomes momentarily less dark for the particular and individual scryer, the man or woman with the sight.

Equally, it is well known that to think of a person one has not thought of for years, is to be assured of a letter from him or her the next morning. Provided, as so often in life, that the assurance is less than entirely conscious, and that the letter is not badly needed, either practically or (still worse) emotionally. To need a thing badly; to be sure one will get it: these preliminaries are fatal to fulfilment.

It is all so complex and unsure, the girls decided in the end, as largely to confirm Miss Rossetti in her claims that what she had to offer would avail those prepared to accept it considerably more than would much of the more regular curriculum.

In any case, there was Aunt Agnes with a huge, costly envelope in her hands, simply cluttered with glaringly continental stamps; and only three days later, though not, it had to be admitted, the next morning. What had happened the next morning had been that Cressida, and even Vivien, had considerably overslept. When Vivien had at last turned up, Dr Blattner had smiled as widely as he could, palpably drawing all the wrong conclusions. Perdita had omitted amiable conversation, even over the sandwiches and éclairs.

At first, Aunt Agnes simply laid the big envelope down on the table, while, with a steady hand, she poured coffee for Vivien and Cressida. But there was a compulsive telepathy in the air, so that before long she simply had to open it. She always kept a paper-knife on the breakfast table for just such communications.

There were pages and pages inside; big pages, which opened like face-towels, except that they were in thin, crackly paper, blue as the sea, or blue as the sea is sometimes.

As she read, Aunt Agnes sometimes scowled with irritation, sometimes smiled slightly, once turned quite pale for a second. There was time for all these events, as Aunt Agnes, unlike her niece, was not a rapid reader. The two girls silently minded their own business.

In the end, Aunt Agnes laid the letter down, abstractedly pushing the sheets into an approximately symmetrical pile.

'More coffee?' enquired Aunt Agnes.

'Haven't quite finished yet,' replied Vivien, her eyes on her eggs, bacon, sausage, and tomatoes.

Cressida gulped down what was left in her cup. 'Please, Lady Luce.'

While she was pouring, Aunt Agnes said, 'Do you girls believe in telepathy?'

'Of course we do, Aunt Agnes,' said Vivien.

'How many nights ago was it that we were talking of Virgilio Vittore?'

'Three nights, I think, Aunt Agnes. But Cressida and I did most of the talking.'

'In that case, you will be interested to learn that this is a letter from him.' But Aunt Agnes did not pick it up and wave it about. She had ceased even to touch it.

'We cast a spell,' said Cressida, demurely spreading an enormous amount of marmalade on her buttered toast, being a stage ahead of Vivien.

'Only half a spell. We don't know the other half.'

'It's the spirit inside that counts, Vivien. You pointed that out yourself.'

'I don't think you should speak when your mouth's as full as that,' said Aunt Agnes. Plainly there was a certain tension.

'I said that it's the spirit in which we do a thing that counts, Lady Luce, not what we actually do.'

'I expect so. Virgilio asks me to visit him in Italy. If that place he's captured can be described as Italy. I suppose that's the whole point of why he's captured it.'

'Are the stamps Italian?' asked Vivien, scooping up the last of the fat with a particle of toast on the end of her fork.

'No, they're not. If you want to see what Virgilio Vittore looks like, see for yourself. His picture's on all of them. Though his looks have been idealised, of course.'

Aunt Agnes threw the envelope across to Vivien, while placing her other hand on the sheets of the letter.

Vivien looked, and passed the envelope over the table to Cressida.

'He must think he's there to stay if he's had stamps printed,' observed Vivien.

'He says in the letter it was among the first things he had done: new stamps and coins, a new flag, new uniforms, some new laws, and a new ceremonial costume for himself. I expect that came first of all.'

'What's he got on his head?' asked Cressida, who had been peering at the stamps.

'That's a laurel wreath, you idiot,' said Vivien.

'Is it really, Lady Luce?'

'I think so, Cressida. He was always rather given to wearing them, even when I knew him. He has very little hair.'

'But he seems to have a small beard.'

'Yes, Cressida. The perfume he put on it seemed to fill the whole room.'

'Is that attractive? I've never heard of it.'

'In those days, women were said to find it so.'

'Did you find it so, Aunt Agnes?'

'That is an improper question from niece to aunt. Besides, you're both late for work again, exactly like yesterday.'

'We hate work, Aunt Agnes.'

'None the less, as your Mothers' representative, I must drive you to it.'

Both girls rose. Cressida handed back the envelope.

'Are you going to Trino, Aunt Agnes?'

'It requires thought, Vivien. Much thought. Besides, I have a responsibility for you two.'

'Will you have decided by this evening?'

'As I have to spend the day helping Lady Walkinshaw with her clinic, probably not. The place is a scandal. It is a good thing that the patients pay so much or it might be closed down.'

'Why can't we *all* go to sunny Italy, Aunt Agnes? Surely that would be best?'

CHAPTER EIGHTEEN

The Boudoir

The rooms upstairs included a boudoir, to which Aunt Agnes withdrew when things had become too much for her and there was nowhere else to go. The walls were hung with boudoir-coloured silk, and there were boudoir-designed furnishings, the colour of dried skeletons on the steppes: a large sofa and a small sofa; two deceptive armchairs; three or four hard seats for older folk; a beautiful, mysterious, pier-glass in what seemed a tortoiseshell frame; likenesses by Vigée-Lebrun and her pupils. Cressida wondered for a moment in what previous apartment she had seen lights so randomly distributed. She remembered that it had been when she had dreamed.

When Vivien had met Cressida that evening after they had returned from work, she had said: 'I don't think we should take the initiative'; and Cressida had replied, 'Well, only if nothing happens'; to which Vivien had nodded.

'We mustn't look as if we're pushing ourselves forward,' Vivien had later observed.

'Especially not me. I'm not related,' Cressida had replied.

'It's not that,' Vivien had remarked. 'It's mainly that Aunt Agnes may have things to conceal.'

And, during dinner, Aunt Agnes had duly vouchsafed nothing to the point: though, in a very small degree, this may have been because there had been a difficulty with the soup. 'Endurance reaches its limit,' Aunt Agnes had said as soon as she once more found herself alone at table with the two girls, 'when we cannot even rely upon what goes with the soup.'

Without giving a reason, Aunt Agnes had ordered coffee to be brought to the dinner table. When it became clear that they were not moving into the drawing room, as they usually did, Cressida, at least, almost fainted with expectation and implication.

'Stretch for the Elvas Plums, Cressida, and pass them round, if you would.'

While Aunt Agnes had poured coffee, it had been as if the breakfast atmosphere had returned, though now she was pouring it into small cups, with wide gold rims.

'You'll be pleased to hear, Vivien, that I've decided.'

'Oh, *good*, Aunt Agnes. We're so pleased.'

'At least, I've decided to have a talk with you two. Not here, though. Upstairs, in my boudoir. Thank God, there's been no bridge planned for tonight.'

'I've never been in your boudoir, Lady Luce.'

'You must tell me whether you like it, Cressida.'

CHAPTER NINETEEN

The Communication

Aunt Agnes reclined upon the large sofa. Vivien and Cressida sank more and more deeply into the armchairs.

Somewhere sandalwood seemed to be burning. At least, Cressida thought it might be sandalwood.

'It doesn't make you cough, Cressida?'

'Of course not, Lady Luce. It's beautiful. It's divine.'

'Everything beautiful is divine, Cressida.'

'We know that already, Lady Luce. Really we do.'

Aunt Agnes had taken off her dress before they had arrived, and lay in her black silk petticoat beneath her black silk peignoir. Her legs were in black silk stockings, and her feet still in shiny black shoes, high-heeled and fanciful.

'It's the most divine room,' said Cressida.

Everything was the very opposite to the open, windy uplands that Cressida normally accounted for bliss. Extremes, extremes; extremes are all and everything, always, reflected Cressida. She had known this but had never before known it so explicitly.

'I want to ask you first,' said Aunt Agnes, 'whether either of you is in love?'

'No,' said Vivien composedly.

'No,' said Cressida with calm.

'That's the truth, the whole truth, and nothing but the truth?'

Vivien and Cressida nodded solemnly.

'I will go further,' said Aunt Agnes. 'Has either of you ever been in love? I do not talk about thinking or supposing yourself in love. Have you ever been in love, Cressida?'

'I don't believe so, Lady Luce. I was, and I am, very fond of my brother, Hugh, but he's dead.'

'What about you, Vivien? Forget I'm your aunt. I'm tired of being anyone's aunt.'

'I don't think so, Aunt Agnes. I suppose it's sometimes diffi-cult to know.'

'I have decided to tell you about Virgilio Vittore—just the little I know about him, of course; and when I have finished, we must all decide what we are going to do about his precious invitation.'

Vivien and Cressida nodded eagerly.

'During the first part of the war, I worked in Lady Balham's hospital in Paris, as you know, Vivien.'

Vivien shook her head.

'Well, I did. It was for the French, of course, because Lady Balham has these links, and I saw terrible things, things about which nothing could be done. It changed my view of life.'

'Yes,' said Vivien.

'But there were other events which changed my view of life also. Virgilio Vittore was certainly one of them. At that time, he was running his famous campaign to bring Italy into the war. I don't know whether that was a good thing or not for Italy. I doubt it very much. But whatever Vittore wanted, he got. Big things, small things.'

'But why was he running the campaign in Paris,' asked Cressida, 'instead of in Italy?'

'One of his ideas was to shame Italy by showing her up in other countries.'

'I don't think much of that,' said Cressida.

'There's a lot about Vittore that people don't think much of,' said Aunt Agnes, looking at her legs. 'But he gets what he wants, none the less, so that what he wants must be right up to a point.'

'Is that true?' asked Vivien.

'Perhaps not really,' said Aunt Agnes, 'but it's the kind of thing he tells you and that you feel when you are with him.

'He came into the hospital one morning—it was a big house in Neuilly, which the owners had lent—and he made a speech in each of the wards, saying that suffering was never in vain and that Italy was coming to the rescue any moment, after which everything would be different. A French girl had been told to go round with him and look after him, because Lady Balham herself had colitis that morning, but I was in the first ward when he spoke, and after that I went round with him too without anyone asking me. His speech was quite different every time, but every time the dying men, and those who were not lucky enough to be dying, cheered him and clapped him, and he went round and kissed them all. After two or three of these speeches, I noticed that the French girl simply wasn't there. That often happens with the French, you know. I daresay she felt out of her depth, and was glad to leave the job to someone else. Until the very end, Vittore never spoke to me. He just followed where I led. His features were set like a statue until he was orating once again, or smiling as he kissed the wounded men. He had very strange eyes, no definite colour or expression, barely human, though not at all animal either; but he had the most wonderful smile. It seemed to overcome Vittore himself, as well as everyone else. He had only to smile, and you fell at his feet. That is something you could go through your lives without experiencing. We went from room to room—they were still much more rooms than wards, very elaborate, though now they smelt—and all the time I took it for granted that Vittore was not seeing me as a person, only as a vague, shapeless guide, doing her duty, as everyone was supposed to be doing at that time.

'I was entirely wrong. But the way in which he misled me was typical of the way in which he misled almost everyone about everything he wanted.'

Vivien and Cressida remained still and silent.

'Outside the last ward, on the landing at the top of the house, he took my hand, very gently, and said, in English, "And you, my lovely lamb, you with your soft and shrinking soul, you suffer as much as many, and more than most!" I could say nothing and it was impossible to smile. "You, too," he said, "suffering will search out and sanctify. Welcome it. Kneel humbly before it. Open your arms to it in your lovely dress of dedication!" I know what I said in reply, that time, but I'm not going to tell you. All the same, I did not for one moment expect his response. It had truly never occurred to me. Vittore took my other hand and said, "Come to my house, 29 Rue Ginestra, at half-past ten tonight. Eat nothing until then. Drink nothing. Do not drink even water. And come exactly as you are, in your lovely dress of dedication!"'

'Aunt Agnes,' asked Vivien, 'did Vittore really have a whole house when he was only there on a sort of business visit?'

'At that time, he had what you call a whole house in every European capital. No, I'm sure that's an exaggeration. Even thinking about that man makes everyone exaggerate immediately. But I think he had six or seven houses. For all I know, he has them still.'

'Has he a house in London?' asked Cressida.

'He *had*.'

'Where was it?'

'I don't know. I never went there. I only knew him for a brief period in Paris.'

'Lady Luce,' asked Cressida. 'After all this time, how do you remember his exact words? It's what people do in books, but it's frightfully difficult.'

'People remember every word of quite long conversations with Vittore. I can remember what *I* said, as well as what *he* said.'

'I wish I could do that,' said Cressida, sticking to it.

'And what did you do at half-past ten? Did you go?' asked Vivien.

'I *hope* so,' said Cressida.

'I owe a lot to Lady Balham,' said Aunt Agnes, shifting her position, and slightly opening her peignoir, as the room grew warmer and cloudier. 'You must always be kind to Lady Balham, Vivien, even when she's at her most demanding.'

'Of course I shall be, Aunt Agnes, but so far I've never met her.'

'And the ways things are going, perhaps you never will,' said Aunt Agnes. 'Anyway, if the place had been run like an ordinary hospital, with strict hours of duty and complicated rules, I should very likely never have seen Vittore again—unless perhaps I'd gone to the Étoile and heard him ranting.'

'Ranting, Aunt Agnes?'

'Yes, Vittore frequently rants. It's what people expect from him. When faced with ten or twelve thousand people, all in the palm of his hand, he's simply unbelievable. But Vittore's almost always unbelievable. Whatever else he is, he is unbelievable.'

'Yes, Aunt Agnes. But did you go at half-past ten?'

'As kind Lady Balham made it possible for me, even easy for me, I went. I stepped straight out of the ward in my nursing dress and went to Vittore as a nun goes to her convent.'

'Is that the way nuns do it, Lady Luce?'

'Yes, Cressida. They go straight off the stage in costume, straight away from the café in a little black dress, straight out of some much worse place, exactly as they are. All of us feel like that sometimes, Cressida.'

Cressida nodded.

'Vittore's house was a dream. Priceless objects, tinkling fountains, strange perfumes (I thought I would do my best for you tonight), and also a certain number of utter horrors: dreadful, unspeakable, indescribable, vile.

'There was a lovely meal, perfectly simple; and the first thing of all that we did was drink a beautiful glass of water. And very soon we were drinking his own particular wine. It comes from that place of his. There was a lot of it. Fortunately, I have always had a good head,' added Aunt Agnes. 'It is a very important acquisition in a woman. Far more important than in a man.'

'What isn't?' enquired Vivien, more or less sotto voce.

'And having decided to go as far as I *have* gone, there's one other thing,' continued Aunt Agnes. 'You must neither of you suppose that my evening with Vittore was my first experience, as people term it. That would be to miss the point that matters. No, it was not my first experience in any such sense. I was engaged to be married to a man I loved very much, and at that time, with everything that was happening, girls did not hold back. But in a different sense it *was* a first experience with Vittore. A first and last.'

'I think we understand,' said Cressida.

'It was Gerald I loved, and it is Gerald I still love,' said Aunt Agnes, 'but Vittore is transcendent, I believe is the word. At least, it's the best word I can find.'

'It is a beautiful word,' said Cressida, uncertain of its meaning.

'Vittore had a Russian servant named Mouchka. At least Vittore said he was a Russian. I don't really know because I never heard him speak.'

'And all this only happened once?' asked Vivien.

'It happened more than once, but yet happened once only, in that it can never happen again, and could never happen more than once anyway.'

'We shall have to think about that rather carefully,' said Vivien. 'But would it be all right to tell us what was the end of it all? What went wrong, I mean?'

Aunt Agnes took a cigarette from an ebony box, elegantly struck a long match, and passed the box to the girls.

'Nothing went wrong, Vivien. It was simply that Vittore had to go back to Italy and I had to remain in Paris.'

'Were you both prepared to leave it at that when it had all been so wonderful?'

'The world was at war, Vivien. Besides, my view of life had been changed.'

113

'In what way exactly, Lady Luce?' asked Cressida.

'Some of it is a little puzzling for us,' explained Vivien.

'What happened was that I had been through an experience which every woman ought to go through once—well, a lot of women ought—but which cannot be expected to develop in any way.'

'That's not what people say,' objected Vivien.

'Why can't it develop, Lady Luce?'

'Because it's perfect already.'

'Oh,' said Cressida.

'And of course it can't last either. Perfection doesn't,' said Aunt Agnes.

'And did you know that at the time?' asked Vivien.

'Not before I entered 29 Rue Ginestra. But soon it was obvious. Only a ninny could have supposed that anything like that would last. And if I had been a ninny, I don't suppose Vittore would have spoken to me in the first place.'

'But he didn't speak to you in the first place, Lady Luce,' said Cressida. 'He just went round looking like a statue except when he was kissing all the men.'

'He knew,' said Aunt Agnes. 'Words were unnecessary. He knew.'

'What did you call him?' asked Cressida.

'Vittore. Everyone calls him Vittore—when they use his name, that is.'

'And what did *he* call *you*? Or is that a silly question?'

'Not at all, Cressida. He called me Agnese, because he saw me as his lamb. I'm hardly *that* any more.'

'It's your name, anyway,' said Vivien, attempting comfort for the change Aunt Agnes feared in herself.

'I think it's a beautiful story,' said Cressida.

Aunt Agnes smiled at her; gratefully perhaps.

'I think you are a beautiful person, Lady Luce.'

Aunt Agnes indeed was beautiful, as she lay there transfigured by her memories and vitalised by the effort of recalling and transmitting them, arranged at once casually and carefully.

Aunt Agnes smiled and extended her hand to Cressida, who took it and kissed it.

'Ton amie est très gentile, Vivien,' said Aunt Agnes.

'Thank God we all have each other,' said Vivien, with no trace of jealousy.

'And now we have to decide,' said Aunt Agnes. 'The three of us. When we have finished our cigarettes, we must stop smoking so that we can decide with clearer heads.'

But the air was as laden as the air in the sorcerer's attic.

CHAPTER TWENTY

The Decision

A few minutes later, Aunt Agnes had sat up, lowered her beautifully shod feet to the carpet, and drawn together her peignoir
across her knees.

'The first thing to be made clear,' said Aunt Agnes, 'is that
we are not invited on a pleasure trip. I doubt whether you will
see much of the pictures and monuments and things like that.'

'*We*, Aunt Agnes. Has Vittore actually *invited* us, too?'

'Not exactly, of course. He's never heard of you. But he has
asked *me* to help with looking after the sick, and to bring along
anyone else I think might be useful.'

'Is nursing the sick what we should have to do, Lady Luce?
I'm afraid I'm no good at it.'

'I *am* disappointed,' said Vivien. 'I'm useless with illness.
Obviously, I'm to have Dr Blattner depending on me for life.'

'You won't necessarily have to tend the sick. I'm not at all sure
how many sick there are, in any case. Vittore seems to suggest
that there are plenty of other things for girls to do.'

'What about men to do things?' asked Vivien.

'Vittore recruits men himself.'

'They come flocking,' said Vivien. 'From all parts of the globe.'

'Precisely. Men cause no difficulty. I am sure that by now there are many more men in Trino than women, and that's always a pleasant situation for women who can look after themselves, which all women who are not ninnies must learn to do in the end, and better soon than late in most cases.'

'I suppose so,' said Cressida, not quite sure what she was supposing, and therefore a little uncertain of herself.

'Aunt Agnes,' asked Vivien, 'are you able to tend the sick? If you don't mind my asking.'

'Not medically, of course, or not in the strict sense. But I am sure there will be doctors for that. In fact, Vittore says so. Doctors of all races and none, he says. I suppose my task will be to do things they cannot do.'

'Then I can't see what we're waiting for,' said Vivien. 'Why linger?'

'But what about your novel, Vivien?' asked Cressida.

'I suppose I can take it with me?'

'You may not have much time for writing it,' said Aunt Agnes. 'And that's just the point. There is certain to be hardship of many different kinds. Vittore say it's the main reason for going. It is testing of the spirit. I daresay there may not be enough food from time to time, and you know what that is like? No, I suppose you were too young during the war to understand. You may both have to wear trousers and do hard physical work of some kind. There may be a shortage of beds. There may be a shortage of almost everything. And it's not as if it's all for our own Empire or anything of that kind.'

'What exactly is it for, Lady Luce?'

'Cressy!' cried Vivien. 'How can you ask?'

'Well, I do ask. It's not exactly like when the school went to Venice and the Adriatic, is it?'

'It's to be in contact with greatness,' explained Vivien fervently. 'It's to Live. Think what will become of us otherwise: you with your flowers and me with Blattner so dependent upon me. It's what we've always wanted, silly. Besides, it *is* the Adriatic, anyway.'

'Yes,' said Aunt Agnes. 'It think it is. That at least is true.'

'We missed it when the school went,' said Vivien. 'Now we shall see it.'

'If only it wasn't so indefinite what we are supposed to do when we get there,' persisted Cressida. 'Not that I want to be a drag.'

'I'm fed up with knowing all the time what I'm supposed to do next,' said Vivien.

'Cressida is quite right to be cautious,' said Aunt Agnes. 'It is always right for women to be cautious.'

'Rubbish!' cried Vivien.

'Vivien!'

'Well, were *you* cautious?'

'No, and I have never regretted it. But in my case there was a world war, which I must admit made everything much easier. I suppose that now we have the coal strike, but it's not the same. What about your parents, Cressida? I suppose they would agree?'

'They might do nothing active if it was a definite job, Lady Luce. Lots of girls take jobs abroad for twelve months.'

'Vittore does mention money. Of course it is of interest to all of us. How foolish of me to forget! Let me see.' She drew forth a small object from the top of her black corselette. She carefully unfolded the thin, tingling sheets, blue as the sea, or blue as the sea is sometimes.

'I don't care,' proclaimed Vivien. 'I'm quite ready to starve in a good cause.'

Aunt Agnes read aloud, 'In Trino there is no payment for service, but the pure are offered an argosy for the sacking.'

'I don't think that would satisfy Daddy,' said Cressida. 'But as Mummy always says nothing will satisfy Daddy, I'm quite prepared to say Yes since Vivien wants to go.'

'You mustn't feel over-persuaded, Cressida,' said Aunt Agnes, rising to her feet. 'Never allow yourself to feel over-persuaded. Sauce for the goose is not always sauce for the gander.'

'Where do we buy our trousers?' asked Vivien.

'They may not be necessary. It was only a possibility. We don't want you both looking like vivandières.'

'Why ever not?' asked Vivien.

CHAPTER TWENTY-ONE

The Journey

Although when the topic came up the next morning, Aunt Agnes, with her usual fairness, had pointed out that her reference to vivandières had been sartorially misleading (when in Paris, she had attended *La Fille du Régiment*), Cressida and Vivien realised in no time at all on the journey from Trieste to Trino that something would have to be done. This was neither the realm nor the season for light woollen dresses, perfectly appropriate beneath light coats at Hurlingham or in Kensington Gardens.

Trieste was still in a terrible state, following the disappearance, upon the destruction of the Austrian Empire, of the main reason for its existence. It had seemed impossible even to find a good restaurant. Eleven o'clock in the morning was an unusual hour to need a good restaurant, but they had all been hungry after the rigours and perils of the night. In the end, they had consumed a dejected repast in a café overlooking the derelict installations, concerning the future of which the world continued to debate.

Vittore had told Aunt Agnes that his car would pick them up outside San Vitale at midday. It was to be hoped that the vehicle would be punctual. Now that the Austrians had gone, it might be difficult if it were not.

The car entered the piazza upon the last stroke of twelve. There could be no doubt as to its identity, because it wore the Italian flag at the peak of the radiator, and Vittore's larger personal ensign from a mast set up beside the driver. Or was it the flag of Vittore's new state? Perhaps, Cressida decided, it was both.

Moreover, though, on the face of it, an open tourer, the car had at some time been armoured and camouflaged for use on a battlefield. Cressida had often seen pictures of such cars, usually conveying senior officers, anxious or plethoric. The camouflage looked the very opposite of protective, nor had it much claim to inherent grace.

Equally, it was easy enough to identify Cressida, Vivien, and Aunt Agnes in the almost empty piazza. The population was still either too dejected or too committed to walk about very much, especially in the morning.

The car stopped with a clank. A youngish man, still quite handsome, alighted from the big back seat. He wore a blue uniform, wind-scintillated. It was a paler blue than that of the familiar writing paper.

The man saluted. 'Lady Luce? How do you do? My name is Terridge. Now Cavaliere Terridge, believe it or not.'

Aunt Agnes shook hands. 'How charming of Vittore to send someone who can speak English.'

'Most of us can by now. Well, more or less.'

'How can that be?'

'It's mainly since we were taken up by Lord Elterwater.'

'What, the newspaper owner? Is he here? I used to know him when I worked in Paris.'

'He's not here himself. He's represented at the moment by his son and heir, Brian. Brian Wicker, you know. But Elterwater's made a big difference. I doubt whether we could have held on at all without him. It's partly the money he puts in, of course. You can't conduct wars in the modern world without money, Lady Luce. Wars unfortunately cost money nowadays. There's no getting away from it.'

They all nodded.

'This,' said Aunt Agnes, 'is Cressida Hazeborough, and this is my niece, Vivien, Vivien Poins. Sorry we're all rather blown about.'

'Not the daughter of Sir Berkeley Poins?'

Vivien nodded again.

'I served under him when I was in the artillery.'

'He's in the West Indies now,' said Aunt Agnes.

'It happens to the best of us,' said Cavaliere Terridge. 'And what about *your* father?' He glanced at Cressida, and then gazed.

'*He* just farms in Rutland,' said Cressida modestly.

'Very beautiful county in England before the war, my uncle used to say. Small, isn't it?'

'Minute,' said Cressida.

'Not too small to produce lovely girls,' said Cavaliere Terridge. 'Sorry, all, about the funny togs. We have to make do with what we can lay our hands on. Mostly captured stuff. Some of us are in Austrian kit, the old white and red, you know. Girls too. At least it's all unworn. You don't dress like that in the front line. And now there's no one to wear it except us. Pathetic, really.'

'*Are* there any girls?' asked Vivien.

'Of course there are! What do *you* think? I must introduce you to Rosemary, Wendy, and Desirée. Gorgeous creatures.' His eyes flickered over Cressida. 'Not that we can't always do with more. There's plenty of hard work for everyone.'

'That's what I told them,' said Aunt Agnes. 'But perhaps we'd better make a start, Mr Terridge? I'm so sorry: Cavaliere Terridge.'

'Don't worry about rank when we're alone, Lady Luce. We're a bit of a Fred Karno's army, and some at least of us know it. We are, and yet we're not. There's that too. But come on, all of you.'

They descended the steps of the church.

'I say, you're going to be frightfully cold.'

'One doesn't somehow expect this kind of weather.'

'Never mind, Lady Luce, I'll tell Eno to drive round the town and we'll capture some rugs.'

'That'll be appallingly expensive in these times, Mr Terridge. When we collect our luggage at the station, we'd better all unpack, and get out something warmer.'

'Vittore's legion, ever valiant, ever victorious, doesn't pay for a thing, Lady Luce. We're adored. They'll fall on their knees, begging us to accept. Well, not quite, but you know what I mean.'

'I'm not sure I do, but I'm awestruck,' said Aunt Agnes.

'This is Eno,' said the Cavaliere, introducing the driver. 'He's one that *can't* speak English, and never will. He's an Albanian. From further down the coast, you know. His language is the most difficult in the world, and it's quite enough to occupy the lifetime of any one man. I manage quite well with him, but you have to raise the voice.'

Aunt Agnes smiled winningly at Eno, and the girls tried to follow suit. He was a dark, knotted, little man, with primeval eyes and a lowish brow.

'I think it's safer if I sit in the front,' said the Cavaliere, as the car drove off. He had to turn in order to shout at the three of them. 'After we've left Italian territory, they sometimes try their hand at an ambush.'

'How long is the drive?' enquired Aunt Agnes.

'Only three or four hours, if we drive fast. This car carried a German Feldmarschall, you know, and really knows how to travel. The road's pretty poor most of the way, but you get used to it.'

Even on the very short drive back to Trieste railway station, they all realised, from their different standpoints, that Sunny Italy had truly faltered. Cressida reflected, however, that where they were was Italy only by annexation, and that even the annexation was not beyond question.

Porters piled on and strapped down quantities of English luggage, and Aunt Agnes gave the Head Porter a large tip, as in times gone by.

'Now for rugs,' cried the Cavaliere, as Eno let in the clutch.

'Are you really sure?' shouted Aunt Agnes. 'Please let us pay. It's entirely our fault.'

'Members of Vittore's legion are not going to start paying for anything, Lady Luce.' The Cavaliere's tone held all the firmness of field rank, and probably of British field rank at that.

The car stopped outside a shop which looked more like a large, sprawling bazaar.

'How wonderful!' cried Cressida.

'Simply leave this to me,' said the Cavaliere. He got out of the car.

'Can't we come in too?' solicited Cressida.

'No, little girl. Only Eno comes with me.'

Eno was already out of the car. Cressida could see that he had two enormous pistols in his belt. She had never before seen such implements except in picture books for children. Eno had a practised hand on each.

'It wouldn't do for us to be too long,' said the Cavaliere. 'But we shan't be.' He strode athletically into the bazaar-like shop, with Eno close at his heels.

From the back seat of the open car, Aunt Agnes gazed up at the sky.

'I hope it's not going to rain as well. I remember spending a week in Venice with the man I loved most in the world and it never stopped raining once.'

'Surely not in Venice, Aunt Agnes?'

'Yes, Vivien. In Venice. The sun sucks up the water everywhere.'

But shady-looking men were accumulating round the large stationary vehicle, though at a proper distance. Men, and, as far as Cressida could see, no women; and some of the men were still unwashed though it was nearly half-past twelve. They were muttering in entirely unknown languages, but they had to find their bearings, so that curiosity had not yet merged into still worse. Most of them looked rather thin, and some had suffered nasty injuries.

The Cavaliere strode out of the shop, with Eno behind him carrying the rugs, which made him look like a koala bear.

'Magnificent pieces, Lady Luce. Sold by the Austrians for food before they went. Sad really.'

'I don't like using them, Mr Terridge. It's embarrassing.'

'It's unlucky,' said Vivien. 'There's probably a curse on them.'

'No good worrying about things like that. We're in a different world now. This is post-war.'

And if it had to be regarded as impracticable for them to change into something warmer, there really was no alternative to travelling with a beautiful rug submerging each of them up to the neck, as if they had been sea lionesses.

CHAPTER TWENTY-TWO

The Breakdown

Bump, bump. Hours seemed to pass.

'I forgot to tell you that this new man in Italy is visiting us today.'

'Benito Mussolini?'

'That's the name. Of course, all we're doing is supposed to be in aid of capturing the place for Italy. We shouldn't have much *locus standi* otherwise.'

'Vittore is a great Italian patriot,' said Aunt Agnes.

'Well, at one time, Lady Luce. He's been very mixed about it for years. Italy has failed him, he keeps saying.'

'Not out loud?' asked Cressida in horror.

'At the top of his voice,' replied the Cavaliere.

'Vittore's voice is like no one else's,' said Aunt Agnes, dreamily.

'He's working to create an entirely *new* Italy,' said Vivien. 'To build a new race. Look at that!'

She pointed to a poster, as the car crashed across the potholes. The poster had been affixed, not quite symmetrically, on the remains of a grey wall that had suffered damage of some kind. It was in Italian.

'What does it say?' asked Cressida. 'I hadn't time to work it out.'

'Something about mingling the Capitoline lion with the Roman wolf,' said Aunt Agnes.

'But that's impossible, Lady Luce.'

'Nothing is impossible where we're going, little girl,' said the Cavaliere. 'That's one of Vittore's most frequent utterances.'

'But we haven't got there yet,' pointed out Cressida. 'Surely the poster's in the wrong place?'

'The kids get hold of them and stick them up everywhere.'

Suddenly the car stopped. There was nothing much in sight but romantic scenery. For a fleeting moment, all was peaceful. Then Eno alighted with a hammer. He began to make new noises far louder.

'Sorry, Lady Luce and girls,' said the Cavaliere. 'This happens every time. It's because we've got no proper spares.'

'Should we get out?' asked Cressida, elevating her pretty chin above the fringe of the rich rug.

'If you wish,' said the Cavaliere. 'Perhaps we might all like to.'

But that was not exactly what Cressida had meant. She felt embarrassed, though aware that it would be more sensible to feel grateful.

The three of them looked at the quite distant rocks, hard-edged vegetation, loose shale. No one set forth.

'I have no wish to pry, Mr Terridge,' observed Aunt Agnes, 'but I should be most interested—I am sure we all should—if you could tell us how you first became involved with Vittore?'

'I blundered through the war, though not in France or anywhere like that. Mostly in Africa, actually. Then I couldn't find anything else. Couldn't think of anything at all, as a matter of fact. Vittore put an advertisement in an ex-service rag, and I answered it. Best thing I ever did in my life—while it all lasts, of course. Right here is the centre of the earth at the moment. You're lucky if you get any pay, but you don't need pay. We do without money. We look like the costume store in the panto-mime, but, my God, Lady Luce, when the time comes, if it ever does come, we'll sell ourselves dear. We've a lot to lose.'

'And do you think the time will come soon?'

'No one knows. Not even Vittore. In the meantime, it's a good life. Better than slaving in a job any day. Less clatter, Eno, if you possibly can. Of course he can't understand a word I say.'

'Is Eno his real name?'

'No one knows his real name. Something in Albanian, I take it. Vittore called him Eno after the bloke in Shakespeare.'

'Age cannot wither her, nor custom stale. Enobarbus,' said Vivien.

'That's dead right, girl,' replied the Cavaliere familiarly. 'And the very same words apply to Vittore himself. We'd all die for the little man, though God knows why, especially as we all probably shall. The males will, I mean of course, though some of the girls are as keen as mustard in their own way. Good man, Eno.'

The engine was once more roaring. In view of the language difficulty, the Cavaliere gave Eno a heavy clap on the shoulder as he resumed his place behind the wheel.

'Thundering clever, Eno. Damned good.'

On the right was the sea, today somewhat muddy in hue; on the left the Dalmatic hinterland, unpopulous, infertile, controversial.

They raced up ridges and dashed down declivities. It went on and on. Only an Albanian could have kept their advance under control. It was as one takes aboard a Mohawk before attempting the rapids.

And there the place was: enormously, incomparably, terrifyingly more lifelike than anything Cressida had ever before seen outside an illustrated book. From this distance, Trino might, indeed, have been designed by Mr Arthur Rackham at his best.

'Don't we have to go in a boat?' enquired Vivien disappointedly.

'No, there's a causeway. It's hell to cross because nothing's been done to it since the Romans, but one can't risk leaving the car on the mainland. They'd be patching up their homes with bits of it within the hour. Makes you think sometimes, I suppose. Now hold on, Lady Luce. Hold on, girls.'

CHAPTER TWENTY-THREE

The Distinguished Visitor

It was terrible while it lasted, but soon they were stopped by a policeman. Apart from the fact that he was not English, he seemed a perfectly average officer of the law, apparently attached to a normally conducted state. He wore a black tunic and scarlet trousers, and a hat with feathers. The costume would have suited Vivien, Cressida thought. Still she wondered where the feathers had come from: perhaps they were artificial.

'Nothing to do with us,' explained the Cavaliere. 'Don't know what he's doing here.'

Vivien and Cressida looked at each other over their rugs; in the eyes of each was the conviction that they were about to vanish from sight until they were all but forgotten, even by their four parents.

There was a conversation between the Cavaliere and the policeman, with the policeman doing most of the talking, if only because he knew more of the language.

'It's simply that the Italian prime minister is leaving, so that the security's been laid on. We've got to get the car off the centre of the highway.'

Somehow this was managed. If it had not been so windy on the causeway, they would this time have taken to their legs, to avoid the further jolts and bruises.

'We should probably twist our ankles instead,' observed Lady Luce with a smile.

They lay at a diagonal, with the Adriatic smashing against the causeway and tearing very slow holes in it just below Cressida's side of the car.

'Does this really go back to the Roman Empire, Aunt Agnes?' enquired Vivien.

'I don't think much of any kind has happened here since the Romans left,' replied Aunt Agnes. 'Nothing constructive, I mean.'

'That's exactly it, Lady Luce,' said the Cavaliere. 'They're too busy fighting to do anything else. Always have been, always will be. That's the point of Vittore's civilising mission. At least, it's one of the points.'

The gates before them opened, even more in the style of Mr Rackham, and a large, black saloon car bumped gingerly out. At the same time, a cannon was shot off, making the most appalling racket.

'Farewell salute,' shouted the Cavaliere, though Cressida and Vivien could hardly hear him through the hands they had pressed belatedly to their ears.

Only Aunt Agnes seemed comparatively undismayed. 'I imagine Vittore does that often?'

'Whenever possible,' said the Cavaliere. 'It braces us up. At the voice of the gun, the soul ceases to weep. You'll soon get used to it.'

By now, the car was edging past them. The Italian prime minister was visible in the rear compartment, where he was seated with two other gentlemen. It was the first prime minister that Cressida had ever seen. As she would have expected he was in morning dress, though the waistcoat was unbuttoned. Aunt Agnes bowed to him and the Cavaliere belatedly saluted as best he could from such a slanting position. The car was perforce proceeding so slowly that the prime minister could easily be seen smiling back. The two girls waved enthusiastically.

Unmistakably, the policeman indicated that they could and should go forward once more.

The gates of the citadel (Cressida at present could think of no other word) had still not clanged shut.

'Hold it,' roared the Cavaliere in English.

'Hold it,' came back the answering voice from afar, also in English.

'Hold it,' cried a helpful bystander on the causeway's edge, still in English.

Cressida realised that the bystander was fishing.

'That's Colonel van Oppé,' said the Cavaliere. 'One of the Devonshire van Oppés. Used to have a place above Ilfracombe, I believe. He fishes with too short a rod.'

'An Incompleat Angler,' suggested Vivien from under her rug.

A legend had been painted on the stonework above the gate:

QUESTA TERRA E REGOLATA DAI DIRETTI DI MUSICA.

They were proceeding so slowly that Cressida had plenty of time to spell it out.

'There you are!' exclaimed Vivien triumphantly. She would have done something dramatic if her legs had not been frozen stiff. The Cavaliere was still erect, and saluting in all directions.

The gates clanged behind them.

Once again Cressida could hardly believe her eyes. The interior of the city was almost as wonderful as the exterior: all history and faded colour and disintegration.

Previously, Cressida had seen only Calais; and that had been on a day trip with her father, who disliked the Continent, so did not wish to go too far from the boat, and there had of course been Trieste looking pointless after the expulsion of the Austrians. Trino was far more what she had imagined things to be. She glanced at Vivien, her eyes glowing; and rubbed her chilly hands together vigorously under the rug.

She noticed that there were poems stuck up everywhere, and promised herself that in due time she would read them. Doubtless there was someone who could explain to her what they all meant.

CHAPTER TWENTY-FOUR

The Allocation

Albanians gathered round to congratulate Eno. It was as if he had motored across the Tundra, or the Puszta, or the Pampas. He was clapped emphatically on the back, often by several men at once. Both of his hands were continually wrung. One man was even offering him a drink of some kind.

'Damned good,' repeated the Cavaliere vaguely. 'Damned good, Eno.'

Soon Eno was dragged right out of and away from the automobile.

The Cavaliere's expression softened. He sprang out.

There were three young women standing in a line.

In a way, Cressida was relieved, because hitherto there had been no locally resident females in sight.

One wore a coat and skirt in quietly authentic tweed. Her bobbed hair was the colour of Cotswold honey. The second wore a most impressive fur coat. Her black hair was very short and fashionable. The third wore a high-necked yellow jersey and navy blue trousers. Cressida drew in her breath and glanced again at Vivien; but Vivien appeared to have gone into a trance. The third girl's hair was mid-coloured, anyway at first glance; and of neutral length.

'Here we all are,' said the Cavaliere brightly. 'Now then.'

The three occupants of the car did what they could to look reasonably dignified, even though they had lost the use of their limbs. The Albanians were still mobbing Eno like birds.

'This is Rosemary. This is Wendy. This is Desirée.'

'Sorry we look such frights,' said Wendy, who was the one in the costly fur coat.

'This is Lady Luce, of course. And this is Cressida. And this is little Vivien.'

'I'm not little,' said Vivien.

'Relatively little,' said the Cavaliere. 'The nearer the bone, the sweeter the meat.'

'Lady Luce,' said Desirée, 'the Commendatore says will you change into your uniform and start tending the sick as soon as you can? He depends upon that very much. I'll come with you and show you where you report.'

'What about my little girls?'

'Rosemary and I shall look after *them*, Lady Luce,' said Wendy.

Aunt Agnes glanced at the Cavaliere.

'Do what Desirée says, Lady Luce,' said Wendy.

Aunt Agnes followed Desirée. The Albanians were extracting and unroping the luggage, arguing in their own language what to do with it.

'I'll stand guard,' volunteered Cavaliere Terridge, 'until you've sorted yourselves out. Better buck up in case there's an alarm, in which case I shall have to dash. Take the rugs with you.'

'Are there lots of alarms?' asked Cressida, as she and Vivien accompanied Rosemary and Wendy across the piazza and up some stone stairs.

'Vittore likes to try it on,' replied Wendy, sinking her hands into the big pockets of her coat.

'Then they're only practice?' persisted Cressida.

'Not always. Sometimes there's a raid from outside. We're not supposed to *be* here, you know.'

They were wending along a rather dark, uneven stone passage.

'What happens then?'

'Our brave boys drive the raiders away. Well, so far.'

'Some of the girls do it too, the man said,' observed Vivien.

'Yes, Desirée lends a hand sometimes. It's expected of her. She's Vittore's campaign assistant, you know.'

'She's not the *only* one who lends a hand?'

'No, she's not.' Wendy smiled equivocally. 'There's a collection of the most frightful little cats over on the other side of the town.'

'Which brings us to the point,' said Rosemary, speaking for the first time. 'There's a decision for you to make.'

They had reached a big, dark apartment in which were single beds. There was a strip of matting down the centre of the room, but much of the floor was covered with clothes.

'The usual ghastly mess!' said Wendy. 'So sorry.'

'You can either sleep in here with us,' continued Rosemary, 'or have a room each to yourselves. There was rather a riff-raff in here originally, but we got them out, and after that it seemed cosier to mess in altogether, just the English girls.'

'It's like school,' said Vivien.

'Quite,' said Rosemary. 'Though I suppose it depends which school.'

'You can choose for yourselves,' said Wendy, walking over to a small looking glass which hung from a nail beneath one of the small windows, and adjusting the Gwen Farrar curls above her ears.

'There's plenty of room. Almost all the proper inhabitants had fled before Vittore took the place over, and some of the rest have fled since. You can live wherever you prefer.'

Cressida and Vivien looked at each other.

Vivien spoke. 'I think we prefer company.'

'Thanks very much for asking us,' said Cressida.

Wendy straightened up. 'Yes,' she said. 'We shall love to have you, naturally, but there are one or two things. Everyone must toe the line in a reasonable sort of way, and when there's any difficulty, what Desirée says, goes.'

Vivien gave a slight start.

'Someone must have authority in a place like this,' Rosemary said persuasively.

Vivien acquiesced.

'Desirée's sweet, really. She sleeps over there.'

Rosemary pointed to a bed in a corner.

Wendy continued her former narrative. 'And there's one thing that must be absolutely clear. If anyone's not here for the night, or anything like that, then no one says a single thing about it.'

'Not unless something's volunteered,' added Rosemary, again softening the position.

'Yes, of course,' said Wendy, 'but often it isn't. I'm sure you understand. We're all grown up now.'

'It's quite clear to us,' said Vivien.

'Crystal clear,' said Cressida. 'Are there any more of us?'

'No, just us three,' said Wendy, 'and now five. There used to be two more English girls, called Victoria and Peter, but they changed their minds and went home.'

'Peter? What a funny name for a girl?'

'She was a funny girl,' said Rosemary. 'She'd been expelled three times.'

'There's no light but oil lamps and candles, because we can't get spares for the generator. Which beds will you have?' Wendy was fastidiously extricating what were presumably her own garments from the mélange on the floor. Cressida could see that they were exceptionally attractive garments.

'I'm there,' said Rosemary, pointing. 'You can have the beds that Victoria and Peter had, or the other two if you'd prefer.'

'Victoria and Peter's beds would be cosier,' said Vivien. 'Which are they?'

'Those two, of course,' said Rosemary. 'Not out in the cold.'

So the order of the day seemed to have emerged as Desirée and Wendy on one side of the room, and Rosemary, Cressida, and Vivien on the other. Actually, there remained not two but three more beds awaiting occupants, no doubt.

Cressida and Vivien spread rugs on their beds.

Cressida wondered about Lady Luce, but Vivien said nothing, and plainly Lady Luce would be out of place here, unless indeed there were an emergency, which might temporarily sweep aside all barriers.

'Talking about cold,' enquired Vivien, 'do we get any heat?'

'Yes,' said Wendy, drawing her fur coat more closely round her. 'The Albanians get a fire going before evening.'

'When they remember,' said Rosemary.

'I never thought it was like this in Italy,' said Cressida.

'This isn't Italy,' said Wendy.

'Don't be silly, Wendy,' said Rosemary. 'Of course we're in Italy. That's what we're all doing here.'

'I forgot,' said Wendy.

'Sorry about the mess,' said Rosemary. 'We all have separate rooms as well to keep things in, if only it weren't so bloody cold. You can have rooms too.'

'It'll be spring in a month,' said Cressida. 'Won't it?'

'Let's hope it will,' said Wendy.

Chapter Twenty-Five

Settling Down

The Albanians had appeared with the luggage.

Cressida wondered whether tips were necessary, and how much to give, and whether the money from Trieste would pass muster in Trino, but she caught Rosemary's eye, and Rosemary seemed to shake her head faintly.

Cressida and Vivien were offered a selection of rooms in which to keep things, and each chose one.

The rooms were all furnished with a curious miscellany of more or less domestic objects, some of them ornate. There had presumably been a steady rearrangement of the town's facilities, comparable with the passage of history itself. In Cressida's room there was a diffuse draught, though the window looked as if it had not been opened since the fourteenth century, or perhaps earlier. For the moment, Cressida did very little unpacking, though her mother had constantly admonished her against leaving her clothes in cases longer than was necessary. She understood why there were so many garments lying about in the room where there was said sometimes to be a fire.

Back in the sleeping chamber, she saw that the Albanians had remained, or other Albanians had taken their places, and were now indeed building a fire, while Rosemary and Wendy sat on their beds and watched. Vivien had not so far re-appeared.

'There's a coal strike in England,' said Cressida conversationally.

'There would be,' said Wendy.

'Is there coal in Italy?' asked Cressida.

'I shouldn't think so,' said Wendy.

'I thought we might have to burn what we could find, like they did at the front.'

'We're not at war here, you know,' explained Rosemary. 'Not unless someone declares war on *us*. We're simply on guard. If we don't make a stand of some kind somewhere, then no one else will. Don't you agree?' She seemed quite anxious to receive a sympathetic answer.

'I suppose so,' said Cressida. 'I don't know as much about it as I ought. Was the coal left behind in the town?'

'No. We captured a ship laden with it.'

'What happened to the crew?'

'They joined us. One of the officers is helping Desirée. She has him properly under her thumb. He comes from somewhere funny, but he's been a Canadian for years. He can turn his hand to anything.'

'That's what *she* says,' commented Wendy.

'That's what *he* says, Wendy,' said Rosemary.

The Albanians were discussing something in their own language, making gestures which expressed paucity, privation, pathos.

Cressida was the first to twig. She opened her handbag and produced a box of matches. The Bryant and May label seemed wistful and bygone.

One of the Albanians said something which might have been Thank you.

The fire roared up. Once a start had been made, the heavy draught in the huge flue sometimes did the rest, provided the wind were not in the wrong direction. There was a heavy fall of objects down the chimney.

Vivien entered.

'Where can we get some warmer clothes? Isn't there a dump somewhere? The man said there was. Warmer and more suitable.'

'More suitable for what?' enquired Wendy. She had risen from the bed and was now standing with her back to the incipient blaze, though still in her fur coat.

'Well, Vittore told my aunt that there was work for everyone.'

Rosemary intervened. 'That's perfectly right. I often work.'

'That's why we've come here,' said Vivien.

'What do you work *at*?' Cressida enquired politely of Rosemary.

'I teach English. I'm perfectly prepared to do more of it, but they don't always turn up. There's no proper discipline.'

'I thought there *was*,' said Vivien.

'You'll soon see.'

'And what do you do?' Cressida politely asked Wendy.

Before Wendy could reply, Rosemary explained. 'She's Brian Wicker's fiancée.'

'How wonderful!' said Cressida. It was what one did say.

'In some ways,' said Wendy.

'And what about Desirée? Was she here when you arrived?'

'Not a bit, she was at school with us. She was a prefect and won the Best Girl in the School trophy. So naturally she's got on.'

'I won the Elocution Prize,' said Cressida.

'That'll help,' said Wendy. 'There's a lot of elocution here.'

'Not from women,' said Rosemary.

'Why ever not?' cried Vivien. 'Cressida and I are fed up with never being able to do anything proper.'

Before Wendy could even smile Rosemary hurried to say, 'So are we all. Desirée will find something for you. Truly she will. I told you she's Vittore's right-hand girl. She's great fun, really.'

But Wendy said to Vivien: 'Did *you* win any prizes?'

'Yes I did. For Latin.'

'Latin!' cried Rosemary. 'That's wonderful. Vittore is always looking for a girl who can speak Latin. You're in, Vivien. You'll be another Desirée.'

'I can't *speak* Latin!' cried Vivien. 'I only said I won at school a prize for it.'

'I expect you speak enough,' said Wendy.

Chapter Twenty-Six

Employment

The Albanians were going after glaring at Wendy's hair, Vivien's legs, Rosemary's bust and everything there was about Cressida.

For no particular reason, Cressida followed them out, at a little distance, into the stone passage, where there was a larger and more accessible window, through which she could see them in the piazza below, already flexing themselves and practising bayonet runs, though of course without bayonets.

She shuddered slightly. The fire, albeit fine and roaring, had not yet had time to make much impression.

Desirée could be seen crossing the courtyard and ascending the stair.

'The days are drawing out,' observed Rosemary.

'I haven't noticed it,' said Wendy, still in her fur coat, and still with her back to the fire.

'If it was England, we'd be having tea,' said Cressida.

Desirée entered, slim and effective-looking.

'Hullo,' she said to all. Then she spoke more particularly to Cressida and Vivien. 'What would you two like to do? Would you like to be settled at something, or would you prefer just to look round for a bit?'

'What's happening to Aunt Agnes?' asked Vivien.

'She seems to be fitting in extremely well,' replied Desirée, 'though the infirmary's only about a quarter full at the moment. The colder weather braces people so they resist better.'

'I've never seen her in her uniform,' said Vivien.

'She looks wonderful,' said Desirée. 'But back to you two. What do you want to do with yourselves?'

'I wish there were some proper chairs in here,' said Wendy.

'Well, go and get some. There are plenty of chairs lying about.'

Wendy made very little movement, beyond a gesture of pique.

'We're not actually trained to anything,' said Cressida. 'I'm not on very good terms with my parents, and Vivien's writing a novel.'

'Well, that's excellent,' said Desirée. 'The prime purpose of the Commandery is submission to beauty. The second purpose is sacrifice for art. The third purpose is adoration of the sublime fire.'

'It's my first book, of course,' said Vivien. 'But I did start it when I was working for a psychoanalyst.'

'That's one of the things we've not got,' exclaimed Desirée, almost with excitement. 'How much did you learn about psychoanalysis?'

'It's supposed to take years and years, and I was only with Dr Blattner for about six months, but he always said that insight was something that no training could bestow. He did really say that. Quite frequently.'

'The Commendatore says the same. One lightning-flash from the soul annihilates ten lifetimes in the schools.'

Wendy sat down on a bed and began carefully feeling her legs, beautifully stockinged but no doubt weakened by standing.

'I'm quite prepared to help as far as I can,' said Vivien. 'From what I saw, psychoanalysis is usually much the same with everyone, once you've got a general hang of it.'

'Provided she has time to write her novel,' put in Cressida loyally.

'Well, of course,' said Desirée. 'That's what the Commandery is for. Individual self-realisation.'

She walked over in order to take Wendy's place in front of the fire, where she opened her trousered legs.

'I'll speak to Dr Bosch about you, Vivien.'

'Who's he?'

'She. Julia Bosch. She's our Chief Medical Superintendent.'

'Well, she's called herself that,' said Wendy, still looking down.

'In fact, I might take you over there when she's had time to finish her tea.'

'Is there tea?' asked Cressida. 'I thought that was only in England.'

'There's a cantina where you can get whatever you want,' said Rosemary.

'It depends what that *is*,' said Wendy.

'And, now, what about you?' enquired Desirée, addressing Cressida. 'Are you writing a novel too?'

'Not yet. I used to be told I'd be better at something more direct.'

'She's wonderful at elocution,' said Vivien.

Desirée seemed once more transfixed with decision.

'Would you like to work in our theatre?'

'I didn't know there was a theatre! How marvellous!'

'It's mainly the Commendatore's plays. They're wonderful. The greatest actresses will give simply anything for parts in them, even though big sacrifices are often involved.'

'Perhaps I ought to drop the novel and start writing a play,' said Vivien.

'And I could act in it,' cried Cressida. 'We could all act in it,' she added, in a rush of generosity.

'There's no shortage of actresses, Cressida,' said Desirée, smiling gently. 'But I expect we could find you something in the wardrobe.'

It was growing dark in the room, as was only to be expected. The fire was achieving new importance.

'Speaking of wardrobes,' said Vivien. 'Where are those warm clothes the man talked about?'

'Follow me,' said Desirée, still gently smiling.

They left Rosemary and Wendy round the fire. Rosemary was seated on the floor, at the end of the strip of carpet.

'They're sweet girls,' said Desirée, as the three of them walked down the passage. 'Brian Wicker's very lucky to have Wendy, and Rosemary's game for absolutely anything.'

'Is Brian Wicker important?' asked Cressida.

'Oh, very. Lord Elterwater is worth millions. He pays for pretty well the whole show, though we don't say so, of course.'

'*Why* does he do that?' asked Cressida.

'He's not in a position to suffer and endure with us in person, so he contributes what he can, even though it's only money.'

Cressida reflected that Wendy's smile seemed very superficial when compared with Desirée's smile, even in the fading light.

'I say,' said Vivien. 'Where's the what-not. We haven't been shown.'

'The one we use is the other side of the dormitorio.'

Ah, Cressida noted: dormitory *was* more or less the word used.

'Do you want to go back?' continued Desirée, no longer smiling now that her attention had had to leave the high places.

'I think I do. So sorry.'

'I do too,' said Cressida.

They returned up the stairs.

'Back already?' enquired Rosemary.

'We forgot to show them the offices,' said Desirée, sharing in the responsibility.

Actually, there was one office only. It had been introduced during the nineteenth century, and a definite style still lingered. Cressida was glad that the apartment was available only to the English girls.

'What about when we want a bath?' asked Vivien.

'We can make an arrangement with Madame Argenti. She's very nice, but mostly we just use the hip bath.'

'What fun!' cried Cressida. 'Lots of people in Rutland still have hip baths. We all love them.'

They were going through the dormitory again. Rosemary was reading *The Illustrated London News* by the light of the fire, into which Wendy, her legs relaxed, was staring with big, sombre eyes. Her trim head was shadowy and perfect.

'We ask the Albanians to bring up the hot water,' explained Desirée.

CHAPTER TWENTY-SEVEN

The Oil Store

Suddenly Cressida recollected: Cavaliere Terridge had said 'I'll stand guard, until you've sorted yourselves out.' How fortunate that there had been no alarm! At least she assumed there had not.

And when, for the second time, they neared the bottom of the external stair, chipped, gnawed, and romantically irregular, there he was, like 'The Blue Boy', in precisely the same position, or very nearly so. Behind him, the sun, not directly visible, must by now have sunk into the Adriatic almost finally.

Cressida and Vivien ran towards him, despite the unevenness of the paving and the very poor light.

'We're so sorry,' they cried with one voice. 'We forgot.'

'That's perfectly all right,' said Cavaliere Terridge, now free to attempt movement of some kind. 'Hope you two have managed to shake down. Lady Luce is gorgeous. You're lucky to have such a fine woman as your aunt, little girl.'

He was addressing the wrong little girl, but, as so much time had passed, neither of them said a word.

'Look!' cried Cressida. 'Isn't that a lamplighter?'

'Vittore dug him out of the Domus Senectudinis. Run by the monks, you know. The lamps are gas really, but first there was no coal, and then there was apparently no one who knows how to make gas. So we've had to fall back on oil.'

'The Commendatore has scientists researching at the gas-works,' Desirée amplified.

'If you can call them scientists,' said the Cavaliere, exactly as Wendy always did.

'Well, Hugh, you know what the Commendatore says about *that*?'

'I do, Desirée, I do, I do. And quite right too, I'm sure. The only point is that we get no gas.'

'When we do, it'll be in a different world from everyone else's gas,' said Desirée.

'I daresay,' said the Cavaliere. 'And now if you're all quite settled, I propose to pop off for some grub.'

'Perhaps we shall see you?' said Cressida politely. 'We're quite hungry too.'

'No, no, little girl. The civil administration eats in one place, the victorious soldiery somewhere very different.'

He leered amiably, attempted a mock salute, as far as the state of his limbs permitted, and stumbled off into the gloom.

'There are whole cisterns full of oil,' explained Desirée. 'They're supposed to go back to the Romans. We're standing on top of them now. If you fall through, the oil closes slowly over your head. There's no possibility of rescue.'

'Does it happen often?' asked Cressida.

'We're trying to strengthen the arches,' said Desirée. 'We've got some Bulgarians on the job. Of course you can't see them, because they have to work in darkness, owing to the inflammability of the oil.'

'Do you think they're nearly finished?'

'I expect so,' said Desirée. 'Everything is beginning to work better and will continue to do so, as long as the Commendatore is spared.'

'And Lord Elterwater too?'

'There are plenty of Lord Elterwaters in the world, Vivien. There's only one Commendatore.'

Despite the dusk, one could be certain that she was smiling the deep inward smile bought by her experiences since she had left school.

'Are you two *really* hungry?' she asked.

'Clothes first,' said Vivien. 'Food afterwards.'

Cressida was not so sure. After all, there had been no food since the rather scratch meal that morning in Trieste. Still, there it was. In any case, she had learned that the Cavaliere's Christian name was Hugh. Oh! Oh!

Desirée led the way. 'Watch where you put your feet.'

'I suppose these poems stuck up everywhere are in Italian?' enquired Cressida.

'Not all of them. The Commendatore speaks twelve languages equally well.'

'How do you learn to speak twelve languages? I should like to so much.'

'The Commendatore just picks them up as he travels about. From books too, of course. He learned three languages simply in order to bring Italy into the war. It's quite easy to do if you have the gift.'

The lamplighter was very decrepit, and so were the lamps. Cressida remembered that of course both were old.

Fortunately they did not have to go very far. In any case, Desirée seemed to manage perfectly well.

They came to a stone structure, three or four storeys high, and of irregular plan. Doubtless it had served some definite purpose at the time it had been built. It might have been anything.

Desirée led the way down a fight of very shallow, very wide steps, each of which sloped forward, after centuries of use, often no doubt by clanking, mailed feet.

'These steps are *very* slippery,' said Desirée.

At the bottom, when all their heads were below the level of the street, were two big wooden doors, ancient and ponderous. Against one of them Desirée leaned all her weight, such as it was.

The door opened and they entered the rugged cellar, perhaps even dungeon.

CHAPTER TWENTY-EIGHT

The Garment Store

There were a dozen battered oil lamps hanging from ropes and chains, none of the lamps very luminous. Such as they were, they glimmered across a boundless sea of garments, strewn across the stone floor. It was the scene in the dormitory, though on a vastly larger scale. Here some of the garments were roped up in bales which had not yet been even breached.

There were persons groping round with lamps of their own and sometimes trying things on. They reminded Cressida of figures she had seen at night on the shores of The Wash, when in early childhood she had spent three weeks there, on holiday, as she had been told. Her father had said the figures were digging for bait: that had seemed to her alarming, but she had always rather wondered whether it had been the whole truth. Down here in the dim dungeon, it was difficult to tell how old the figures were, or of what sex or social group. Of course it had been like that, too, in childhood on The Wash. Cressida suspected that in the cellars of Trino, here full of clothes, there full of oil, farther on full of mystery, it was not to be expected that the essentials of a person would be as instantly definable as in sunny Bond Street. She felt a faint frisson; from fear and from fascination.

Upon a pile of sacks in the centre of the wall at the far side of the dungeon squatted a woman. Probably the sacks had once contained clothing, now appropriated. The woman had her legs drawn up under her in a way which Cressida would previously have thought impracticable in one so old. The woman had almost no hair, was smoking a very small, rather dirty pipe, and appeared to be arrayed simply in rags. Her sex was apparent only in a rather embarrassing way.

'She's a Montenegrin,' whispered Desirée.

The odd thing was that Desirée's whisper susurrated all round the stone walls. Cressida had heard of such acoustic phenomena helping to while away the time of unfortunates confined indefinitely during the Dark Ages. Cressida realised, however, that none of the groping figures was uttering a word.

'Montenegro's disappeared, hasn't it?'

Cressida whispered too, though it seemed almost pointless.

'Yes, Montenegro has been merged. That old lady will be one of the last of the independent Montenegrins.'

Cressida gazed across the ill-lit dungeon with interest. Vivien was picking up garments and peering at them.

'The man said there were lots that were unworn. These aren't unworn.'

Vivien spoke in a more or less normal voice. It is often so difficult to decide when one should whisper and when one should not.

Inwardly, Cressida made another comparison. This cluttered floor was as the floor of her room when she and Vivien, so very recently, had strewed it with the ingredients for the spell, without which they would not have been where they now found themselves. Until then, she had almost forgotten about the spell.

'Some of the clothes have come out of the houses since the original people left,' explained Desirée. 'But if you stick to it, you'll find something you want. Selecting clothes always takes some time, doesn't it? And shouldn't it?' Desirée smiled suitably.

'Did you find what you're wearing here?' enquired Cressida, in a tone of light incredulity.

'Certainly I did. These yellow sweaters used to be for the riding school. If you can find a sweater like this with a high neck, you'll stop worrying so much about the cold. I believe the trousers were meant for naval cadets. They're very warm too. I'm lucky to have the figure to wear them, but you two don't have to worry about that either.'

'What about Rosemary and Wendy?'

'Yes, they brought more clothes from London. Wendy is Brian Wicker's fiancée in any case. Now plunge in, Cressida. Have a good look. It's all free.'

Vivien was a third of the way across the room by now. There she had found a red silk party dress. Her colour. She was holding it against herself, what there was of it. It was completely fashionable.

'What do I do?' she called to Desirée in a perfectly normal voice.

'If you will both bring the things you want to me, I'll look after them until you have enough.'

Really, Desirée might have been far, far older. Responsibility had matured her at every detectable point. She was seated on a stone ledge that continued all round the dungeon, but had first laid several empty sacks on it, much as the aged Montenegrin had done.

Cressida had come to believe that her present appearance was so inappropriate to be positively silly.

All the same, she could not find a single yellow sweater or, for that matter, a single pair of trousers, blue or in any other colour. She found a pair of breeches, but that, she knew well, was a garment that simply had to fit, and she did not feel, in the present circumstances, like trying it on, even though such delicacy could no doubt be overcome in due course, because, quite near her, there was a young man, a man beyond doubt, who at that very moment was trying on the tight lower part of what Cressida supposed to be the costume of a professional jester, or, in the world of today, probably of Harlequin. When he was girdled up, the young man actually spoke: 'Hola!' he said, and touched his right cheek with his left forefinger. It was not clear whether or not he was intending to address Cressida; who therefore deemed it unnecessary to respond. The uncovered upper part of the man's body was quite hairless, and so white that it almost shone through the murk, as a fish shines in a cavern.

Cressida dropped the pair of breeches. She picked up a grey evening dress in some material that went dull in streaks and patches when not properly attended to, but which in the right circumstances would have shimmered all over. She went to the trouble of holding the garment against herself, but it went on for miles. It was more suited to Jack and the Beanstalk than to a girl who only a year ago had been at school. She threw it away. The young man in the cubist tights picked it up and held it against him instead. His pallid features changed as the fabric touched his skin. For a second he might have been a quite different person, and doubtless was.

Cressida found several nondescript dresses, almost exactly like her own. This made her feel embarrassed once more. Then she found a V-necked sweater in ribbed white wool, with club colours round the V, plum, cedar, and cream. It reminded her of what the girls in the tennis team had worn when off the court, and she had no intention of flaunting colours she had not earned. Then she found an exceedingly elegant mackintosh, black and silky: a lady's mackintosh indeed, not merely a woman's. Cressida even tried it on. It fitted like a dream. It must have been worn by a Countess at least, or perhaps by—Cressida blushed. All the same, her confidence was augmented.

She went back to where Desirée reclined upon her sacks, almost mathematically opposite the taciturn Montenegrin.

'That's beautiful!' cried Desirée. 'You see what can be done.'

'I can't find a yellow sweater.'

'It doesn't have to be *yellow*. Better not, perhaps. We don't want you all to look like me.'

'I can't find *any* suitable sweaters.'

All the same, she noticed that Vivien had assembled an impressive pile of all kinds of likely and unlikely things.

'I'll give you a hand,' said Desirée.

'Will Vivien's things be all right?'

'No one steals when everything's free.'

Things like that seemed so simple. As in the case of what her father had said on the shores of The Wash, Cressida wondered if it were true. She suspected that people did not always do horrid things only because they had to. Once more she trembled slightly.

They passed an old person who, with a tiny lamp, was fumbling through discoloured undergarments, and crooning.

Desirée soon lighted upon a roped-up bale of sweaters. In fact, there were several such bales. Some of the bales were of dark blue sweaters, some of white. None were yellow.

Desirée produced a knife from the pocket of her trousers and opened it. It had been unexpected, but it must have been very sharp, because Desirée was through the ropes in a flash.

The sweaters seemed to be ideal.

Cressida tried on a number of them, quite recklessly. She herself selected one blue sweater and one white, and, on Desirée's suggestion, added another of each.

'Vivien,' cried Cressida. 'Look!'

All idea of keeping down the voice had been forgotten.

Vivien picked her way across the littered floor, and herself took two of the blue sweaters, comparatively at random. She declined a white sweater, because it would need so much washing.

'What *happens* about washing?' she said. 'I suppose we can't get out of it altogether.'

'There are people who do it,' replied Desirée. 'Greeks, mostly.'

'Women, of course,' said Vivien ironically, but Desirée only smiled.

Now several people were not merely talking loudly, but shouting at one another. In such cases, the trouble always is that when two or three start, then in no time everyone follows. It was hard to believe that anyone could understand some of the things being said, and, as a matter of fact, there was no evidence that anyone did.

'I *must* find some trousers,' cried Cressida, almost in a panic.

'Here you are,' said Vivien, merely swooping.

As well as everything else, Vivien appeared to have that gift for instant selection which is so rarely found in women and which is so promising when it is.

They were corduroy trousers, slender, and, as far as could be seen, of no colour at all.

'Better try them on,' said Desirée.

'No,' said Cressida. 'No, really. I'll take a chance.'

'Better take another pair as well, then,' said Vivien, this time looking a little longer.

And so on: with the consequence that when it came to re-ascending the steps worn away by so many capitani in heavy armour and an even greater number of contadini in heavy boots, the three of them could hardly carry all that had been assembled.

'We'll take it back to the dormitorio,' said Desirée. 'And then I'll show you our cantina, where I shall have to leave you.'

'Was it always the dormitorio?' asked Cressida. 'I thought it was called the dormitory because it's so like school.'

'It depends which school,' said Desirée, as Rosemary had done earlier. 'But it's not that. It used to be dormitorio of a convent. That's why we've been put there. The convent of Madonna della Porta. Very unusual that there should be nuns so near the gate, I'm told; but in any case they all disappeared long ago, though there's the ghost of at least one of them. Or rather of a novice. She's supposed to have been walled up, though no one really knows. Wendy's seen the figure. She's terribly psychic, you know.'

'I hope to see it,' said Vivien.

For herself, Cressida left the matter open.

'They joined the old convent on to the next houses, where all those rooms are,' elucidated Desirée.

The darkness was thick as soot, through which the oil lamps spied polyphemically from the tops of their poles. Cressida had never before had to carry so many clothes down such ill-paved streets in such poor lighting.

'The chapel's still there,' went on Desirée. 'We all drop in from time to time. Quite often, in fact.'

'More things are wrought by prayer than this world dreams of,' said Vivien, her utterance muffled by woolly fabric piled up in front of her mouth.

'There are very few people about,' said Cressida.

'That's what I like about Trino,' responded Desirée. 'I simply loathe crowds.'

CHAPTER TWENTY-NINE

Changing

The lamps burning in the dormitory gave more light than the lamps on posts in the streets. Wendy and Rosemary had departed.

'What beautiful vessels!' cried Cressida, throwing her armful of clothes on the floor, in accordance with custom.

'The Commendatore allowed me to take them from the museum. They're Greek. Proper Greek, I mean, of course.'

'Do we ever see the Commendatore?' asked Vivien. 'That is, Cressida and me.'

'You mean intimately?'

'Or at all.'

'You may not see him intimately for weeks. Perhaps never. He's seldom his own master. He moves as the spirit compels. But whatever the obstacles, he shows himself publicly from the Torre Grande each morning. He feels it his duty. It's rather high up, but you can see him quite well on most days.'

Vivien in turn dropped her heap on the floor.

'Why doesn't he appear lower down?' asked Cressida.

'He has to remember that we all depend on him absolutely.'

'Oh, but doesn't everyone adore him? It said they did in the paper I read. He goes everywhere quite unarmed, and at the slightest danger a thousand blades will flash as one.'

'Yes of course,' said Desirée, 'but one of his plays is called *Et tu, Brute*, and you know what that means. Some people think it's his very greatest play. Gugginesco played it once in the Roman Colosseum before a hundred thousand people.'

'There's daggers in men's smiles,' confirmed Vivien.

'I acted Brutus, and Vivien acted Cassius,' said Cressida, 'though only in Shakespeare. The new English mistress acted Julius Caesar in a toga with real blood.'

'Will you two buck up and change, if you wish to? I should be on duty already. It's just as well the Commendatore has no sense of time.'

'But how can he fly his aeroplane and go down in his submarine and all he has to do, if he has no sense of time?' asked Vivien, taking things off.

'He can't even distinguish between night and day,' said Desirée, smiling almost fondly. 'It's quite a pity you have to take that mac off, Cressida. You look super in it.'

'Do you see Vittore every day?' persisted Vivien.

'Yes,' said Desirée with pride. 'It's my work.'

'Do you get fun out of it?'

'It's exalting, Vivien. You may find out for yourself if you're very fortunate.'

The corduroy trousers which in the uncertain light of the dungeon had seemed without colour, now proved to be the most delicate possible grey. Furthermore, they were actually lady's trousers. Like the silk mackintosh, they must have belonged to an unhappy countess, or to— Anyway, they fitted Cressida perfectly. In fact, nothing had ever before fitted her so well.

Vivien looked less sophisticated, though exciting too.

'Where was that poor woman walled up?' asked Cressida.

'Nowhere really, Cressida,' said Desirée reassuringly. 'It's just what people say.'

CHAPTER THIRTY

The Canadian

A man stormed in.

'Hell, I can't knock.'

Cressida considered him with some interest. He was plainly not one of the Albanians.

The man was considering Cressida with reciprocal interest. He had slightly staring eyes at the best.

'What is it, Harry?' asked Desirée, with faint irritation.

'The Commendatore is rapping for you.'

'This is Cressida Hazeborough and Vivien Poins. Harry Crass. He's a Canadian now.'

Perhaps for that reason, the man shook hands vigorously. His hands were enormous and very hard. Cressida remembered that he could turn them to anything. From the right hand part of a finger was missing.

'Pleased to meet you. Pleased to meet you, lovely lady.'

It was invidious for Vivien, but she gave no sign.

'Rosemary mentioned you,' said Cressida.

'The hell she did,' said the man.

As far as she knew, Cressida had never before spoken to a Canadian, though, like everyone else, she had seen them about during the war. This one was very dark, with red hair that was at once receding and unruly. He had a very prominent and curvaceous nose. He was still dressed for the sea, with loose, salt-caked boots and earrings.

'What did she say about me?' asked the man in his funny accent.

As Rosemary had of course said he was under Desirée's thumb, which was why the whole matter had come up, it was difficult to answer politely.

'Well, tell me, lovely lady. I want to know. What did Rosemary have to say about me? Tell me her words.'

'You mustn't press for confidences, Harry,' said Desirée. 'Girls don't like it.'

'I'm sorry, Desirée,' said Harry. 'I guess that's just right.'

'I'm always telling you; girls are quite different from men.'

'Sure you are, honey. And I knew it already too. You observe a lot when you're at sea.'

'Were you at sea for long, Mr Crass?' asked Cressida. This was a much easier matter to be polite about, but the lack of expression in Mr Crass's eyes upset her, especially when coupled with their attentiveness.

'A lifetime, lady,' Mr Crass answered.

Cressida forthwith added at least twenty-five years to her idea of his age.

'Never have escaped a grave beneath the deep waters if we hadn't been captured. Best thing that ever happened to any one of us. Fighting, liquor, and lovely ladies in tight pants. What more can any son of the sea expect?'

'Now, Harry,' said Desirée. 'You must remember that you hardly know Cressida.' All the same, she was not so much smiling as simpering. Cressida was surprised at her.

'Didn't you like the sea, Mr Crass?' she asked.

'Awesome,' he said, 'just awesome. Especially when you're on the dawn watch. Just you and God. Just the pair of you sweating it out together, and settling everything between you. A man can't carry so much knowledge inside one skull.'

'What about a woman?' asked Vivien.

'Maybe she could. Never say that I sell Woman short.'

'We never have,' said Vivien.

'I'm right under the thumb of any woman who cares just to stretch it out. Always have been. And let me tell you, I like it that way.'

One of his eyes seemed about to flash faintly, but it was probably an effect of the Old Hellenic lighting; Greek Fire, as one might say.

'I'm just going to take Cressida and Vivien to the cantina, and then I'll be with the Commendatore. Run across and leave that message, will you please, Harry?'

'Yum, it's good in there. Better than comes to us rough sailors. Sorry I have to leave you . . . '

He whipped out his huge right hand, with the partly missing finger.

'I guess it's been nice talking to you.'

Cressida never knew the form of rejoinder to remarks like that, though she was sure there must be one.

'It's been nice talking to *you*,' she said feebly.

His foot slipped on something intimate and slithery as he departed on his errand.

'Harry's quite harmless really,' explained Desirée. 'When you've learnt to know him, he's just like a great child.'

'Are you his mother?' asked Vivien.

'The maternal side is very strong in me,' said Desirée, quite seriously.

Chapter Thirty-One

The Acting Minister

The Cantina was almost opposite. But as they crossed the ill-lit street, they encountered a white-haired priest. It would have been difficult to miss him, as he was loudly talking to himself. Cressida was not used to priests wearing cassocks everywhere, instead of blazers or overcoats, as in England.

The priest raised his hand in benediction, and muttered some words even more rapidly.

Desirée paused, and the other two followed her example.

'It's best to stop for a moment,' explained Desirée.

But the priest wended his way, wringing his hands and moaning.

'Is he all right?' asked Cressida, looking after him as she might after a distressing denizen of the hedgerow.

'He's a little strange, as you can see. That's partly because he's not a Roman Catholic but a Greek Orthodox. The Commendatore found him in Crete and attached him because he has the gift of tongues. He's been with the Commendatore for years in order to be resorted to when all else fails.'

Cressida had supposed that in anything called a canteen there would be continuous pandemonium, as in the Dining Hall at school, but in fact there was almost complete silence.

'This is just like Daddy's club,' exclaimed Vivien, in more or less her normal voice, as in the garment store.

'All the seniors come here,' said Desirée, 'but we are allowed to come whatever our age because we're English girls.'

'What about the girls who aren't English?' asked Cressida.

'I don't think they'd want to come,' said Desirée, smiling. 'Now I shall just settle you at a table and then I shall have to leave you on your own.'

'Don't *you* want to eat?' asked Cressida.

'I'm on duty now, Cressida. Since about half an hour ago actually. There'll be sandwiches and cakes for me.'

'Ham sandwiches?' asked Cressida.

'Caviare more likely, or foie gras.'

'Foie gras's cruel,' said Cressida.

'English people sometimes think so. I don't care for it much anyway. Still, one can't expect roast beef of Old England *all* the time. Now eat what you like, and do what you like.'

Cressida noticed that almost everybody else in the room seemed to be a man.

Desirée went, exchanging nods with various people at tables. One man even threw her a tempting kiss. Cressida could see only his back, which looked solidly soldierlike, though in a foreign way.

Vivien could not see that, as she was seated opposite to Cressida. There was a lighted candle on each table, and all the chairs were gilded. Either the establishment had been the best restaurant in Trino, or the chairs had been brought from the club set up at some time by the Austrian officers. In the nature of things, the Austrians had left Trino before they had left Trieste. There were even a few very early flowers in a scrolled crock. Had it been in England, Cressida would have supposed them to be croci and perhaps even snowdrops. Here it was hard to say.

Where Desirée had stood now stood a sallow man in a very white jacket.

'This is like Daddy's mess,' observed Vivien. The man could obviously not speak English, so that one could say anything.

All the same, this was once again where abroad really began; as when stepping on to the train at Boulogne, as when stepping off the train at Trieste, as when the gates clanged at Trino. Now Cressida and Vivien had no one to intercede, to interpret, to interfere; even to instruct.

Their situation was confirmed when the man offered each of them a menu which, though frilly round the edges, was printed entirely in French. Cressida had not been particularly good at French; which, naturally, had not been particularly well taught. Whatever was a *flétan*. And did not *queue* mean tail? *Escargots* she knew about, but she knew also that she was still far too young for them.

However, they ordered perfectly well, as regularly happens unless one is a complete goose, or, worse still, gander.

The man produced a folio of wines, bound in tooled leather, with a dark ribbon emerging from the spine, as if after an operation.

Cressida, who had been given the album, because she was the elder, ordered a bottle of Bollinger, a fluid which she could not only identify but which she had enjoyed very much in past years, albeit on rare occasions. She knew, moreover, that it was just the thing with the sole and fricassee that lay ahead.

'Do we wake or dream?' enquired Cressida.

'It's exactly like a place Daddy goes to in Soho,' said Vivien.

'He must be fond of it then?' said Cressida.

'Yes, but he always says you have to watch the actual food.'

'There's not much light for food-watching.'

'There's enough,' said Vivien firmly. 'You must remember why we're here.'

A man in uniform loomed up. Cressida had neither heard nor seen him approach, and was upset for a moment. None the less, though his uniform was of a different colour from that worn by the man who had thrown the kiss to Desirée, this man looked solid too, and in much the same way. This man had hair white as lard, shining and glistening: in texture quite unlike the priest's white hair. This man's face was red, his eyes blue. He moved with some difficulty but with the elegance that no art can confer.

'You are newcomers,' he said in an accent quite different from the Canadian's accent, and much more worldly. 'May I sit down?'

While remaining polite, it would have been difficult to stop him.

He drew up a gilt chair from the next table, and sank between them.

'I am the Acting Minister for Foreign Affairs,' he said. 'What in England you call Foreign Secretary. Only Acting, I must emphasise. None the less, it is right that I should act while I may. It is expected. It is also pleasant.' He chuckled affably.

'My father is in the Colonial Service,' said Vivien. 'He's a Governor.'

'Your great empire is a wonderful thing,' said the Acting Minister. 'It gives opportunities to so many, who would not otherwise have them.'

The champagne was arriving and being poured for Cressida to sample. The sparkle was exciting.

'Won't you have some?' she said to the Acting Minister.

'That's charming of you. Indeed I will.'

He made a gesture and the dark waiter drew a third champagne glass from the air. Already there had been three different glasses beside each place at the table.

As no food had yet arrived, they all began to lap champagne.

'I should have introduced myself by name,' said the Acting Minister, 'only here we no longer have names.'

'Well, we must call you something,' said Vivien, glass in hand.

'That is true. To my colleagues I am known as the Marchese, so address me so by all means. And how may I address you?'

Vivien caught Cressida's eye, and Cressida caught Vivien's.

'I am Miss Vivien Poins,' said Vivien.

They spelt themselves out.

'Poins!' cried the Marchese. He is known to all of us. He is the Welshman with the leek.'

Neither Cressida nor Vivien would have thought it polite to attempt correction.

'Like Mr Lloyd George. We find him difficult too,' said the Marchese.

'We've got rid of him now,' said Cressida.

'Too late.'

Wide glass receptacles arrived. They were set on the slenderest of stems. The delicate bowls contained delicacies of some kind: the first course.

So often chance guides us so much more profoundly than guidance.

Cressida addressed the Marchese.

'What about you?'

'Thank you, Miss Hazeborough,' said the Marchese. 'I have eaten already. I have eaten well. I and my colleagues also.'

'Are you one of a whole government?' asked Cressida, spooning up her delicacy.

'And have none of you names?' asked Vivien.

'Do you not understand?' enquired the Marchese.

His faded but far-sighted eyes reflected the bubbles in the lifted glass.

'We don't understand a thing,' said Cressida confidently.

Every moment she was spooning more strenuously.

The Marchese considered.

'How often do you regard the sea?' he asked.

'We were talking to a Canadian sailor only just now,' said Cressida.

'Ex-sailor,' corrected Vivien.

'And naturalised Canadian,' said Cressida, remembering.

'You will be walking along the white cliffs of Dover,' said the Marchese, 'as you English do so often. The waves of the sea are heaving tempestuously, wildly, uncontrollably, as heaves the human heart. You shout with laughter at the plight of the passengers on the little steamboat. What, do you not fail to enquire, can stand against Mother Nature when Mother Nature is angry as Mother Nature is now? But if you look over the cliff's edge, and if you look closely, you will see little pools of peace. Into these pools has floated all the wreckage of the world. Driftwood, I think you call it.'

He enunciated the word in two clear and distinct syllables.

'And, what is more, the driftwood, once it has been drawn into the peaceful pool, cannot escape again into the wild waters, even if it wishes. The different pieces of worn and weakened timber grate gently up against one another. Oh, so very gently. The sound is so muffled, so monotonous that if you climb down the cliff in order to sit by the pool, you cannot for long endure it. It seems a sound sadder than sadness itself.'

Cressida refilled his glass; and, *en passant*, her own and Vivien's. They were beautiful glasses, so thin and clear as, in the manner of good silk stockings, hardly to exist.

'Everyone in Trino is driftwood, borne in to the peaceful pool by the great storm which your Welsh Wizard, Miss Poins, has raised with his leek. We are nameless because our names have no meaning without the realm, the structure of which we were part. Framework might be the better word. Quite literally meaningless, Miss Hazeborough and Miss Poins. What meaning has the name of a great ship when it appears only on a single floating plank, however deeply it is scored into the timber?'

But before either of them could attempt to answer that, their second course arrived, and there had to be an interlude of application.

Cressida was pleased to discern that set before them was neither too little nor too much. Most rare, in her experience.

'Are you *quite* sure you won't join us?' asked Cressida, inspired to new solicitude by the watering of her mouth.

The Marchese shook his head. The movement was the perfection at once of courtesy and of abnegation.

'Indeed, a single drifting plank with a name scored on it is often the sole evidence of a leviathan that has vanished.'

'Are you really a Marchese?' asked Vivien. 'Really and truly?'

'What, in the circumstances, is really, Miss Poins? What is truly?'

'Well, *were* you a Marchese?'

Everything about Vivien was becoming pinker, even by candlelight.

'I was assuredly born one.'

'You can't be born a Marquis,' said Cressida. 'You have to wait until you inherit it.'

'That is usually the case in England, Miss Hazeborough. It's not the case anywhere else.'

'You mean,' said Vivien, 'it *wasn't* the case. There, that's caught you.'

Cressida frowned slightly.

The Marchese bowed across the table, then struggled up again.

'What happens in the end to the driftwood in the pool?' asked Cressida, more romantically.

'In the end,' said the Marchese, whose glass was again empty, 'men—quite ordinary men wearing sea-boots—come along the beach and start a bonfire, omitting only a few boards that they take home for their children to make into hutches and traps. Then the sad sound ceases, and on the beach there is only the screaming of the killer gulls and the smiting of the treacherous waves.'

'The man in sea-boots we met earlier wasn't like that at all,' said Cressida. 'He said he preferred it here. Much better than the sea.'

'This land is regulated according to the laws of music,' the Marchese reminded them.

'We don't quite know what that means,' said Cressida.

Alas, the champagne was finished. Cressida was dubious about ordering more; even in the interests of hospitality to a former nobleman and present Acting Cabinet Minister; even had she been sure how best to set about it.

'Music,' said their guest (and surely that was the term for him, even though no consideration passed in any discernible direction?), 'music is at once infinitely fleeting and infinitely enduring. Such airs as "Tannenbaum" or "La Carmagnole" spring up everywhere, like groundsel, but perish on the instant each time they flood forth from human throats. A sophist might claim that music fails to comply with the criteria basic for the establishment of bare existence. Yet our senses tell us that music does exist, and so, by the same standard, does the musical republic of Trino. Indeed, I should offer up a toast to Trino's continued existence were there available the *de quoi*.'

'Please,' cried Cressida. 'Let us have some more. Tell us how to attract the man's attention.'

Now Vivien frowned slightly.

'You, Miss Hazeborough, and you too, Miss Poins, can count upon attracting attention wherever you are. No, I shall drink no more, though I am grateful to you for proposing it.'

Plainly, he was about to heave himself up and depart from them.

'There's one more thing,' cried Vivien. 'While we've got you here.'

'More than one,' said Cressida. She had nearly cleared her plate.

'Tell us,' Vivien persisted. 'Does Lord Elterwater really pay for all this? Pay for everything?'

'Honestly, Vivien!' protested Cressida.

Vivien was pinker still, but by now the whole room was pink.

'Not for everything,' said the Acting Cabinet Minister, with professional reserve.

'What else is there then? Are there taxes?'

'Mankind is bid,' said the Acting Cabinet Minister, 'most earnestly bid, to take no thought of the morrow. I remind you of that.'

'That's only for the people of that time. Well, in practice.'

'I imagine it depends at any time upon the reality and the intensity of one's faith.'

But now he had managed really to get up.

Before struggling away, he kissed their hands, and, with the help of the Bollinger, neither appeared in the least slow or gauche, though it was the first time that beautiful thing had ever happened to either.

CHAPTER THIRTY-TWO

Alarm

They were drinking coffee; even though one thing about which all four parents agreed completely was that coffee should be eschewed after a certain time in the evening, because it kept one awake.

'I think there are only two kinds of people in the world,' said Vivien telepathically. 'Those whose lives are regulated according to the laws of music, and all the rest.'

'I wonder what's happened to Wendy and Rosemary?' Cressida speculated.

'Need we ask? Wendy's with her fiancé and Rosemary's teaching English.'

'I suppose Wendy and her fiancé are eating quietly somewhere?'

'Perhaps they're not eating at all. They're in love, remember.' Cressida reflected.

'Do you consider that Wendy regulates her life according to the laws of music?'

'Well, music's the food of love, isn't it? As you told Aunt Agnes.'

'Have some more coffee,' propounded Cressida. 'It's so good. I wonder what's happened to your aunt?'

'She'll be quite safe.'

'But not necessarily contented?'

'More contented than she was yesterday. Well, more than she was a month ago.'

'Why,' cried Cressida, 'there she is!'

It must have been telepathy for the second time. Cressida and Vivien were possibly ascending to some simple degree of the higher awareness.

'Is she in her uniform?' asked Vivien, whose back was still firmly to the door.

'No. She's in the most wonderful evening dress. Mignonette.'

'Can't remember a mignonette one. I expect she bought it for the trip.'

'Don't you want to look?'

'She'll have sat down by now.'

It was telepathy for the third time.

'I'm not sure it's proper to wear mignonette,' resumed Vivien. 'It's supposed to be serious our all being here. *We're* both in trousers.'

Cressida burst out laughing.

'And look at all the men. The way *they're* dressed. Almost all in some kind of uniform.'

Cressida continued to laugh.

In fact, it was infectious, because now Vivien herself was at least smiling.

'You *are* a devil, Cressy,' she said. 'I hadn't thought it of you.'

Cressida stuck out a leg on each side of the table.

'Is she alone?' asked Vivien.

'No, she's got several men with her. All with Orders and things. They keep standing up and bowing to her.'

There was the most tremendous report or boom. It came from somewhere in the outer world. The venerable stonework vibrated and things began to fly about. One of them, flying low, extinguished several candles.

'Golly!' said Vivien, though both girls had managed to return elegant coffee cups to elegant saucers without fracture.

'Bats,' cried Cressida. 'They're flapping round our heads.'

There was a second, and at least an equal, report or boom. The two girls acted as one and dived beneath the table.

In any case, it seemed the thing to do. Most, if not all, of the men in the room had fallen beneath tables after the earlier explosion, for one reason or another.

'I expect the poor creatures are still half-asleep', said Cressida.

'They ought to be waking up,' commented Vivien. 'Bats are supposed to be nocturnal.'

'So few animals lead natural lives,' said Cressida.

There was a third boom. The flying things were putting out more and more of the candles, sometimes knocking candle and stick right over, so that there were eerie little thuds and crashes from all over the room.

'It must be an alarm,' said Vivien.

Cressida raised her head above the level of the tablecloth. 'Lady Luce is still sitting there,' she reported, 'and some of her men too.'

'Is anyone else?' asked Vivien.

'Not that I can see. It's gone quite dark and the room's absolutely full of creatures.'

'You're supposed to take cover immediately firing starts,' said Vivien, doing what she could to comply.

There was a whole sequence of rattling noises, confident though less reverberant. They split merely the ears, instead of the whole head.

'That'll be us making a reply,' explained Vivien. 'I used to hear about it from Cousin Mark before he lost his leg. He never talked about anything else, even to a babe.'

'I don't think this table gives much cover,' said Cressida. 'Except from the bats.'

'If they really are bats,' said Vivien.

'Of course they're bats. What else could they be?'

'Perhaps they're some kind of new weapon we haven't been told about.'

'Oh, Vivien, do you really think so?'

The booming from outside the stronghold and the banging from within it were now advancing into a confused methodology, as when church bells are rung by keen but unpractised holidaymakers and one is trying to read the parochial records hung in frames at the foot of the tower.

'We just don't know, Cressy. We're only women.'

'Fancy having this for four years on end, Vivien!'

Cressida was reflecting that the discharge had not yet continued for four *minutes*.

'And all the mud and bad food and vermin as well,' Vivien pointed out.

There was now almost no light at all.

'Daddy says that bats are verminous. That's why you shouldn't let them get in your hair.'

'You shouldn't *have* all that hair, unless you're a goose. Women don't have to provide nests for bats as well as everything else.'

'I could go somewhere,' said Cressida.

'That's only because you're in a funk. I feel the same but I'm determined not to.'

'I wonder how long an alarm lasts?'

'I wouldn't mind if there was something we could *do*.'

'Vivien!' Cressida almost shrieked. 'There's a big animal crawling along the floor.'

'There's not enough light to see whether there is or not,' said Vivien.

'I can smell it, and hear it,' cried Cressida. 'I can *sense* it. Vivien, I'm frightened.'

Vivien presumably took experimental action of some kind, because she was able to make a report.

'It's a man.'

'How can it be, Vivien?'

'He's crawling away on his hands and knees. I think there's another one coming.'

'I hope they don't crawl into us.'

Cressida shrank up against Vivien quite tightly. Both girls made themselves as compact as possible under the small table. If only, when the room had been so empty, they had been settled at a larger one!

Two, three, four men, at least that number, managed to crawl past without touching them. Nor did they utter a word, apart from the usual grunting.

'I daresay it's the right thing for them to do,' remarked Vivien. 'We're under fire, you know.'

Cressida was noticing that Vivien seemed to derive positive satisfaction from compliance with the rules book, even though she had no actual volume. It was most unlike her generally questioning attitude under other circumstances in which Cressida had known her.

'Perhaps they are going to their stations,' said Cressida.

Conversation had been made difficult by the military din. If one whispered, the second half of one's sentence was lost. If one shouted, the whole room could hear the second half.

'Every time they start again, I jump,' complained Cressida.

'Cousin Mark said you soon get used to it. He read the complete *Grimms' Fairy Tales* in German during a bombardment on the Somme or somewhere. It lasted two months.'

'What a funny thing to do when he was supposed to be fighting the Germans!'

'Cousin Mark said there was very little actual hate.'

'Do you think there's much hate here?'

'I don't know. It's politics here, not war.'

'How do people tell the difference?'

'A match against another school is war. A match against another house is politics.'

'Goodness, Vivien, you're super sometimes! I should never have seen it like that.'

CHAPTER THIRTY-THREE

The Fiancé

'It's dying down,' said Cressida.

She put her head above the tablecloth.

'Lady Luce is still sitting there. She's still got two men and two candles.'

'We couldn't have seen *anything* unless there'd been a light of some kind somewhere,' Vivien pointed out. 'It would have been frightening.'

'I was quite frightened anyway,' said Cressida, joining Vivien beneath the table again.

'So was I, but I'm determined not to be.'

'There's still a bang every now and then.'

'The distant and random gun, that the foe was sullenly firing,' cited Vivien.

'I'm not looking forward to the rest of the night,' said Cressida. She shuddered slightly.

'Perhaps we should have voted for rooms of our own?'

'I don't think that would be any better. Desirée and Rosemary are quite nice really.'

'I don't think Desirée will be there. She's on duty, remember.'

'Vivien! I suppose she's all right?'

'I expect so. If she's with Vittore, she'll be in the safest place there is.'

'And Vittore has to think of others, anyway. That would include Desirée.'

'I suppose so,' said Vivien. 'It's quite different from Elsie Churchill's article.'

Uncomfortable though she was, Cressida reflected rather seriously.

'Vivien,' she said. 'I'm not sure I really know why we're here at all. You were so keen on it.'

'Well, you didn't want to work in Perdita's little shop for the rest of your days, did you?'

'Perhaps only until I got married?'

'No girl is ever wise to count on marriage achieving much. Except perhaps girls like Wendy.'

It was quite extraordinary; but no sooner had Vivien spoken than a door opened, a man entered, and, advancing upon their table, addressed the two girls beneath it with the words, 'You must be Cressida and Vivien, and some time you must tell me which is which. I'm Brian Wicker and you can come out now.'

Cressida had been able to project her head on two occasions, but the rest of her was almost as insensible as it had been in the cold car, or as Cavaliere Terridge had been after standing guard for so long.

'Very wise to bob down, all the same,' said Brian Wicker pleasantly.

Cressida felt that her beautiful, shapely trousers must have rumpled pitiably, perhaps irreparably; but when she was more or less erect, she saw that men were relighting candles, and, that even though Brian Wicker was looking at her legs, the damage appeared to be much less than she had feared. She had often heard that this was one of the reasons why it always paid to have only the best quality clothes.

'How do you do,' said Cressida. 'Sorry we can't shake hands but we're both numb.'

'How do you do?' said Vivien. 'We've met your fiancée.'

Where Tweedledum and Tweedledee were circular in most respects, Brian Wicker was rectangular. His trunk was a rectangle. His legs and arms were each elongated rectangles. His head was square.

He wore a black jacket and waistcoat, and grey striped trousers. He had a gold watch-chain. He had a platinum pin with a pearl end. His more intimate garments were snowy. His mouth was a further rectangle, elongated in the other dimension.

'Goodness!' cried Cressida. 'Where are all the bats?'

'I expect they've gone back to their homes,' responded Brian Wicker, in his same pleasant way.

'There were hundreds of them!'

'I'm sure there were. Very old place this, you know. Historical. Still, we've got to stand by as long as we can. The alternative would be far worse, as the Governor always says.'

'What governor?' asked Vivien.

'My pop,' said Brian Wicker. 'But I'm sure you both know all about it, or you wouldn't be here.'

'Not as much as all that, actually,' said Cressida.

'Well, you will in the end,' said Brian Wicker.

'Hullo, you two,' called out Aunt Agnes from afar.

CHAPTER THIRTY-FOUR

The Officers

The two men with her rose to their feet as one. They had been so brave that there was no simile accessible for all their decorations.

It seemed proper for the girls to step forward.

Other men were slowly dragging themselves upwards and resuming seats or selecting new ones.

Aunt Agnes introduced the two girls. The men clicked their heels fiercely, as if glad of the exercise.

For Cressida and Vivien it was a further experience; and surely a second major one that evening, for any female struggling, like a pupa, from happy girlhood towards responsible womanhood.

One officer had a thin face, hard eyes, a big moustache, and very little hair. The other man was blonde, with eyes to match Aunt Agnes's dress. His face was bigger, fatter, redder.

'The Colonel and the Major are our sabre and broadsword champions,' Aunt Agnes explained. 'Respectively, of course.'

Cressida could think of absolutely nothing to say, but Vivien managed an impromptu comment.

'There must be an awful lot of practising. Like playing the oboe or ballet dancing.'

The two officers turned quite the same colour with rage.

'Yes, Vivien,' replied Aunt Agnes, quite calmly. 'The Colonel and the Major normally have to spend hours each day training with their volunteers, of course.'

Now the officers flushed with pleasure.

However, they still lacked authority to sit down. What is more, the girls were still standing also. Only Aunt Agnes sat. As always, Cressida thought that Aunt Agnes's bosom was enviably beautiful in repose.

'How are you getting on?' asked Aunt Agnes.

'We're all right,' said Cressida.

'We're fine, Aunt Agnes,' said Vivien, more definitively.

'Got somewhere nice to sleep?'

'We're sleeping with the other English girls, Lady Luce.'

'You both look like Amazons,' said Aunt Agnes. 'Don't they look like Amazons, Colonel?'

Apparently, the Colonel was the blonde with the matching eyes. He bowed and clicked.

Possibly he had very little English.

'Got something useful to do?' continued Aunt Agnes.

'I'm going to work in the theatre, Lady Luce, and Vivien may be doing psychoanalysis, though she has to have time for writing her novel, of course, and what she really wants is to do something more warlike.'

The two officers, instead of looking gratified, as one might have expected, looked indignant.

'I knew you'd both soon get settled,' said Aunt Agnes. 'One can depend upon Vittore for everything.'

The officers clicked again but more dreamily. Their eyes, whether blue or red, looked ethereal.

'But who's this?' enquired Aunt Agnes.

Cressida was thrilled by the way Aunt Agnes's elaborate gown cascaded downwards as she rose.

'Has one of you found a beau already?' asked Aunt Agnes.

Cressida looked sorrowful and Vivien looked contemptuous. Cressida at least could not have imagined Lady Luce asking such a thing in England. Life at the infirmary must already be lowering standards.

All the time, Aunt Agnes was referring to Brian Wicker, who had been hovering pleasantly in the twilit region behind.

Cressida pulled herself together.

'This is Brian Wicker, Lady Luce. He's here to represent his father. You remember. The man told us.'

'Brian Wicker!' cried Aunt Agnes, her voice like tiny silver bells. 'Brian, I used to know your father when I worked in Paris.'

The officers had not forgotten to click.

'I'm sure I've heard him mention you,' said Brian Wicker.

'And who's *this*?' cried Aunt Agnes.

Already there were six of them on their feet.

Cressida knew at once who it was.

It was the man, indisputably a man, who had said 'Hola' in some language or other while touching his right cheek with his left forefinger: Hola Harlequin, as one might at that time have denominated him.

Everyone seemed to be getting in tonight. Perhaps it was the alarm.

'I am Trifoglio,' said the young man in a clear but suppressed voice. It was as if he were enunciating, quite beautifully, from a sewer far beneath; if, of course, there were sewers of that kind in Trino.

'Is that your real name?' asked Vivien.

'No,' said Trifoglio.

'Most people here are called something else, Aunt Agnes,' explained Vivien. 'Cressy and I have been told about it by a Minister.'

Aunt Agnes's eyes flashed in the twinkling light of the two candles. 'It is the same everywhere with Vittore,' she said. 'People bear names as shields against our recognising them.'

'Is that what Vittore says?' asked Trifoglio, in the same suppressed voice.

'Surely we all know it is,' said Aunt Agnes.

'Vittore was not the original person to say it,' said Trifoglio, without expression.

Cressida thought it was the first faintly implied criticism that had crept past her ears. The impact, however distressing, was not unbracing.

'No one ever suggested that he was,' said Aunt Agnes, gaining considerably from her erect posture. 'Vittore is but the Ionian harp on which the world's breath plays. That was the way he put it himself years ago when I was working in Paris.'

'*Aeolian* harp, Aunt Agnes,' said Vivien.

'Not all of us have been to school as recently as you, Vivien.'

'Vittore is not the first to say that either, Lady Luce,' said Trifoglio.

'And how do you know my name?' She did not wait for an answer. 'Whatever are you wearing?'

The officers wheeled and inspected Trifoglio.

'It is for when I practise, Lady Luce.'

Cressida might have known it. Bayonet practice; broadsword practice; oboe practice; whatever it was Trifoglio practised: in this world it is almost impossible to be merely natural, completely untutored, simply oneself.

'Well, I suppose we might as well sit down,' said Aunt Agnes, at long last.

But there were seats for six, not for seven. What was more, the six of them packed fairly closely, especially as a margin had to be left on each side for Aunt Agnes's dress.

Trifoglio was seatless.

The fix had something in common with the shuddery situation at Perdita's party.

'I say, old man,' exclaimed Brian Wicker, almost rising.

But Trifoglio merely croaked, made his gesture, and flitted off.

'That's like Hamlet's ghost,' said Vivien. 'Just the same sound. You remember, Cressy? When the Fourth did it?'

By now it was hard to believe that anyone in the world ever uttered anything authentically for the first time, least of all a groan; let alone ever did anything.

'I think he's all right,' said Cressida. 'In his own way, of course.'

'He's just a type,' explained Brian Wicker. 'Perfectly harmless.'

'Anyway, wasn't it the ghost of Hamlet's father, not Hamlet's ghost?' persisted Cressida. 'Under the floor, I mean?'

'So it was. I was over-excited,' replied Vivien contritely.

Cressida could hardly recall a previous occasion when it had not been Vivien who had retained the better grasp.

'Canst work in the earth so fast?' speculated Cressida.

'Do you go in for Shakespeare a lot?' enquired Brian Wicker.

'They're both mad about him,' said Aunt Agnes, answering for them.

Of course all of it was quite beyond the two officers, because they spoke so little English, and because the German they had learned at their Academy had not included Schlegel's wonderful translations.

Chapter Thirty-Five

Bye-Byes

The gun was still firing every now and then. There seemed very little system to it.

'Does this go on all night?' enquired Cressida. 'Vivien doesn't sleep very well.'

'Sometimes,' said Brian Wicker. 'It depends on the immediate situation. The weather too, of course. Besides that, the gunners have to practise, you know.'

'Is that our gun or someone else's gun?'

'Oh, it's our gun. The other guns are made by a different concern. You can tell at once.'

'Isn't it a waste of money to keep firing it when we don't have to?' asked Vivien.

Cressida confirmed that. 'The man went on about how much it was all costing. You remember, Lady Luce.'

'I think we should leave that sort of thing to the people responsible,' said Brian Wicker.

The officers sat on, rigid as idols, and as highly glazed.

'Is there a general of some kind?' asked Vivien.

'Of course there is,' said Brian Wicker in a serious voice.

'Where did he learn about it?' asked Vivien.

'It depends which one,' said Brian Wicker. 'We have some of the best generals in Europe.'

'As many generals as soldiers?' suggested Cressida.

'Cressida,' interrupted Aunt Agnes, quite sharply. 'I'm afraid you're looking a little flushed. What I suggest is that we all have a possetto and then you two go off to bye-byes.'

Cressida could hardly believe that such a term as that last should fall from the lips of her adored Lady Luce, and within only a few hours of Lady Luce's arrival in these new scenes. Indeed, Cressida was far from sure that she had actually heard the term before. Assuredly, it had not been the preferred term for slumber at Riverdale House. She was not even sure how it was spelt.

'We all know,' said Aunt Agnes, 'that Vittore is responsible for all the generalship that matters.'

The officers looked faintly ethereal once more, but neither made movement nor remark. Doubtless a long day behind them; another before them.

'What's a possetto?' asked Vivien. 'Outside *Macbeth*, that is.'

'Well, it's a sort of old-fashioned local drink,' said Aunt Agnes. 'I've been giving gallons of it to everyone in the infirmary.'

Vivien caught Cressida's eye and Cressida caught Vivien's eye. Of course they were seated on opposite sides of the table.

'I don't think I want anything else,' said Cressida. 'Thank you very much, though.'

She rose to her feet as firmly as she could. Instantly, the officers shot up too.

'Nor me,' said Vivien, rising also. 'See you in the morning, Aunt Agnes. At least, I hope so.'

Her finality had brought Brian Wicker, the third man, to his feet.

'Well,' said Aunt Agnes. 'If you both prefer.'

One might almost have thought that she was gladdened by their departure. She was, of course, standing surrogate for two mothers, one of whom she had never met.

Brian Wicker was proffering Goodnight handshakes, so that the officers clicked more tentatively and less clatteringly than at the beginning, the operation being now difficult to time.

'What do you think that man meant by the noise he made?' asked Vivien, looking squarely into Brian Wicker's almost square eyes, even though he was engaged to someone else.

'I shouldn't worry about what he meant,' replied Brian Wicker in his comforting way.

The girls bent over Aunt Agnes and kissed her: Vivien, as a relative, on the cheek; Cressida on the mouth.

'You both look like Amazons,' repeated Aunt Agnes affectionately.

'*You* look absolutely beautiful, Lady Luce,' responded Cressida.

All the same, she had been shaken by the change in Aunt Agnes.

'Can you find the way back?' asked Aunt Agnes.

'Shall I come with you?' volunteered Brian Wicker.

'Nothing in it,' said Vivien.

The matter was not pressed.

As the girls went out into the night, the four others—beautiful Aunt Agnes with no fewer than three men, two of field rank—once more settled down: probably not, Cressida reflected, to a possetto.

'I wish that every single man one meets wasn't called Brian,' she said.

'Men!' said Vivien; and was silent until they were under the stars, even though the stars were no more visible than before, owing to the ceaselessly scudding wrack.

CHAPTER THIRTY-SIX

Night or Day?

In the piazza, and by a single lantern, of which the light was the colour of egg-yolk, Trifoglio was doing one of his dances: leaping and capering without regard to the intriguing irregularity of the immemorial stones.

Perhaps, having found no seat in the cantina, he was keeping himself warm.

The girls stopped for a moment or two, as Desirée had suggested at the encounter with the Orthodox priest; for both were obscurely aware of something almost hieratical about Trifoglio too.

Vivian spoke quietly to Cressida.

'Do you know what time it is?'

Cressida had a watch, but Trifoglio's eggy lantern spread little effulgence, so she simply shook her head.

'It's past two.'

'Does that allow for the adjustment this morning?'

It had been something which came to Cressida quite unexpectedly.

'It certainly does,' said Vivien.

'They turn night into day in Trino,' said Cressida.

She had heard the expression often, but here was Trifoglio, whatever his reason, apparently acting upon it.

Vivien shrugged her shoulders in the darkness: at least, Cressida suspected that this was what Vivien had done. Scepticism seemed to be advancing within Vivien; parallel perhaps with extroversion.

'Goodnight,' said Cressida politely to Trifoglio in the end.

'Goodnight,' said Vivien, more sceptically.

One sound he made might have been a submerged gurgle of acknowledgement, though it was so hard to be certain with him; especially when his feet, minute though they were, pattered up and down so fast, and when his every muscle squeaked like a toy mouse.

Or like a full-scale bat, thought Cressida with sudden alarm; though she did not think she had ever knowingly heard a bat. As far as she knew, the bats in the cantina, if bats they had been, had not peeped once.

'If you find him attractive,' said Vivien, when she thought they were out of earshot, 'you can have him.'

'I'm a little sorry for him,' said Cressida.

'You'll see a lot more of him if you work in the theatre.'

Within the dormitory, the full radiance from Hellas had been dowsed, but a single candle burned. Cressida liked such still beauty.

The candle stood in a flat metal holder, presumably modern and looted from some attic. Vivien picked it up and passed with it from bed to bed.

'You look like Florence Nightingale,' whispered Cressida, giggling.

'She was another aunt of mine,' Vivien whispered back.

Vivien often said that kind of thing. She was widely connected, as well as widely informed.

'Well, a sort of aunt,' Vivien whispered.

It transpired that Rosemary was silently asleep. Wendy was absent; and hardly, as Cressida could not but realise, with her proper fiancé. Desirée of course was on duty.

Ignoring the special, but now dark, apartments allotted to them, the girls dropped their clothes on the floor. It would be inconsiderate to awaken Rosemary.

'Some day we've had,' whispered Cressida, in the new transatlantic intonation.

At least they had pyjamas for many occasions.

Briefly they kissed. Swiftly and tenderly they slithered into their serviceable beds.

'What about the candle?'

'Leave it,' directed Vivien.

Perhaps that was the reason why Cressida began to dream almost at once. She was quite unaccustomed to falling asleep with any light in the room beyond the gleam of the night sky. Here, though there were draughts, there was not even an open window.

Cressida dreamed that she and her mother were visiting Westminster School, where Hugh was to have been a pupil, had not something which Cressida never understood prevented it, so that in the end he was sent to another place, where, as we have seen, he had soon excelled in all kinds of different directions. Cressida's mother wore an indulgent expression and a red dress, though the red was so unlike Vivien's red as hardly to count. Her mother was watching the boys at their pancake game, and

Cressida was compelled to watch also. On the far side of Henry VIII's beam, the cook was compounding his mixture. He was a beefy man, with clumps of hard grey hair, like wire-wool or dead gorse bushes. The sleeves of his shirt were jagged at the elbows. His clown-shaped trousers were smeared with animal mess. He kneaded and churned massively in a dark wooden bowl, such as was used in Rutland cottages for washing clothes. The boys were expectant and exuberant. Some were all but men, fully grown or overgrown: assured, commanding, muscled, in need of a shave. At the other extreme were urchins not yet shaped, with marks on their faces, and untamed hair. Every intermediate stage of growth was no doubt represented also. Everywhere the bigger boys were looking after the smaller boys in accordance with the public school tradition. Cressida flinched. It was like going behind the scenes on a farm. Now the cook had transferred the mixture from the bowl into a large frying pan of iron. The sizzling became relentless, while the cook tried ever more desperately to keep the smoke from his eyes, and the fat from the hair on his hands. As the climax approached, Cressida felt almost emetic. The mighty shape of the cook drew itself together as with ropes, and then threw, forwards and upwards, with all its confused strength. The full sweep of the arms was vouchsafed, matted, mottled. The unformed mess left the iron pan and, in large part, winged across King Henry VIII's beams, dispersing and dispensing itself like Shrapnel's bullets among the boys on the other side. At once, the boys were beyond all control (had control been even contemplated). Lust had suffused them, and, in its igneous grip, they fought with arms, legs, and teeth. Cressida knew what the object was: that the boy who emerged, after however long a period, with the largest lump, received, a week or two later, when he was on the way to recovery, a golden guinea from the hands of the Monarch, together with a signed commission in whatever regiment his father might select for him. Cressida could give little thought to this consummation: a significant portion of the cook's mixture had failed to traverse the Tudor beam; had, instead adhered to it; and was now, before Cressida's mesmerised gaze, transforming itself into something so hideously awful that there were no words, mercifully not even thoughts.

'Whatever's the matter, Cressida?'

Wendy was standing over her. She was holding the lighted candle. She wore the most beautiful crêpe-de-chine nightdress, sleeveless and the colour of crystallised violets. There was a darker violet ribbon at the neck, and a girdle in the same colour. It seemed unfortunate ever to submit such a garment to the displacements of slumber.

'You *are* Cressida, aren't you?'

'I'm Cressida and I was having a dream.'

'Do you often have dreams?'

'Quite often.'

'Well, try not to so much.'

Cressida's head felt as if something medical had been done to it.

'Were you pulling my hair?'

'I had to wake you up. When I came in, you were fretting like a hunter.'

Cressida managed to abstain from any direct question.

'Aren't you cold with no clothes on, Wendy? You are Wendy?'

'Frozen. I'm now going to try and get some sleep if I may.'

'Is Vivien asleep?'

'I suppose so.'

It was another change in Vivien. Hitherto, it had been she who awakened first, when Cressida dreamed; she who had entered to rescue Cressida, to reinvigorate her.

'I'm sorry to cause a fuss,' said Cressida.

'Well, don't do it every night,' said Wendy.

She was returning the candle to its shelf. Her movements were as austere as those of a temple acolyte.

'Do we leave it alight?' enquired Cressida.

'We do,' replied Wendy. 'Otherwise I see the novice's ghost.'

Cressida had forgotten.

'I have my troubles too, you know,' said Wendy.

But Wendy seemed to fall asleep in no time, if one could judge by her high-pitched snore. At school, snoring had regularly been a problem. It always seemed peculiar that girls should snore at all. Someone having discovered that snoring is aimed at frightening away wolves and bears, men seemed more than ever the people who should do it.

Cressida wondered how Brian Wicker would accommodate Wendy in the long years to come.

When, in past days, Vivien had soothed Cressida after one of her dreams, Cressida had always slept again at once, and slept more than usually long and peacefully.

Now she found it difficult. She wondered how much longer the candle could last, and what was the expected procedure when it guttered, because, on the present occasion, she might well be the person called upon to adopt it. Moreover, as it was her first night, there was no criterion for judging whether or not she was among those qualified to see the poor, dead, misused novice.

Vivien had been very matter-of-fact about that, but Vivien had been matter-of-fact also about what Cressida felt had been a quite extraordinary day for the two of them, when taken as a whole. She reflected, as one does at such moments, that soon it might have come to seem an entirely average day, perhaps even an unusually quiet day. As in the matter of the novice, Cressida was not at all sure what she thought about that; or about several other things, mainly that both Vivien and Aunt Agnes seemed already so changed. She was very much the more disconcerted because she was quite sure that she herself was not changed in the least. It came to her that here was what was wrong with life: other people change, while we do not change.

'Three o'clock in the morning courage,' Miss Hobbs had said; or some such pre-breakfast hour. Cressida looked at her watch, and immediately felt more wakeful than ever, now that there was a datum to judge by.

After a dismal lapse of time, there was a happening.

Rosemary roused and glided from the room. Her night garment was pink and quite plain. What was more, she had floated away not towards the bathroom but towards the piazza.

Cressida recognised at once that Rosemary was sleepwalking; something else that was not uncommon at school. Despite what had been so clearly said that afternoon, she wondered whether she ought to intervene. She abstained from again looking at her watch. It would have been too much like a detective.

How cold Rosemary must be! Cressida knew so little of these girls among whom she had been placed. For example, Rosemary had pattered out much more swiftly than had been customary among the sleepwalkers at Riverdale House. There might be danger in that, even though everyone knew that sleepwalkers never come to harm.

If Rosemary had at least put on her dressing gown!

Soon Cressida could bear it no more. Disregarding all pledges, she put on her own blue dressing gown, and her slippers too, and walked over to Rosemary's bed.

Yes, Rosemary's brownish dressing gown unmistakably lay on the floor. Even if it were someone else's dressing gown, did it really matter in Trino?

Cressida placed Rosemary's dressing gown over her arm and, far from warm herself, descended the historical steps to the historical piazza. At that hour it would be icy.

But it proved not to be. It was quite uncanny. Out here, the weather was changing and becoming quite warm.

The air around was tinted with the first, faint lilac dawn, and the historical buildings looked such stuff as dreams are made on.

Cressida threw back her head. Quite unselfconsciously, she opened her heart for a moment. There was no one in sight. There was no sound.

Then distant seagulls began to rave; or Cressida became aware of their raving. It was very unlike the dawn chorus in England. Cressida knew that when it came to birds who tweet, Italian sportsmen, with gun or lime, slew everything that moved, and then, together with their families, ate the carcasses; feathers, beaks and all. She shuddered, even though it was so surprisingly far from cold.

Rosemary could hardly have flitted through the town gates. Cressida turned her back on them and gazed down the street leading away from them. She advanced through the pink mist, carefully lifting her slippered feet. The lamps on poles, even at midnight never much more than symbolical, now made one sad.

Cressida had passed the cantina and was drawing near to the garment store, beyond which she had never previously passed. Her slippers might be suffering, but down those steps were presumably new ones, if on the morrow she were to look long enough.

Cressida perceived that the short streets to the left all ended at a high wall, and that the short streets to the right all ended at the sea. Each time the buildings became rougher and more utilitarian as the sea was approached. There seemed to be no marine promenade such as one is entitled to expect in Great Britain.

At the end of the street was a church with a dome and a pillared porch. The central doors were open, so that Cressida could see right through to the illumined altar.

She ascended the steps and entered. The illumination was mainly from candles impaled on spikes by petitioners. There were two big stands of them, like Spanish chestnut trees, one near the altar. Some of the candles were long and fat, but most were humbler, so that they had nearly consumed themselves. None the less, Cressida had never before seen anything more truly religious.

Catholic church though presumably it was, she sank on her knees and prayed fervently though briefly. The hassocks (as they would be called in England) were thin and skimpy; the back of the chair upon which Cressida's elbows rested was a little too high. Of course the Church of Rome deemed all suffering to be beneficial. How Miss Close, the physics and chemistry mistress, had disagreed with that! Whole lessons had been devoted to her expressing and explaining her disagreement. It had been the most fortunate of diversions.

Cressida sat back on the chair and examined the knees of her pyjamas. They were seriously grimed, but it was a small price to pay. All garments come to grief in some such way, having often achieved little else. Fortunately Rosemary's dressing gown, safe on the chair beside her, was not of a colour to show the dirt very much.

Cressida was not in the least frightened by being alone at dawn in an alien church. The reminders of mortality enmarbled on tombs crept nearer as daylight waxed, but, to Cressida (for the moment) they seemed acceptable abutments of the single, divine plan. Only the plastery figure of St George disconcerted her: the poor dragon had such human suffering eyes, and St George such un-English hair.

Cressida noticed that behind the altar was an open door, rectangular as the entrance to a distinguished family's vault. Through it now came the intensifying light, the pinkness and blueness of Heaven. The advent of an angel would hardly have surprised.

Trying to disregard the grime, Cressida knelt for a further prayer; a prayer upon departure. 'There are two kinds of prayer,' the retired Bishop had said, after they had wheeled him in; tucked in his wrappings; and altered the positioning of his neck-rest. 'There is a prayer for a bicycle and there is prayer into the blue. Never despise petitionary prayer; only remember that the petitions are usually granted. But it is prayer into the blue that brings bliss.' To Cressida it had seemed plain enough though faintly unofficial, and afterwards Vivien had explained that this particular retired Bishop had at no time been more than a Suffragan Bishop without a proper cathedral. That went some way to explain; and, moreover, the Bishop had finally died less than a month later, and received only an inch and a third in *The Times*. One of the other girls had measured it.

Heavens, what about Rosemary, still sleepwalking?

Cressida's devotions had carried her too far. An awakening sense of the numinous can be as ambivalent as any other awakening apprehension.

But Cressida simply could not leave without once looking through the rectangular door which lay open as a revelation before her.

She hurried towards it and, as she did so, became aware of a throne, topped by an enormous gilded mitre, which stood between the petitioners' candles and the altar. This was no church merely, but a cathedral! Cressida knew that Roman Catholic bishops were far sterner and more involved than Church of England bishops, and might hope one day to be Cardinals, then Pope, at which point imagination ceased.

She looked out.

It was, indeed, like Heaven.

There was a beautiful garden, though in need of attention, the grass being too long, and the evergreens uneven; and beyond that, on three sides, the sea; and, on the left, the chariot of Apollo, advancing imperiously; and, at the very extremity of the little peninsula, a tall, vague, crumbling monument, beside which stood Rosemary in her simple matching nightdress, and with her fair hair looking really lovely from a distance in the sunlight.

Cressida ran towards her, once more taking care not to trip. There was a narrow, stony path from the church to the extremity, lined by box hedges run half-wild.

Cressida seized Rosemary's hand, even though she did not know her very well.

'Are you all right?'

Rosemary rejoined with a counter-question. 'Isn't it gorgeous?'

She seemed alive; and more or less awake.

'I came after you because I thought you were walking in your sleep.'

'Oh, I was,' said Rosemary seraphically. 'It brings me all my best experiences.'

'Have you seen a doctor?' After all, it was the kind of thing one was expected to say when addressing a comparative stranger.

'Yes, of course.' For that matter, it was the expected kind of reply.

'Would you like me to take you home now?' Indeed, Cressida was still holding Rosemary's hand.

'Yes, it's all over now.'

'Was it wonderful?' asked Cressida, holding out the dressing gown.

'Super,' said Rosemary.

'What's this monument?' asked Cressida.

'It's for the ships to steer by.'

'A very seamark and journey's end,' said Cressida.

'That's right. Shakespeare, isn't it?' said Rosemary, joining in.

Cressida thought she had better go first, as Rosemary might not yet be fully herself. At first, therefore, she towed Rosemary.

An elderly man had appeared with some very simple horticultural tools in a worn bag. He greeted the two girls politely in his own language, and Rosemary replied in the same language.

'You'd never get people to start work at this hour in England,' remarked Cressida.

For better or for worse, it was beginning to happen all down the street, even though the sun was hardly more than seven-eighths risen.

Everybody spoke politely, calling the girls Signorita, or other things in other languages. Cressida thought it best again to take Rosemary's hand, though this time it was she, rather than Rosemary, who seemed to need support.

'I once sleepwalked along there,' said Rosemary, pointing steeply upwards. 'Not long after I got here.'

'Surely it's only a ledge?'

'No, it's a parapet. The guards used to walk round it in the Middle Ages.'

'Is it all there?'

'Most of it. There's the most wonderful view.'

'But not if you're asleep.'

'At the crucial moment, I usually wake up.'

'Do you sleepwalk often?' asked Cressida, thinking of what must be Wendy's view on the subject.

'Quite often,' said Rosemary.

'It's perfectly safe really, isn't it?'

'All my family do it, or nearly all,' said Rosemary. 'And it's quite common among the people here, actually.'

'There's an opera, isn't there?'

'That's right, and it's all based on fact.'

They passed two little boys industriously plaguing one another, early though it was.

'I've never seen an opera,' said Cressida.

'Heard.'

'Yes, I suppose so. Sorry.'

'Well, you're going to work in the theatre so I expect you'll hear dozens.'

Cressida tried to assume a suitably expectant demeanour. She did realise that she was a complete beginner.

'This street would be pack-jam soon if the town wasn't half-empty, thank God. I can't stand crowds.'

'Desirée said that too.'

'We all feel it,' said Rosemary.

'Where are the soldiers who are defending us?'

'The military establishment's at the back. Turn left at the cathedral, if you really want to go there. I shouldn't.'

Cressida was relieved to see that Rosemary at least had something on her feet. To walk barefoot over these old stones would be too much of a Roman Catholic exercise for almost anyone. She reflected that sleepwalkers usually manage to put something on, as Lady Macbeth did.

'You're not a Catholic, are you?' enquired Cressida.

'No,' said Rosemary, 'though I think there's an awful lot in it.'

Back in the dormitorio, there was Desirée in her bed, but awake none the less, and with one arm lying on the blanket. Desirée, like Cressida and Vivien, was in pyjamas, though not like Aunt Agnes's pyjamas.

'Where've you been this time, Rosemary?' enquired Desirée over the edge of the sheet.

'A long way,' said Rosemary.

'We've been right out to the point where the monument is,' Cressida expanded.

But then she realised that Desirée's question had been purely formal, like an enquiry after someone's health. She blushed faintly.

Vivien was still asleep. It was unbelievable.

Wendy's snoring was perhaps less loud as the first nocturnal stupor abated.

'Goodnight, all,' said Desirée, even though it was almost full day, with half a town doing things and disputing about things outside.

'Oh, bed,' said Cressida to herself: gratefully this time. At once she was sleeping deeply.

CHAPTER THIRTY-SEVEN

Preparations for Work

Cressida looked at her watch. It showed twenty-five minutes past twelve. She wondered if the works had been affected by the foreign air; sea air at that. Perhaps an adjustment of some kind was always necessary. She shook her wrist tentatively, but the time shown remained the same.

She had never in her life slept until that hour all on her own; only when enduring the inevitable sicknesses of immaturity in various forms, rashes, whoops, migraines.

She looked at the other beds. Only Desirée was still in position. She was also still asleep. The beds, including Vivien's, were in a tumbled state. Perceptibly, Vivien was being drawn into some accepted collectivity, to which Cressida still felt impervious—or was still uninvited.

Cressida realised that a scrap of paper had been stuffed under her pillow. 'Having a look round with the others. Love, Vivien.'

Cressida felt excessively wakeful, as one always does when one is in bed and does not know how to proceed. She wished that Desirée would wake up. She simply did not fancy putting on her clothes and setting forth alone.

There was a clatter. A man, palpably a man, was leaping up the stairs. Harry Crass flung back the door of the dormitorio and flung himself in.

'I'm sorry, Cressida,' he said, with real Canadian contrition, 'I should've knocked.'

Cressida was inclined to agree with him.

'Rise and shine, Desirée girl,' cried Harry Crass affably.

Desirée continued to sleep.

'She works so hard,' explained Harry Crass. Then he respectfully touched her on one of the carotid arteries with the hand from which the half-finger was missing.

Desirée screamed girlishly. Then she exclaimed, 'Harry!'

'Come on up as soon as you can will you, Desirée? We're like a box of mixed biscuits without you.'

'I'll come soon,' said Desirée, turning over on to her back. 'Now, go away, Harry, *please.*'

'It's real nice in here,' said Harry. Cressida was a little relieved that his eyes seemed mainly for Desirée.

'You can't be on duty again as soon as this?' Cressida speculated as soon as Harry Crass had clattered out and shut the door.

'I could quite easily be up there night and day,' said Desirée. 'It's a privilege really.'

'Where exactly is "up there"?'

'In the Residency. It stands high, you know.'

'Is that where the Tower is that Vittore comes out on each morning?'

'Right at the very top.'

'It seems a long way off?'

'A natural leader always keeps a certain mystery.'

'What's the Tower for otherwise?'

'It was built so that the ladies could watch the naval battles in the old days.'

'If I'm to work in the theatre, will you show me where the theatre is?'

'Of course I will, Cressida. I spoke to you about Vittoria last night.'

'Who is Vittoria?'

'The theatre's under a man named Colossi. He is one of the biggest theatre people in the world. I'm sure you've heard of him. But Vittoria does most of the actual work. She's frightfully nice.'

'Can she speak English?'

'Fluently. She was brought up in Alexandria.'

'Does anyone *go* to the theatre? When the town's half empty, I mean?'

'The Commendatore goes. That's the great thing.'

'But isn't that because he writes most of the plays?'

'They're not like other plays, you know. They make no attempt to be commercial. They have a sacramental quality. They're often acted in marble quarries and disused cathedrals and places like that.'

'But, still, if no one goes to them—' said Cressida doubtfully.

'They go with joy. It's one of their principal forms of self-expression. Besides, all the seats are free.'

'I'm not sure that I *want* to work in the theatre if attendance is somehow compulsory. It's too like school.'

'Don't be so silly, Cressida. The most famous people come from all over the world. Osbert Sitwell's here now. He arrived last night.'

'Is he an American?'

'He's English, I think. Yes, he must be. He's very good-looking. He's going to model for Apollo in the National Gallery.'

'Is there a National Gallery here too?'

'No, the British one. It's in Trafalgar Square, you know.'

'I went there with Mummy when we were in London, but she had to spend most of the time in the Ladies, and I was too young to be left alone.'

'It's wonderful, really,' said Desirée.

'Do you and Wendy and Rosemary all go to see Vittore's plays?'

'Wendy and Rosemary, actually, can't be expected to go, because they're English girls and have other things to do. I go quite often for an hour or so. As for you, you'll see for yourself. When you're to be involved with putting things on, of course you'll want to go. You won't be able to stop yourself.'

'It doesn't work like that with everything,' said Cressida, looking towards the ceiling, distant and vaulted.

'Of course you will,' said Desirée, 'and your friend, Vivien, as well. Isn't she very fond of things like that too? You'll both love it. It's a great privilege even to be able to say you've been under Colossi.'

It depended upon whom one was speaking to, reflected Cressida.

'We're a bit late for breakfast,' she said.

CHAPTER THIRTY-EIGHT

Sources of Supply

None the less, they had no difficulty in being served with the most excellent croissants, although most of the other people were eating more elaborately, or, in some cases, just drinking in that way. The coffee was a dream, as on the night before.

'We bake the bread and churn the butter ourselves,' explained Desirée.

'Is there any room for cows?'

'Yes, there are cows in the Public Garden, though of course they don't yield enough for everybody. If the town were full up, it would be quite impossible.'

'What happens to the rest of the people?'

'There are goats. Goats will eat absolutely anything, you know, and need very little space.'

Cressida looked dubious.

'And they yield absolutely gallons of milk daily. People don't know what to do with it all.'

But it was really the goats that Cressida was worrying about, rather than the people.

'I didn't know there *was* a Public Garden,' she said.

'Oh yes, it's beautiful. It's full of the Commendatore's war trophies. Battleships, aeroplanes, artillery, tanks: everything he's ever captured. Even camels. He's had them stuffed.'

'Don't they frighten the cows?'

'Oh, it's all right,' said Desirée. 'The trophies are surrounded by wire. The sappers put it up.'

But Cressida was worrying about the cows, not about the trophies.

'What time did you say Vittore shows himself up the Tower?' she asked in order to divert her mind from suffering of all kinds.

'Midday.'

'Then I've missed him.'

'Better luck tomorrow.'

Plainly Desirée was unprepared to proffer anything more personal: an introduction, a presentation, whatever it was called; not even a peephole.

'I hope it's not misty tomorrow,' said Cressida.

'I'll lend you a pair of field glasses. They're very good. The Austrians left hundreds.'

Soon they were walking down the main street. It was less crowded than at dawn.

'How do you get through that wall?' asked Cressida. 'When you're going to work, I mean?'

'I have a key to a little gate of my own.'

'I hope I'm not taking you miles out of your way.'

'Of course not. I must hand you over properly. That's the cathedral.'

'I know,' said Cressida. 'It's where Rosemary walked in her sleep. It's beautiful.'

'The theatre's opposite it.'

'I didn't notice.'

'It's no longer an ordinary theatre. It's a shrine. The player's spear and the centurion's spear inflict the same divine wound.'

'My brother, Hugh, carried a spear in his first school play. Everyone thought it rather a joke.'

Desirée said nothing.

'But later he acted Angelo and Malvolio.'

If only she were about to see him do one of those things now!

The theatre looked more like a Town Hall or a place where merchants assembled in days when merchants had the time to assemble. It was quite unlike what Cressida had seen in Shaftesbury Avenue. There were only a very few, very small, very factual posters, which Cressida had no time to read, especially as they were printed in black on paper the colour of plums.

'Vittore doesn't put his name up much,' she remarked.

'He's the incarnation of self-effacement, Cressida. He once said that, and then he laughed at himself, because a thing which is effaced can't be incarnated at the same time.'

Desirée was walking straight in, as if she owned the place.

CHAPTER THIRTY-NINE

The Repetition

It was beautiful inside, with plaster ladies and flowers painted on the walls, almost ethereal in technique.

In other directions, there were actual women sweeping, cleaning and polishing.

Desirée pushed open the main doors from the foyer to the auditorium. Both doors bore full-scale representations, the one of Faust, the other of Marguerite. Faust was carrying a guitar with ribbons attached.

'This is what we call a repetition,' explained Desirée.

There were people sitting or lying in almost inconceivably sustained inactivity, and other people screaming and arguing, but Cressida had taken part in rehearsals before this one.

'It's the Commendatore's new play.'

'Does he still have time to write them?'

'Plays, poems, guignols, romances, they fall from him whatever else he may be doing, and that's often several different things at once. I've heard him say that the pen is even mightier than the sword.'

'I should think it depends what you're trying to do with it,' said Cressida.

'Of course, his manuscripts fetch thousands of pounds in the salerooms, though most of them have now disappeared, but nowadays he dictates mostly. He's a superb dictator.'

'What's the play called?'

'*La Donna Riscattata Dalla Vergogna.*'

'Goodness!' said Cressida. 'I haven't got much to offer if it's in Italian.'

'Vittoria will find something to do with you, I'm certain. In fact, she's seen us already.'

Certainly no one else had taken any notice of their arrival, but now the most alarming looking woman that Cressida, at her still tender age, had ever seen, was ascending the slope of what in Shaftesbury Avenue would have been called the stalls. There were ugly lights upon and around the bare stage, but no lights at all where Cressida and Desirée were conversing.

'How wonderful of you!' said Vittoria, looking deeply into Desirée's eyes through the darkness.

She took Desirée's right hand between both of her own, which were disproportionately large. Or was disproportionate the word? Cressida immediately debated.

'Let me embrace you,' said Vittoria to Cressida. 'It's not every day I embrace a person called Cressida.'

All Vittoria actually did, however, was kiss Cressida on the lips. It was a most skilful kiss, neither too much nor too little. Nor could it be denied that Vittoria smelled glorious.

'Leave her with me,' said Vittoria. 'Here she will learn.'

It was quite true that Vittoria had an Alexandrian accent. At present, Cressida found it rather stimulating.

'Goodbye, Cressida,' said Desirée. 'I must go back to work. See you some time.'

Really Cressida would have preferred something more definite.

Vittoria put her left arm gently round Cressida's shoulders. 'This is a new play of Virgilio Vittore which we are preparing,' she said.

'If it's in Italian, I'm afraid I can't help very much, as I only know a little French,' said Cressida, 'and not really enough of that, honestly.'

'You can help *me*,' said Vittoria, 'and in that way help more than anyone.'

'I hope so,' said Cressida, modestly.

'I am in no doubt of it,' said Vittoria.

'Is Vittore here?' asked Cressida. She blushed. 'I don't know how to speak of him.'

'That's the proper way to speak of our hero,' said Vittoria. 'He likes nothing else. He rejects all distinctions, even between man and woman, even between warrior and poet. But, no,' she continued. 'Here he is not. He gives his work to mankind, but he lives more and more in his thoughts.'

One hears so many things as one goes through life, reflected Cressida; all so inconsistent with one another as to imply a quite new consistency, different, but possibly more exhilarating. Assuredly one might hope that.

'Does anyone *ever* see Vittore?' asked Cressida. There was something about her new employer (if that was the proper term) which already she found emboldening. 'Except up that tower, I mean, where you can't see him anyway. Does Vittore exist?'

'That is an excellent question, little Cressida. Already you are learning. But it is not true that Vittore cannot be seen up the tower. Where he is, there is light always. You cannot have looked for yourself.'

'That I must admit,' said Cressida. 'Tomorrow I must make more of an effort.'

'But tell me', said Vittoria, 'what are your impressions of our republic? Tell me while the first bloom is still upon you.'

Vittoria had taken away her arm, and was gazing into Cressida's eyes, as previously into Desirée's. They had come to a standstill halfway down the stalls.

'I can't really understand everything being free, and all of it so good. It's quite the opposite from England.' There: in some way Vittoria had lent her strength to put it into exact words.

'The body must be fed on lotus and clothed in samite if the spirit is to disengage, to soar, to penetrate.'

'I expect that's true,' said Cressida, struggling with it, 'but surely it can't go on for ever? It's uneconomic or something?'

'The world itself can't go on for ever. This may be the end of the world, Cressida.'

'My father keeps saying that something or other is the end of the world. The new postal rates and letting women into clubs and things like that.'

'Your father is right. He places in the palm of his hand a postage stamp and sees the entire condition of man. He is a seer.'

'I don't think he can manage quite so much, actually.'

However, it was rather embarrassing. Almost all the bickering and screaming, the very essence of the working theatre, had by now dried up; all activity (and even conspicuous inactivity) had abated: presumably because the central and compelling force had been turned aside.

223

In consequence, Vittoria's next words rang through the whole auditorium.

'The human race is at an end, Cressida. We are the last of it.'

'We few, we happy few,' murmured Cressida, partially entranced. She blushed and dried up. For a second, silence was total.

Then Vittoria uttered conjurations. The turbulence took over. The repetition of a great play forced itself forward.

Cressida could not understand a word. She was far from sure that she would have understood much, even had it been in sixth form English.

That was not to be expected, she tried to reassure herself by reflecting. Surely there must be *something* more to be learned when one has left behind one's teens, even one's early twenties? Other than dodges and attitudes, that was to say? At heart, Cressida was far from sure that she thought there *was*. For a moment, she felt as if quite dead.

However, here she was; seated under a nasty, glary light at the end of a row of stalls. She could not help remembering how much such seats would cost in Shaftesbury Avenue. She had never sat in the stalls outside a theatre's hours of public business, and all too seldom within them. Cressida expanded a little, despite all hazards; slightly lounged.

Vittoria was seated three seats away to her left; every now and then rising to her feet and speaking clearly. She was so endowed as to make shouting unnecessary. It occurred to Cressida that if ever Vittoria came to shout, it would be a once and for all incident; the single death-dirge of a lovely black swan.

Cressida had been stealing glances at Vittoria while the two of them were picked out in the glare. In the end, she was looking at little else.

Vittoria's body was very brown, and one could see an unusual amount of it, because her black silk shirt was unbuttoned all down the front, with nothing but brown body visible inside it. It was almost as if it were the shirt of some other and smaller person, casually borrowed for a working day. The sleeves were rolled up, exposing the brown forearms. Vittoria had very big bones, very big eyes, a very big nose, a very big mouth. She was a big lady in every respect. Her bosom was that of a goddess: robuster and more elemental than Lady Luce's beautiful bosom. Her neck was strong and columnar: a neck one would notice and gaze upon, as the neck of an immense Greek statue.

At that point, it came to Cressida, and quite disregarding the traffic of the stage, that very possibly this was what the goddesses were like (or had been): dark rather than marble-white or milk-white; of a bulk to cause awe (assuredly not ridicule); maternal and paternal simultaneously; utterly universal, breath-depriving.

Cressida was awestruck by her insight. It was something entirely different from what had been fostered at Riverdale House. None the less, it had always been a part of her, though hitherto unoccasioned.

Cressida felt scared once more. Vittoria had again become the most alarming woman that, at Cressida's tender age, she had ever seen.

Cressida pulled herself together a little and awaited a comparative pause in the all-comprehending drama.

'Can I do anything?' she timidly enquired.

'Watch,' replied Vittoria, 'and learn, always learn.'

Even Vittoria's black hair recalled the Classics; for it was tied loosely with what Cressida was almost sure must be a fillet.

Cressida tried to concentrate more on the play that was coalescing into immortality before her eyes. Really, she should.

This, after all, was the ambiance in which she would be working for some time to come; she who had hitherto worked only in a flower shop. For some reason the thought that there too, in its way, was art, only depressed. Perhaps it was the best in the way of art that an ordinary English girl could sensibly aspire to? Seated where she was, it seemed very probable. Cressida wished that Vivien were there to remind her that she was not ordinary, that neither of them were. She wondered what on earth could be happening to Vivien.

The repetition had reached a point where one of the characters was about to be mercilessly maltreated. He (or rather, perhaps, the actor) was a quite young man, with hair so fair as to be almost silvery, so fair that it was hard to see where it began and ended, where the lines were to be drawn, so to speak. Possibly he (or, rather, perhaps the character) was a famous martyr of some kind. History is filled with most terrible events.

'You look pale, piccina,' said Vittoria.

'I'm all right,' said Cressida, trying to suit the action to the words.

'I think you're going to faint,' said Vittoria.

'I have never fainted in my life,' said Cressida.

It was a thing that only silly geese went in for, and she, who had so long faltered beneath the miseries of domesticated mammals and of poor sexless bees, was certainly not going to make an exhibition of herself because a pale-haired actor was about to be tortured to death on a stage.

'Perhaps it is that you're going to be sick,' said Vittoria.

And, oh goodness, perhaps it was.

'Fermato,' exclaimed Vittoria.

There was silence again, and to secure it, Vittoria had hardly needed to raise her voice.

The pale-haired actor began to lounge about, looking peevish; but Cressida could not claim that this made things any better for her. Such, she reflected later, is the greater power of imagination (once disagreeably roused) than reality.

'Maddalena!'

To Vittoria's call came a dark, serious-looking girl in a dark dress. Vittoria spoke to her. Then Vittoria spoke to Cressida.

'Maddalena will take you to my bedroom.'

For Cressida there was no alternative, no option; especially as Vittoria had already gestured for the repetition to continue, and the horrors were once more imminent. Cressida had long known it was useless for people to say it was only acting, or words to that effect. Appearances count far more than realities, when the two are set in the scales.

Cressida followed Maddalena up many stone stairs, ascending uncarpeted between stone walls. Maddalena skipped up with the grace of a gazelle. Cressida, in her confused condition, found it difficult to sustain the English equivalent.

Maddalena said nothing. Ascending behind her, Cressida was impressed by Maddalena's beautiful stockings and shiny shoes. It was sometimes difficult to remember how much still lingered of the privation left by a world war.

When it seemed impossible to go higher and probably was, Maddalena threw open a wooden door. She stood back for Cressida to enter. Maddalena was expressionless.

Opposite the door, and above a big fireplace in the stage-classical style, was a painted portrait of Virgilio Vittore. Cressida identified him at once, from the likenesses on the stamps sent to Aunt Agnes.

'Il fratello della Signora,' said Maddalena in the helpful way of all Italians.

That much of the language Cressida thought she could understand.

She gasped and sank upon the bed, which, unlike beds in England, stood, unprotected, in the centre of the room. She reclined.

She apprehended that when one lay on one's back with one's head on the pillow, exactly as she was now doing, Vittore stood inescapably before one.

It was, however, only a half-length of him. The portrait stopped just beneath the bottom button of Vittore's jacket. Or perhaps tunic was the word.

Maddalena, unable to add very much, had shut the door and gone.

CHAPTER FORTY

The Lover

Why had not Desirée told Cressida that Vittoria was Vittore's sister? Or was the relationship only conceptual, as in a monastery? Could anyone really be called Vittoria Vittore? And what further names might Vittoria have? Cressida recollected that Vittore was only an adopted name anyway.

The bed was very big, and with high carved ends. The bedcover was very closely and heavily woven: presumably four Albanians had to be sent for if there was any question of removing it. It reminded Cressida of the cover which was rolled back and forth over the billiard-table in her uncle's house, a ceremony quite as strenuous and ritualistic as any part of the game itself. The cover upon which she now lay was far more beautiful than that had been. There was a skinny, silver lion in the middle of it, with staring eyes and slavering mouth. Perhaps one made no attempt to stable the lion, except on special occasions, but simply slid in beneath him. His background was fadedly golden, and looked as if knit from silky female hair.

On the walls of the room were tapestries, but never yet had Cressida succeeded in guessing the subject of a tapestry, or even in working it out when she had been told: 'Boscobolus and Arcite', or whatever it might be.

There were wonderful cupboards, chests, and presses: mostly in dark wood bizarrely carved or significantly inlaid. Each one of them would have accommodated more cadavers than Cressida cared to count on her fingers. There were big rugs, on which the stains were so old that by now they had almost disappeared.

There were four fine windows on Cressida's left as she lay on her back. The glass was of that beautiful kind that is difficult to see through.

There was no likeness of the Virgin; nor anything to recall the Great Captains of the past. There was the one face only, as Cressida remembered that A.E. Housman had expressed it.

Of course this room had not been built when the present theatre had been built, but was far older. The movement from the one to the other had been made possible by the way in which all the necessary structures of life used to cling and cluster together, so that it was often hard to define exactly where one stood. Off colour as she was, she found the thought stimulating; the way of life, engaging.

In the same way, every activity that mattered clustered about and clung to a single person who mattered, or to a very few persons. Cressida felt not merely stimulated but moved.

She glanced up at the portrait again. It had been Miss Rossetti who had said that painting a good portrait had become totally impossible. Information like that was far more important than the proper curriculum; far more useful when one came to real life.

She wondered whether she was supposed to take off her clothes. Vittoria had been very kind in her own way, but Cressida hesitated to start opening drawers and doors in order to find pyjamas or nightdress. Besides, Vittoria was so much bigger than she was.

Cressida had never in her life lain naked in bed, though some of the other girls had gone in for it. Still, one could not be regarded as properly ill (however transiently), when one continued to be fully dressed.

Cressida turned on to her side.

Was she properly ill now that she had evaded that terrifying repetition? She might have doubted it, but the thought of what had been about to happen in the theatre still made her shrivel. It was a thought that she had succeeded in keeping from her mind, since Maddalena had shut the door; and successfully converted into physical malaise. Now that she felt better 'in herself', as her mother would have put it, she was assaulted by the thought once more.

Cressida was looking across to the windows, when suddenly there was something outside one of them, the one at the furthest end of the line, which she could see least well.

There was a crash, a casement flapped about, and, quite unexpectedly, a man was in the room with her.

However, it was only Trifoglio, still in his practice dress.

'Hullo,' he said at once; so that Cressida found it impossible actually to scream, even supposing she could have managed it in any case.

'Same old face,' said Trifoglio; referring not to himself but to the portrait.

'Did you come down or up?' asked Cressida.

'Up, apparently,' said Trifoglio. 'Yes, up.'

'I don't believe you.'

Trifoglio smiled modestly, but Cressida realised that she had at no time actually looked out of the windows.

'I don't want you in here, you know,' said Cressida. 'I'm ill.'

'What with?' asked Trifoglio. 'Shall I examine you?'

'No,' said Cressida. 'Are you English?'

'I'm nothing,' said Trifoglio. 'Nothing at all.'

'Why do you use an Italian name when you're not an Italian?'

'When in Rome,' said Trifoglio.

He took a step towards her.

'Do you still work in the theatre?' asked Cressida.

'In a way,' said Trifoglio.

He was doing something to himself.

Cressida sat up.

'Would you mind going?' she said. 'I've told you. I'm ill.'

But with one of his leaps, though the distance had seemed impossible, he was upon her. He had drawn off the lower part of his costume.

It had been widely believed at Riverdale House and elsewhere that in these circumstances girls experience a sudden unpredictable release, a blissful, compulsive capitulation. The event, now that it had occurred, was proving, as so often in life, quite otherwise.

Trifoglio was disgusting: sallow all over and sticky.

But he had power in his arms almost equal to that in his legs. He was dragging at Cressida's corduroy trousers; and not wildly, but skilfully.

She raised her knee steeply between his legs. As many sharp teeth appeared in his mouth as in the equally skinny lion's mouth, but Cressida managed to butt at him with her head, so that he failed even to snap at her, this time at least.

She had no experience of wrestling, whereas he had very probably been trained. Furthermore, she was in the disadvantageous position of being beneath him.

However, both his hands were committed to holding down her shoulders, and his legs he felt compelled to keep close together, in view of what had just happened. His whole body was as overextended as dragged-out elastic.

Finally, he was, after all, a lightweight, totally harlequinesque.

Cressida chose her moment, then gathered together her whole frame and heaved upwards at him. He slid off the slippery cover and dropped, feather-light, on to one of the priceless rugs.

Cressida slithered herself off the bed on its other side, but was still on her feet. Trifoglio attempted another of his great leaps at her, but fortunately his brow struck the elaborately carved bedhead. Pale blood oozed down his features, already moist, already dingy. His overt physical excitation seemed not one whit diminished.

Cressida looked round the room for a weapon of offence, with which to retain the initiative more firmly.

There was only a black, serpentine, silky thing, depending from a peg above the dressing table, and of unknown function, if of any function. Cressida snatched at it and made use of it.

She could never have predicted the upshot. Instead of attempting in some way to strike back, or perhaps simply to escape, Trifoglio merely cringed and crumpled.

Cressida struck at him again. She saw that now he was quivering.

Cressida struck a third time, though it was becoming pointless.

Trifoglio collapsed upon himself in a curiously tiny heap, holding himself together with his long arms and emitting a steady, gurgling whimper.

There was an assessable pause.

Then, from the floor, he looked up at her.

Giving him a final sharpish flick, she turned her back on him, waiting for him to go. Surely he must understand?

Apparently, yes. She heard him get up, seize hold of the garment he had discarded, and again clatter as when he had entered.

Still holding the serpentine object, she turned. Trifoglio was at least wearing his practice costume in its entirety once more.

Without meeting her eyes, he leapt lightly out of the window.

At once, she crossed and looked out. As she had supposed, there was a quite immense drop.

She managed to look down.

There seemed no reason for concern (even if Cressida had felt in the mood for concern). She could see Trifoglio squirming away, adequately on his legs and feet, in and out among the groups in the piazza before the cathedral. His progress resembled that of a disturbed crustacean on the shores of The Wash. Soon he had disappeared down an alley; as a crab, small and scuttling, disappears between rocks. No one seemed to be taking much notice of him.

For the first time in her life, Cressida felt faint, after all; though she managed first to reach the bed, of which the heavy leonine cover was still almost undisplaced.

CHAPTER FORTY-ONE

The Sickbed

Still, there is a limit to the amount of time during which anyone can continue to feel faint without something else happening, negative or positive. Soon Cressida was beginning to wonder where her next meal was coming from.

The black serpentine object which had done so much to restore order, still lay conveniently on the bed beside her. She examined it more closely. Though silky in the extreme, it had a core as of steel, if steel so flexible could be imagined. Cressida simply did not know whether it could or not. She held the object to her face, then she rose once more from the bed and returned the object to its peg, arranging it with care so that it looked much as she thought it had looked before she had snatched at it.

Even though the weather had turned so much warmer, she next shut the window. Despite the distinctive noise made by the intruder upon both entrance and exit, she was much relieved to find that the small panes of ancient glass seemed intact. It was merely that they rattled.

Cressida was relieved also that she had come to no premature decision about undressing, and she saw no reason to undress now.

There was a full-length looking glass in an ornate painted frame. It was so magnificent that Cressida had previously abstained from looking into it, indisposed as she was. She had been absurdly unsure who she might see in it.

She plucked up her courage: a process that was becoming continuously necessary, as all along Vivien had half-predicted and half-yearned for.

It was mercury-backed glass, so that Cressida looked even more beautiful than ever before, and beautiful in a quite different way. On the instant, she was all but spellbound by her own image. Without motion, she gazed and gazed; though in the end she managed fleetingly to smile at herself. Moreover, the exquisitely cut female trousers she was wearing were something she had never known before, or thought of, though with Vivien it might have been different. Cressida even liked the reflection of her funny little figure inside the high-necked jersey. Time must pass before there was even the possibility of her looking like Aunt Agnes or Vittoria; and, of course, Time, while scything the grain upon which we live, simultaneously scythes the meadow flowers. Though the sun was shining sturdily outside, Vittoria's bedroom was mercifully opaque. Every image in the great mirror was refined by shadow and by age.

Included among the reflections was a shelf of books which Cressida had not before noticed in the room, perhaps because it was set so near the floor.

Gathering herself together, Cressida set out to see what she might find. How had the sister come to have been brought up in Alexandria, when the brother presumably had not? Cressida knew quite well that the enormous Alexandrian Library had been simply razed to the ground.

But before Cressida reached the dark corner where the books dwelt, the door had opened and Maddalena had entered without in any way knocking, just like Harry Cross.

She was bearing a quite big tray which she set down on the bed, innocent of what only just now had transpired thereon.

'La Signora say you stay,' said Maddalena with a single stirring gesture towards the skinny lion. The gesture, together with Maddalena's eyes and face, implied reproach that Cressida had been discovered walking about fully dressed.

'Thank you,' said Cressida. She had not particularly intended to sound perfunctory, but could not help herself.

'La Signora e la sorella del Commendatore,' said Maddalena, now pointing imperatively at the portrait instead of at the bed.

'Si, si,' said Cressida, quite surprised at herself.

Though, with the single-minded concentration common among Italians, her whole aspect and bearing emitted doubt, Maddalena could do nothing but depart.

The food and drink on the tray were perfect: of nothing too much, and of very few things too little. Cressida smiled once more, remembering the trays that were brought to the sick in Rutland, or even in her uncle's house in Huntingdonshire, wherein once, to her fury, she had sunk beneath German Measles, and, on another occasion, beneath ant-bites.

After the most delightfully delicate luncheon she could remember (though having to eat and drink from the tray on her knees or on the bed beside her had been the drawback that life seldom forgets to provide), Cressida strolled back to the window, as people do when they judge themselves replete.

The piazza was almost empty. Doubtless the bulk of the reduced population had ceased work in order to eat with their families. Cressida found it impossible not to wonder once more how long things could last.

But for the present, Trino seemed even to accommodate tourists. There were three of them now, with dirty dresses and fretful faces. One appeared to have twisted her ankle, and Cressida could hardly wonder.

Cressida sank down upon her knees before the shelf of books.

It had struck her that probably they were all by Vittore. But it was not so. There were even three books in English. One was the second volume of *Dombey and Son* in very small print. One was a work of some kind by Dornford Yates in much larger print. The third was the Badminton Library book on *Archery and Falconry*.

Unfortunately, Cressida had failed to conclude even G.K. Chesterton's Introduction to *Dombey and Son*, though at the time Mrs Gropewood had chided her quite harshly; Dornford Yates she knew to be a writer mainly for boys, and falconry she thought a loathsome pastime. Almost at random she drew out a fattish book which seemed to be mainly illustrations, and therefore ideal for a sickbed.

Cressida suddenly wanted to go somewhere. She cautiously opened the door by which she had entered, and looked around as one does in the passages of a theatre. There was nothing but the stone steps, with the theatre on one side, and this much older building, on the other: nothing more than Cressida had recollected from the first period of her infirmity.

She shut the door again, and realised that, manners or no manners, she would have to open the other doors in the room. Not even the Vittore family could be exempt from all life's demands.

Happily, the very first door provided more or less what she sought. The matter was always such a blight in foreign countries. Her father joked about it, but her mother grew grim. Nor had Cressida's recent experience falsified such attitudes. Even here, immediately off Vittoria's gorgeous bedroom, there was more of a smell than in England, and very much less water. Cressida realised that abroad there were curious problems about water. She reflected that she had been lucky to have solved her difficulty so instantaneously; though there is often an instinct in such matters.

Cressida tried to settle herself on the bed once more. There were several chairs in the room, but, apart from the fact that they looked more beautiful than comfortable, Cressida reflected that while, on the one hand, the sick are normally expected to be in bed, yet, on the other, resentment might arise if she were to be found seated in a chair with her feet on the bedspread, as would surely be de rigueur from a health point of view. In practice, the matter could be even more delicate than the necessity to open doors.

On the dark red cover of the book was a family blazon, with the motto 'Semper Crescens'. The illustrations proved to be woodblocks of men and women doing exercises, and, consequently, in all kinds of attitudes. When one had examined the first thirty or forty drawings, one became conscious of a certain sameness. Moreover, the artist had made little effort to differentiate the features of the individuals depicted. Deep within her, Cressida had sometimes wondered whether nudity did not soon become rather boring. Indeed, she had wondered that ever since she had started wondering at all about things.

She turned back to the date of the book. 1895. The clothes of that period were gorgeous; at least the women's clothes. She would gladly have been made to wear them herself.

It was odd that only about thirty years ago, the brief explanations in the book should have been written in Latin. But Cressida realised that Latin and Italian had an enormous amount in common. Though she knew almost no Italian, she now realised that neither did her Latin fully suffice for the construing of a book encountered at random. It is a saddening moment, however familiar, in one's contest with any language.

Cressida laid the book on the floor and went to sleep.

CHAPTER FORTY-TWO

The Tear

The room was full of sunset fire.

Vittoria was there, smiling at Cressida. She wore a chamois leather jerkin over her black shirt.

'Sorry to disturb you,' said Vittoria, in her fascinating Alexandrian accent.

'I had very little sleep last night,' said Cressida, blinking.

'Now it's evening once more,' said Vittoria.

'The bright day is done, and we are for the dark,' said Cressida, still only half awake, if that.

'It's the afterglow,' said Vittoria.

'Red sky at night,' said Cressida.

'It means a storm,' said Vittoria.

Cressida sat up a little, and looked out more anxiously. It was true that the dusk had a farouche aspect.

'John Ruskin used to be carried in a basket to the top of a mountain every evening,' said Cressida. 'He was mad by then, of course.'

But Vittoria, unlike Mrs Gropewood, showed no sign of any full response to John Ruskin.

'It's so beautiful,' said Cressida. '*Must* there be a storm?'

'Nothing is more beautiful than a storm, piccina,' said Vittoria. She had picked up the illustrated book that Cressida had left on the floor, and was bearing it quietly to its shelf.

Cressida now felt she was sufficiently awake to ask another important question.

'Are you really the Commendatore's sister?'

'They say I am.'

Cressida could not think what to ask next. She had often been unable to grasp the complexities of relationships in families.

'Neither of us knows who were our parents,' explained Vittoria.

'Neither parent? In neither case?'

'We are children of the storm.'

Vittoria sat down on the bed.

'Isn't that a film?' asked Cressida.

'Every artist naturally aspires to chronicle our hero.'

'You've been very kind to me,' said Cressida. 'Letting me lie down, and not making me watch the man in the play being tortured, and sending up lunch.'

'It's partly that you remind me of my sister,' explained Vittoria. 'Or, rather, of my half-sister.'

'Where is she now?'

'She was raped by the French during the war, and swallowed poison.'

'But weren't the French your allies?' cried Cressida.

'We were theirs,' said Vittoria.

'How *awful*!' cried Cressida.

'The French are without the sacramental attitude.'

Cressida was far from sure that at present she knew exactly what that was, but it was no proper moment to ask.

'She looked much like you,' said Vittoria, 'though even more virginal.'

Cressida blushed as she basked in the sunset.

'Such eyes, such lips, such tiny, undemanding breasts.'

Really, Cressida could again think of nothing to say.

'Such fragile feet, such frail fingers, such filigree hair.'

Cressida could think only of the faded background to the skinny lion.

'Such hair, such hair, such hair.'

Vittoria stretched out her hand and began reminiscently to stroke Cressida's substitute hair. Cressida thought it best to lean her head slightly forward.

'I'm so sorry,' said Cressida. 'I know about it. I lost my brother, Hugh, in the war.'

Though she was having to speak into her chest, Cressida, as always when that name was spoken, found it difficult not to shed a few tears. Oh, Hugh! Besides, the stroking of the head tends to melt inhibitions.

But at once Vittoria stopped stroking. Cressida looked up timidly: almost certainly her hair had proved utterly inferior to that of the girl who had poisoned herself.

But she saw that a single simply enormous tear was very slowly descending Vittoria's own right cheek, big, brown, and bone-structured. The tear kept its lovely shape from start to finish of its course, like a pearl that happened to be transparent instead of being translucent. Previously, Cressida could not even have imagined such a perfect tear. In the end, it dropped formally on to the collar of Vittoria's shirt, and dissolved in the blackness. Cressida could only gasp.

'War is to man what childbirth is to woman,' said Vittoria, but her voice was so unusually low that Cressida wondered how far she really meant what she had said. Could she be speaking from the heart? So perfect a tear proved that Vittoria *had* a heart.

'Do you know about childbirth?' asked Cressida.

'I have known about it four times.'

'Oh,' cried Cressida, aware that it was the right cry to utter. 'Boys or girls?'

'Veronica, Vitellia, Vespasiana, and Vittorina,' said Vittoria.

'What sweet names!' cried Cressida, again aware that one always did. 'Where are they now?'

'They are serving.'

'Young maidens now are level all with men,' said Cressida. She at once fancied that the quotation was a bit wrong, but doubted whether Vittoria would know that; Vittoria who had given no sign of having so much as *heard of* John Ruskin.

What Cressida really had on her mind was whether all four chicks had (or had ever had) the same father! If there had been more than one sire, what men there must still be in the world, when one gazed upon and reflected upon Vittoria! Cressida felt quite a thrill.

'How old are they?' enquired Cressida, still sticking to the expected thing.

'How can I remember that?' rejoined Vittoria, as if it had been the most childish of questions.

But of course it set Cressida speculating once more upon Vittoria's own age.

'I am myself forty-eight,' said Vittoria, no doubt by telepathy.

Cressida would never have thought it possible. How old then was Lady Luce? As always, one made such errors.

'Our hero is ageless,' continued Vittoria.

'Yes, of course,' said Cressida. 'I understand that.'

'You are ageless too,' said Vittoria, 'and you should perish before you become otherwise.'

'My friend, Vivien, and I have sometimes thought that,' replied Cressida solemnly.

'At this moment you are perfect,' said Vittoria. 'But for how long?'

Cressida tried hard not to blush once more. There was quite enough red in the room already.

'You may call me Vittoria. In fact you must. I require it.'

'I should love to, Vittoria.'

'Not for nothing am I said to be sister to a hero.'

'I like you very much,' said Cressida. 'Really I do.'

'And now,' said Vittoria, 'I, in turn, have three questions for you.'

She said it again, 'I for you.'

CHAPTER FORTY-THREE

La Couture
Assez Grande

'First,' asked Vittoria, 'are you better, are you well?'

Cressida reflected that already there had been two out of the three questions, but all she said was: 'Yes, thank you, Vittoria, I am quite well, provided I don't have to watch any scene of horror.'

What, Cressida wondered, would Vittoria do if inflicted with the narrative of Trifoglio's behaviour that afternoon, at once so absurd and so disgusting? Cressida found herself unable even to imagine the answer.

Vittoria looked a little doubtful about Cressida's reply. In her mien, the solicitude she had shown in the theatre conflicted with the stern sense of reality she had manifested in the bedroom.

Cressida wondered what it was in the life of a man that corresponded to a girl being required to witness spectacles of torture and mutilation. Something required at his public school, she supposed. Or perhaps, later, in hospital. Training would be needed.

'Second,' asked Vittoria, 'would you like me to lend you a costume in which to attend the banquet?'

'Very much,' said Cressida. 'But I didn't know there *was* a banquet.'

'There's a banquet all the evenings.'

Cressida could detect the words 'while it lasts' as they hung in the pink and purple air awaiting form, awaiting death. One pinkness at dawn, quite another at dusk.

'And tonight there's a ballet.'

'In the theatre?'

'Yes, but no scenes of horror. Or not in the schoolgirl sense.'

'I'm not a schoolgirl.'

Vittoria only smiled.

'I should love it, though I can't really speak a word of anything but English. I thought I could, but I can't.'

'Speech will be unnecessary.'

'What's the third question?'

Vittoria rose from the bed and opened one of the doors other than the door that Cressida had opened earlier. She stood there and beckoned.

Within was another bedroom; not tapestried, and ormolued, and grand, but white and pale blue and pale pink; almost as in a good family at home, though perhaps the effect was attributable in part to the afterglow which here struck full in the eyes, instead of striking only sideways.

On the opposite side of the room was another door, which stood open already. Through it, Cressida saw a further room, and a still further, and a further still: virtually rooms without end.

'Would you like to remain?' asked Vittoria.

'Thank you very much indeed,' replied Cressida gratefully. 'But I think I really should go back to Vivien and Rosemary and Desirée and Wendy, or they'll wonder what has happened to me. Vivien especially.'

'Possibly you would prefer to go back at once?' asked Vittoria edgily: really her fifth question.

'Oh no, not at once. I'd like to wear a costume and go to the banquet. And I've hardly ever been to a ballet. Only once to *Bluebell* at Loughborough when I was a kid.'

Vittoria really was someone in whom it was quite easy to confide. Probably, like her brother, she had the simplicity of the truly great. Cressida had heard of that often.

There was even a sweet little picture of ducks, but Cressida resolutely turned her back on it.

They returned, and Vittoria closed the door irrevocably behind them.

'How would you like to be a slave girl?'

'You don't mean black all over?'

'Oriental, rather than transatlantic. You have been captured by pirates and sold in the public market to the Bey of Tunis.'

'Will he be kind to me?' asked Cressida doubtfully.

'Rapidly you will achieve a complete ascendancy over him. You will be an invisible autocrat.'

'How shall I manage that?'

'By pandering to his every whim.'

Cressida looked more doubtful than ever.

'That is the route to power. Give men what they ask, and they are once more as babies at the breast.'

'Or at the bottle?' suggested Cressida, giggling a little, but remembering, indeed unable to forget.

'The people of the Prophet are forbidden the bottle.'

'I shall alter that,' said Cressida, still giggling.

Vittoria had opened a huge drawer. It contained everything wonderful: like the play chest at home, but incomparably more so, because here everything had been of much better quality in the first place, because everything was more delicate and fragile and peculiar, and because, simpler still, there was far more of everything.

'I could go for a swim in that drawer,' said Cressida, surprised at herself. 'And perhaps drown.'

'One day. One day soon,' promised Vittoria. 'Not tonight.'

When Cressida was arrayed in her little tunic and comical pantomime trousers, gathered tight at the ankle, and all of course, in black, she saw, in the ancient looking glass, that, through the slave garments, she herself was excitingly, whitely visible.

Cressida recollected once more that very costly fabrics were often the cheapest in the long run. Unsuitability for work is relative.

'What would my work be?'

'Pleasing,' said Vittoria.

The memory returned of Trifoglio squirming around. Cressida had nearly forgotten the incident for a few moments.

'Could I have a cloak, please?'

Without a word, Vittoria opened a lacquered armadio and gave her one.

It was black, but with a high golden collar. Though as opaque as Cressida could have wished, it was marvellously light on the shoulders. It was exactly the right length.

'Vittoria. Do you keep slaves of all sizes?'

'Of one size only.'

Cressida strayed over to the window. Her feet were bare. Previously she had been wearing yellow socks from the garment store but they did not harmonise with diaphanous slave trousers, and she realised that the golden collar made her carry her head better—truly like a slave-girl autocrat, in fact.

She perceived at once that the element of menace in the sunset had increased.

'Perhaps you'd better rest?' suggested Vittoria.

'No thank you. I'm watching the storm gather.'

If it had been her mother who had suggested a rest, Cressida nowadays would positively have snapped at her. There are perils in maternity, as well as pleasures. But now it came to Cressida that her mother and Vittoria had a surprising amount in common. It was simply that in her mother all of it had been lost.

But in the end curiosity overcame Cressida as to what Vittoria was up to. And what costume could she have in mind for herself?

Cressida wheeled.

Doubtless it was because her eyes had become accustomed to the sunset that the room seemed much dimmer than before.

In the dimness, Vittoria stood naked. She was stretching upwards to the top of the cabinet.

The highest beauty is impossible to imagine, but this does not mean that we do not identify it if ever we encounter it . . . if ever we do.

For some time, Aunt Agnes had been more or less the pattern to which Cressida had hoped, when the time arrived, to attain. And of course Aunt Agnes remained soft, charming, and delightful; but Vittoria was unique in the world. Cressida knew that at once.

Cressida pulled herself together. She caught hold of the fact that whereas Aunt Agnes was a not completely inaccessible ideal, Vittoria was beyond all emulation. The thought saved trouble too.

Cressida gulped. 'Are you going to be the Bey of Tunis?'

'I am outside the revels. I provide the revels.'

'Like our hero?' Cressida was falling into the idiom quite unconsciously.

'Like our hero,' Vittoria confirmed.

'I should prefer that too. When I am old enough, of course.'

'If you fail, you will be trampled without mercy.'

'Like Mr Lloyd George?' illustrated Cressida.

'And in the end you *will* fail. You *must* fail.'

'It hardly seems worth it.'

'When you are called, there is no choice.'

'Then, what *are* you going to wear, Vittoria?'

'My puppet-master's dress. It is quite grand enough.'

It proved to be as simple as a dress possibly could be, though the skirt fell to Vittoria's strong ankles instead of ending at her knees. It was in some kind of glazed material which rustled and crackled as Vittoria moved. It was all she wore and she wore no cloak.

'You are Artemis!' cried Cressida, inspired to her very furthest stretch of simile.

'*Diana*, among the Latin peoples,' corrected Vittoria.

Cressida realised that they had changed almost without light, though for both of them the task had been simpler than in England, albeit with results greatly more diverse.

Now there was little in the sky but livid, dusky threat.

CHAPTER FORTY-FOUR

The Wildfowlers

Vittoria opened still another door. Cressida realised that in former times the rooms had to be big in order to provide ingress and egress for such different activities, with at the same time space for so many armoires and credenzas.

'I know death hath ten thousand several doors for men to make their exits,' she said under her breath.

There was a really wonderful staircase, with blazons, persons in armour, lighted lamps everywhere, and a carpet of which the pile erupted between Cressida's bare toes.

'Ought I to go back for my shoes?'

'Slave girls aren't allowed shoes.'

There was a picture on or in the carpet from top step to bottom.

'Is it a very old carpet?'

'The old carpet was worn out. Our hero designed a new one. It was woven by the women of Scythia.'

'What's the picture?'

'The Massacre of the Innocents. Herod is in the likeness of our hero, and the Blessed Virgin is the Queen of Italy. She comes from Montenegro, you know.'

'Then she must have been merged,' said Cressida knowledgably.

For the moment, Cressida had seen enough of Vittore's likeness, but she turned to seek that of the Queen. However, Vittoria was stalking on, and Cressida had to accept failure. There were cruel soldiers woven in at every step, and the quantity of blood depicted was almost unbelievable considering the extreme immaturity of the victims. Still it all made a splendid splash of colour.

In the hall below were immense stuffed monsters on stands of ebony, or mock-ebony. All of them had their mouths open, displaying rows of teeth (in certain cases, parallel rows), inches long. Some of the creatures seemed to wink and slaver as Cressida slunk past them. A few of them still had lances stuck in them, mementoes of men who had passed. These victims also had generative organs in a state of animation: something that Cressida had never noticed in the Natural History Museum. That had been the afternoon when Cressida's mother had lost her cashmere scarf in the Underground and they had spent most of the time trying to trace it, including a journey all the way to Baker Street.

It struck Cressida that now Vittoria was striding out like a great huntress, while she, Cressida, really was creeping along like a creature in bondage. Such is the power of apparel, of aspect. Cressida sighed ambiguously.

At the far side of the Hall of Monsters, steps ascended, perhaps a dozen of them, long, low, and largely ornamental. They were tiled with representations of the last hours or minutes of holy martyrs, but the tiles were not large enough for proper inspection of the different scenes without descending to one's knees, which both time and her cloak made difficult for Cressida. How glad she had been, though, for the cloak's protection already! One trouble now was that the tiles were not only cold to the feet, but also rather uneven, after so many years of use.

At the top of the Martyr's Staircase was a triple entry: a large entry in the middle, with smaller entries at each side, separated from the main entry by stout stone columns. Against the two columns were stationed persons in heraldic garb.

Cressida was intensely surprised to perceive that one of these persons, the one in front of her, was Vivien.

Forgetting even the sudden chill in her feet, Cressida dashed up to her. 'You look like the knave of diamonds,' she said.

'You look like Guy Fawkes,' said Vivien. Of course only Cressida's cloak was visible. 'Are you in a play?'

Cressida's eyes could not help dropping to Vivien's feet. But Vivien was all right: she was wearing heraldic boots, ascending high.

'No, I'm going to the banquet, and then to the ballet. What about you?'

'I volunteered for service, but the woman made me dress up and ordered me to stand here.'

'*Ordered* you, Vivien?'

'Oh yes, I'm under orders.'

'What's the woman called?'

'Isolde. She's German.'

Cressida looked around wildly. Naturally, Vittoria had gone forward without her.

'Heavens, Vivien, I must rush.'

But she peered slantingly at the other herald. It was impossible to make out whether it was a man or a woman. Cressida realised that a function of a herald is to be impersonal.

'Shall I see you tonight?' asked Vivien.

'Yes. I've refused to move into Vittoria's spare room.'

'Is it horrible?'

'No, it's like Daniel Neal.'

'Bye,' said Vivien resignedly.

'Bye, Vivien. I'm a slave girl.'

Cressida threw open the lower part of her cloak for a moment so that Vivien could see how enslaved she was and then darted up the remaining steps, her feet forgotten.

At the top of the steps was another large hall, unfurnished except for tapestries, and, beyond it, a curtained arcade, through which could be heard the babbling and burbling of the banquet.

Should Cressida throw off her cloak with a single shrug before entering?

She decided not to. After all, she was belated, and entirely through her own fault. As a first move, she prised her head between two of the heavy curtains.

Vittoria was sitting with her back to Cressida and with an empty chair to her left. The table was long and wide and marble, and, among those seated round it, Cressida could see several people she knew: the Colonel and the Major, the Acting Foreign Minister, even Brian Wicker and Wendy. There were many females, all more or less ravishing, and, as far as Cressida could see, all in costume: a pierrette in black and white bobbles, a vivandière with fine eyes and a prominent bust (just as Aunt Agnes had implied), a slim blonde wearing nothing but feathers, an unlaced milkmaid, Cleopatra, Circe, Aimée

255

Dubucq de Rivery (in a costume similar to Cressida's own), all the usual things and people. Sure enough, only Vittoria looked her day-to-day self, at least from the back. None of the men had gone to much trouble, of course, not even the very young ones, though perhaps the addiction to uniform of some kind tended in a decorative direction. Brian Wicker was in a dinner jacket from the Savile Row area and Wendy in a little black dress from Marguerite's. It was *so* little that the cost must have been prohibitive.

Where was the Commendatore?

Cressida glanced at the occupant of the chair on the other side of the one which was presumably intended for her. She could see only the back of a male head, quite faded. The man was in uniform like that of a police inspector.

The numberless lamps and candles had already made the banqueting hall very torrid. A cloak was impossible. With a wild gesture, Cressida threw it aside, whatever the consequences.

She tripped to the feast. She sat down.

'I'm so sorry to be late,' she whispered in Vittoria's left ear. 'I was delayed by meeting a friend.'

Two Albanians in fullest national costume drew back her chair.

'This is Madame Magda Ciasca, one of our greatest actresses and sculptors,' said Vittoria, introducing the lady on her right, to whom she had been speaking, and who was arrayed as Lucrezia Borgia (though in one of her simpler styles, with less than half the complete array of jewels). 'Madame has no English.'

Perhaps for that reason, Madame Ciasca merely glowered at the world; or at least Cressida. Her eyes seemed even yellower than her dress.

'But this,' said Vittoria, introducing Cressida's neighbour, 'is Brigadier Barker-Henslow, a countryman of yours.'

How thoughtful Vittoria always was!

'Just call me Horatio,' said the Brigadier.

Cressida had never before encountered such informality in a man with grey hair. But she had heard that the English often tended to relax after living for some time on the continent.

'Is it your name?' she enquired.

'No. My name's Brian.'

Even above the general hubbub, Brian Wicker looked up and bowed politely to Cressida. Next, Wendy smiled slightly. Cressida smiled back at the two of them.

'But it's not always convenient to use one's real name in this place,' said the Brigadier.

Cressida had again been forgetting that.

'My name's Cressida Hermione Helena Hazeborough,' she said, picking up a silver spoon with a very long shaft, a hook at one end, and a rather small bowl at the other. She began to poke with it at the contents of the silver goblet standing before her on a damask mat.

'The girls have all the luck,' said the Brigadier, staring neutrally through Cressida's diaphanous couture.

On the Brigadier's other side was a lady with a face like a greeny-brown almond, who was costumed as Aspasia. One could tell that she had no English either. The poor Brigadier! However, the lady had the most complex jewelled earrings instead. They made Cressida's own ears ache to look at.

'Who's the lady on the other side of you?' enquired Cressida in a whisper.

'I believe she's a thinker of some kind,' said the Brigadier.

'And a lady mountaineer too. Speaking for myself, I can't reach her.'

Involuntarily, his eyes and shoulders twitched towards the lady. She glared across him at Cressida.

'What am I eating?' asked Cressida. It was really rather good: a bit like an end of brawn, only with something more.

'Larks' tongues. It's the same every night. They're pounded into a purée, of course. A sort of forcemeat. I once lived on it for a month.'

'How disgustingly cruel!' cried Cressida, putting down her spoon.

'We're in no position to pick and choose. In a sense, we're at war, you know, even though in another sense we're not.'

'What's the matter with *you*?' asked Vittoria in her Alexandrian voice.

'I thought eating larks' tongues was only a sort of joke,' said Cressida, white all over, very visibly so.

'Only when the singer has been in our own mouth can we truly hear,' said Vittoria.

'I don't want any more,' said Cressida.

'There's quails to follow,' said the Brigadier helpfully, 'though on some evenings we only get thrushes.'

'You can't *eat thrushes*!' cried Cressida her heart abrim with Robert Browning.

'Not if you can get quails,' said the Brigadier.

'What exactly are quails?' asked Cressida, quailing before the answer.

'Stupid little birds you catch with sticks,' replied the Brigadier. 'When I was with Allenby we caught hundreds, many more than we could eat. They're thick, are quails.'

'Oh!' gurgled Cressida.

Then she became aware that all the time Trifoglio had been in the room quietly doing his tricks for any who might be interested.

Mercifully, the Albanians were removing the goblets without giving heed to how much or how little had been eaten from them.

She took a long pull on the glass of wine before her. Both the wine and the glass seemed hard and clear and impersonal: as reassuring as diamonds. Cressida set down the glass with a gasp. She would have liked to cough slightly.

'Steady on,' said the Brigadier. 'Leave some room inside you for the Tokay.' He gazed at Cressida's delicately pretty stomach in a military manner, as if to check its capacity.

'What's *that*? Is it something to do with Japan?'

'It's Hungarian. The blood of live bulls goes into it.'

'Oh!' gasped Cressida. She already knew too much about what happens to bulls.

'It's mainly a wine for men. We used to drink bottle after bottle in the mess and then see how far we could throw the empties. A great pal of mine managed to kill a sheep. Unintentionally, of course.'

The Brigadier took advantage of the pause in the service to look at the ceiling, the better to recall old times. As one does, Cressida looked up too.

There was a glorious representation of Eurydice in purest white re-emerging from Hades and looking down on them, while multi-coloured Orpheus passed the time twanging away to entice the wildlife.

The trouble was that Cressida knew perfectly well what happened next: Eurydice went back because Orpheus had failed her, and all the birds and beasts were swatted. Mrs Gropewood had read Virgil's story to the class, translated quite freely by someone in the eighteenth century.

'Are you in the army?' asked Cressida. Vittoria was conversing intimately with Madame Ciasca; and one had to say something to one's neighbour at table, or so Cressida had always been told.

'I was,' said the Brigadier with solemnity, and slowly bringing down his eyes. 'These days it's the police. I'm a Deputy Chief Constable, you know, but the Chief's laid up more or less permanently, poor chap, so there's work enough for three. It's just as well my shoulders are strong.'

'Then what are you doing here? If you don't mind me asking?'

Cressida couldn't see why he should mind, seeing that she didn't mind hearing.

'Seconded,' said the Brigadier, as if the odd-sounding expression explained something.

'What's that? Sorry I'm so ignorant.'

'It's a man's word,' rejoined the Brigadier tolerantly. 'It simply means that old Vittore thought he could use a few tough and experienced bobbies and had the sense to look for them in the right place.'

'Are you here officially, then?'

'Sort of,' said the Brigadier. 'It's best not to pry too far.'

Cressida formed the impression that he had attempted an actual wink. Anyway, his eyeglass fell out.

Happily, she had no more wish to pry than to wink. It had simply been that she had doubted the Brigadier's interest in anything that lay too far from himself.

The dreaded quails had still not appeared, nor, for that matter, had glasses been refilled.

Cressida became aware that many of the men round the table were feeling in their pockets or in other places.

There seemed to be not so much a deficiency in the service as a pause deliberately inserted; contrived for some definable purpose. With a faint chill, Cressida remembered the like phenomenon as Perdita's party had drawn to its climax.

Perhaps ever rising, though polyglot, excitement could be sensed.

And then the whole room was full of birds in flight. Last night it had been mammalian bats, but tonight it was tiny fluffy songsters in blue the colour of happiness, yellow the colour of art, green the colour of nature, and red the colour of passion. What was more, Cressida could see the birds being released from an open door high up under the Orpheus ceiling. An evil face, with a long nose imperfectly centred, could be discerned among the emerging twitterers. The birds flew wildly, hitting the walls, hitting one another, sometimes dropping to floor or table, maimed or cataleptic or dead.

Many of the men were firing upwards with small silver pistols. Some rose for the purpose. Others were unable to and fired from their chairs. The pistols emitted a pop rather than a report, thus leaving no doubt that all was in play, entirely for fun.

Many of the costumed women seemed to understand this: they emitted little appreciative shrieks when their neighbours hit; tiny sympathetic groans when they missed. Others, however, among the women showed signs of stress and shock. One or two had fainted or had heart attacks, though their neighbours were too excited to attend very much.

In no time the table was covered with blue, yellow, green, and red bundles, heaving and cheeping and defecating whitely in death.

It would have been quite senseless to have brought in the second course before the fowlers had exhausted themselves.

'Damned unsporting!' grunted Brigadier Barker-Henslow under his breath, which smelt of spirits.

Even in the midst of such a scene, Cressida had noticed the reserve of Brian Wicker also, though Wendy had begun by slightly slapping her hands.

'Damned foreigners,' grunted Brigadier Barker-Henslow.

'It's *horrible*,' cried Cressida, fearing to lose control of her manners, and clutching with both hands at the heavy table, lest that happen.

Vittoria's hand was on hers: warm, dry, carrying the burden.

'The slaughter of the innocent is the strengthening of the just,' she said.

Cressida slowly withdrew her hand and stared into Vittoria's wise eyes.

Never before in her life had she felt so completely unstable.

'The symbol equips us for the ordeal,' said Vittoria, gazing back at Cressida but not attempting again to take her hand. 'We all have to die. We all have to kill.'

Presumably, that was true. Most people acted as if it were.

But it was when the Albanians in national costume began to sweep away the dead, dying, and mutilated birds that Cressida could accept no further argument. This time the Albanians were assisted by their wives and daughters, also in national costume, and carrying baskets.

Trifoglio was lending a hand too, throwing up the dead birds and catching them again, three or four of them in an endless, multi-coloured ring, a rainbow with all the hues in the wrong order.

Cressida rose discreetly and flitted through the curtains at her back.

She fell over something, and for a moment thought she'd be sick.

But it was only the cloak she had discarded because of the heat.

She no longer fancied it, and let it lie. She ran barefoot down the tapestried hall, in full retreat, until she came to Vivien at the top of the stairs in her heraldic dress.

CHAPTER FORTY-FIVE

Conditions at the Depôt

Thank goodness Vivien was still there: though, of course, the other and unknown herald was there also. Both were gazing glumly at the stuffed monsters on ebony, or mock ebony stands. The lighting had been considerably reduced. The need for economy was sometimes paramount.

Cressida threw her arms round Vivien.

'Oh, Vivien, it was horrible!'

Vivien tried to comfort her. 'What was horrible?'

Cressida did her best to explain, though she felt constrained by the other herald being only a few feet away.

The banquet was a distant hubbub through the thick curtains, and the monsters before them nuzzled and grazed no longer, but were menacingly silent.

'I've seen things here I don't like either,' said Vivien.

Cressida sought no details. The things must have been terrible for Vivien to speak like that.

'Cressy, where are your proper clothes?'

'Upstairs in Vittoria's bedroom. Where are yours?'

'At the caserna.'

'What's that?'

'It's the depôt. I'll show you.'

'Just at this moment, I only want to get away,' said Cressida.

'Put on your clothes then, and come back here,' said Vivien.

Cressida hesitated.

'Vivien, won't you come with me?'

Vivien hesitated.

'I'm supposed to be on duty until the end of the evening, but I don't think it matters very much. I don't think I'd have been told to do it, if it did.'

Cressida glanced at the other herald, who had stood totally motionless and noiseless, emitting neither a groan at Cressida's broken narration, nor even a personal hiccough: splendidly trained, in fact.

'What about—' enquired Cressida in a whisper and with a shift of her eyes.

'It's a dummy,' said Vivien bitterly. 'When women are given a job to do, it's with a dummy.'

Cressida stared at the imposing figure. 'Are you certain?'

'Have a go,' suggested Vivien.

But Cressida did not feel in the mood. In any case, she had been in doubt about the creature since first she had set eyes on it.

'Come up with me, *please*, Vivien. I'm afraid of Vittoria coming after me.'

'Don't you like Vittoria?'

'I do in some ways. She's wonderfully made.'

They were ascending the Scala Grande; trampling on more massacred innocents, dodging Herod, showing deference to the Queen of Italy.

'Vittoria runs the theatre, doesn't she?'

'And a lot of other things too. She's immensely able.'

'In what way?'

'She's supposed to be Vittore's sister.'

They entered the bedroom. There were four lamps burning beautifully.

'How did you first get in here?' asked Vivien.

'There was a disgusting scene in a play. Vittoria let me lie down because I felt ill.'

'You're becoming very fanciful, Cressy.'

'Do you think that different creatures fly about *every* dinnertime here?'

'I expect so. It's having all these men.'

'Why men, Vivien?'

'That's after a day at the caserna. It's like a brothel.'

'Don't be silly, Vivien. You don't know what a brothel's like.'

'Let me look at you, before you take it off.'

Cressida posed, tempting but enslaved. The lighting was almost perfect.

'How did you come to put it on?'

'Vittoria lent it me, just for this evening. It does something, Vivien.'

'I can see.'

Suddenly Cressida began to undress.

'Would you like to try it on yourself?'

'Too much fag getting all this off. I feel like the knave of hearts.'

'Of tarts, you mean,' giggled Cressida.

Vivien had walked over to the portrait and was examining it as closely as conditions permitted.

'There ought to be some kind of light for it,' said Cressida, beginning to look round semi-proprietarily.

'Never mind,' said Vivien. 'I can see.'

'I suppose there are more men than girls at that place you're talking about?'

'No, but Isolde lets men come in because the girls get so bored with nothing else to do. I don't think she can keep men out really. Most of the girls can't even read or write or make their beds.'

'Are they nice, all the same?' Cressida had often heard her great uncle say that illiterates were the nicest people, and often the cleverest too, when it came to the point.

'They're the most frightful little cats. You remember what Desirée said.'

So, as usual, *British* illiterates must be different.

Cressida shuddered. She doubted whether she would *ever* tell Vivien about Trifoglio's visit that afternoon.

'What are you all supposed to be doing?' she asked.

'We're standing by. We're not exactly at war, but every now and then there's one of those alarms and people get injured. The idea is to freeze us out without actually massacring all of us, which of course they easily could if they decided on it.'

'They can't hope to freeze us out in this weather, so perhaps they *will*?'

'It's been going on for more than a year now. Us versus The Rest. Isolde calls it a Battle of Nerves. I could do with more action. So could most of us.'

'It's quite nice here really, Vivien, when you've learnt to pick and choose.'

'Picking and choosing is not what I came for,' said Vivien petulantly.

'Well, you *are* under orders. You managed that. It's like me being a slave girl.'

'The only order I've been given was to stand about for hours in fancy dress.'

'They also serve—' began Cressida.

'And it's an order I'm now going to disobey,' interrupted Vivien.

'People like being told what to do in theory, but none of them like the orders actually given them.'

'Or people in theory hate being given orders, but are waiting to be told what to do for most of the time.'

'How sophisticated we have become, Vivien!'

A shadow crossed Cressida's lovely features.

'Let's go, Vivien. Hurry up!'

'I'm waiting for *you*,' said Vivien, tearing her gaze from the picture, almost without effort.

CHAPTER FORTY-SIX

Sight-Seeing

They couldn't well go out though the Banqueting Hall, where there was now only one herald on duty, so that they had to go out through the theatre.

There was no difficulty. Instead there was delight.

The auditorium was empty even of grumbling auxiliaries, the curtain was up, and there was a single dancer, in the whitest of tutus, going through her solitary motions in a state of trance. All utilitarian working irrelevancy had disappeared, and behind the dancer was a crenellated, pinnacled castle, palely lit.

'Stop,' whispered Vivien.

The two girls stole into a shadowed niche whence they could see everything.

'Only when she's alone can she dance like this.'

Cressida was awed both by the truth and by the simple words Vivien had found for it.

'Only when she's in the half-light.'

'Or the half-darkness.'

Cressida and Vivien linked hands.

'Other people spoil so much,' whispered Cressida, with the very lightest of sighs.

'Perfect solitude or perfect sympathy,' whispered Vivien.

'Who said that?'

'André Maurois.'

Of course they had both read *Ariel*, though with different results. Everyone had read *Ariel*.

Cressida and Vivien whispered nothing more, and it was hard to estimate how long they stayed.

The dancer had a face by Murillo and faint lights gleamed intermittently from her satin tunic. Her body was so soft that she no longer had boundaries. The movements of her arms, legs, and entirety drew towards, but then retreated from, the infinite.

Cressida and Vivien dissolved sympathetically. It was not so much that all their troubles had, even in illusion, ceased to exist; but rather that, while they watched the dancing, they stood outside them, above them, in a new dimension of being. Each almost forgot that she was holding the other's hand.

But in the end their legs began to ache. Without a word being whispered, they both became aware that it would be a mistake to linger until the dancing had actually ceased: better far to assume that it continued for ever.

Without need for words or gesture, as when birds wheel, Cressida and Vivien stepped out of the niche and crept from the theatre.

A high wind, heavy with wet, swept the piazza. Cressida looked surreptitiously towards the spot where Trifoglio had landed after he had leapt from Vittoria's window.

'Vittoria said there was going to be a storm. You could see it coming. I wish I had my mackintosh.'

'It's too frail for weather like this.'

'Better than nothing.'

'It's not actually raining yet. Let's run.'

Immediately, they ran into the priest with the gift of tongues, but Vivien refused to stop even for a moment, as Desirée had recommended. The priest was visibly prophesying, and there might have been much to be learned, especially as he did it in all languages at once, as normally happens only at Whitsun.

Cressida realised that Vivien's new experiences must be expected on occasion to translate her from the commanding to the headstrong.

They were running into an area of the town which Cressida had not previously visited. She had, in fact, entered such areas only in books, for example by Dumas; but now it was a case of she who runs may read.

The people were poorer, less healthy, more numerous. Some of them ventured upon what might well have been opprobrious comments upon Vivien's costume; probably, Cressida realised with a shock, upon hers also. The females here wore loosely knitted black shawls, skirts to the ankles, and babies at the breast, often several at a time, so that one wondered how their arms managed to hold them all.

'I'm panting,' gasped Cressida.

'All right. Let's walk. We're nearly there.'

'How can you *tell*? I'm lost.'

'Cressy, you *are* growing soft.'

Cressida blushed. But she had been unfed since her lunch-time tray, except for a small spoonful or two of purée.

'Better not walk too slowly,' said Vivien.

Cressida could see that for herself. Males of all ages were beginning to sidle, just as if they had not, for the most part, wives already, let alone wives with multiple infants at suck.

'No, we mustn't loiter.'

'Nor let them think we're afraid of them.'

'I'm sure they imagined we were running away.'

'I hadn't thought of that.'

In the teeth of all prudence, Vivien perceptibly slowed a little.

'We mustn't let them think we're leading them on,' said Cressida.

After all, the two of them in their different ways must look vastly different from what men were used to, and it was well known that men were always avid for new experiences, hence Magellan and Drake and Isaac Newton with his apple, and Captain Scott with his Pole, and Debroy Somers with his Orpheans, as on the ceiling.

'What a bore all this is!' muttered Vivien.

'It's much better to be a woman than a man,' Cressida reminded her.

There was a crash and a scream. A young nursing mother had been hurled out of a window by her spouse, who then stood, wearing only a dirty vest in the aperture, and continued to rail at her, conceivably in Serbo-Croat. It was just as well that it had been only a first-floor window, and that the ground floor rooms were so low.

Cressida happened to notice the name of the narrow street where gaslight fell on it: Via Funebre.

'Do you think we ought to help?'

'No', said Vivien.

And indeed, a thick, black, noisy crowd had instantly clotted round the presumably damaged woman, and was fattening momentarily.

At the same time, the first drop of what Vivien had called actual rain, fell on the very apex of Cressida's head; on the cavity where her third eye had once been.

'We're there!' cried Vivien, pointing.

It was a long, stone building of four storeys, with many windows, rectangular, identical, and dirty. Sentries in various uniforms were pacing up and down the roof with long muskets. Of course the rain, heavy though it was, had only just started.

'Why aren't the sentries at the door, like Buckingham Palace or the Tower?'

'There's too much coming and going,' explained Vivien.

And, in fact, as she spoke, Harry Crass strolled out in his seaman's rig. He looked completely relaxed, but then became aware of the rain.

'Oh, Christ-in-Hades,' said Harry Crass.

Then he recognised the girls as they were going in.

'Do you two work here? That's nice.' But he seemed surprised. 'Guess I'll be coming back.'

'You wait, Cressy,' said Vivien as soon as they were inside. 'Don't wander away. I'll be very quick.'

She left no time for Cressida to argue. She went straight ahead and up some stairs.

The room extended an equal distance to the right and to the left. Girls and women in assorted military costume were sitting about and lying about; some of them on broken chairs, but a larger number on the stone floor. Cressida assumed that they were waiting for orders. It was true that, as Vivien had said, few

273

of them seemed to have any present occupation. The scene was very picturesquely lighted with lamps and candles. Every now and then, a man either descended the stairs up which Vivien had disappeared, or emerged from a door at one or the other end of the apartment.

All the men whom Cressida saw departed without ado, without asking to be excused as they swept past her, without saying Adieu to a soul. They made a mixed company, but every single one of them swore as he encountered the weather in the streets. Cressida was at a promising starting point for the compiler of an all-language dictionary of colloquialisms: *Popular Swearwords of the World*, in twenty-six illustrated parts.

She felt that she was unduly conspicuous as she stood there by the door, but no one, male or female, seemed to take the slightest notice of her, and indeed her aspect was restrained and mousy when compared with that of the exotics strewn about within.

What could Vivien be doing? Was she all right? How ought Cressida to act if another twenty minutes passed without Vivien re-appearing?

Cressida wished there was a seat. She was finding it more and more impossible to dispose her limbs. She knew how difficult it was for a beautiful young woman in trousers to stand about without looking alluring. On the other hand, the problem was unlikely to be solved by her sitting on the floor, as so many of the others were doing. Moreover, she had been repeatedly warned of the nasty malady one contracted if one seated oneself on any kind of cold stone.

There had been a number of departures, but now there was an arrival. Good heavens! It was Cavaliere Terridge, soaking wet. What a relief! And Eno came in behind him; wetter still, as duty bid.

The Cavaliere seemed even more pleased than Cressida, because he blushed the colour of a rotten tomato. Cressida had never seen a blush on the features of a grown man, and felt quite warmly towards him.

'Well!' said the Cavaliere.

'Well!' said Cressida demurely.

'I just looked in,' said the Cavaliere.

'I'm waiting for Vivien,' said Cressida.

'*Really!*' said the Cavaliere. He seemed more surprised than ever.

'She's just putting on her clothes.'

'Upstairs?'

Cressida nodded. 'Up there.' She pointed to the staircase.

'Have you been up there yourself?'

'Vivien told me not to.'

'Quite right.'

'She's been gone more than half an hour.'

'Some people will hang on so.'

'Vivien says that no one here has enough to do.'

But the Cavaliere's mien was growing ever more shifty. Suddenly he made a gesture, at once sweeping and command-ing, as one does to a fox terrier when one has at last got him to the Recreation Ground. Eno scuttled across the room and darted out of sight up the staircase, as Vivien had done. Plainly, it was an errand.

'And what are *you* doing?' enquired the Cavaliere politely. 'I mean if your friend is working here?'

'I'm working in the theatre,' said Cressida, proudly, as the occasion seemed to dictate.

'I suppose that's much the same when it comes to it,' said the Cavaliere reflectively.

'Vivien's very keen on our doing something serious.'

'I used to be mad about Gilbert and Sullivan,' said the Cavaliere.

'Daddy's like that. He can hum all the tunes, though of course he can't remember the words.'

'The moan of a merry man moping mum, his step was sad and his glance was glum, he sobbed all day and he soaked up rum, and all because of a lady.'

One of the women took off her tunic and proved to have nothing on underneath except a mass of hair which was turning grey round the edges, though she could hardly have been much more than fifty.

The Cavaliere looked like a tomato once more.

'You really oughtn't to be here, you know,' he said with an entirely new firmness.

'It's very hot in here,' said Cressida deprecatingly. 'Especially now that it's turned so cold and wet outside.'

'This is a place for men only,' said the Cavaliere, with nearly the same firmness.

'Don't be silly,' said Cressida. 'There's not a man in sight. Apart from you, of course. They're only dressed up rather like men. It does something.'

The Cavaliere was aghast. 'You're not supposed to know things like that,' he said. He was really quite indignant with Cressida.

A young girl did the same, then another, the latter a very young girl indeed: third form, Cressida would have said under other circumstances.

It was a working model of Fashion's power: one female after another blindly following.

The Cavaliere's eyes rolled as they migrated from the very young girl to Cressida and back to the very young girl and back again to Cressida.

The Cavaliere eyed Cressida before speaking further to her. His intention was to evince unshakable will; directed to some aspect of the situation. The expression on the two sides of his face was quite different.

In the end, the words burst out, as if they were alive.

'You're much too sweet to be in a place like this. I think I'd better speak to your aunt.'

'She's not really my aunt, you know.'

'Oh God,' said the Cavaliere, utterly revolted.

By now, half the women in the room had done it. The more attractive girls were wearing all kinds of things underneath. It was rather like an illustrated catalogue. Cressida had to remember that it took all sorts to comprise even a paramilitary force.

'She's my *friend's* aunt.'

'And your friend's upstairs!' responded the Cavaliere in a last extremity of bitterness.

Eno came scuttling down again, nodding decisively. He stood in front of the Cavaliere, still nodding.

Cressida noticed that he seemed to have no eyes for the changed scene around them.

'Sufficient unto oneself is the evil thereof.' She quoted inside her head, because there was no one present who seemed likely to love literature as she did.

But, honestly, what *was* Vivien up to?

Suddenly Cressida knew the answer, knew it by intuition: Vivien was arguing about something.

The Cavaliere had stopped Eno nodding, as one does with a Chinese figure; and Eno just stood there like a newt, interested in none of the gorgeousness on the floor, but merely awaiting the next event. It was the secret of happiness; Cressida knew that.

The women were taking off more and more. Sometimes there is no limit to the demands of the mode.

Only a bigot could deny the loveliness of much that was on view, evanescent though it must be, embellished though it already was.

The Cavaliere snapped like one of the thinner sticks of Mablethorpe rock. After a scorching perusal of Cressida—desire fighting on all too equal terms with disapprobation—he snatched at Eno's collar and propelled the two of them into the tempest outside, the original purpose of his visit to the caserna forgotten.

The rough handling of a subordinate proved him to be all but unmanned.

Cressida, deprived of compatriot companionship, felt more and more out of place, out of her depth. She resolved to go up after Vivien, despite the unnamed perils.

Vivien might even be at risk. Besides, Cressida felt curious.

CHAPTER FORTY-SEVEN

The Professor

But Vivien appeared round the turn of the staircase and dragged Cressida back down again. Vivien was once more in her clothes from the garment store.

'I've given in my resignation,' said Vivien.

'Yes, it's far too hot in here for work.'

'It's that woman, Isolde,' said Vivien fiercely.

'You've been arguing with her for hours.'

'Foreign women use more words than we do. Let's go, Cressy.'

It could not be said that either of them was particularly successful at getting on with her employer or even at remaining within her place of employment.

However, Cressida, reassured of Vivien's safe return, could hardly tear her eyes or herself away from the fascinating scene. She felt it was a scene that might not recur in her life very often, even if she were to live to be as old as poor Miss Waddon, who had long been over ninety-five.

'It's not even up to the standard of the Guides,' said Vivien. 'It's more like a baby show.'

'Whatever *becomes* of the babies?'

Instantly Cressida feared for what the answer might be: all those heavy sacks that impeded navigation through the Bosphorus.

But Vivien only replied, 'Aunt Agnes gets them.'

'How many are there?'

'The Infirmary's full of them. They're almost the only patients now. The smell's frightful.'

'No wonder Lady Luce has to get away sometimes.'

'Oh, there are Macedonians to do the work.'

'Some speak of Alexander,' said Cressida.

But a perfectly enormous man was lumbering down the stairs and, as far as Cressida could see, accosting the two of them.

'He's a professor of some kind,' said Vivien. 'He's gaga.'

'Hullo, boys,' yelled the Professor cheerily. His height was as excessive as his bulk; and his bald head was most excessive of all. Visibly a virtuoso.

'He kept calling me Boy upstairs,' said Vivien. 'He's in business of some kind with Isolde. He's bonkers.'

The Professor threw his arm round Vivien's shoulders, before anyone could stop him. It nearly went twice round, like an anaconda.

'And who's this?' enquired the Professor. 'Present your friend to me, come on.'

'This is Cressy,' said Vivien under duress.

The Professor's other arm circumambulated Cressida.

She did realise that it had been her inability to tear away her eyes which was responsible for the two of them being thus enwrapped.

Moreover, Cressida might have said he was a cockney if he hadn't been a Professor.

'Who are you?' asked Cressida.

'I'm Colossi from Rome.'

'Then you're here to run the theatre?'

'You may say so.'

'I'm one of your staff.'

'Which one?' The Professor bellowed with laughter.

'I'm only a beginner.' The Professor bellowed again.

'This is no place for beginners. Come to my house.'

'It's raining,' said Vivien.

'It's opposite,' said the Professor.

Standing upright was nearly impossible, however narrow the street. The gaslights had all blown out long ago, so that mass asphyxiation was likely, as soon as conditions eased. Water lapped around Cressida's ankles. Even in the short time taken to cross the street, she heard the crash of a falling house.

The Professor opened the picturesque front door with a kick.

Two slim figures in black sank pleasingly to the floor as they all entered.

'My pupils,' said the Professor.

Everything was very original. Cressida was reminded of Vittore's house in Paris, as described by Aunt Agnes.

'Did Vittore design all this?'

'——,' said the Professor, in some language or other.

It was the second criticism of Vittore that Cressida had heard.

'Take everything off,' commanded the Professor.

'We're all right,' said Vivien, 'except for our socks.'

Cressida rejoiced in Vivien's presence of mind, though of course she might have expected it. To strew wet clothes across these exquisite silks would indeed have been unaesthetic. Even the carpets were silky: the spoils of Cathay, of Cardinal and

Harford. Besides Cressida was tired of taking off and putting on clothes.

'This place belonged to a maniac,' explained the Professor. 'It's inhuman. Come in here.'

There were two big tin beds; a small desk in imitation wood, badly chipped; a hard chair standing at the desk; a single sad green light.

'I sleep there,' explained the Professor, pointing.

And indeed, one could see the bulge.

'My pupils sleep there.' He indicated the other bed, which had no bulge.

It was interesting to learn how other people lived, as Cressida had so often overheard.

'The man used this room as his dungeon. Countless people died here, many of them guests.'

'What happened to the bodies?' asked Vivien in her sceptical way.

'He ate them. Him and his cats. He had more than forty cats in one of the rooms upstairs. Would you like to see the marks?'

'I think we ought to dry our socks first,' said Vivien.

Cressida could see that dry socks would be better than nothing, since the weather prevented their making their way home, as she would greatly have preferred.

'Go on, boys. Do whatever it is you want to do.'

There was a fearful clap of thunder.

Cressida and Vivien sat side by side upon the second bed, removing their wet shoes and socks.

As soon as she was seated, Cressida felt extremely wet all over. She hoped they would not leave pools on the bedding.

'The Austrians got him in the end, and he was rended.'

'That sounds unpleasant,' said Vivien.

'You have to be cruel if you wish to be kind,' said the Professor.

'Did Vittore say that?' asked Cressida.

'——,' said the Professor; and this time in perfectly clear English. Cressida had not previously heard the expression except, as we know, in a dream.

Cressida and Vivien raised their eyes from their wet feet.

'Do you come from London?' they asked in chorus.

'I was dumped as a kid,' said the Professor. 'I started in the Yiddish Theatre, the Palais we called it, and worked up, until now I'm the greatest theatre artist in the world.'

'I know you are,' said Cressida. 'Desirée told me.'

'The boy who gives Vittore his dope and all that?'

'I expect so. Desirée's his secretary. But she's not a boy.'

'You're all boys,' said the Professor.

It would, of course, have been simply absurd to argue.

It was thundering all the time now. The weather was becoming worse and worse, as Vittoria had predicted.

Another trouble was that once more Cressida's bare feet were very cold indeed, even though they were an inch or two above the cold floor.

'Why are you a Professor?' asked Vivien, in order to continue the conversation.

'I'm Professor of Applied Dramaturgy and Playhouse Administration in seven universities, if you count the one we all know about.'

'How can you give all those lectures and do your work at the same time?'

'I delegate. That's what administration is. That's what life is. That's what success is.'

Cressida and Vivien looked as impressed as their chilly feet permitted.

'What's your real name?' asked Vivien.

'Cohen,' said the Professor, quite without display. 'It means king.'

Cressida had not known it meant that, but there were very few Cohens in Rutland.

'I'll tell my pupils to give you their shoes and to cook us some salt meat.'

There was simply no alternative other than death by drowning and thunderball.

'Thank you,' said the girls in unison, suppressing all thought for the pupils, let along for the morrow.

'You don't mind kosher?'

'I don't think we know,' said Cressida.

'Then you'll know soon. Wait there.'

He lumbered out.

Cressida looked at Vivien, and Vivien looked at Cressida. Again, there was nothing else for them to do.

The Professor came back with a pair of ropey sandals in each hand. Without being firm enough to keep their shape or the foot's shape, they were not yielding enough to be comfortable. They were such as are to be seen on such as the pupils. The girls gratefully made the best of them, though they were spiky without socks.

The Professor himself had discarded his wet suit and indeed his wet shirt, and over a thick carmine vest, possibly a liturgical garment, now wore a mantle in many colours, as of a patchwork monk.

'You've changed very quickly,' said Cressida.

'I'm the greatest at everything. You know that.'

But Cressida was reflecting that she was seeing quite enough of men in their vests. Even girls did not always look their brightest in their vests, though perhaps a few did.

'Come up and I'll play to you while you're waiting.'

The girls followed him back into the highly decorated part of the house. There were peacock feathers, and spirit reproductions of Fra Angelico, and shrunken heads on shelves.

'Why do you go to bed in the dungeon?' asked Cressida.

'I'd lie out in the street if I could. The gutter.'

'Why can't you?' asked Vivien.

'Don't be silly, Vivien. Look at the weather,' Cressida pointed out.

'There's nothing in this house that's mine except what you've seen,' said the Professor. 'I'm a hermit crab compelled to live in a shell full of pearls.'

Cressida reflected that there was indeed something of the crab about him; one of those enormous dressed crabs she had seen in coloured illustrations of lovely City dinners. Her mind was returning again and again to food.

In the room where the piano was were also perfect chairs of the kind one associates with Madame de Maintenon: so hard inside as to be quite inconsistent with use, let alone enjoyment.

The piano, a modest half-grand, was inlaid with teeth, and toenails, and strangely preserved eyes. Hair hung from its edges. Plainly it had been created by the house's previous tenant.

The Professor opened the keyboard. The keys were very indelicate.

The Professor lifted the lid and a carnival head shot up in place of the usual stay. The expression was almost obscenely lifelike, though the eyes had crossed with disuse.

The Professor played dreamily: without sheets of music and, one would have said, without conscious thought, conscious expression, conscious exertion.

The girls were soon slipping unobtrusively from the hard chairs on to the hard, but at least level, floor. Moreover, there were furry skins of animals strewn about. Cressida did not like sitting on skins from real animals, all dead; but there it was. At least the skins had probably been disinfected of parasites; so often the problem with living beasts of all types.

The crumpling roar in the sky confirmed the prudence of indoors.

Cressida identified one of the pieces. It was by Chaminade, but she herself could once have played it far more accurately, though not now, as she had given up music when she and Vivien decided to concentrate on literature. It was called 'Moments'. Once it had been among her very favourites.

Other composers represented were Chopin (inevitably), Mr Irving Berlin (irregularly), Isidore de Lara (ingeniously), Stephen Foster, and Amy Woodforde-Finden. Sometimes the Professor played loudly, sometimes softly, assisting these effects by the use of the pedals; sometimes slowly, sometimes rapidly. The variety was immense. There was something for everyone, if everyone had been present.

One trouble about sitting on the floor was that Cressida had become aware of further eyes on and around the ceiling. The ceiling was a composition of finest plaster from the dix-huitième siècle; la douceur de vivre, however far from either Trianon.

By now the eyes on the piano itself were actually glowing.

The thunder rolled drearily on, even though the lightning was kept out by the straggling French curtains, hung before windows doubtless equally French. The curtains seemed to be made of faded dresses cunningly tacked together.

Vivien, as a matter of fact, was quite plainly in full slumber. It seemed to be happening again and again: extraordinary how she had changed!

'La cena!' shrilled the two pupils, bobbing in, and speaking as one, much as Cressida and Vivien had done earlier.

The Professor stopped in the middle of a bar, indeed in the middle of a chord.

'Talk English,' he commanded.

The pupils dropped their heads penitently. They wore black tights, an ideal costume for work; but of course their feet were blue.

The Professor rose, the girls rose, and they all surged into the Sala da Pranzo, which was at the back of the house, where the Salon de Musique was at the front.

'Roger and Sam,' said the Professor. 'Percy and Victor.'

Of course, the sweet little shapes of the two pupils were totally inconclusive. It was something that one of them was not called Brian. Or both.

Anxiety was reawakened by the embellishment of the Salon with paintings by Wouwermans and bronzes by Barye. Cressida was glad that the forthcoming baked meats were to be distanced by salting and koshering, whatever that latter process might in modern times amount to. Some of Barye's creatures, though smaller and tighter, were worse than any she had seen in the Hall of Monsters.

While they all stood reverently, the Professor spoke grace before meat, in Yiddish. Cressida thought he looked exactly like Solomon in the Temple. It was much more theological than at home or school.

First, they ate rather hard fish. Then they ate rather hard meat.

Of course there were supply difficulties. One sometimes tended to forget that.

With the meat came botanical products, fibrous and flavourless, one pale yellowy-grey, another pale greeny-blue; all noticeably fresh, as if just gathered at a Holman Hunt roadside. There was also melted kosher butter to put on things: at least Cressida was sure it must be kosher.

People said it was nice to eat at home sometimes.

Vivien, though she was now awake, was silent.

The pupils brought things in and dispensed them; unvociferously and unassumingly, as befitted.

There was thin wine, which also somehow brought back Holy Writ. It was light red in colour, like ichor. It was presented in a decanter which had possibly belonged to the former tenant, as it was of shape not to be put into words after one had considered it closely. Cressida almost blushed after considering it closely, but was checked by the wearisome thunder, which kept her continuously pallid.

'Isn't that Madame Dubarry?' enquired Vivien, rallying, when the coffee was brought in. She was referring to an illustration on the side of the pot.

'Poor boy! He ended by losing his head and things,' said the Professor.

'Wasn't it because she tried to do someone a good turn?' said Vivien, showing off a little.

'An eye for an eye and a tooth for a tooth,' said the Professor.

For Cressida's taste, there were too many eyes and teeth in the house already.

The pupils had been encouraged to sit down with them for coffee and to drink it out of the Pompadour-de-la-Vallière-Dubarry cups that everyone was using, but almost as soon as they were settled, their mentor had them on their feet again looking for the former tenant's liqueur.

'He made it out of snake-venom. Antidoted, of course. A bit different from the Old Kent Road all the same.'

In the end, it was found, but everyone declined, even the Professor himself, who called simplicity in aid once more. It looked grey and cloudy: as if it had gone bad.

'Vittore's always talking about the importance of things like austerity and agony,' said Cressida, 'and how much they do for all of us. Is that why you've come here?'

It was a question that puzzled her in so many cases.

'Nothing so fancy, boy,' said the Professor. 'I was on the run. Most of the folk here are on the run, when you know.'

Really: almost every hour one encountered a new view of the same situation!

'This place is regulated according to the laws of music,' said the Professor.

'Yes, we *know*,' said Cressida.

'Make hay while the sun shines shall be the word of the law,' said the Professor with extreme inaccuracy.

'Or even the moon,' said Vivien, breaking her long silence.

Chapter Forty-Eight

Walking on the Water

They were back in the Salon de Musique.

Probably the pupils were washing up. Their contribution to the evening had so far been entirely practical. Because they were unable to speak English, they had very sensibly said nothing. Silence in a foreign language can be especially golden!

There could be no doubt about the advantage to any sensitive household of two pupils as neat and unobtrusive as these were.

'I'll sing to you,' said the Professor. 'Can either or both of you play well enough to accompany me?'

'I can play a little,' said Cressida, 'but not well enough for that.'

'I've got cramp,' said Vivien.

'Then I shall have to accompany myself,' said the Professor.

He sat down, tinkled away, and bawled out several songs, not all of them closely related to the accompaniment. They included 'Rock'd in the Cradle of the Deep', 'There Be None of Beauty's Daughters', which he had to give up because he had temporarily forgotten the words, 'On with the Motley' more or less in Fred Weatherly's translation, 'Dreamland Faces', and 'Roses of Picardy'. The last made him cry so much that the excess fluid penetrated his bronchi and he modified to quadruple pianissimo, like Richard Tauber.

'I'm sorry, boys. We used to sing it in the rest huts and then there would be a Hun surprise of some kind and only the song was left.'

There is poetry in everyone, Cressida remembered.

Vivien merely looked perverse. However, this made her jaw-line even more classical.

'I'll tell you what I'll do,' said the Professor. 'I'll paint your portraits. The studio's upstairs.'

Cressida knew that when one is being entertained, one has to adapt oneself continually.

Now they could see lightning, because the studio had a north light, a west light, and a top light, which made it coldest of all. Not that Cressida and Vivien cared about cold, of course. Tentative endeavours of the former owner were propped against the walls: here a 'Fleurs Mortes', there a severed head on a plate, beyond it the uncompleted likeness of a swarthy Zouave.

There was a stretched canvas already on the easel lest inspiration strike someone suddenly. The easel had curiously monstrous feet, at which it was best for the sitter not to look.

Opportunely, the model throne could accommodate two: something Cressida had not seen before, though she had once taken an art course for several weeks in Kettering, at the suggestion of her uncle, who had unexpectedly wanted the run of his house.

'Sit down,' said the Professor. 'Together.'

He picked up an immense palette and a very long brush. In his patchwork robe, he looked much as Rembrandt must have looked when painting pictures of Saul and David. He had exactly the same hair difficulty as had Rembrandt, especially after he went bankrupt.

'Look at one another,' said the Professor testily.

The throne had a scarlet back and arms and a wicker seat on which it would have been difficult to sit in a short skirt, as the wicker was springing round the edges.

Cressida and Vivien disposed themselves, one over each red arm, and gazed at one another with determination.

Cressida was quite upset by what she saw. Disillusionment, she fancied: again as in Rembrandt. Oh dear, what could she do for Vivien, whose expectation was always intense in the degree that it was imprecise? If only she could find more time to work on her novel! The imagination provides the only outlet for so activist a temperament as Vivien's.

'I really ought to be roughing out something for *Die Jungfrau von Orleans* in Anvers,' said the Professor.

'Who wrote that?' enquired Cressida, without looking away from Vivien.

'Schiller did,' said Vivien, without looking away from Cressida.

The Professor, who was painting away like a maniac, looked up for a second and appeared to take in what Vivien had said.

'It's the usual stuff about a woman being done for,' amplified Vivien. 'She's burnt up in the end. Schiller wrote another play about Mary, Queen of Scots.'

'Mary, Queen of Scots had her head cut off at Fotheringhay,' said Cressida. 'We used to go there every Whit Sunday for a picnic. I don't think I told you. Daddy always loved it.'

'Whatever you do is wrong. Edith Cavell was shot for doing nursing. Served her right too.'

'Vivien! What about your Aunt Agnes?'

'She just thinks Vittore likes the costume.'

'I don't believe Vittore exists. I'm going to watch for him exposing himself tomorrow with Desirée's Austrian field glasses. I don't believe I shall see a thing.'

'——,' ejaculated the Professor from force of habit.

It had been impossible even to imagine that anyone could paint so fast. Already Cressida and Vivien, had they looked away from one another, could have seen themselves one on each side of the canvas; which the Professor had begun by shifting from the vertical to the horizontal for that precise purpose. Moreover, he was making rapid progress also with the view of Amalfi in the background; with the ocelot in the foreground, sleek and winsome; and with a dense tangle of bougainvilleas and passion-flower surrounding all, in order to give atmosphere. Really, he must remember to leave room for his signature! Architects readily forget even the staircase.

The rain was lashing down on the top light, which was oozing in several places. Against the north light the lightning was hurling itself like the frustrated Rothbart in the Ballets Russes. Every now and then the floor gave a faint seismographic heave, so that Cressida had to repress a tiny scream, and the Professor to steady himself with his other hand. Cressida had never seen such weather, as her mother said on six or eight occasions each year, especially during the school holidays.

For much of the time, it was almost daylight; which was just as well, since even the Professor might have found difficulty in painting two portraits by no more than that number of oil lamps, picturesque though they were.

'Finito!' exclaimed the Professor, and threw his long brush on the floor, as Rubens latterly did before resuming work at the next easel but one, each lined out in gold-leaf that was real, there being at that time no alternative to what was real on the market.

Had the Professor really completed the picture? But, then, had Rubens? Much must, perforce, be left to pupils.

'Ah, bello ritratto dei due ragazzi bellissimi e fragranti!' exclaimed the Professor. 'Not bad, is it?'

Cressida and Vivien tried to look away from one another and to step down from the throne.

By the next lightning-flash, which came in an instant, they examined their likenesses.

Ragazzi, indeed: perhaps some elements of likeness, if one were charitable, as the English nowadays are to portrait painters, but truly not very much. On the other hand, it was hard to be sure that Amalfi looked much like that either, when one had not yet been there; or that the verisimilitude of the abundant passion-flowers could be assessed when one was so unparticularised about passion.

Cressida thought that possibly their soft mouths, damask cheeks, chic and fashionable coiffures, and open expressions had been captured up to a point.

'Do you know many great painters?' she asked the Professor.

'All of them. Without exception.'

'Where were you trained?' asked Vivien.

'On the pavement, boy. You learn not to be afraid of your colours. I write poems too. Long poems.

294

'When the Trojan Horse is neighing,
Drink deep and damn the cost.
When the Hounds of Fate are baying,
Think that Love is best when lost.
When your chair is pulled from under,
There's nowhere like the floor.
When the Gods begin to thunder,
Just try and reach the door!

'There's hundreds of lines of it, maybe thousands. All philosophical. All based on what I've seen of life. It pours out of me like piss. They can hardly get it down fast enough.'

'It's the writing down that's the difficult part,' confirmed Vivien.

'I can do anything,' screamed the Professor, 'just anything. I'm amazing.'

He stared at Vivien by the lightning flashes. 'Here, wait a moment. I haven't quite caught the look in your eye.' He commanded Vivien back to the throne and picked up another brush.

But what Cressida was thinking on the sudden was how like to the Professor Vittore must be: the same almost universal talent; the same masterful though unassuming manner; even, she supposed, the same dismissive attitude to the perennial problem of boy or girl, and, if so, which? At all points, the Professor was a splurged image of the unique concentrate: a fifth carbon copy, as Cressida might have put it if she had been learning to type.

Perhaps it was now less than urgent for her to behold Vittore himself; which might be just as well.

Vivien was declining to sit any longer.

'We really must go,' she said. 'They're expecting us. Would you please lend us something that will keep out the rain?'

'And the lightning,' added Cressida anxiously, though falling into line. It had, of course, been a brainwave that was characteristic of Vivien.

It proved that the former tenant had a whole cupboard full of things like that. He had hung them in rows from hangers, as a fashionable woman hangs evening dresses.

Cressida and Vivien each found a garment suitable for the deer forests on a typically foul day: and each drew on boots suitable for freshwater fishing in conditions of flood. Cressida had never before seen so many boots in a private house. Could the weather here be worse than at home? However, the accumulation suggested that shooting and fishing had their justifications after all, at least for selfish humanity!

The Professor was offering to sing to them again, or to show them how to make paper flowers, but Vivien was firm as a rock, and here they were in the hurricane. They had not even said Goodbye to the pupils, who by now were probably studying once more.

Though the caserna opposite still had a light in every window, the sentinels on the roof had long before taken shelter, so that one would hardly have thought it was a military establishment at all. It looked more like a church indulging in Midnight Mass at the wrong season: a lone beacon through the darkness and the storm.

By now the water was positively swirling down the street, carrying with it quite heavy objects such as cradles and coffins, lifebelts and artificial limbs, which it behoved the pedestrian to dodge. It was hard to decide whether mankind's detritus was being swept out to sea, or whether the sea was unloading its spoils on to the city authorities, whether the circumambient waters were poisonously salt or just ordinarily polluted. Probably they were both, in that at such times the rivers mingle quite indistinguishably with the oceans. Every now and then, the lightning knocked off a chimney pot or chimney stack, already hanging by a thread. The people were huddled in upstairs rooms, united in family prayer.

The girls ploughed forward through the shin-high water more and more exhilarated, despite Cressida's reservations about the thunder and lightning. Never before in their lives had either of them been so near to reality, but at the same time so shielded from it in their boots and burberries.

'The ghosts do sheet and gibber through the Roman streets,' remarked Vivien.

'Are you going back to that monkey-house tomorrow?'

'No, I've quarrelled with Isolde. She's horrible. Are you going back to the theatre?'

'I'm not sure. I can't make up my mind about Vittoria.'

'We're not cut out for subordinate positions,' said Vivien.

'I think it's even worse having to run things.'

Cressida had already mused on the several people she had already met who were running things. Could any of them be described as buoyant?

'Perhaps we ought to be shepherdesses in pretty rags?' suggested Vivien.

'And far from the madding crowd.'

'And the sky the limit.'

'And not too many sheep.'

'We'd need enough sheep to keep us in clothes and books.'

'Sheep get horrible diseases, Vivien. Bronchitis every winter, and foot-rot every summer. They're only sweet when they're very young and agile.'

'Rather like us,' said Vivien gloomily.

'Oh, I don't know. Look at Aunt Agnes.'

'I'm not sure I wouldn't rather look at a sheep.'

Cressida realised that there might have been elements last night which were disillusioning to a relative. None the less, she was resolved to hold firmly, though silently, to her ideal.

In the piazza, small waves were breaking against the cathedral steps, wearing small holes in them.

'Suppose it goes on for forty nights and forty days?'

'It won't, Cressy. Make the best of it while it lasts.'

CHAPTER FORTY-NINE

The Anthem

There was a light in some upstairs windows to the right; one of which might well have been that from which Trifoglio had descended. Probably Vittoria had accepted a period of peace in which to do accounts.

So far they had seen no one.

But now a commotion was approaching down the street which led to the town gate and to their abode.

'It's a ship!' cried Vivien. 'It must have sailed in from the sea.'

'No,' corrected Cressida. 'From the Public Garden. Vittore has a whole fleet there apparently, as well as some aeroplanes and camels.'

Round the bend it came, and proudly into the piazza. It bore port, starboard, and masthead lights, in confident compliance with international law. Fundamentally, however, and though camouflaged and militarised up to the nines, it was but a very small and quite obsolete armoured launch, adapted at best to use by customs officials in a secondary locality.

'Look out for the wash!' cried Vivien. 'It might come over the top of our boots.'

The two girls dashed for safety up the cathedral steps. The way things were going, even the level area at the top could hardly be guaranteed as a refuge.

The thudding of the vessel's engine was as irregular as that of an old and broken heart.

'They're quite good at navigation!' cried Cressida impulsively.

As so often when that is said, she had reason to modify her belief almost immediately.

It had become apparent to whoever was responsible that the street along which the girls had just waded was too narrow to pass a vessel of that beam without sweeping away ornamental balconies and flowerpots, in so far as any of the latter were still in position at this phase of the storm.

There was a big blaze of lightning; projection, perhaps, of the steersman's objurgation. One thing the lightning did was dowse the masthead lamp, so that, on top of everything else, the ship was now in breach of the maritime code.

The engine went into compulsive reverse, generating a diffuse and formless tidal wave which bumped round the piazza, to say nothing of the adjoining streets, and duly washed over the pavement at the cathedral doors, swilling beneath them into the sacred structure, but mercifully not rising so high as to fill the girls' boots.

'Men in boats always carry on like that,' commented Vivien, from experience with her father in more than one continent.

'Whoever are they?' asked Cressida.

All she had been able to pick out during the seconds of brilliance had been Trifoglio flittering around the deck and mast, but palpably contributing nothing. Most of the other Argonauts were doubtless under hatches. And now there was, as for most of the time, almost no visibility at all.

'The outside world, I should say,' vaticinated Vivien.

The ship grated on the bottom and juddered to paralysis. It must have struck some object of beauty or utility (though in this land the two were hardly to be differentiated) on the lustrous floor of the piazza. Probably this was just as well, since the ship was plainly out of control and might well have broken open the theatre box-office (to use the English term), or spattered seaweed before the high altar.

There was silence; apart from the inevitable cursing below decks and in the wheelhouse; apart from the slate-pencil peepings of Trifoglio.

Nothing came to the girls' ears of the solid and competitive jocularity which normally attends occurrences of this kind.

That, however, was explained by what happened next; and all, it could hardly be doubted, within a matter of seconds.

From within the hull came a unified eerie anthem. Muffled though it was, all hands must have been mustered for the music; most mournful through the murk.

Despite the almost total darkness, Cressida could see that Vivien's face was white.

She clutched Vivien's arm.

'What is it?' she gasped.

'It's the *Internationale*,' Vivien murmured. 'I heard it with Daddy in Nicosia.'

CHAPTER FIFTY

A Further Augury

They heard the anthem through to the end.

'It's not very inspiring,' commented Cressida.

'I don't think it's meant to be,' said Vivien. 'It's more that it's inevitable.'

All was now silent aboard the mysterious vessel. No one had even seen fit to hoist the I'm Aground signal. Little waves splashed miserably against the hull.

'Won't they rape and then murder people like us?'

'I expect they're up to something.'

'People like that are up to something the whole time, Daddy says.'

'We ought to be up to something too,' said Vivien. 'But we're not.'

By this time Cressida did see what Vivien meant when she said things like that.

'Oughtn't we to be running away before they come out?'

'We can't run, Cressy. The water's too deep.'

'Then let's just go. Why wait to be raped? It's horrid.' But of course, Vivien didn't really know that, not as well as she did.

Suddenly, Trifoglio slid, like a fireman, down one of the pillars that supported the cathedral porch; but this time there was a curious gleam around his head, as of a halo. It glinted through the surrounding gloom.

It was impossible to see what he was about. Cressida despised Trifoglio and his tricks, but it was necessary to be alert.

In the darkness, Trifoglio spoke. 'Beware,' he said in his underground voice. His usual thing.

Vivien took a step towards the sound, and Cressida thought that she should go too.

Then Cressida realised. Trifoglio was squatting there with a knife in his mouth.

'Look out, Vivien,' she cried. 'He's foul.'

'I'm Jack the Ripper,' said Trifoglio, as if from his sewer.

Cressida was nothing less than astonished by Vivien. Vivien had said nothing but she had made a single, quite casual plunge, and the knife was in her hand.

There was a tremendous rumble and flash, and Vivien was revealed standing histrionically with the knife in one outstretched hand, rather like the figure at the summit of the Central Criminal Court, though far from blindfold.

'We'll keep it,' said Vivien. 'Now let's go, as you say.'

They descended the lapping steps and waded off across the piazza.

'Well,' said Cressida, 'at least we didn't have things dropping from the roof during dinner.'

Still, when they re-entered the dormitorio, Wendy, who was the only one there, was having hysterics, and was unable even to comment in the usual way upon how wet Cressida and Vivien were.

303

Cressida reflected that it was no joke having hysterics all by oneself and took Wendy by the shoulders even before she had removed the soaking garment she had been lent.

'Whatever's the matter, Wendy?'

But Wendy writhed away from her and screamed, 'Have you come out of the sea?'

'Of course not, Wendy. Whatever is it?'

'You're both ghosts. You've been drowned.'

She said it with such conviction that Cressida could not but glance enquiringly at Vivien, who had now removed her soaking garment and was struggling with her boots.

'We're absolutely alive, and you're alive too, Wendy,' said Cressida; hesitating, however, to draw nearer once more, lest she drench Wendy in rain water and sea water, as do sheepdogs and seadogs.

'Slap her face or something,' said Vivien.

'Wendy, you're perfectly all right,' said Cressida. 'You're not alone now.'

Wendy was truly transformed. She was wearing the same beautiful nightdress, or, more likely, one of its sisters, but every fibre of her short hair was on end, and her eyes were quite filled with expression.

'Calm down,' said Vivien, still struggling with strange boots.

'I've seen the novice,' said Wendy, 'and if you see her three times, it means you're going to join her.'

'Do you mean join her in the cloister?' asked Cressida, regardless of the pool that was spreading around her on the floor.

'Or in death,' said Wendy. 'It's very nearly the same thing.'

'*Have* you seen her three times?' asked Vivien.

'No. Four times now.'

'Well, there,' said Cressida comfortingly. 'And you're still alive and you're not in a cloister.'

'It means something awful,' moaned Wendy. 'You two don't understand. It's all because I agreed to marry Brian.'

'Let me get you a hairbrush,' said Cressida.

'You're much too wet,' said Wendy, beginning to return to her normal, discriminating self.

'I'll take this off,' said Cressida. 'We've been having dinner with my employer, and it began to pour.'

'How *long* have you been engaged to Brian?' asked Vivien.

'Last spring after the boat race, at the Nègre Bleu. You know, behind Rupert Street. Or *do* you know?'

'I've lived mostly abroad,' said Vivien, though it was a big exaggeration.

'Here, have *my* brush,' said Cressida, before commencing her own contest with unknown boots. 'Did Brian row in the boat race or was he cox?'

'Of course he didn't,' said Wendy. 'He's far too old. His father sponsors it.'

Cressida had not realised that the boat race required sponsoring, but of course she had never actually seen it. The only time they tried, they had arrived after it was over, and it had been very wet then too, and there had been a dreadful episode with a retriever.

'Who won?' asked Cressida politely.

'Cambridge, of course,' said Wendy, trying simultaneously to press down and fluff up her locks with Cressida's brush.

'Cambridge won when I went,' said Cressida.

'Lord Elterwater says that Cambridge will always win until they decide it's not worth holding the race any more.'

'It doesn't seem very fair,' said Cressida, still struggling away.

Vivien was lying back, victorious but worn. Now that Cressida and she had reached sanctuary, the storm was, of course, dying away.

'When are you going to marry Brian?' asked Vivien.

'Don't ask me,' said Wendy. 'Not ever, I should think. I told you I've seen the novice three times and that's the end of me. I never wanted to be dragged out here in the first place.'

Wendy made clear that this most of all was an index of superior discrimination.

'We're none of us doing much good here,' said Vivien.

'I haven't decided yet,' said Cressida. 'There's a funny side to it all as well.'

'We weren't supposed to come here for merriment,' said Vivien crossly.

'I should say not,' said Wendy. 'Thanks for the brush.'

'I suppose Desirée's on duty,' said Cressida, 'but what's happened to Rosemary?'

'Don't ask me,' said Wendy.

'Are you all right to go to bed again? Shall I look for Brian?'

'No, thanks very much,' said Wendy. 'I'll be as all right as I can be.'

When the three of them were in bed, and reduced to the single lamp, Hellenic and hieratical, Cressida spoke again to Wendy, addressing her across the void. 'Wendy, does this kind of thing happen to you often? Things like the novice, I mean?'

'All the time, if you really want to know.'

'Do you ever get anything useful out of it?'

Naturally, what Cressida would have asked a different person was: Do the things ever come true?

'Of course not. I only get warnings.'

'But they might be *useful* warnings.'

'Don't make me laugh,' said Wendy.

Cressida reflected that here they all were, what people would call five perfectly average English girls from quite good schools, and yet one was a somnambulist, one had the most terrifying dreams, and a third received frequent supernatural monitions. Three out of five: it put into proportion the singing she had heard from the grounded boat—if, of course, proportion was a consideration among people of that kind.

Midnight struck. Could Rosemary be somnambulating already? Cressida felt that she really could not undertake to go after Rosemary every single night.

But this time Rosemary might well have become very wet as well as very cold.

Cressida remembered that when, that morning, the thought of how cold Rosemary must be, had moved her, she had discovered that really it had become quite warm. Not that for a single moment would she ever regret praying in the beautiful cathedral and floating out to the very seamark and going to Rosemary's rescue generally.

On the instant, moonlight filled the dormitorio. It was as if Professor Colossi had arranged it in one of his opera houses. It was glorious, though one had to remember that on the missing Rosemary the effect might be incalculable.

Wendy shifted irritably. 'Could one of you please draw the curtain?'

'There is no curtain, Wendy,' said Cressida calmingly. 'You know that.'

'Then we're none of us going to sleep,' said Vivien.

Cressida surmised that after a short period of being very nearly someone else, Vivien was resuming her familiar identity.

But the immediate problem, that of Vivien's insomnia, had always been one before which she, Cressida, had been helpless, even though Vivien had been able to help with her, Cressida's, dreams.

'Let's talk quietly for a bit,' was all she could think to contribute. 'Wendy will soon drop off now that she's seen the novice and got it over.'

'I wonder how *long* I've got?' asked Wendy.

'Now it's happened four times, I'm sure that proves there's nothing in it,' said Cressida.

'I once drew the ace of spades and the next day my cat died,' said Wendy.

'Whatever of?' asked Cressida, sincerely concerned.

'Worms, or so they said. I don't want to talk about it.'

'If people play cards, they must all draw the ace of spades sometimes,' Vivien pointed out.

'I wasn't playing cards,' said Wendy. 'I was only playing about with them. It was horrible.'

'What other warnings have you had?' asked Cressida.

'I saw a woman in a silk dress who'd been hung.'

'You didn't!' cried Cressida, suppressing a small yell, as she remembered her dreadful dream. Inside herself, she never forgot any details of her dreams.

'Hanged,' said Vivien. 'That's one of your episodes, Cressy, isn't it?'

'How can it be?' enquired Wendy petulantly.

'And what happened?' enquired Cressida.

'Need you ask? It was the day before Brian proposed to me for the last time.'

'Nothing like that followed in my case,' said Cressida.

Wendy made no comment.

'Why did you accept Brian?' asked Vivien, 'if you don't really like him?'

'I was bored,' said Wendy. 'I still am.'

'It's not *boring* here, Wendy,' Cressida remonstrated. 'It's sometimes comic and sometimes horrid. Not boring for a minute.'

'*I'm* bored,' said Wendy.

It was frightening to think that, for some people, being so pretty, having such a sweet nightdress, and being engaged to be married to the perfectly amiable, perfectly average son of a rich peer did not suffice. Perhaps the novice was right, and Wendy would be better off in a cloister? Cressida shivered internally.

'Are you always bored?' enquired Vivien.

'Mostly.'

'It's easy to feel like that,' said Vivien, 'if you let yourself.'

But Wendy was sitting up in bed. Her expression in the moonlight was one of horror.

'She's coming back,' croaked Wendy.

And now, indeed, Cressida could hear steps. It was impossible not to be scared, though perhaps possible not to show it. She remembered some such ideal as that being put forward in chapel.

But an answer offered. It was hard to say whether it was a relief or an anticlimax.

'It's all right, Wendy,' said Cressida. 'It's not the novice coming back. It's Rosemary.'

But Wendy seemed not to hear. Her eyes, full of terror, followed the figure along the dormitorio.

Cressida had to speak again. '*Wendy, it's all right!*'

Rosemary was pattering along in the moonlight, both arms outstretched in front of her. She did not turn towards her bed, but pattered out at the other end of the room. Cressida had not realised that the far door was open, nor could she see why it should be. Rosemary's very short steps made her seem to be moving faster than she probably was. It was as if her feet went round and round on a small wheel, as in the case of Marie Tempest.

With a sigh, Cressida drew on her familiar dressing gown, and went after her. Wendy was still sitting both upright and petrified.

CHAPTER FIFTY-ONE

At Work on a Yacht

Cressida had previously been only a short distance that way down the passage.

This time it was quite easy to overtake Rosemary, and to keep up with her.

The difficulty was to know what to do next.

At school one had been told that if one awakened the somnambulist, the shock could be fatal. If one even touched the somnambulist unnecessarily, the result was unpredictable. The thing to do was to follow the somnambulist upstairs and downstairs, but in a protective rather than authoritative posture. It was quite likely that in the end the somnambulist would return to her own bed of her own accord, and then fall into a dreamless sleep. That, assuredly, was what one must hope and pray for.

But here, Cressida reflected as she edged along behind Rosemary, conditions might be different. The somnambulistic instinct

for gliding intact across wires and along edges might only operate when the somnambulist had waking knowledge of where the
wires and edges led. On the other hand, Rosemary might well
have that exact knowledge of this lone, gloomy passage, even
though Cressida had not.

Now Cressida had crept past the rooms from which she and
Vivien had yesterday been invited to select quarters of their
own. It was impossible to surmise what happened in the apparently endless further apartments, some with rusted padlocks on
the doors, some with doors that had been stove in for defence
purposes (as people put it).

At the very end, the usual flight of ornamental stone steps
descended to a stone quay, white with moonlight. When sleepwalking, Cressida reflected, Rosemary seemed drawn toward
water; exactly the opposite to what could have been expected
if she had been bitten by a mad dog, something now illegal in
England but still allowed abroad.

Rosemary automated faultlessly down the steps, even though
they were as historically rough as the flight at the other end of
the building; and pattered to the edge of the quay, against which
the sea was flapping and bashing, ruffled by the recent storm.

Attached by silver ropes to stout bollards was a huge white
yacht, everyman's ship of dreams—and, even more certainly,
everygirl's. The carved figure at her prow was of a weeping
woman, only in part robed: Niobe, perhaps, notoriously all
tears. But the name of the yacht, painted at several major sites
in lustrous black ended all speculation as to ownership. The
yacht was the *Pericoloso*.

No faint thread of steam crept from the white funnel, touched
out in gold. As far as one could see, neither the Ancient

Mariner nor the Flying Dutchman lurked in the baroque wheel-house.

Rosemary stood, ahead of the yacht, at the verge of the high quay, gazing sightlessly at the billows. Her arms had dropped from their doll-like elevation and now drooped peacefully at her sides. All the same, one sightless step more and Rosemary might be beyond rescue, though Cressida had twice won the Captain Webb Annual Bronze Medal for Girls.

Going on all the time was a steady chipping and scraping which much impaired the perfection of the scene. Almost always there is something of that kind: almost must one be glad when there is no more than one such irritant.

Creeping up behind Rosemary, Cressida realised that there was a boatful of men at work on the yacht, down there near the water-line, though the water-line went up and down appreciably. By the light of little lamps, the men were trying to make holes and stuff something in and generally wire it up. Cressida knew too little of marine architecture to reason why. She reflected once more that in England it would be difficult to persuade tradesmen to work at that hour. Obviously it must be a commission of some importance. The cursing confirmed this. Cressida had noticed that men curse even more when confronted with a task that matters in any way.

'Rosemary,' said Cressida in a low voice; perhaps too low to be heard above the stormy billows. All the same, one knew it was essential to avoid a shock.

Rosemary turned slowly and looked at her from eyes that had lately been seeing an entirely other world.

'Do you often do this two nights running?'

'Not often,' said Rosemary. 'I think it's because something's going to happen.'

At that moment, the men in the boat saw them standing there in the moonlight.

As with one throat, the men started to whistle, hoot, and jeer. Quite unexpectedly, the girls had found themselves at the centre of a political demonstration.

As so often in Trino, at least one of the workers was not merely English-speaking, but English born and educated. People often said that the whole world was becoming Anglicised.

'— the —ing whores!' bellowed the English worker.

He was the only one whose exact words were comprehended by Cressida. But in politics words are merely the glints one picks up from the surface of things.

'We'd better lock the door when we get back,' said Cressida to Rosemary as they re-ascended the steps.

'It's Wendy who always wants it open,' explained Rosemary. 'She sees a figure sometimes, you know, and she's frightened of being shut in with it. Isn't the moon wonderful?'

'Too good to be true,' said Cressida.

Pessimism was seeping through at more and more places.

Cressida, safely returned, was having no nonsense about that door, especially as Wendy had fallen asleep, despite the moon, in the light of which she looked unearthly.

Alas, there was no lock, not even a padlock.

'What's going on?' whispered Vivien, as Cressida was creeping into bed, having said goodnight to Rosemary.

'There were some men mending Vittore's steam yacht.'

'That's so he can hop it,' whispered Vivien.

'They were beastly,' whispered Cressida. 'To me and Rosemary.'

'We shall have to tie Rosemary to her bed.'

'That would only excite them, Vivien.'

'It's a pity we didn't arrive here sooner. It can't have been like this to begin with.'

'Everything's different to begin with. Everything's like this in the end.'

'I wonder how long it lasted?'

'The older we grow, the less things last.'

'It seems a pity we can't live backwards.'

'We've only been here two days,' said Cressida.

'I'm already unemployed,' said Vivien.

'I suppose I may be unemployed too. After running away from the banquet.'

'It's just like home really.'

'Oh, Vivien! There's a black cloud coming over the moon.'

CHAPTER FIFTY-TWO

Cressida Finds Herself

The cloud remained in position long enough for Cressida to go peacefully to sleep.

Still, it must have soon moved on again, because, when Cressida stirred, the sun had burst forth instead.

Someone was weeping. Perhaps it was that which had awakened Cressida.

She elevated herself an inch or two and looked cautiously around.

This time it was Desirée who was in trouble. It was impossible to know at what time she had been released from her duties, but now she was lying on her face and sobbing into her pillow. Desirée, of all people!

Rosemary and Wendy had already needed Cressida's support, and Vivien, she was beginning to realise, needed it in her own way, almost all the time. Cressida was really more and more surprised. Was her destiny in life to be one of those stronger persons upon whom others, albeit possibly more gifted, would need to lean and even depend? Very possibly it was. She was not at all sure about such a prospect.

She stepped out of bed and confirmed that everyone other than Desirée seemed asleep. She crossed to Desirée's bed and put her hand gently on Desirée's shoulder. She said nothing.

'He's so sad, Cressida,' said Desirée, suppressing a gulp.

'How did you know it was me?' After all, Desirée's face was flat into the pillow.

'He can't move, or eat, or speak any more. I'm not sure he can even think.'

'We mustn't talk about it here,' said Cressida, speaking low into the back of Desirée's ear. 'It's not fair to wake everyone up.' Vivien was shifting about already.

'He can't even *write* his orders. We tried that. It was awful.'

'Let's go for a little walk,' said Cressida, 'and you can tell me. There's a beautiful ship at the end of the passage.'

Still gulping, and very pale from long hours of toil and responsibility, Desirée struggled from bed. The two of them set off in their pyjamas; strictly working pyjamas in both cases, and in single, simple colours. At that moment, the light and air were exactly as when one ascends to Heaven; exactly as they had been in the cathedral.

'It's Vittore's own yacht, isn't it?' asked Cressida, when they had gone some little distance from the dormitorio. She put her arm round Desirée's shoulder.

Desirée nodded.

'Vivien says he's going to run away in it.'

'It may be too late.'

'But, Desirée, everything seemed perfectly all right yesterday?'

'It wasn't all right, Cressida. It *wasn't*. We were just acting.'

'I don't believe it.' Nor could she.

'I was putting a face on it. It seemed the proper thing to do. You know how one learns?'

Cressida considered. The air was full of inapprehensible golden motes: some vegetable, some mineral, some animal.

'How long ago did it stop being all right?'

'I'm not sure it ever *was* all right. Not really. I've been feeling more and more doubtful about that for a long, long time. I was simply kept going by Vittore. All of us were.'

'If that's true, it'll be terrible for Vivien.'

'It's terrible for *me*, Cressida.'

'Yes, of course it is.'

'I don't think he can even *feel* things. His nerves have seized up. Every single one.'

They had reached the end of the passage.

Well might Cressida be stunned by the beauty of abroad before breakfast! Such intensity as this was never to be seen in England; or at least had never been seen by her, neither on Exmoor nor in Charnwood Forest, not on the shores of The Wash, nor of course at home. And she had, once or twice, been up early enough for it in almost all those places!

'Gosh, it's lovely, Desirée!'

For a moment nothing else mattered. Even death; even cruelty.

'Yes, but it doesn't *help*,' said Desirée.

'Oh, it *does*.' Cressida tightened her grip on Desirée's shoulder, then lowered her arm.

'We can go aboard, if you like,' said Desirée, managing to smile a little.

'Yes, please,' said Cressida.

There was no one to be seen, neither the nocturnal shipwrights, nor the local population. Perhaps the area had been cleared.

Cressida withdrew her arm and Desirée led her up the snowy gangway. They roamed round the deck and, descending, penetrated austere cabins for the officers and crew, and succulent saloons for the owner and his guests. Either way, every way, all was perfect.

'Which is Vittore's own cabin?'

'We mustn't enter.'

'What's inside?'

'Paintings and models of the great sea monsters he's caught at different times.'

'Why shouldn't we look at them? No one will know.'

'The price of disobedience is despair.'

'I love stuffed fish. They make Vivien and me giggle.' But Cressida knew it would be unkind to persist when Desirée was already so shaky.

'We can't go down among the engines without boiler suits,' said Desirée.

'I'd like a boiler suit, but I can't really stand engines,' said Cressida.

'Vittorio flies, swims, and of course drives about, faster than anyone else. He holds all kinds of world records. Permanently, I believe.'

They had reached the billiard cabin: tribute to the glazed inertia at times of southern seas, though not at the moment, when there was a gentle but steady breeze blowing. Over the rack of cues hung a coloured photograph of the Commendatore making a record break in the costume of a professional. But Cressida saw at once that this table was of less than standard size.

'What kind of thing do you mean, Cressida?'

Cressida brought out the word, though she had never known quite what it meant, except when applied to tabbies and pekes. 'Strokes. People are always having them at home. Either because they have nothing to do, or because they're overworked.'

'No,' said Desirée, 'it's not any sort of ordinary illness. Vittore will never permit illness in anyone, least of all in himself.'

'It's just that he's feeling blue?' suggested Cressida, mainly from the wish to command the situation at least intellectually and thus help Desirée.

'How could it be *just* anything, Cressida? Not with Vittore. You couldn't use a word like that if you knew him.'

'I should *like* to know him. Or at least to set eyes upon him before I have to go home.'

'We can only hope and trust,' said Desirée, gazing solemnly at the billiards photograph.

The Commendatore and his costume filled so much of the foreground that it was difficult to tell whether the table was this one or another, perhaps even in Leicester Square, the world capital of the ancient game, as Cressida had read in the gardener's *Sporting Times*.

'Before you go you ought to see the Creation Cabin.'

It was on the opposite side of the companion way to the billiard cabin.

The walls began deep blue near the floor, passed through horizontal gradations of yellow and orange, and towards the ceiling became Pompeian and purple. The ceiling itself was a whirling green, here frog, there hemlock. In the very centre was a blobby symbol of duality. Splashed about on all sides were tersely monochrome esquisses of persons undergoing experiences.

'This is where the Commendatore writes, composes, paints, directs: everything. When he's at sea, of course.'

'Did he do the decoration?'

'He designed it. It symbolises peace and pandemonium interfused.'

'The people don't look happy,' said Cressida doubtfully.

She was beginning to realise that for some reason it was not the proper criterion. Of course, the chaplain had all along told them it was not.

'They're all submitting to the love experience,' explained Desirée. 'Each in his or her own different way.'

'I might have guessed,' said Cressida. She looked uneasily around her.

'It's for everyone and for no one,' explained Desirée. She was doing what she could to be a good guide, but Cressida could see that inside her simple pyjamas she was shaking, despite this glorious haze of warmth, spiced with just the right amount of breeze, whistling in through the portholes.

'Never mind, Desirée,' said Cressida. 'If you really have to go back to England, I'm sure Vivien's Aunt Agnes won't mind if you latch on to us.'

Desirée looked at her so gratefully that Cressida wondered about herself once more.

She had often heard that, at times of real crisis, true leaders emerge from quite unexpected places.

CHAPTER FIFTY-THREE

Tars on
the Taffrail

Upstairs (though Cressida was almost sure that was the wrong expression), they saw that a great grey ship with long grey cannon was very slowly steaming into the bay, systematically puncturing the sunshine. Very heavy grey smoke gushed from all four grey funnels, as if there was something wrong with the ship's inside. There was a wireless aerial stretched between the masts, for use in wartime and in deep-sea rescue operations, and to enable the officers to talk to one another.

'If the wind changes, the *Pericoloso*'s going to suffer,' remarked Cressida sagely. She had picked up remarks like that from weather-beaten acquaintances made by her father at estuarial ports, such as Boston and Wisbech; brief encounters every one.

'We're *all* going to suffer,' responded Desirée. 'It's been sent by the Peace Powers to blow us up.'

'*She*,' corrected Cressida primly.

'If you must,' said Desirée.

'Anyway, she won't blow us up. Can't you see she's British?'

It was not an altogether fair question, as the once-white ensign, no doubt rent in many a sudden, sullen trial of arms, was but intermittently visible through the effluvium. Seagulls were flying out to engorge rations cast overboard by ratings.

'Britain *is* a Peace Power. One of the worst. That's why we're here. Haven't you heard of Lloyd George?'

'He's out of office now. Daddy says he's gone for good.'

'But not his work.'

'The evil that men do lives after them,' confirmed Cressida, without thinking.

But the tars had spotted the two girls all alone on the white yacht in their pyjamas. The tars began to whistle through their fingers and ejaculate. More and more and more of the tars were pressing against the taffrail (as Cressida fancied it was called). Cressida had never seen such a crew, or not all at once.

Back in the dormitorio, the other girls were up and dressing.

'We're going to be blown to bits,' announced Cressida.

'I told you I'd seen the novice,' said Wendy, who next to her skin was wearing something obviously most desirable in fit, texture, hue, everything.

'At least it's action of a kind,' said Vivien.

'How long before it begins to happen?' asked Rosemary. 'I wish to spend ten minutes in the chapel, if the rest of you don't mind.'

'I bet there's an alternative,' said Vivien. 'There always is. Learn "Christabel" by heart, or mend all the holes in the strawberry nets.'

'We can give in, I suppose,' adumbrated Cressida.

'Yes,' said Desirée quietly. 'We can always do that.'

Desirée was already fully dressed in her familiar blue trousers and jersey, high-necked and yellow. Cressida doubted whether she herself would ever cast such an aura of efficiency, try as she might, and even though one was beginning to suspect one might have other qualities.

Restored in some degree to herself, Desirée walked out of the dormitorio without a further word.

'Do you think we *shall* give in?' asked Rosemary.

'Of course we shall,' said Vivien.

'That means a nursery governess's job for me.'

Cressida tried to smile at Rosemary sympathetically. She knew there were such fates.

Brian Wicker entered. He had of course knocked, but he had hardly awaited the response. Wendy had assumed a dreamy coat and skirt in sand-coloured velvet over a crêpe blouse from Paris, and intermittently flecked with tiny pimpernels.

'Hallo, Wendy. Hallo, girls. I'm afraid it's bad news. In fact, we may all be blown up if we don't look out. I thought it right to tell you. Forgive my barging in.'

'What are you going to do about it, Brian?' demanded Wendy, looking at the seams of her stockings.

'Well, I've put through a call to my father. It should come in before midday. Unfortunately he's in Ross and Cromarty just now, stalking. The beaters and gillies will have to find him.'

'You do realise,' said Wendy, 'that we are all girls?'

'I do indeed, Wendy. And very pretty ones. You first, of course, my sweet one.'

'We're *all* pretty,' said Vivien.

'Yes, of course,' said Brian amiably. 'You may have to be evacuated.'

Cressida started. It was a term she had only come upon in a medical book, and in a context so disgusting that she had put the book back on the shelf at once.

'Well, hurry up about it,' said Wendy. 'And see that our things are properly looked after. We can't turn up in England looking like kitchen maids.'

'It may not come to it,' said Brian. 'There's usually a way out if you look behind and under things. Have a good breakfast all the same, just in case. Build up the old body.'

He went.

'We might be wearing crinolines in the Crimea,' said Vivien.

'Rosemary, hadn't you better eat before you pray?' suggested Cressida.

'I don't propose to pray, Cressida. Rather to meditate.'

Cressida felt faintly regretful. She had been so thankful that she had prayed in the cathedral; and at a time when the whole adventure had been vaguely new.

'And you can't meditate on a full stomach,' added Rosemary. 'You must be as transubstantial as possible.'

'Isn't that rather blasphemous?' asked Wendy, unexpectedly but somehow characteristically.

'Of course it's not blasphemous,' said Vivien, now fully dressed, and very much available for action. 'Though some things are.'

'We'd better look for breakfast,' said Cressida tentatively. 'It may be our last meal.' She did not really want Wendy to make a third, and palpably Vivien did not.

Outside, serving sailors were already swarming. The ship must hold hundreds of them, thousands, even. Cressida wondered why. What use could so many be? But she realised that this might not be the right question.

For that matter, she would not have supposed, and judging by what she had seen elsewhere, and from what Vivien said, that the ship could yet be properly attached, or anything like it. It always took hours and hours; and probably longer still when there were so many to help.

All the sailors wore summer sailor suits. Now that they were more or less out of the wind, most of them also wore sailor hats inscribed HMS DREADFUL.

Cressida realised that many were striplings who had been assigned to Neptune instead of, like Hugh, to Mars.

The cantina was divided between those who seemed over-excited in their different languages and those who seemed silently morose.

Wendy asked for Post Toasties and, when the man brought muesli instead, said, 'It looks like vomit' and refused even to attempt it.

The Acting Foreign Minister passed their table.

'Good morning, lovely ladies.'

He was gazing awestruck at Wendy's hair and couture.

'This is Wendy Twyford-Blair,' said Cressida. 'The Acting Foreign Minister, Wendy.'

He would have kissed Wendy's hand, had she not been buttering rolls.

'I am no longer that, Miss Hazeborough.'

'Is that why you're not wearing your uniform?' asked Vivien.

'There may be epochal events ahead, Miss Poins. I regret them, as we all do, but it is necessary to be fluid, to be flexible. If I survive the change, you may all count upon my protection.'

'Thank you very much,' said Cressida politely.

'The English presence is among us so I am wearing my English suit. See for yourself.' The ex-Acting Foreign Minister attempted to twirl himself.

'You look like a day's shooting,' said Vivien.

'We must all hope it does not come to that. You ladies may wish to spend the day in prayer.'

'Our friend Rosemary Lawton-Smillie is already doing that,' explained Cressida, not quite accurately.

'More things are wrought by prayer than this world dreams of,' Vivien reminded them all.

The ex-Acting Foreign Minister bowed his head to each of them, then shuffled forward to his new destiny.

'Old has-been,' said Wendy, with butter coming out of her mouth.

Because Wendy was there, Cressida and Vivien had to talk about clothes and shopping; and about both from points of view that were not their own. Also, Wendy sometimes talked familiarly about people. As Cressida and Vivien knew none of these people, they found it impossible to tell whether Wendy knew them either.

'What's the commotion?' asked Wendy.

Cressida had been aware of it for some time, but they had been analysing Harrods; merits and blemishes as defined by Wendy's mother, who lived quite near.

Wendy even asked one of the men in white jackets.

'It's the English sailors, Fräulein. They are sacking the town. I advise you to conceal yourselves. They are filled with ferocity.'

Certainly they seemed to be besieging the doors of the cantina. With Vittore inert, there was neither heart nor co-ordination in the resistance to anything.

It was hard to think of a standard that might not be threatened.

But suddenly Cavaliere Terridge was there, though of course he had no right to be, according to what he himself had said.

He strode down the room in his scintillating, though now discoloured, uniform. He hauled back the cowering guardians of the portals. He addressed the tars.

'Fair's fair,' he said. 'Let the terrier see the bunny. Other people have their work to do too. Just one more heave and then you'll all be home. Remember Lloyd George. Remember what he promised? Come on then, who's first?'

Restored to normal decency, the sailors broke and straggled. A group of them even raised a small cheer. Cressida wondered what they could possibly do next with their time, however well intentioned they might for the moment be. Also she was upset by the Cavaliere's reference to a poor rabbit.

Breaking through the cluster of men in miscellaneous uniforms who, in their foreign way, were almost fighting among themselves to thank and congratulate him, the Cavaliere strode, brisk and matutinal, straight to the three girls.

'Wendy. Vivien. Cressida. I'm so glad you're all chums.'

Wendy spoke. 'You were wonderful with the men.'

'It's just a knack. You've either got it or you haven't,' said the Cavaliere disclaimingly.

'What will they do now?' asked Cressida.

'Make whoopee elsewhere, I expect. You have to give and take. It's all strange to them, you know.'

'When do they start blowing us up?' asked Cressida.

The Cavaliere quickly looked serious. 'The enemy we've got to think about is here already. The bluejackets have been sent to protect us.'

'Desirée didn't seem to know that,' said Vivien. 'She's having kittens.'

'It's very complicated,' said the Cavaliere seriously. 'But don't worry about it. That never does any good. It'll all come out in the wash. Brian Wicker's speaking to Lord Elterwater at midday.'

The wash! Childhood impressions last for how long a day!

Chapter Fifty-Four

The Emblem

Midday!

The way things were going, it might easily be Cressida's only chance of even setting eyes on Vittore, who had brought them all here, at least in a sense. She had not yet worn a boiler suit, but she had eaten through the two very best breakfasts since she and Vivien had (as people insisted) grown up. In general, the food had been even better than at Lady Luce's. And of course there had been so much else: wearing trousers, music, theatre, the cathedral, the sea, two dawns, a bombardment, strange men in uniform, a near-ravishment impressively resisted, the sense of being far nearer to the heart of things than ever before; or, almost certainly, ever again. It had been a lightning course in finding oneself. She had so much for which to thank Vittore, if only she could do it.

'Have a cup of coffee,' said Wendy to the Cavaliere.

'Thank you very much, Wendy. But I mustn't. Not here. There's protocol.'

'Have you some field glasses that I could borrow?' asked Cressida. Desirée's promise had simply been forgotten. But of course Desirée had so much on her mind.

'I could scavenge,' said the Cavaliere. 'What do you want them for?'

'I want to look at Vittore when he comes out on his tower.'

'It's not fair to examine a man too closely.'

'Why not?' asked Vivien.

'Vittore's not English, you know. They don't last out in the way we do. No fault of theirs. Too much of the wine, women, and song. Don't get me wrong. I'm not one to hold back. But enough's enough.'

'Enough is never enough for Cressida and me,' said Vivien.

Aunt Agnes entered in her nurse's uniform, buttoned tightly and becomingly over the bosom, and with a stiff collar: the ensemble in the palest of blue, paler even than the Cavaliere's blue; the wimple involved and snowy.

'Getting on well with your jobs? Mr Terridge is still looking after you, I see. That's extremely thoughtful of you, Mr Terridge. And who is this?'

'Wendy Twyford-Blair,' said Cressida. 'This is Vivien's aunt, Lady Luce, Wendy.'

'How do you do?' said Wendy. 'Are you a real nurse?'

'Well, I'm certainly not a children's nurse, Wendy,' said Lady Luce, smiling. 'I used to know Vittore in the old days, and he wrote inviting me to take over the Infirmary here. I'm making myself thoroughly useful. It's very good for me.'

'I'm sure it's very good for the patients,' said Cressida politely.

'It's you two I'm mainly concerned about,' said Aunt Agnes. 'And, of course, you also, Wendy. Isn't it wonderful having a

British battleship in the bay? Many of the sailors are under my care already. Sent straight in by the Admiral. Some of them have contracted a very nasty disease. They're being well looked after by the porters.'

'It's not a battleship,' said Wendy, in her unexpected way. 'It's not big enough.'

'However big or small it may be, Wendy, it's there to see that we come to no harm, and that's the great thing.'

'Aunt Agnes,' said Vivien, utterly exhausted by all this optimism, 'it's here to tell us to surrender and to blow us up if we don't.'

'I think you can safely leave things like that to the Admiral. I knew him when he was our naval attaché in Paris, after his big breakdown. Of course he was only a Captain then, though a Captain in the navy is something quite different from a Captain in the army. I expect you know that, Wendy? We'll all be quite safe in the hands of Togo Broadfoot. They called him Togo because he looked so Japanese. Did you find some useful work to do, Vivien?'

'It wasn't useful. It wasn't proper work. I've left it.'

'I think you had better come and join me. There are plenty of openings now that we've got the sick sailors.'

'I think that's a splendid idea, Lady Luce,' said Cavaliere Terridge unnecessarily.

'And what about you, Cressida?'

'I've got a job in the theatre, but I don't like it much.'

'You can't expect to like any new job for the first weeks or months. If you do, there's something wrong. One has to be broken in.'

Cavaliere Terridge looked doubtful.

'Come along, Vivien,' said Aunt Agnes. 'I'll show you the ropes.'

And such was Vivien's despair that she actually went. Cressida tried to visualise her dressed as a nurse. As yet, she had hardly the shape for it.

'Can I come to the theatre with you?' The Cavaliere was addressing Cressida. 'Lady Luce will be all right anywhere in that rig, but your clothes may have just the opposite effect.' Wendy smiled cynically.

'I'm not going to work just yet. I want to see Vittore.'

'I should lay off the field glasses. They mightn't be popular. There's a spy scare, naturally.'

'Why has everything suddenly gone off?'

'It's this new thing. Internal subversion breaking through at the moment of climax. There's some rough characters arrived in town. With the intellectuals hidden away behind them, of course. It did for the Tsar, you know. Now everyone's going in for it.'

'Is it going to do for us?'

'Not if you keep your chin up.'

Cressida pulled up the collar of her sweater.

First of all, she went back with Wendy to the dormitorio; in her own case, simply to assess the lie of the land.

As the land seemed to by lying much as usual, she then walked down to the cathedral square. Of course the theatre was there, so that she ran the risk of being required to resume her employment, but, in view of all that had been said, she simply had to see what had happened to the camouflaged ship.

The square was littered with rusty tins, sodden hay, and putrid fish, proving that the tide had indeed flowed and ebbed; but there was not a ship in sight.

Possibly the men had succeeded in pushing the vessel out to sea again. Possibly the vessel had just been carried away, dragging with it the men trying to hold on to it. Possibly by now the vessel had even sunk, and was in need of being properly marked as a menace. Cressida knew perfectly well that such characters as had been under discussion that morning took care to cover their tracks on all occasions, let alone their identities. Her father was always talking about it, and peering about.

There was a huge crab, still alive, poor thing, and looking for its natural habitat. Without all these confirmations, Cressida might have wondered whether the whole incident had not been one of her dreams. She stood behind the crab, trying to drive it in the right direction without actually touching it. But it is always difficult to propel any form of life in the right direction.

Cressida looked at her watch. Still three-quarters of an hour to go before the revelation.

She entered the cathedral. There was a dingy lifebelt lying on one of the steps with straw protruding, like entrails.

Alas, it was but a forerunner. As Cressida crossed the threshold, she saw that the entire cathedral had been, as she took it, sacked. The enmarbled dead were at rest no more. They were protruded like the straw. Some might even be described as strewn. However, the remains were for the most part, fortunately, ancient and sparse: here a shapeless bone, there a ring with the jewels lugged out by the subversionists, not much more.

Some of the wonderful coloured glass had been smashed, or there would have been very little light. It was all too apparent what had happened to the candles, short or long. They had been piled on the altar steps and melted down into a broad, squidgy scab, which had ruined the rich carpet, and overflowed into the aisles. Perhaps the object had been total incendiarism? Symbol struggling into substance?

Cressida could not but glide forward, appalled. All mortality was here, for what it amounted to, and as far as the patchy daylight permitted.

She gazed in revulsion at the swollen raft of wax, dotted with chewing-gum globules. Then she realised that, from the Episcopal throne to her left, the huge mitre had disappeared, and that upon the upholstery of the back, where the diocesan was wont to recline in his lacy surplice, had been incised an emblem of the militant toilers. The workmanship was rough, but Cressida had seen the thing in the supplement to the *Children's Encyclopedia*.

It was the first such sight she had seen, three-dimensionally. At once she doubted whether it would be the last. She gulped.

She hastened from the edifice. Even the high altar had been rearranged as a mockery, and Cressida nearly fell over a substantial object which had no business to be on the floor of the nave.

She realised that it was St George, lying on his back. Despite his odd hair arrangement, exceptionally un-English, his plight seemed the nearest to one's heart of all the atrocities. His head was loose, or even about to leave the body, as with so many British folk figures. Cressida forgot even to look for the poor dragon.

And, lastly (or so Cressida hoped), there was a thing on the floor where the light from the door fell upon it. Cressida picked it up. It was unquestionably nautical. Possibly a marlin-spike. She had so often read of them. They were used as instruments of inhumanity, for example against cabin-boys and cabin-girls. Not wishing to drop the object on the stone floor and thus make a crash, Cressida laid it on one of the chairs which had not been overturned. No one would be likely to sit on it, as there was no one but she in the cathedral, and very naturally.

In the full light of the portico, Cressida perceived that the sacred lance of St George had lightly penetrated her left thigh, making a tiny hole in her trousers. On top of everything else, she would have to change; perhaps this time into a soberer and more practical hue. Now that Vivien had virtually abdicated from serious activity, she, Cressida, might have to bear a twofold burden. They might all have to flee in the night or early morning with nothing but their hairbrushes.

CHAPTER FIFTY-FIVE

The Exposure

As the tower mounted in a quite random manner from an inchoate and ascending jumble of more or less mediaeval buildings,
and as no one was permitted to pass within the walls of the
citadel unless, like Desirée, they had a key, or, like the Italian
prime minister, a special passport drawn according to the laws
of music, therefore there was no particular viewing area which
could be allotted to tourists, students, and loafers. There was
simply no space for it. The mediaevalists had not supposed that
these categories required any special provision.

None the less, Cressida found that six or seven people were
already waiting about, doubtless expectantly. One was purple
as a prune, one as grey as a public servant.

Cressida thought that she might as well be in good time. It
was quite a maxim on her mother's side of the family. If she
had not supposed herself to be in the city partly in order that
she might set an example, she would have sat down. After all,
it was still quite a wait.

About eleven more people arrived in a group, all with the anxious, inturned, tied-together look usual among pleasure parties from the United States. As always, they were comparing exchange rates in subdued voices.

There seemed very few citizens of the town who were interested, but of course they were in a position to be interested every day, if they felt like it. Cressida wondered if in case of rain Vittore used an umbrella; probably with silver spokes and an ivory knob at the extremity of each. This, of course, was sheer fantasy, but, as a matter of fact, it had been looking like rain for some time. Unfortunately, Cressida had again left behind her exquisite silky mackintosh. The usual faint frisson flitted through her as she recalled its touch.

But then, right on cue, the clouds parted and the full southern sun scorched forth, like an immense Japanese demon. It was once more as if Colossi had been responsible in person; or perhaps one of his better assistants.

An American removed his Rob Roy jacket, and stood there in his tartan braces (or suspenders) looking corpulent.

'Don't do it, Hiram. How could you? Put it right back on.'

Three minutes to go. How terrible if among those attending there should be an assassin! No one could claim that there had been no warning: there had been Wendy's too-manifold novice; and that had been only to start with.

Cressida wondered how far the bullet could be counted upon to ascend. From the corners of both eyes she reviewed as many of her neighbours as possible. If one of them should on the instant drag a carbine from his shirt, would she be expected to throw herself all over him? What she needed was a bread knife, with which Charlotte Corday had served the state so well.

All the ecclesiastical and municipal clocks started to strike twelve. The cohesion was absolute—so far. But the big cathedral bell struck only seven and then broke up. However, the subversionists had failed to silence it totally, for all their up-to-dateness.

At the top of the world, a door opened and a man stepped out. In an outpouring of the fullest (and hottest) possible sunshine, he stood there smiling graciously to the parted clouds above him and to the crumbling roofs below him. The human spectators were too distant for applause, and perhaps not quite sufficiently numerous.

Within Cressida there was a transformation scene, and explanation streamed forth. Often had she dreamed of, say, Queen Alexandra, and seen, perhaps, a tall, stout figure in a low-cut ball gown. 'But,' people would say, her mother for instance, 'but Queen Alexandra was slender, and rather short, and never wore a low-cut dress, never.' 'I know,' Cressida would reply, in actually spoken words or otherwise, 'but, all the same, the lady in my dream *was* Queen Alexandra, so that we must all have been mistaken in what Queen Alexandra looked like, I really can't tell you how.' Nor could she even imagine how, but there it just was. And the same with Dame Nellie Melba, or anyone else: at least once it had been with old General Booth of the Salvation Army, in his knee-long beard and tall hat.

And here it was in real life, as people put it.

Far off though he stood, Cressida could see quite well that the man smiling up there was of godlike beauty and stature: wholly apt to the station he occupied. His features were those of a marble figure in that boring book about Greece. Not only his architectural but also his personal altitude was exceptional.

His plenteous hair was exquisitely deployed above and around his imposing brow. His nose predated the Lacedaemonian captivity. He could hardly be less like the picture of Vittore on the stamps, and yet here he was, Vittore in person, the truth at last, wholly beyond explanation or real need of it, just as in those dreams. The man even wore an ordinary heliotrope suit, however good its cut.

Cressida gazed with the rest, gently holding in her little bosom.

A small voice spoke, seemingly at the level of Cressida's elbow.

'It's not Vittore. It's Vittore's guest, Osbert Sitwell.'

Needless to say, it was Trifoglio speaking; the public sceptic and disillusioner, the public enemy.

Trifoglio crossed himself in reverse. The effect was deeply evil.

A murmur began to circulate among the Americans, Cressida squinted at Trifoglio with loathing. But already he was erasing himself like an eel, impossible to hold in the hand, even if one had wished to.

'Oh!' said Cressida, not merely out loud, but quite distinctly.

Not only would she now never see Vittore, but also she had lost an illuminating quasi-explanation. Trifoglio had taken it from Cressida. For if something impossible, experienced in a dream, more or less repeats itself, impossibility and all, when we are awake, then something akin to explanation hovers in the air; and what that is so denominated, ever truly does more?

CHAPTER FIFTY-SIX

Twilight
at Midday

Terribly disillusioned, Cressida decided that, after all, she might just as well return to work.

Back she went to the square in front of the cathedral.

There had been a further development. From the campanile, the yellow and white ensign of St Peter had been replaced by a sailor's red petticoat with holes in it. Democracy was emerging above the heads of the people. 'In hoc signo vinces,' the Emperor Constantine had directed at a similar moment. Cressida had been unable to forget the terrifying illustration of this incident.

And on the outer door of the theatre was a notice. Hastily typed in four languages, it had been pasted on the inside of the glass. 'Paralysis of Will. Owing to impending events, the theatre is closed in the interests of safety prior to demolition by fire and rebuilding on a smaller scale under popular management. Present personnel are advised that their services will never be required again. Advice, help, and medical accessories are sometimes available at the infirmary. After the fish comes the waterman. Take the darkness as a lover, and cross swiftly.'

Cressida looked about her. It was indeed true that the clouds had sealed up again and now presented a united porridge-like front, as in England. A few enthusiasts were hard at work setting up barricades. Fortunately, there was never all that much traffic. At the moment, there seemed to be very little interest in either.

Life really was impossibly antagonistic when one had somehow left one's appointed place in it. Cressida wandered off, deep in thought. She remembered Aunt Bolsover saying at her, Cressida's, fifteenth birthday party: 'The happiest moment in my entire life was when I saw on the board that I had been given my colours.' And indeed, after that, all that Aunt Bolsover had done was to marry a monger, who had proved tragically unable to expand beyond the one shop, however long he wrestled. Cressida's father had often expressed the view that the monger was a man who had no right to marry at all. But it had to be remembered that Aunt Bolsover was not truly a relative; not by blood, that is to say.

Very young men kept pressing leaflets in Italian on Cressida. She accepted politely, but many of the leaflets were very poorly printed, with the words not fitting properly on to the page. They were laced with expressions in capital letters, such as MORTE, CASTIGO, and UNITA. Sometimes the last of these words even had an accent, as in French; sometimes not.

And there before her, without her having in any way purposed it, was the Infirmary! INFERMERIA was carved over the doorway. Almost certainly she had been guided there by the instinct that takes over so imperceptibly when two or three have been gathered together, and supersedes the need for individual reflection and decision.

Across the front of the Infirmary, which was another bleak building, like last night's caserna, only larger and more penal in aspect, stretched a dirty banner or streamer with inscribed on it in letters of blood, QUESTA TERRA È REGOLATA DAI DIRITTI DI GIUSTIZIA SOCIALE. At each end was a crude skull and bones, though one could tell that the bones were not traditional English bones. Cressida translated without difficulty.

Giustizia was one thing, and impossible anyway. Sociale was quite another thing, and not necessarily desirable. But politics is the art of compromise: there had been an elderly Member of Parliament who had come down and said so, while the class did its knitting and embroidery. He had gone on to say it was the art of the possible.

Cressida wondered whether Aunt Agnes might be available for luncheon. There must surely be privileges attached to the position of Principal or Superintendent or whatever she was?

It seemed difficult, however; because the shapeless and somewhat slummy space in front of the Infermeria was filled with excitable people. No doubt the new ideal brandished before them was having the effect that so many new ideals have for a period. Here and there, men were already standing on things, sometimes back to back, and attempting oratory. Even if Cressida could have understood them, she would not have listened, as she never liked the faces and gestures of people making speeches of that kind.

Vivien appeared; as so often in the past at critical moments. What a relief!

'Everything's out of hand,' said Vivien. But she herself looked much the same as at breakfast.

343

'Aren't you being a nurse?'

'Couldn't find a dress to fit me.'

Cressida had suspected it from the first, even known it.

'Not your thing, anyway.'

'Nothing *is* my thing.'

'Have we got to go back to England?'

'If we can.'

'Have we any ideas?'

'We're not being asked. Aunt Agnes has taken over again.'

Cressida could not decently express a feeling of relief, however qualified.

'She's retired from her job,' said Vivien. 'Now she's changing, and we're to meet her for lunch in the cantina.'

God moves in mysterious ways to perform exactly the same wonders!

'If we can get there.'

'Of course we can get there.'

What a joy that spirit had revived in Vivien! All the same, the streets were appallingly crowded. It is only at times of protest and revolt that one realises how many people there are about. These neighbours were even rowdier than neighbours are normally.

'It's pretty overcast for quarter to one,' remarked Cressida.

'So bad begins, but worse remains behind,' predicted Vivien.

'Do you mind if we look in at the garment store? A lance made a hole in my trousers, and I might as well get an extra pair.'

'You can't have too many pairs.'

Cressida had always known it was true, and soon there was double confirmation; because the garment store was shut. There was another of the notices stuck on the door, though as it was on the outside, it had been already disfigured by scrawlings.

Doubtless they were political as well as pornographic, if one only could decipher them, let alone translate them.

'Do we understand it?'

'Something about normality. Or perhaps they mean the opposite.'

The old Montenegrin woman was standing there in her familiar rags, looking as lost as Ben Gunn, and much the same colour. Even her little pipe was being smoked upside down, as if it were raining again. She could hardly have been five feet high, but of course she had no shoes on.

'E chiuso,' she said, in a Montenegrin accent. 'Mamma mia!'

'Si, si,' attempted Cressida comfortingly.

'Povera voi,' commented Vivien, quite launching out. Of course she must have picked up some valuable idioms at the caserna, and even briefly at the Infirmary.

'Never mind, I've got a spare pair.'

'Let me see the hole.'

Cressida raised her leg, as if she had been in the gym. People stood and stared.

'It's very small.'

'There's blood round the edge.'

'Not much.'

'It's *my* blood, Vivien.'

'We probably shan't be able to take many things with us anyway.'

'Do you mean we've got to run away in our dresses?'

'Ask Aunt Agnes.'

Far, far worse: the cantina proved to be not merely shut but locked. Wicked people had nailed on what Cressida believed was called a hasp, and from it a closed padlock depended, keeping everyone from his or her food. It was the sort of fitment that restrains the cows from the hearthstone. Even the nails were a bit of a job lot.

'What do we think the notice says this time?'

'I can't be bothered to read it.'

'It's signed by someone called the Commissario Popolare del Cibo.'

It was the first of the notices that had been actually signed by anyone.

But Cressida had fallen into a state of agitation. 'Vivien! I believe it's signed by Trifoglio.'

'Just what I'd expect of him.'

'I'm not *quite* sure. The writing slopes backward so much.' Everyone who had ever confronted a copy-book knew how dreadful that was: weak, untrustworthy, doomed to failure, and almost certainly common.

'I'd expect it to,' said Vivien.

And, really, there could be almost no doubt about it, because at that very moment there were shouts of 'Liberta! Liberta!' even hoarser than the usual ones, and a sort of procession had appeared, though really it was only a crowd of men carrying a scratchy wooden shutter, probably part of a house, upon which was squatted Trifoglio in person, though no longer in practice costume of any kind but in the full array of a manual worker. He even wore an improvised red thing for which his head was ideally elfin. For the moment, he had emerged decisively, as Cressida had to realise. Even as he was borne in triumph, he was signing papers such as the one upon the door of the cantina. A natural leader can (and will) do many things at once almost without noticing. Generally, he has to.

A rush of pity for Vittore carried Cressida away for a moment, even though she had failed even to set eyes on him.

Her tear-torn gaze returned to Trifoglio.

'I'd like to throw something at him.'

'It would go straight through him.'

'You must feel even sorrier for Vittore than I do, Vivien. It was you who first thought of him.'

Vivien looked at her enigmatically, but before she could speak, in the same or any other sense, Aunt Agnes had appeared for their luncheon date. She too was now wearing trousers. They were of sky-blue canvas, and matched well with her cerulean short-sleeved blouse.

'It's locked up, Lady Luce,' said Cressida.

'I'm sorry,' said Aunt Agnes, 'but we probably shouldn't have had enough time, anyway. Vittore has offered us all cabins on his yacht, so that we can get away in comfort. Isn't that exciting?'

'Is he coming with us?' asked Vivien.

'I'm afraid we may have to decide that for him,' said Aunt Agnes. 'He just put his hand on my arm and fell back, poor fellow.'

Cressida gazed at Aunt Agnes's bare forearms, shapely as the rest of her.

'Did you actually set eyes on him, then?'

'Of course I set eyes on him, Cressida. I've known Vittore since childhood.'

The exaggeration had to be forgiven, allowing for the circumstances. Nasty-looking men were advancing in all directions breaking windows and tearing down or tearing up everything that was attractive.

'Now you two hurry up and pack. Guards are standing over my luggage on the quay. The Albanians will bring yours down, and then we can all go aboard together.'

'What about Rosemary, and Wendy, and Desirée?'

'You girls always want to bring all your friends. We can't expect Vittore to find room for everybody. After all, it is just his private yacht. I've got to say goodbye to one or two people and then I'll see you on the quay. It's just the other end of where you've been staying. The whole area is surrounded, so you've nothing to worry about if you buck up.'

Aunt Agnes floated off, ignoring all hostilities, like a blue rose at its moment of fullest bloom: provisionally omnipotent.

Between the cantina and the steps to the dormitorio building was really horrid. Homes were being desecrated everywhere, and many other things too. Men and even some debased women glowered at Cressida's and Vivien's costume. Someone had painted MUTAMENTO on the wall of an obvious monastery, long disused.

'What's that mean?' asked Cressida.

'Something to do with physics, isn't it? I don't expect it's meant literally.'

'Nothing here ever is meant literally,' observed Cressida. She was beginning to wonder whether the dormitorio might not have been looted, might no longer be even accessible to two young girls from England.

On a public building of exquisite Renaissance design but characteristically uncertain purpose someone else had painted ALTERAZIONE, by way of a change. It must have been a different person, because the writing was less regular. Plainly, the entire community had begun to find expression as one man.

In the piazza between the gate and the dormitorio building, bombs and grenades were being handed out, small and palpably home-made; no doubt the evening work of dedicated hands during the recent winter. It was hard to believe that people had been attending plays and operas as well, even though these last *were* free. There was also a machine being assembled by committee; at which Cressida thought it best not to look too closely. Novelty was simply everywhere. Even the big gate stood open, though a corps of lusty subversionists was taking care that no one passed through it in either direction.

Bang! Some wight had proved momentarily intransigent in that very matter.

Cressida put her hands to her ears. Too late, of course.

But she fully realised that the opening of the gate was as symbolical as the report. Ancient boundaries, natural reserves, had gone with the nineteenth century. Vigilance and promptness were continuously necessary to keep everyone in position.

Vivien put her arm round Cressida's shoulders. 'Sorry, Cressy. It was all a bad idea.'

'It was your aunt's idea, really,' responded Cressida, strictly fair.

'It was *my* idea,' said Vivien.

'Then there was Rossetti's spell. That was mainly me.'

'It was my idea at bottom,' insisted Vivien. 'I thought it would solve things, but it's only made them worse. We've lost even our hopes.'

'I've not lost *all* hope, Vivien.'

It was hard to tell who was comforting whom.

Mercifully, Cavaliere Terridge was holding on at the foot of the stairs. He was backed by a platoon of hairy men in uniforms so unlike his own that it was hard to believe that he was effectively in command of them. They looked like the chimpanzees' tea party.

'You'd better get packed up, girls, before the fun begins.'

'Hasn't it begun?' asked Cressida.

'Not properly,' said the Cavaliere.

'Have you seen Rosemary and Wendy?'

'Wendy's gone home with Brian Wicker. He's returned to report. His father told him on the telephone. I expect they'll take the opportunity to get married. Lucky them!'

'What will you do?'

'Die with my boots on, I suppose.'

Involuntarily, Cressida glanced at them.

'Won't you come with us? I'm sure Lady Luce would be glad to have you.'

'If you're going to die, you're going to die,' said the Cavaliere.

Cressida looked doubtful.

Harry Crass materialised from somewhere.

'It's awful, just awful.' He croaked. His diction was impeded by his hands being pressed against his face. As far as one could see, he looked pale and grubby, but he had gone almost as soon as he had come.

'The Yanks!' said Cavaliere Terridge with a smile. 'Saw something of them in the trenches.'

'Mr Crass is a Canadian,' corrected Cressida.

'Oh,' said the Cavaliere. 'That's different.'

'Cressida,' said Vivien. 'Stop gossiping and come along.'

As she spoke, the first drop of morning rain fell. It made a circle on the ancient step about an inch and a half in diameter.

CHAPTER FIFTY-SEVEN

All Aboard

Needless to say, it then began to thunder. The first crash came before they were up the steps. Possibly it was also the loudest crash, so that the worst was already over, even though no one knew it.

Moreover, one problem solved itself immediately they entered the dormitorio.

Rosemary was there, packing quietly, in her obviously authentic coat and skirt.

'I've been offered a lift,' she said. 'It's rather a small car, but I expect we could fit you two in with a squeeze. You won't mind making your own arrangements after we reach somewhere civilised?'

'Thank you, we've got a lift,' said Vivien. But the thunder made such a noise that she had to say it again. 'Thank you, we've got a lift.'

'Oh, good,' said Rosemary. 'Then perhaps one of you would like this? I'm afraid I've only got two copies, and I rather want to keep one until I'm completely out of peril.'

Cressida accepted it at once. 'Thank you,' she said.

She looked at it. It was a small four-page leaflet, entitled *As Life Goes On*. There were violets and forget-me-nots on the cover, and faint intimations of dawn or sunset.

'We'd better exchange addresses,' said Rosemary, squeezing at her suitcase in order to shut it. 'Mine is 24 Oates Avenue, Chingley, Essex. Oates with an E, like the South Pole man. We're on the telephone. I won't bother you with the number, as you'll find us quite easily in the directory. Daddy is a Lloyds underwriter.'

'Ravensfoot, Rutland,' said Cressida.

'Is that all?'

Rosemary had now lifted her suitcase to the floor and was kneeling on it, risking her stockings.

'Rutland is a tiny county. You mustn't think we're anything in the least grand. Daddy just farms mainly. We're not on the telephone at all.'

Rosemary looked up at Vivien, in so far as her exertions permitted.

'My parents are always out of the country. Cressida's address will reach me too.'

Vivien had herself begun to pack with industry.

'Shall I kneel on it beside you?' Cressida asked Rosemary.

'No, I think I've managed.' For the moment, Rosemary's face was a pretty pink. 'Well, goodbye all.' Rosemary extended her hand and they shook it, one after the other.

'Will you be all right?' asked Cressida.

'Of course I shall. Hugh Terridge is taking me.'

'Really? When?'

'Now. I'm sure we could fit you both in. Are you sure you won't?'

'We've been given places on the *Pericoloso*,' said Vivien.

'I shouldn't think that's safe at all.'

'Well, we can't get out of it without upsetting my Aunt Agnes.'

'Lady Luce is very sweet,' said Cressida.

'I do hope you'll be all right. Well, goodbye, finally. Or rather for the present. We might all meet one day for tea in Gunter's or somewhere.'

It was hardly necessary to wait for her to be out of earshot when there was so much thunder in the air.

'That man Terridge wasn't speaking the truth,' observed Cressida, as she too began applying herself.

'He was covering up, like a perfect gentleman,' replied Vivien.

'From now on we might both be murdered, and without his even attempting to protect us.'

'I'm nearly packed,' said Vivien. 'I've decided to leave a lot behind.'

'It'll come in for the refugees. There are always millions of them.'

'Starting with us, I daresay. And normally the new people try to wipe them all out. It's called turning your back on the past. For God's sake, Cressy, you can do without an evening dress.'

'I can't, Vivien. Nor can you. It's the one thing you need on a ship. You know that as well as I do. Look at all the dresses your mother took when she sailed on the *Periphrastic*.'

'But we're not going for a trip on a liner. We're running away.'

'It's a private yacht. And it's white. You'll need your evening dress.'

'I refuse to open up again.'

'Just put it over your arm.'

'What about the rain?'

'Oh, Vivien. Do *try*!'

But four Albanians were coming down the stone passage from the direction of the quay. They made gestures intended to indicate that they had been sent by Aunt Agnes to carry the luggage. Cressida thought their expressions questionable, but acquiescence was the only possibility. In any case, Cressida simply hated carrying almost anything.

The rambling old place was at its most typical with thunder banging, rain flooding, and lightning intruding horizontally in double sheets.

Suddenly Cressida darted back to the dormitorio.

'What now?' enquired Vivien.

'Sorry,' gasped Cressida. 'I just wanted a last look.'

It hardly took a moment, but now the Albanians were well ahead and beginning to bawl at one another, whereas previously they had been silent. Of course there was nothing like enough for four strong men to carry. Virility was being under-utilised.

'If you'll stand under the arch at the end, I'll come back with an umbrella or something to keep your dress dry.'

It was not the silk party dress from the garment store, but a pretty garment from Harvey Nichols, where Vivien's mother had an account. It did not matter about the account being overdrawn as, at the worst, there was the Colonial Office, the numerous Colonial Banks, all those things. Cressida had been present when Vivien had chosen the dress and had chosen one for herself too, indeed the one she had just packed. Both dresses were much nicer that most of the things on offer down in the garment store, but Cressida had doubts about their being sufficiently sophisticated for a steam yacht. Sophistication was always the most terrible problem, if one was honest, which most girls managed not to be.

Cressida dashed down the steps. At the bottom, she turned for a second, excited by the deluge, threw up her arms, and grinned back at Vivien. Standing in the crumbling old archway, Vivien resembled one of the saints who carry their skins over their arms.

Cressida's hair was like that of a beautiful mermaid, and now her trousers were soaked, as well as pierced by a lance.

Aunt Agnes was standing under cover at the top of the gangway. She was gazing back at the town and looking very sad. However, a handsome man stood beside her, towering terrifically, and dressed for the sea in a blue doeskin jacket, white trousers, and a stiff collar. He wore chocolate and cream canvas shoes.

The first thing Cressida did was to stare where Aunt Agnes was staring.

She saw that, all over the place, clouds of smoke were rising, and making the prospect darker than ever. On the other hand, there were tall flames rising also, which doubtless had the contrary effect. Cressida had never seen such tall flames, except in the London Museum diorama, one half-term.

'Has something been struck by lightning, Lady Luce?' Cressida never under-estimated that possibility, however strenuously her father and most of his friends poo-pooed it.

The tall, handsome man seemed to smile for a moment. It was like the rotation of the beam at the top of a lighthouse.

Aunt Agnes spoke. 'It's not a thunderbolt, Cressida. It's a revolution.'

'Insurrezione,' said the tall man; quietly wistful as one who knew all, regretted all, accepted all, acknowledged all.

'But surely you can't have a fire in weather like this? Not a proper fire, anyway?'

'The old workhouse went up when I was a girl and my sister and I watched the firemen struggling with their hoses all day and it made not the slightest difference. Several other girls watched too. They were staying with us for the holidays. That was years ago, of course.'

'But you can't burn down stone houses.'

'You can burn down anything, Cressida. Even the Tower of London might burn down one day. Even the Crystal Palace.'

'Lady Luce, do you think I could borrow an umbrella or something to keep Vivien's dress dry? She's carrying it over her arm.'

Aunt Agnes spoke to the handsome man in Italian.

Cressida had quite realised that umbrellas are not issued at sea, owing to the strength of the wind.

'It's Vivien's *evening dress*,' she explained.

A common sailor slid past, saluting, trying to smile at the ladies.

The handsome man spoke to him. In no time he returned with a special sea umbrella with two garments in yellow oilskin.

Cressida clambered into one of them. It was as inflexible and enormous as a lobster shell: absolutely too big and vague to be exciting in any way. Moreover, it stank of salt. The clothes that one had to borrow when abroad! She descended the gangway and arranged to raise the sea umbrella against all odds. She conveyed the other garment to Vivien, who by now was looking impatient.

'I'm feeling hungry,' she said.

CHAPTER FIFTY-EIGHT

Midnight at Teatime

They were in the dry once more. The sea umbrella had been lowered, the oilskins removed, and all the luggage safely stowed, Lady Luce's included.

By now there were urban explosions to augment the divine rumble. It was like the last ten or twelve minutes of a long symphony when everyone begins to wake up again, having lost the thread hours before, or what seems like hours.

'When do we cast off, Lady Luce?'

'When Vittore makes up his mind, Cressida, or when someone makes it up for him, poor man.'

'Might it be Desirée?'

'If that's a friend of yours, I think it would probably be someone a little older.'

'Why don't *you* try again, Aunt Agnes?'

'I've already done all a woman can, Vivien. Besides, I've got you two to look after.'

'I'd like us to go, Lady Luce,' said Cressida, with unmistakable sincerity.

'They were always blowing up houses in the war, weren't they? It was the way you could tell the Germans were getting nearer and nearer.'

'During the Risorgimento, signorina,' said the handsome man unexpectedly, 'Garibaldi, our national hero, blew up one house in six. At times of social change it is necessary.' The handsome man had the most romantic possible accent. Valentino would have spoken like that had Valentino been able to speak. Not that Cressida any longer cared all that much for Valentino after Vivien had made some comments.

'This is Captain Nessuno, master of the ship,' said Aunt Agnes, a little later than convention required, as so often with her. 'This is my niece, Vivien, and her friend, Cressida. Captain Nessuno went with Vittore in a miniature submarine right under the polar ice-cap. He is a man of mystery.'

Captain Nessuno bowed pleasantly to each girl. It was as when a poplar feels the south-west wind.

'Did you go in winter?'

'It makes no difference, signorina. The darkness is eternal.'

'It's pretty dark here and now,' said Vivien.

'This is nothing, signorina. Niente.'

Cressida thought it would be sensible to go inside. There seemed no reason to continue just standing about on deck, even though technically they were out of the rain. Also she would like to see where the Albanians had taken her and Vivien's luggage; where they were to sleep and do their little chores while the voyage lasted. She tried to glance significantly at Vivien.

'What a pretty dress your mother chose for you, Vivien!' said Aunt Agnes.

'I chose it. Mummy was in the East.'

'Well, you'd better hang it up.'

'We're hungry, Aunt Agnes. Is there tea or something?'

The Captain spoke. 'I will take the signorine to Minimo.'

'And mind you're very kind to him,' said Aunt Agnes. 'He can't help being as he is.'

It seemed best not to know too soon what that was, but before they could go below or whatever might be required, a figure had burst through the guards, or presumably so, because Cressida had not seen any guards, and darted up the gangway before anyone could stop him. Sure enough it was Harry Crass again.

'Give me passage, lady. Let me work. I'm a certificated seaman.'

He was on his knees, with one hand on each of Aunt Agnes's lovely thighs.

'Well, I'm not sure.' Naturally, Aunt Agnes looked to the master of the ship in matters of this kind. She looked now.

'The government's disappeared. The whole lot of them. The soldiers and sailors have killed their officers. All the drains are blocked.'

Oh, thought Cressida, the poor nice old Marchese! And several other people like that too. But when she came to think of it, perhaps they could not latterly be described as the government? Latterly, if ever? There might be hope still.

'My life's not worth a handful of dimes.'

Surely they were American currency, not Canadian? But of course there was no proper border between the two countries. Coins must stray about continually.

'I can see my head on a pole, lady. Give me a chance to get to Manitoba. My sweetheart's on the farm there.'

Well, there could be no doubt about where Manitoba was.

Aunt Agnes turned to the Captain. 'What do you think, Captain Nessuno? It's your ship, you must remember.'

'Plead for me, lady!' said Harry Crass, his grip tightening, even though one of his fingers was there only in part.

He had been looking up at Aunt Agnes, as in a picture by El Greco, but on an instant his eyes fell to the deck and he pressed the hard top of his head between her knees.

'I'll *show* you my certificate.' One felt there were no limits to what he might manifest.

Certainly it seemed extreme behaviour for a Canadian, but of course he had not been a Canadian always.

Aunt Agnes wriggled gracefully backwards a little. 'Well, Captain, what do you say?'

But the Captain said something in Italian.

'English, English,' cried Harry Crass. 'Have mercy.'

'I said that I ought either to throw you overboard to the sharks or to clap you in irons.'

Cressida could only giggle. 'I don't believe there *are* any sharks.'

'There are gelatine with tentacoli thirty feet long, one touch from which is death.'

'They're called Portuguese men-of-war,' said Aunt Agnes seriously, 'and you two must remember about them if you do any bathing before we reach home. You can see them bobbing about in the distance, because they're all the colours of the rainbow. My grandmother's French maid got into a serious situation with one at Juan. Her name was Germaine. Now, my man, get up at once, stand properly, and kind Captain Nessuno will find you work of some kind down in the hold.'

'Lady, I'll never forget. I'll die for you, lady. Even when I'm an old, old man.'

The curious part was that now he actually looked older. Not that one could see very much in this absurd light. More accurately, it was darkness shot with flames. Of course there were sometimes very long thunderstorms in England too, even though never a full revolution.

Cressida was relieved that someone had decided something. After all, there might be little actual harm in having Harry Crass on board. He would quite possibly come in useful for some purpose or other.

Suddenly she gasped. 'Vivien! You haven't forgotten to pack your novel?'

Vivien shook her head.

'I'm glad you've brought something to do,' said Aunt Agnes. 'At sea there are very long periods without occupation, except of course when one's being ill.'

'Work's a bit like that too, Aunt Agnes,' said Vivien.

Captain Nessuno had handed over Harry Crass to the bosun, or some such person, who was concerned with things actually happening. Was the Captain about to hand over the girls to the steward?

'I wish we could go,' said Cressida, glancing once more at the scene of storm, incendiarism, and, almost certainly, mayhem.

'I feel hollow,' said Vivien superfluously.

'Well go, you ridiculous girls,' said Aunt Agnes, smiling affectionately.

Cressida was quite prepared to excuse whatever had to be excused in the steward, but she thought it best not to peer too closely for what that might be. After all, it might soon be diffi-cult enough to keep her food down without anything more to worry about.

There was a large teapot, supported by caryatids with clothes falling off them. The fluid within was leafy and smoky. There were peculiar yellow and brown cakes, which looked at the same time plain and rich. There were mixed bonbons in the upturned mouth of a chimaera. There were even spring flowers in ornamental sieves.

'Pane e burro?' enquired Vivien tentatively.

The steward shook his head. Drops of sweat fell off it onto the white table cloth.

'Pane e burro e *marmellatta*?' persisted Vivien, quite at her best.

But the steward only shrugged and lumbered off.

'Do you think they haven't got any bread,' enquired Cressida, 'or didn't he understand? There's no milk either.'

'I'd like a boiled egg,' said Vivien. She had placed two of the cakes on her plate, and was attempting to eat them, as starving prisoners eat snails off walls. 'Sorry, Cressy.' Vivien had forgotten to pass one of the dishes before making do herself.

'Why's he called Minimo? He seemed enormous to me.'

'It's like Elephant. Only the opposite. *You* know.' Vivien's mouth was full.

Elephant had taught chemistry, and was as limpid as a test tube. She ate nothing at all, and when she was missing for more than a full school year, was understood to be undergoing treatment of some kind in Harrogate, necessarily lengthy.

'What's peculiar about him? I decided not to look at him.'

'I think he's a eunuch,' said Vivien.

'They were in Biblical times.'

'Daddy knew bushels of them when he was in Smyrna. He said they were the only people who got anything done. Rather what you'd expect of course.' Vivien took in more than usual of the cake in order to finish it off. 'That was before they shunted Daddy from the Foreign into the Colonial, of course.'

'How can you tell a eunuch when you see one? I mean, with his clothes on, of course?'

'They bulge all over, and perspire a lot, and lose their hair sooner than ordinary men, and have to be very charming all the time.'

'I didn't think Minimo charming.'

'We have nothing to give him in return. Eunuchs are like cultured pearls. These cakes are foul. I'd pay anything for a couple of proper buns.'

'We'll soon be home.'

'Shall we?'

'It's very pretty in here, Vivien.'

'The food doesn't feed.'

But Cressida could quite easily gaze round with admiration.

Fundamentally, it was a décor in the Louis Seize taste, with pilasters, the most subtle strawberry pinks and mint greens, and pictures of women on swings and in hammocks, as well as the usual likenesses of Vittore, now in the most emollient costumes also, here of a shepherd, there of a swain, and only once of Jupiter himself in a golden chlamys and shiny diadem, the points in the likenesses of rams and of other horned things.

The lights were held by arms coming through the walls.

'That clock's stopped!'

And even though it was in the fashion of a gilt octopus with jewelled eyes towards the top of the dial and a beak where one inserted the winder!

'Clocks are no good at sea. You have to use chronometers.'

'All that stuff about ascertaining longitude and someone getting a prize for it?'

'Monica Dixon-Scott got the prize. *The Complete History of Logarithms*, with illustrations.'

Cressida rose and crossed to the shelf where the clock stood glowering.

'It's been screwed down.'

'Naturally. Even the cups and plates have to be screwed down sometimes.'

And, indeed, if one were honest, the boat had never been in exactly the same position for two seconds running since Cressida had boarded her.

'Let's get out of here, Cressy.'

'I could try to find you some proper food, but I think we ought to see where we're sleeping.'

Vivien was at the door. 'We *can't* get out. We're locked in.'

'Why on earth should we be?'

'Well, look!'

Vivien was pointing to the town, even though there were only small portholes through which to view it. The town was in retreat; because the *Pericoloso* was on the high seas.

For Cressida, Trino disappeared in a bigger-than-ever winding sheet of lightning, from which it was but prudent to avert the gaze, let alone the mind.

Crash! That time it was not Jupiter's wrath, but something falling to the floor. One of the ornaments had been imperfectly secured.

Then Cressida realised that it was her own little pochère, which she had, from habit, been carrying even when wearing trousers. She picked it up.

'Vivien, we shall need money again soon!'

Just as the sea was settling down to its business, there was the sound of a key turning. The door opened and Aunt Agnes entered. She was wearing much thicker blue trousers and a blue sweater over her cerulean blouse.

'Have you had a nice tea?'

'No,' said Vivien. 'Sick-making. Though I daresay it doesn't matter much.'

'Captain Nessuno thought it best to lock all doors while Vittore came aboard. Of course you didn't know. I was locked up with the rest, as I was preparing myself for sea.'

'You look just like a sailor, Lady Luce.'

'When you're a little older, Cressida, you'll have learnt that's one of the best things a woman can look like.'

Aunt Agnes caressed her arms slightly, the one with the other, and glanced down at her legs.

'Is Vittore all right now?'

'I fear not. Captain Nessuno tells me he's completely inchoate.'

'Are we all going to be seasick?'

'Not if we make up our minds in good time not to.'

Cressida could not doubt that the time was coming soon. The motion was becoming more and more like that afternoon at Sutton-on-Sea.

'Do you think the ship will hold together, Aunt Agnes? Cressy saw it being patched last night so that Vittore could do his bunk.'

'You shouldn't use common expressions, Vivien, and of course the ship will hold together. Vittore's been round and round the world in her. He's always doing it.'

'Are we still within sight of land?' asked Cressida. It seemed unwise to look for herself. In any case, soapy water was covering the portholes all the time now.

'I'm sure we are,' said Aunt Agnes soothingly. 'The Adriatic is quite narrow.'

They were all still in the saloon. This was because no one felt very inclined to go anywhere else at the moment.

As so often before, Harry Crass burst in.

He flung himself at Aunt Agnes and gripped her arms in a vice. Despite her thick sweater, it must have been quite painful, but Aunt Agnes was too considerate to complain.

'Ma'am, I swore to save and keep you, and the little ladies too. You've got two to three minutes. The lot of you.'

'Are we already sinking, Mr Crass? I believe that is your name?'

'The crew's turned bolshie. The ship's been mined. It's inside her now and ticking.'

For two or three seconds, Cressida was paler than at any thought of mal-de-mer. She realised that at the very, very bottom of her being she had known all the time. She had known and she had not spoken!

'Oh,' she gulped.

'This is really *not* the moment to be sick, Cressida,' said Aunt Agnes.

'We saw them putting the mine in,' cried Cressida. 'It's true. We'll be like the *Lusitania* and the *Titanic* and the *Deutschland* and the *Camperdown* and the *Royal George*': emotion bringing literature to her head in a rush.

'And the *Birkenhead*,' added Vivien.

'Mr Crass. Have you told the Captain of this?'

'He's fighting for his life at the moment, ma'am. They've even got the cutlasses out.'

'Surely cutlasses belong to the past?'

'They're held by for emergencies, ma'am. You can take the word of a certificated seaman that far.'

'We really don't want to be cut to bits,' protested Aunt Agnes. 'Is there *no one* we can depend on?'

'Not many, lady. This is a revolution. There's always me, of course.'

'Well, Mr Crass, and what can *you* do for us? You say you have the experience.'

'We must lower a boat while everyone's fighting and row to the land. It's quite near. You can see it sometimes.'

'And what about poor Vittore?'

Aunt Agnes's expression resembled that of the Tragic Muse; and her posture also, in so far as her present clothes were consistent.

'He can come too, I suppose, if he bustles.'

'I'll tell Vittore myself, if it's the last thing I do.'

'Oh no, Lady Luce, not the last thing!'

'Well, naturally I hope not, Cressida. But Vittore's one of the great men of our time. Far, far more important than any of *us*.'

'That's right, Aunt Agnes,' said Vivien, though her intonation was difficult to define amid so much excitement and noisy surf.

'I shall remain loyal to Vittore though all others fail him,' said Aunt Agnes.

Cressida and Vivien nodded their heads as if momentarily propelled by the same clockwork.

'It's the very least I can do,' said Aunt Agnes, concluding the dialogue.

Chapter Fifty-Nine

Clutching at Straws

'Let's get moving, folks,' said Harry Crass. 'We only have seconds.'

They all hurried up on deck.

'It's stopped raining,' cried Cressida. 'The storm's over.' Goodness, the weather abroad was changeable!

'The first thing to do,' said Harry Crass, 'is to bolt down all the hatches, so that they have to fight it out below decks.'

He began to dart about doing it. The girls got the idea at once and helped enormously, especially as they had the full use of all their fingers.

'But,' cried Aunt Agnes, 'what about poor Captain Nessuno? And, I imagine, his fellow officers? We can't just clamp down on them.'

'Needs must, ma'am, when there's revolution. Reckon there's a transvaluation of all values, as Nietzsche put it.'

'He was German,' said Aunt Agnes firmly.

For her part, Cressida had merely found Nietzsche rather silly. Three pages were quite enough when there was so much else to read in the world before one was dead. Of course the three pages *had* been in translation. All those Gothic letters, looking like thistles, were even more impossible.

'Next thing is to slay the guy at the helm and whoever else may be around in the wheelhouse. See you in a jiffy.'

Harry Crass had a nasty-looking gun in one hand; an even more nasty-looking knife in the other. There was little evidence of where he had obtained such objects. He sprang aloft. Not every day could his technique of sudden entry prevail so potently.

He was back.

'What happened?' asked Aunt Agnes.

Though the storm had passed, it was still gusty, and one might have thought she spoke too low to be heard.

But Harry Crass answered: 'Only one man there. The good old K.O. settled him.'

'He'll be all right?'

'Lady, there's a revolution. You keep forgetting.'

'Well, what next?' asked Vivien.

'Get that boat loose. We're running before the wind and don't want the ship to break up before she blows up.'

On the empty deck, the four of them set about it, with Vivien decisively the second in command. All know that when at last the British find themselves, it is usually in order to retreat. In such circumstances, all their coolness comes into play.

'Couldn't we stop the engine too?' asked Aunt Agnes, as she pulled at ropes. 'So that we can get off more easily?'

'The engine room bell won't necessarily be answered, just now,' replied Harry Crass. 'They've got other things to deal with.'

'When I've helped with this, I'm going to look for Vittore. I really am.' Aunt Agnes paused for a second, rubbing the tips of her fingers. 'Mr Crass! I hope he's not one of the people we've locked in?'

'The owner of the vessel usually occupies the deckhouse, ma'am. He and his lady friend and so forth.'

'Vittore has no lady friend, Mr Crass!'

'To think of so lusty a man being brought that low. It's pitiful.'

The boat had begun to descend on its lines, stale though they were from disuse. Harry Crass tied it off while awaiting the final assembly.

'The sun's coming out,' remarked Cressida.

She gazed across the taffrail at the coast of Croatia, or was it Herzegovina? The scenery was mostly rocks, and very beautiful. People came great distances to look at it.

Gannets and such things were emerging from natural shelters and beginning to scream and fly about.

'Perhaps it will be easier than we thought,' suggested Vivien, looking at the sea.

'A swell like this often lasts for whole days after the wind's dropped,' observed Harry Crass. 'Sometimes it even gathers force. You can't do nothing about it. It's Nature's own way with things. It's how things are.'

Plainly he had emerged as a natural leader, and instinctively was using more and more of the language proper to that status.

Aunt Agnes was tapping politely at the deckhouse door. Within, all the blinds were down, which, Cressida realised, might mean anything or nothing. Each blind had a big V at its centre, circumferenced by a glory. The blinds were in a very nautical blue, and the embellishments in crushed gold.

Aunt Agnes tapped politely again.

'Hurry, lady. Mines wait for no man.'

Cressida was quite startled by his peremptoriness; but she was startled also to note how far she had forgotten about the mine she herself had seen being installed.

Aunt Agnes tapped a third time; more forcibly, because more despairingly.

There was the most tremendous crash that Cressida would have thought possible. It was as if Aunt Agnes had been the chambermaid knocking to bring in a full breakfast, and then dropping the entire tray: only far louder.

In no time they were all in the water. It could not be said that Harry Crass had failed to give them warning: quite ample warning, all things considered. Cressida could see him now respectfully dragging Aunt Agnes into the boat. How fortunate that the boat had been loosened by the four of them! And whose idea had that been too? Almost, whose directive?

'There's no art to find the mind's construction in the face,' Cressida reminded herself, expelling sea water from her mouth, and devoutly wishing she could eject it from her ears also. Everyone knew there were no tides in the Mediterranean and its contiguous parts, so that the sea must be far fouler than the sea round Britain, especially as it was also far older.

She thought it was probably a good thing she was not wearing a skirt, as on the outward journey. She had always been told that learning to swim would stand her in good stead one day, and here it was standing. If only monitions of that kind were always so dependable!

The sea was heaving up and down unpredictably; like life itself. Cressida knew that the thing was to offer no direct resistance; rather to relax, as far as possible to float.

She could see that Vivien was now in the boat too. There seemed to be no one else around. The man at the wheel had been defeated pugilistically; and most or all of the others locked up, partly by her. Cressida began to feel confused and upset. She knew perfectly well that it was no moment for self-examination, but could not altogether desist.

As far as the toppling waves permitted a view, the ship seemed to have disappeared. So, for that matter, had the flaming towers of Trino. In the latter case, a sensation of relief was possible.

'Cressida!' It was Vivien calling for her.

Cressida could from time to time see the boat with three people in it, but found it curiously difficult to swim towards it, even to keep constantly in mind where it was.

'Cressida! Cressida!' The anxiety in Vivien's voice—the *kind* of anxiety—was beautiful, was wonderful, was moving. Cressida would have liked to weep.

She flapped and floundered about. Thank goodness there was no long hair to tickle and obstruct her eyes. At least, one couldn't actually drown with rescue so very near. Even the rocky coast was within her accepted swimming range, she reflected; at least if conditions had been more like a swimming bath. Of course, there had been Aunt Ramuz, Aunt Bolsover's half-sister, who had deliberately drowned herself in an ornamental pool not eighteen inches deep, not four feet square, and (as so often) full of supposedly ornamental fish. 'The will power!' everyone had exclaimed, aware in themselves of lacking it.

Cressida's will power, at least under present circumstances, was being exerted in the opposite direction. A chubby little boat bobbed past her; much smaller than Vivien's boat. She had noticed it lying on the deck, rather like a flagon in a wooden cradle. Presumably it had not needed loosening, but, when the ship fell apart, had just floated off with the other debris that littered the sea.

'Cressida!' Now Aunt Agnes was participating.

'Miss Hazeborough!'

'Cressida! Cressida!'

Kicking vigorously downwards to keep herself in position, Cressida managed to raise her left arm and to stop the little boat by gripping the gunwale with her hand.

She was aware that clambering aboard would be a very different matter. She was far more likely to overturn the fat little craft. Even then, however, she might conceivably contrive to mount the keel and squat there like Hope in the famous picture, whose harp, she had always thought, was pathetically lacking in strings.

She pulled down the nearer side of the boat, and transferred her grip from her left hand to her right. The boat proved small enough for her to reach the far side of the gunwale with the left hand she had released. The discomfort was great and she could not have lasted for long, but by determination, and by treading water furiously, she managed to avoid overtoppling the boat until the swell she was waiting for lifted her aboard, and at the same time so flooded the boat that the first need was for a baler.

The calling for her had stopped. Aboard the other boat, all could see what was happening to her.

Why, she wondered, did they not make towards her? The distance and the bluster were too great for a question to be heard; or an answer either.

As far as she could see, they were playing about among themselves and taking no external action.

Vivien shouted something to her. Duly, she could distinguish not a word; nothing but the anguish.

Cressida smiled back as warmly as she could.

What was her proper course? To make signs, as in old posters, that she needed rescue; or at all costs to find something with which to bale.

She decided that the second activity was the more imperative.

In the bottom of the boat was a boathook, which had neither toppled out nor floated out. Cressida realised that this was because it had been prudently secured with twine in two places. Within a short distance of her were miscellaneous objects, still afloat: buckets marked INCENDIO, hats marked PERICOLOSO, tins marked HEINZ.

From her horribly soggy trousers pocket, Cressida drew her penknife. It was just like the penknife with which Desirée had cut the ropes round the bales of sweaters. Cressida even managed to open it without splitting her nail. She tweaked at the twists of twine. A knife had hardly been needed. The twine was debilitated by numberless changes in the weather.

Cressida found the boathook heavier than she had expected. Though shorter than the boathooks hired out on the lagoons at Skegness, it was also far stouter, and somehow of heavier wood. None the less, Cressida tried to flourish it before starting to fish about with it.

In a moment, she had aboard with her exactly what she needed. It was the bottom part of a tin inscribed TE CINESE and, despite exposure to the briny, smelling intoxicatingly of cocoa. How Cressida, wet as she was, would have welcomed several successive cups at that moment!

It was absurd. The sun was now shining so blatantly that soon she might well be too hot, especially with all the physical work to which she was unavoidably committed: on the other hand, the sea was still bumping about so steeply that water was probably being shipped at least equal in volume to that which was being so laboriously hurled forth. On the other hand again, Cressida could at the moment see no alternative. Not to anything.

And at that same moment she realised why she was not being rescued properly. Almost certainly poor Vivien's craft had been set afloat without oars.

When the two little boats were for a second fully in sight of one another, Cressida waved cheerfully.

The next time it happened, Cressida's theory was confirmed: Harry Crass was seen to be mounting a sail made from ladies' undergarments. Black and red, it was a pirates' sail.

Cressida giggled. In any case, she was slowly winning her struggle with the elements, even though she might be making the ocean smell of Cadbury's in the process.

Goodness! Where was Vittore?

It was curious how every time he seemed to be the person one failed to think of first, however true it might be that one would never have found oneself here at all but for him—though possibly, when one came to think of it, but for Elsie Churchill either.

Cressida baled on: more soberly, but no less vigorously. After all, the weather might change again. It almost certainly would. There seemed no fallacy more total than the belief that in and around Italy the sun shines without a second thought.

The boat was nearly empty, but the dregs were resistant. Alas, Cressida had been observing for some time that Vivien's boat was sailing in the wrong direction. Harry Crass, certificated or otherwise, was accomplishing less than he had promised; or at least implied. Cressida could imagine what Vivien was thinking.

She had no oars herself. She had undergarments for only one woman, not two. She had no idea how to sail even a model boat in any case. On her one visit to a full-scale yacht club, she had fallen dead asleep: something that rarely happened to her at that sort of hour.

She shivered quite violently, so that her teeth chattered against the gusts of wind. Heavens! If she remained in these wet clothes, the next thing would be pneumonia. Pneumonia was always the next thing; far ahead of the next thing but one, which latter was always the more obvious thing, and what one would expect.

For throwing off wet garments there were reasons, therefore, even more cogent than the need for a sail. Always, always, take off even one wet shoe as soon as you possibly can, as had been done last night. And now both Cressida's shoes were as wet as they could be.

She took off more and more.

There was no one in sight to worry about, except, she supposed, Harry Crass, who by now hardly counted.

The degree of warmth, the quality of the air, were delightful, as they so often are when one puts everything at risk.

Cressida gazed much in awe at her marine self. If only the sea would lie down properly. After all, the sea was the lion, and she the lamb, nacreous and prelapsarian.

She peered over the gunwale, the edge of the boat. Vivien's craft was still going round in small circles. She could see Harry Crass fussing: Vivien must be deeming his seamanship compromised beyond hope. Cressida was gratified to note that her own little eggshell, all on its own, and without her doing one thing, was unmistakably though imperceptibly drifting inshore. Her father's term for it would certainly be 'undertow'. Then, she reflected: one thing she *had* done; Leda had unlatched to the swan; a proper ritual act.

In fact, a flight of what might well have *been* swans hurtled through the atmosphere at that moment. The noise was like the creaking of bellows.

For a second or two, Cressida judged herself indifferent as to whether she was rescued or not.

'To cease upon the noontide in a boat,

'To die within one's beauty ere it's stained.'

For a flash, Cressida was even more closely at one with a poet than ever before.

She saw what she took to be a sack with something inside it; almost certainly something nasty. The whole thing was floating, or perhaps not quite.

She averted her eyes. She concentrated upon her knees. Nothing availed. She had been most harshly returned from the paradise of poetry to the tension and anxiety of living.

She knew it must happen: the sack was bumping against her boat.

She tried to shrink so far within herself that she might well have turned inside out.

Worse still: the sack had been lifted on a wave and had lowered at her. It was like something in Sinbad.

Still worse again: as it sank almost beneath the surface, the sack had uttered a cry.

Cressida was appalled by the need, the utter duty, to release some poor creature from a watery end; very likely a quite large obstreperous creature, rampant with life force.

A pair of eyes appeared over the gunwale. They were strange eyes, but, being beneath an enormous brow, were strangely human too. Above the brow, or across it, the sack resumed.

As the owner of the eyes showed no sign of pulling down the sack, Cressida tried to turn her back. When the eyes had sunk down once more, she stretched out for a garment, but there had not been enough time for anything to dry, even in air of such purity.

'Bellezza!'

Not only the eyes had ascended once more: this time there was the fullest of faces, apart from the regions shaded in soaking sack.

Neither the visible features nor the voice could be misascribed; even though Cressida had not before actually heard the latter.

'I'm afraid I don't speak Italian. I'm so sorry.'

'Naiad incarnate!'

'Let me put on some clothes, then I'll help you aboard.'

'Help me now or I die!'

There was nothing else to be done, and at least it was simpler than having to cope with a young bullock or a smelly goat.

'I am Vittore!'

'Yes, I know. I am Cressida Hazeborough. How do you do?'

'You are Beauty!'

'Hadn't we better talk about getting ashore?'

'You are Anadyomene!'

'Green and gold,' supplied Cressida, without thinking.

'You are Sappho!'

Cressida could only giggle.

'Your realm is the sea!'

'It does look like it, I know.'

'Your belly is a flower, your thighs are a prayer, your breasts are peaches!'

The most extraordinary thing then happened.

Vittore touched each of Cressida's breasts with his lips, lightly, in order not to chill them; and she neither spoke nor moved.

CHAPTER SIXTY

Go Back at Once

Came the dusk. Cressida had never been so uncomfortable. By now something called rheumatic fever might well be threatening.

Hours ago Vivien's boat had disappeared from sight, slowly, picturesquely, conclusively.

In Cressida's own case, the undertow seemed to have given up. Cressida now recollected that undertows normally draw the swimmer away from the land, not towards it; so that his case becomes hopeless. That was the whole point.

Besides, there was more weight in the boat now.

'We really must make an effort. I'm terribly hungry.'

'Effort no longer has effect!' And, indeed, our hero did seem strangely exhausted. Cressida was quite surprised by him.

'But you're primarily a man of action! Everyone knows that!'

Cressida realised that she too was beginning to converse in exclamation marks. It was well known, among girls and mistresses alike, how catching such tricks were.

'No more! I am now a monk!' Vittore pointed to the wet sack.

He had the most beautiful hands she had ever seen, even on a female.

Cressida wished he would put the sack on again, unbecoming though it was. There was a limit to having to look at the gashes on his front, however triumphant. There was one place where a bullet had gone right through him, like a weevil.

'What did you hope for when you started all this—though I'm not at all sure what all this is?'

'For my death to equal my life! It is your privilege to join me! You alone!'

'Certainly not!' She smiled at him. 'Look what happened just now!'

'That is always a half-death!'

Cressida was perfectly well aware what he meant.

'I'd much rather try to swim ashore. I think I could get there, but I shouldn't be able to manage when I landed, with no words and no clothes.'

'Life ends at twenty-six.'

'Yes, I know,' said Cressida, remembering what Dr Blattner had said. 'But I'm nothing like twenty-six.' However, she was guiltily aware that Dr Blattner had said twenty-five. Vittoria might well have bid even lower. Life and death are a Dutch auction.

'I have given you life! Only death can equal it!'

The trouble was that part of her knew how right this might be. For one reason or another.

'Have you always been like this, Vittore?'

'I am a messiah! The messiah of doubt!'

He began to talk somewhat in the manner of old Mr Gulliford, whom Cressida and Vivien had met in a wood, and had often been back to, so that he had taught them almost all they knew that was important, showed them things too.

'The world is will and idea,' said Vittore, in his curious, improbable voice; 'but not as Schopenhauer used those terms. There are no facts. There has never been anything claimed as a fact, which has not been argued, at the time or later, and usually disproved, often reversed. About all things, there are only ideas. And ideas are chosen and organised by will: collective will when the people are weakening; individual will when the people are strong. Science is an illusion, a mistake.'

'Yes,' said Cressida. 'I know.' But she added politely, 'Though of course I couldn't have explained it so well.'

'Questions are what matter,' said Vittore, 'not answers. Questions are for the strong, answers for the weak.'

'Is Vittoria really your sister? I thought she was sweet.'

'She and I lived together in a crater and strangled all our enemies. When we were children.'

'Where was that?'

'In the Apennines.'

Cressida nodded knowledgably. They descended from between Italy's shoulders all the way down to her high heel and arched foot.

'I had left my sister the future,' said Vittore, his eyes gleaming with past power.

'You believe in proper jobs for women? So do I. Well, in many ways.'

'The course of history has made men superfluous.'

Cressida gleamed back understandingly. If there was any discovery that she and Vivien had packed meticulously into their bundles, their very rucksacks . . .

But Vittore, protean always, was again being Mr Gulliford.

'Men,' said Vittore, 'are designed to live savagely in a crater or a gully and at intervals to slay a dragon. It is not ten seconds ago. I am that man. I am Saint George with his lance; his eyes now hard, now soft. There have been wars. There have been bad weather, bad crops, bad houses, bad taxes, bad men, bad generals; even bad kings. Always a fight, always a struggle, a contest, a challenge; and in the end, always a defeat. Now we have seen the last of the wars, or the last but one. The final fight, the final struggle is very close. All will be security, as in the byre. There is no longer reason for a man to be a man. Men are unnecessary.'

'You're leaving a lot to your sister!'

'I have cut to pieces my testament with razors! I have burned it with hot coals! I have ground it beneath my iron feet!'

'I'm sure Vittoria will take charge very well.'

Vittore shook his head. Cressida was surprised to notice that after all the time that had passed and all the things that had happened, distinct drops of moisture fell from his sparse hair on to his gashed, though sculptured, thighs.

Perhaps it was merely perspiration. The evening was becoming warmer every minute.

'Power is going too! Rule will soon be obsolete also! People will be placid, reasonable, managed.'

'When did all this begin to happen?'

'Prophets have prophesied it for two thousand years. It is known as the Millennium.'

It *was* a coincidence. Mr Gulliford had spoken of that too, though of course in the British way, hazy from word-shortage, heavy with airborne damp.

'You speak English wonderfully,' said Cressida, really meaning it.

'Everything I attempt becomes perfect.' It was *very* like Professor Colossi.

'But I should never take you for an Englishman!'

'I am what the English call a Hyperborean!'

'I don't think they do,' said Cressida. 'Or not where I've been. I'm terribly hungry. I've had nothing to eat for hours and hours. Can we *please* go ashore?'

She had no idea of how it could be done, but felt an irrational trust in him, despite all the evidence.

He arranged himself in the manner of an important statue by Michelangelo, hands on thighs, expression superhuman.

'I have offered you death!'

'Yes, but not *now*!'

He seemed at least to hear her; because Cressida could observe him deflect for a second from the course set by his will, from the history of the race.

He spoke once again.

'There is a thing more! Be wise! Imagination is henceforth prohibited, and only facts permitted. Only lies.'

'I'm going to put my clothes on. They're almost dry. I'm sorry *you* haven't got anything nicer.'

She had never before donned anything so private with a man looking at her. She was surprised by how little difference it made. She wondered where Vivien could be by now.

'Now please get me ashore. I have to find my friends and go back to England. Only for a little while, of course. It's quite dull there compared with everywhere else.'

He gazed at her with impressive sadness, as if throned in marble at the top of a staircase in the Vatican.

Cressida had a brilliant idea. 'Would you like to come too? You already know my friend, Vivien's aunt, Lady Luce. She thinks you're fascinating. Do come.'

Vittore remained ineffable.

'I believe you had a house in London once. You could take a flat while you make up your mind. Everyone's doing it.'

But it was as if Vittore had passed beyond speech, beyond thought.

'Lady Luce would like it so much.'

Cressida half-paused. 'It would be nice for me too.'

Vittore responded in a low mutter; the voice of a cracked statue in the desert. 'Life now holds nothing and no one. There is no future for man. There is only death.'

It was impossible to go on arguing with a hero so wilful, so specific. Cressida was aware that young children, when being difficult, often displayed those precise attributes, and thus presented the same problem.

Cressida's eyes ranged round the hot horizon; her mind round the possibilities. At home, it took hours for first twilight to become final darkness: something, somewhere, between the two was the normal background to everyday living. Abroad it was different. More in the way of decision was needed the whole time.

In Vittore the god of power had become the god of wounds. Cressida offered transfiguration, had postponed it: Vittore lay materially depleted, but perhaps in some other way glorious. His scars, the hole in him, suggested that it was so. Who could be sure?

'Is that another storm coming up?'

Powers as ultimate as Vittore might be moving in to a final settlement. Cressida gave Vittore's drying robe a squeeze.

Maddeningly, it was still humid. However did the religious manage in the olden times?

Cressida had second thoughts. 'It's not a storm! It's clouds and clouds of black smoke!'

'The Greeks fired all Troy,' said Vittore. 'Men were betrayed by a toy horse.'

'I love reading,' said Cressida, placing her hand momentarily on his calf. 'My friend and I hope to read *everything* before we die. Everything that's worth reading, of course; not *The Way of an Eagle* and needlework books. Are all your plays and poems and things translated into good English?'

'Into every language,' said Vittore, 'but soon they will be proscribed. There will be only voices and pictures and a majority. The world is dying of compassion.'

But Cressida had cried out, interrupting his oracle quite rudely. 'It's nothing to do with Troy! It's the navy coming to rescue us.'

'Rescue is obsolete.'

'I'm sure that's what's happening. You'd better put your thing on even though it's still a bit damp. I wish I could lend you something.'

Osiris in extremis, he stirred and peered over the gunwale, as when Cressida had first sighted him.

'With my iron heel I shall stamp both of us into oblivion.'

He really seemed about to do it, whether Cressida agreed or not.

'That's no use. You'll never be forgotten.' She was quite surprised at what she felt to be a new resourcefulness.

'I'm forgotten already. Everything that has happened hitherto is forgotten. History is obsolete.'

'There's a new world waiting round the corner,' said Cressida, unable, as so often, to stop herself.

He raised his limb, in beauty as in strength, presumably proposing to hole the bottom of the little vessel.

For better or for worse, a muscular twinge of some kind delayed him. After all, he had been exposed to the weather for what seemed hours, and there had been all those other things as well. What they did to a man, Cressida just did not know. She lacked the experience.

'You'll only hurt yourself,' said Cressida. Not that she wished to make it sound a challenge. Still, breaking up a boat was notoriously as difficult as carving a duck.

Vittore seemed to have tied his muscles almost in knots. Of course, one feels the same when contemplating the works of most artists devoted to sculpting the male form in male format.

'Let's just allow ourselves to be rescued,' said Cressida. 'For the present, I mean.'

Vittore was struggling more and more desperately with the potentially rheumatoid consequences of the unusual action he had attempted.

Cressida could not but realise that it was touch and go how soon Vittore could recover control of himself.

She dragged her handkerchief out of her trousers pocket. Unfortunately, it was still damp, and refused to wave properly.

Cressida realised that what she needed was one of those Union Jack handkerchiefs on sale everywhere at the Lord Mayor's Show; the larger size.

Then she reflected that even if Vittore succeeded, she ought to be able to float about for long enough to be picked up. Despite Harry Crass's attitude, the sea was much calmer now; following the events in her life that afternoon. Presumably events of that kind tended to work in that way. Moreover, the Royal Navy was equipped with all kinds of dodges for rescuing people. One began learning about them in the Guides, and those who were interested could in the end compete for certificates.

All the same: Vittore might hold her tightly, tightly, in his steel arms and drag her downwards. Seldom does life offer but a single possibility.

'What a gorgeous sunset!' Cressida pointed out. Surely that must appeal to any artist? But, like so many people, Vittore was not Ruskin, however regrettably. It had been just the same, of course, with Vittoria. A family characteristic.

Moreover, the sunset was being desperately diminished. Cressida knew that the navy used only the very best South Wales silkstone, and had not supposed it would make quite so much smoke. After all, it was shipped everywhere, for taking aboard in sacks by endless files of coolies. But the *Dreadful* possessed a long line of funnels, and they were all belching. There was absolutely no other word.

Of course, of course! It had been Full Steam Ahead to rescue Cressida! Probably All Hands To The Pumps too! She should be *glad* of the smoke; as is the housemaid in a burning attic of the noisy fireman's bell.

Through the murk, Cressida could see that what she thought might be a whaler was approaching, energetically rowed by bluejackets. An officer stood at the stern, playing on a pipe.

She could not entirely look forward to the return trip aboard the craft. She knew how bad she was at all repartee. Was she, even in the most general way, what the girls called 'good with men'? She doubted it.

She glanced sidelong at Vittore.

What a relief! He had ceased to struggle. There were some Roman Catholic words which related to such conditions. Not being a Roman Catholic herself, Cressida could not remember what they were.

But she thought it best to avert her eyes reverently; not least to keep dead mum.

'What ho? What ho?'

It was a difficult question to answer, just as she had known it would be; but at least rescue had happened. And before Vittore had recovered the use of his death wish and muscles.

Cressida could see that the man with the pipe was not an officer but a Petty Officer. The coloured pictures that she and Vivien had pored over did not confine themselves to commissioned ranks, as so many do, but went right down to private soldier and able seaman and flying apprentice. However, she realised that even pettiness must be a matter of degree, just as, in the case of a seaman, must be ability.

Arms tattooed with anchors, hearts, and other quaintnesses soon lugged her aboard. Perhaps, indeed, the craft was not a whaler but a lugger?

'Would you care to come aboard too, sir?'

'You know not what you ask.'

'Quite sure, sir?'

'In our end is our beginning.'

'Very well, sir. If you say so, sir.'

The Petty Officer bawled an order, and the able seamen responded with the unanimity of Tiller Girls in their boys-of-the-bulldog-breed scene, lately so popular.

It had proved so simple. Vittore had risen to a final decision, and without even putting on his vesture. It is choice that distinguishes the artist from the common herd.

Cressida wondered what the Petty Officer could think of the scene that had been disclosed—and, indeed, of her. If there had been more light, she might have blushed.

The Petty Officer, however, had plainly been trained to think of nothing but the matter in hand, and the bluejackets to think of nothing at all except, of course, when on furlough. The former looked serious and responsible, as if Cressida had been snatched from cannibals. The latter confined themselves to squinting at her.

The Petty Officer began to play once more on his pipe, a melody at once functional and febrile, as in a Mozart one-act opera.

It was very thick when they reached the stationary ship. Perhaps the stokers had damped down the furnaces with dust, as Cressida's father did at home, and with the same consequences.

There was a rather fragile staircase suspended at the side of the ship and Cressida was expected to go up it. The Petty Officer stood aside for her, but then followed too closely.

Cressida could see the rolling main between each pair of steps, because there were no risers, as in a house; and the main looked more mischievous the further one rose above it. If one *didn't* look down, one could make a bad mistake with the placing of one's feet. Also there was no proper handrail, but merely a rope, on one side only, and with too much give in it. The motion of the waves became more noticeable under such circumstances as these.

Cressida felt a nervous wreck before she reached the top, but of course gave no sign of it.

Aunt Agnes was once more standing there to welcome her.

But by now Aunt Agnes was in full fig: navy blue jacket with the brassiest of buttons, navy blue skirt, white shirt and expensive black tie, the most beautiful black silk stockings, always Aunt Agnes's particular thing, as Cressida fully realised.

Aunt Agnes threw her arms round Cressida, and kissed her several times. The brass buttons stuck into Cressida, but Aunt Agnes always kissed most beautifully; gently, tenderly, with immense meaning.

'Yes,' said Aunt Agnes, with a proud smile, only faintly deprecatory; 'Admiral Sir Wilmot Broadfoot arranged for me to embrace the service: in an honorary capacity, of course.'

'You look more wonderful than ever, Lady Luce.'

'I have a command of my own, though a very small one, of course.'

'You can command me, Lady Luce, any time you choose.'

'Dear Cressida! Since you may not be my daughter, I must think of something else that would be suitable.'

Vivien was standing there in a girl's sailor suit; assuredly an official issue also.

'Cressy! You must be starving! I'll take you to the eats.'

'Stop!' exclaimed Aunt Agnes. 'Let me first introduce the Admiral, our saviour.'

Another of Aunt Agnes's particular things seemed to be a very tall, very nasal, very commanding man to be continually by, beside, and with her; to implement her every wish, even the lightest and slightest, for it is those wishes that are nearly always the really important ones.

'But,' cried Aunt Agnes, 'wherever is Vittore?'

She actually clutched at the Petty Officer, who was standing by, his pipe held against the seam of his trousers, even though it was a wandering seam, the stuff being so stout. Aunt Agnes had unquestionably committed a breach of the regulation that prohibits an officer from touching another rank, however great the urgency.

'Gentleman preferred to remain in his own craft, ma'am.'

'But what will become of him? Admiral, we must set sail after him, full steam ahead!'

'No need for that, ma'am,' said the Petty Officer. 'Gentleman was only a few hundred yards from the shore. He could swim it easy. If the gentleman knows how to swim, of course.'

'If Vittore knows how to swim!' cried Aunt Agnes. Her voice was all silver bells. 'He once swam the Merganser Straits four times running on a single evening. Back and forth.'

'Don't know where that is, ma'am, but I don't expect he has anything like so far to go this time.'

Cressida knew that comforting the distressed was a prescribed obligation among naval ratings, and especially among the non-commissioned officers. She had nothing to add on the subject of Vittore, even though there had been things which now made her smile slightly, and of course involuntarily.

It would have been quite dark, if it had not been for the ship's coloured lights, which made her look like a Mardi Gras ball passing Baton Rouge.

'We've picked up everyone,' exclaimed Aunt Agnes. 'The Admiral's been quite wonderful. Not a soul left except the revolutionaries.'

'What's to be done with *them*?' enquired Cressida; perhaps Trifoglio at the outer edge of her mind.

'We can't stand in the way of progress, young lady,' proclaimed the Admiral definitively. His voice was somehow like the voice of all the tons of coal that were kept downstairs. 'If you don't mind my calling you a young lady,' he added, looking at Cressida's trousers.

Carnival costume, she feared, at that time of the evening.

Cressida was once more at a loss for words: the rank within the service seemed to make no difference. Not for nothing was the navy called silent. It had that effect on her every time.

'The British government is not in a position to rescue everyone in the world from their own foolishness,' expanded Aunt Agnes.

'Oh goodness!' cried Cressida. 'Whatever can have happened to Vittoria?'

But, of course, no one knew who Vittoria was, except Vivien; and Vivien only slightly.

'She'll turn up,' predicted Vivien.

'And now for England, home, and beauty!' exclaimed Admiral Sir Wilmot Broadfoot. 'Blow, bugle, blow! Let the silver trumpet sound!'

The noise was appalling, but at least something had become concrete.

Conclusion

Vivien had been perfectly right. Vittoria re-emerged in no time, pioneered a strange form of untheatre in remote places, and ended an Honoured Artist of the People. She died, like many another, rather prematurely. The state funeral was all red roses, even though changed conditions was somewhat inadequate for the enduring commemoration of the burial place. Cressida wondered for a moment what had become of Maddalena?

The poor old ex-Acting Foreign Minister was (perhaps quite logically) 'executed'. Doubts had been indicated by interested parties about how ex he had really been; and complaints had been laid, by friends of the same parties, about things he had done, not done, thought of doing, given no thought to doing: all before he could even claim to be ex. How far was his Acting an act? And, of course, his English suit weighed heavily in every sense.

Professor Colossi, as one might expect, was simply murdered by his pupils while trying to escape.

Trifoglio reaped the whirlwind. He climbed higher and higher, while the authorities popped off at him and covered all retreat with lime. In the end, the sirocco or the mistral or the levanter or some other local breeze caught hold of him, and he was blown out to sea like a scrap of discoloured paper.

Eno joined the Motor Cycle Section of the Security Police: a big chance for the right man.

The Albanians soldiered on.

Vittore enlarged 'that place of his' as Aunt Agnes had termed it, the place where the wondrous wine had come from; and went on enlarging it, until the day he ascended to Heaven. He enlarged the house, the castello, the palazzo, the tempio, however one might term the structure; ring upon ring upon ring, expanding the whole as a tree expands. Concurrently, he enlarged the demesne as opportunity arose, or could be contrived; and he transformed the demesne into desert: thorny, scrubby, rubbish-strewn, infested with hungry dogs and the strangest snakes. Never again was Vittore to be beheld by human vision; he was resolved upon it; and it is well known that in such cases no architecture can be entangled enough, no cordon sanitaire sufficiently boundless. When, early one May morning, Vittore floated upwards, there was no one who could possibly detect; indeed, no one who even knew. Long ago every person in the world had eagerly forgotten Vittore's existence, exactly as he had prophesised, except for a few specialists, whose lips were sealed. There was, I suppose, the singing on Magdalen Tower at about the same moment, but no one takes that very seriously either, and one wonders how long it will continue.

Their wider experience enabled Cressida and Vivien to find better paid jobs, so that they were just able to meet the costs of a shared flat in W.2., until something else should happen, if anything else ever did. The worst trouble was, as usual, the kitchenette, though the bathroom made its contribution from time to time. Soon they found themselves knowing many perfectly normal, average people of about their own age. Wendy flashed by occasionally, like a beautiful shooting star. Desirée had found a promising position in a Department, just as people expected. Rosemary became a fairly close friend.

Aunt Agnes won six dozen bottles of Château d'Yquem playing cards with Togo Broadfoot's brother-in-law. She often came round with one of these bottles, and the tripartite understanding was so intense that she usually stayed the night. Then, one day, she joined an expedition to look for Colonel Fawcett in the Matto Grosso, or wherever it was that the man of power and mystery had disappeared finally. She sent the girls coloured photographs of herself in khaki breeches, and looking much slimmer: the Consul stood, tall and tailored, at her side. In the end, she even became quite a close personal friend of Colonel T.E. Lawrence, who had as many names as anyone in Trino. Never did she lose her soft sympathy for Vivien's friend, Cressida. Never did she cease to be Cressida's ideal—at least among the people Cressida had so far actually met.

Too late Cressida realised that she had never read a single one of those poems stuck upon walls. Oh, dear: life! life!

Thus one kind of world became a quite other kind of world, without anyone but Cressida and Vivien much noticing. Many of the others, of course, were in no position to do so. Vivien never quite finished her novel. Suddenly all the material seemed to have raced down the drain. So perhaps really this is it?

Dear readers,

As well as relying on bookshop sales, And Other Stories relies on subscriptions from people like you for many of our books, whose stories other publishers often consider too risky to take on.

Our subscribers don't just make the books physically happen. They also help us approach booksellers, because we can demonstrate that our books already have readers and fans. And they give us the security to publish in line with our values, which are collaborative, imaginative and 'shamelessly literary'.

All of our subscribers:

- receive a first-edition copy of each of the books they subscribe to
- are thanked by name at the end of our subscriber-supported books
- receive little extras from us by way of thank you, for example: post-cards created by our authors

BECOME A SUBSCRIBER,
OR GIVE A SUBSCRIPTION TO A FRIEND

Visit andotherstories.org/subscriptions to help make our books happen. You can subscribe to books we're in the process of making. To purchase books we have already published, we urge you to support your local or favourite bookshop and order directly from them — the often unsung heroes of publishing.

OTHER WAYS TO GET INVOLVED

If you'd like to know about upcoming events and reading groups (our foreign-language reading groups help us choose books to publish, for example) you can:

- join our mailing list at: andotherstories.org
- follow us on Twitter: @andothertweets
- join us on Facebook: facebook.com/AndOtherStoriesBooks
- admire our books on Instagram: @andotherpics
- follow our blog: andotherstories.org/ampersand

ROBERT AICKMAN (1914–1981) was the son of an architect and the grandson of Victorian Gothic novelist Richard Marsh. A novelist, critic, editor, memoirist, literary agent, and saviour of the British waterways, he is regularly acclaimed as the most singular, alarming, and accomplished writer of supernatural fiction in the twentieth century.

BRIAN EVENSON is the author of a dozen books of fiction, most recently the story collection *The Glassy, Burning Floor of Hell*. His collection *Song for the Unraveling of the World* won the World Fantasy Award, the Shirley Jackson Award, and was a finalist for the Ray Bradbury Prize.